Deborah Carr, *USA Today*-bestsellin̶ lives on the island of Jersey in the husband and three rescue dogs.

Her Mrs Boots series is inspired by another Jersey woman, Florence Boot, the woman behind the Boots (Walgreens Boots Alliance) empire. Her debut First World War romance, *Broken Faces*, was runner-up in the 2012 Good Housekeeping Novel Writing Competition and *Good Housekeeping* magazine described her as 'one to watch'.

Keep up to date with Deborah's books by subscribing to her newsletter: deborahcarr.org/newsletter.

www.deborahcarr.org

twitter.com/DebsCarr
facebook.com/DeborahCarrAuthor
instagram.com/ofbooksandbeaches
pinterest.com/deborahcarr
bookbub.com/profile/deborah-carr

Also by Deborah Carr

The Mrs Boots Series

Mrs Boots

Mrs Boots of Pelham Street

Mrs Boots Goes to War

Standalones

The Poppy Field

An Island at War

THE BEEKEEPER'S WAR

DEBORAH CARR

One More Chapter
a division of HarperCollins*Publishers* Ltd
1 London Bridge Street
London SE1 9GF
www.harpercollins.co.uk
HarperCollins*Publishers*
1st Floor, Watermarque Building, Ringsend Road
Dublin 4, Ireland

This paperback edition 2022
1
First published in Great Britain in ebook format
by HarperCollins*Publishers* 2022
Copyright © Deborah Carr 2022
Deborah Carr asserts the moral right to be identified
as the author of this work

A catalogue record of this book is available from the British Library

ISBN: 978-0-00-853458-5

Printed and bound in the UK using 100% Renewable Electricity
by CPI Group (UK) Ltd

To my mum, Tess Jackson.
For her constant support for my writing and for making me laugh
almost every single day.

Prologue

DECEMBER 1917, BELGIUM

Jack

Captain Jack Garland held his breath, not daring to move. The icy cold mud had hours before seeped deep into the patched woollen coat and worn trousers he had stolen from the bombed-out farmhouse close to where they were hiding. His muscles ached as he crouched low in the dense bush metres from where he had escaped earlier. He clamped his teeth together in a vain attempt to stop them from chattering and alerting the German soldiers who were scouring the woodland looking for him and his corporal, Falkner. Jack longed to be back in England with his darling Pru enjoying their first Christmas together but he had to survive this nightmare first.

Finally, the soldiers' footsteps began moving further away. After waiting another two minutes to be certain, he allowed himself the luxury of rotating his shoulders before stretching his arms and then his legs to ease them. He heard the shot that

1

slammed into his arm just below his elbow at the same time the pain exploded. Bastards. They had been thorough in their interrogation methods but Jack had no intention of giving them any information about the British lines. He would rather die in this putrid mud than betray fellow soldiers. No, he thought, picturing his British angel. He had promised her he would return and he would do his best to make that happen. He might be struggling to keep Falkner's spirits up but at least this time he didn't have to look after Monty, too.

He instinctively pushed his bloodied hand into his trouser pocket, looking for the lucky piece of twig Pru had given him when he left to return to Europe. It had been all she could think of to give him when he told her he would be unable to take the photograph of her. He hadn't had the heart to tell her that this mission was to be his most dangerous one yet.

He pictured Pru, wishing he *had* been able to bring the photograph of her. The pain of being held captive in what was once a magnificent chateau these past three months, and not being able to return to her, almost succeeded in shattering his resolve. The thought that she wouldn't know he had been thinking of her at the end, that she would never know what had happened to him, sent fury coursing through his veins. He had no intention of letting any vicious officer stop him returning to his darling girl. The image of Pru's pretty face came into his mind. He pictured that dimple in her left cheek and smiled. Then the sickening pull of pain on his swollen chin from his last beating reminded him that he still had a long way to go if he was to outsmart his captors and get back to her. If only his Sopwith Camel was nearby he might still have a way to fly out of this cesspit.

2

The dull thud of German military boots neared again. Jack crouched further down into the undergrowth once more. He needed to focus all his attention on his predicament if he was to get out of here alive.

Part One

ONE

Pru

Pru sat back in the comfortable leather armchair in front of the open window of the sitting room where the nursing staff went to rest between shifts. It was cooler than she had realised when she was busy looking after the injured men in her care, but the cup of steaming tea warmed her hands nicely. The hospital had been more chaotic lately with nurses having to set up some of the larger rooms into extra wards and she was glad of a little peace.

Lord and Lady Ashbury weren't at all like she had imagined people of their class to be when she and her best friend Jean had arrived at Ashbury Manor soon after finishing their training. The Ashburys were slightly authoritarian and scared her a little at first, but she soon discovered that their hearts were in the right place. Her friend Milly explained soon after their arrival that the aristocratic couple had lost their oldest and middle sons to the war and were concerned about their surviving youngest son who they believed was fighting somewhere in France. The women felt certain it was these

7

experiences that were behind the Ashburys' decision to open their magnificent home as a hospital for injured soldiers and their care to ensure the medical staff lived as comfortably as possible.

Pru closed her eyes, determined to make the most of the few minutes' peace, and turned her face up towards the winter sunshine, relishing its slight warmth. She wriggled her toes as best she could in the tight shoes they all wore, wishing she could take them off and massage her throbbing soles, but she'd learnt the hard way that to do so meant a delay arriving at the ward if she was sent for and she didn't want to risk the wrath of Matron again.

Tyres crunched on the gravel driveway and she could hear distant, calm voices as instructions were given. New arrivals. She tried to picture her maman, papa, and grandmére at home with her younger brother Frank in Jersey and wondered when she would be able to spend time with them again. Right now though, she was relieved that Frank was too young to enlist. She took a sip of her tea, relishing the sight of the sun in the azure sky. If she tried hard enough, she could almost imagine she was back at home relaxing in the garden at their family-run guesthouse at La Rocque with their views across to the small, pretty harbour with its rocky estuaries and waves rolling in to shore.

Hurried footsteps behind her along the hallway's polished floorboards alerted her to someone's imminent arrival.

'You're wanted,' Milly said breathlessly from the doorway, a slight panic in her gentle voice.

Pru didn't ask why. She didn't need to. It was obvious that the new arrivals needed to be settled in and her assistance was required. She stood and hurried over to the sink, taking a quick last sip of her drink before regretfully tipping the rest away, quickly washing her cup and leaving it to dry on the draining board.

They ran along the empty corridor before slowing to a walk as they reached the busier areas near the wards.

'The first ambulance has just left but another couple are expected imminently,' Milly murmured, stifling a yawn. 'It's a bigger intake than we're used to and Matron wants everyone helping.'

The arrival of new patients always made Pru a little anxious, although she had been a qualified nurse for almost two years. She had gone through training with Jean Le Riche, her best friend from Jersey, and they had met Milly on their arrival in England. The three had been firm friends and roommates ever since. Pru recalled her excitement at the sight of the impressive house where they would now work when the three of them arrived that first morning. She had been stunned to learn that the family had readily donated their panelled ballroom and baronial dining room to the Red Cross to treat wounded soldiers being brought back from the Front. Now, though, she understood why Lord and Lady Ashbury were so keen to help in any way they could.

The novelty of living away from home hadn't worn off yet but she wished her fear of seeing new patients for the first time would diminish. Not that anyone would guess how she felt, she reminded herself, calming slightly as she hurried to do Matron's bidding. Pru prided herself on her professionalism and ability to reassure the men brought in to be nursed by them, despite some of the stomach-churning injuries she had seen over the previous months, which had given her a few nightmares and shocked her to her core.

Matron glared across the reception area at them as Pru and Milly entered the Great Hall. 'Nurses Le Cuirot and Denton, good of you to finally join us.'

Pru was used to Matron's scathing tone and although she sometimes wished she could answer back with a snappy retort, she focused on keeping her expression neutral.

'I want you outside with the first two ambulances,' Matron continued. 'Lead the porters into Ward Two. Doctor Parslow is waiting in there with Nurse Le Riche to receive the men and to decide which wards he wants them sent.'

Pru and Milly hurried along the corridor and outside just as the first two ambulances slowed in front of the main entrance. They stood and waited for each of them to park. Pru braced herself for what she was about to be confronted with. 'Here we go,' she said, almost to herself.

The ambulance driver stepped out of the vehicle and walked around to where Pru was waiting for two hospital orderlies to open the back doors.

'Good morning, Nurse.'

'Good morning,' Pru answered, only half aware that she was speaking as she watched the patients' stretchers being withdrawn from the ambulance. She gave her best welcoming smile to the first patient, unable to miss the wince as his movement to return the smile caused him more pain. She took the list from the driver's hands and scanned down over the details. 'Thank you.'

The first soldier was carried out of the ambulance. His eyes moved in her direction and she immediately spotted a dark shadow of fear she had become familiar with since her arrival at the hospital. 'I'm Nurse Le Cuirot,' she said, keeping her voice level and faking a confidence she didn't feel. 'Welcome to Ashbury Manor. We'll take you inside where Doctor Parslow will speak to you and we'll settle you into a ward shortly afterwards.'

He seemed reassured by her comments, so she turned her attention to the porters. 'Please try to carry these men with as little movement as possible.' She checked the label tied to the first man's lapel. A leg injury. 'If you would go to Ward Two, please,' she said to the porters carrying the first patient. 'I'll follow on.'

The porter at the front of the first stretcher smiled. 'No problem, Nurse.'

Pru stepped over to the second stretcher. Checking her list, she saw that he was suffering from a leg injury as well, but also had a shrapnel wound to his arm. She greeted him and then waited for the next patient to be lifted from the back of the vehicle, wondering where these poor men had returned from. It could be many places, but she had heard a few of the nurses discussing reports in one of the newspapers of yet more casualties at the Front in France and suspected this influx of casualties might have come from there.

'How much longer do you think this dreadful war is going to continue?' she asked her friend Jean as they went to replenish their supplies of dressings later that morning.

'Probably until there are no young men left?' Jean replied,

opening the supply room door and holding it back for Pru to push in the trolley. 'I'm finding it a struggle to deal with all this suffering. I wish we could have a break from it. Even a few days would be welcome.'

'I'd love that,' Pru said, reaching up to take bandages from the shelf. 'It gets a little too overwhelming sometimes, doesn't it?'

'It does.' Jean counted dressings before placing them on the trolley and turning to fetch more.

'But I remind myself that we're the lucky ones,' Pru added miserably. 'Our aching feet get to have a break whenever we're off duty, unlike these poor men, who might have to wait months for proper relief.'

'And some of them will never get it.' Jean sighed. 'Right, I think that's all we needed,' she said, lowering bottles of saline solution carefully onto the trolley. 'We'd better get back now.'

'I'll just fetch the two larger basins Matron specifically asked for and then we can get back to the ward.'

She hoped the allies would find a way to beat the enemy into submission, and the sooner the better as far as she was concerned. It was heartbreaking to witness these damaged men being brought in day after day, especially as most of those who survived were too badly injured to ever be able to lead the life they had been used to before enlisting.

'Nurse Le Riche.' They jumped to find Matron waiting for them outside the supply room. 'Why are you both fetching supplies? I feel like I'm dealing with a pair of nitwits sometimes.' She groaned. 'Surely one of you could have done that.'

Pru was too shocked to laugh at the woman's strange

description of them. She went to explain that they each needed different items, but knew that one of them could have handed the other their list, so instead kept quiet. She could tell her superior that it was nice to take a moment every once in a while to catch up with her friend and talk openly, but didn't think Matron would appreciate the sentiment.

'Nurse Le Cuirot, take the trolley back to the ward.'

'I want you,' Matron added, turning to Jean, 'to go outside. A private ambulance is due to arrive soon and I want one of my nurses ready and waiting for it. It's bringing in a special patient and I want him taken to the private part of the house. Do you understand?'

'Yes, Matron.'

'The porters will wait with you. They've been instructed about where he's to be taken.'

Pru glanced at Jean, frightened on her friend's behalf to think how injured the soldier must be if he was to be kept away from the rest of the patients. She couldn't help feeling relieved she wasn't the one being sent out to greet him. She mouthed a *good luck* when Matron had turned her back to leave, and then pushed the trolley back to the ward.

TWO

Pru

JANUARY 1917

P ru was helping three other nurses set up a room at the back of the house under Matron's watchful eye.

'Remove those pictures carefully,' she ordered. 'They're to be placed on the rug over there, one behind the other, ready for the footmen to take them away to be stored.'

The nurses did as they were told. Pru assumed the room they were clearing had been someone's study or sitting room. It was smaller yet prettier than the rooms they already used for the three wards. The small sofa and armchairs were covered in a delicate floral material and the lamps and pictures were somehow more personal than the more austere furnishings she'd seen in the areas of the rest of the manor house that she had had access to.

'Stop dawdling, girls,' Matron snapped. 'This room should be ready by now.' At that moment, the door opened again and a hospital bed was brought in by two porters. Pru knew they had been footmen before the war. 'Place the bed near to that window.'

Matron believed that fresh air helped cure many ailments.

Having finished helping with the pictures, Pru walked over to Matron. 'Shall I fetch the bedlinen and pillows now, Matron?'

'Yes.' She waved Milly over to her. 'You can bring in a tray with the carafe and a glass for the patient, then fetch two chairs for visitors.'

Pru heard her instructing the porters to bring a screen for the room, although she wasn't sure why as the room was to be for single use only.

'I want a desk and chair for nursing staff placed in that corner,' Matron instructed.

'I wonder who the patient can be?' Milly whispered as she and Pru hurried down the corridor. 'He must be someone special to have a room all to himself.'

'Hmm,' Pru replied thoughtfully. 'Or he's more badly injured than the others and needs to be kept by himself.' She wasn't sure that was the best way for a patient to be treated. Surely, she mused, being alone with no other company or distractions to take a patient's mind off their situation couldn't be a healthy choice.

'I suppose we'll find out soon enough,' Milly said, stopping in front of the linen cupboard that was the size of one of the smaller rooms at Pru's parents' guesthouse. 'Whoever he is will be arriving in about a quarter of an hour.'

'You're right. We'd better get our skates on if we don't want Matron giving us the third degree.'

They were used to coming across Lord and Lady Ashbury around the manor house and sometimes when they visited the wards, but something felt different about their behaviour today, although Pru couldn't pinpoint what it might be. When the room was almost ready, Pru and one other nurse were instructed to go and wait with Matron by the front door while Milly and another finished up. Pru stood at the large arched doorway and watched Jean waiting to lead the porters outside when the private ambulance arrived.

Pru was becoming restless. She had been on her feet since dawn and was desperate for a few minutes' respite and to be able to take off her sensible shoes. As the welcoming committee stood silently, she heard the distinctive sound of an engine coming down the driveway and saw Lord Ashbury take his wife's hand in his own and whisper something to her. The usually self-contained woman appeared tense, her expression taut with contained emotion as she stood silently staring out towards the parking area. It occurred to Pru that the reason their host and hostess were acting differently today might be because whoever was being brought to the manor was someone close to them. This time it was personal.

She withheld a gasp. Could this arrival be Viscount Montgomery Ashbury – the Ashburys' youngest son?

The motor ambulance slowed and stopped.

'Nurse Le Riche,' Matron said, not needing to give further orders for Jean to do her bidding.

Pru watched her friend calmly lead the porters outside and then glanced sideways at Lord and Lady Ashbury, wondering why they didn't hurry out to meet the ambulance. She realised that it was probably because they didn't want to be seen acting in any way that might be construed as lacking in self-control. She thought of her parents, also rigid in their ways, but believed that if this was her younger brother coming home injured, then both would be outside ahead of Jean, determined to be with him as soon as they possibly could.

Jean gave Pru a brief wide-eyed glance from where she stood next to the ambulance and Pru could see that she had been right and the patient must be Viscount Ashbury. Jean was always calm and Pru realised it was why Matron had instructed her to be the one to go out to greet the ambulance. Carrying the patient on a stretcher, the porters stopped in front of Lord and Lady Ashbury.

The top half of the man's head was bandaged with only his nose, mouth and chin showing, and Pru's breath caught as she witnessed Lady Ashbury's anguish, as she took her only surviving son's hand in her free one, the other still clasped by her husband's grip. Pru wasn't sure which of the two of them was finding their son's homecoming more difficult.

'Welcome home, Montgomery,' Lady Ashbury said, bending to kiss his bandaged forehead. 'We're so happy to have you back with us.'

'Thank you, Mother,' he said, his voice croaky. 'I wish I could see your face, but I can picture it well enough.'

He sounded friendly, Pru thought, wondering if he knew how many people were standing nearby in the hallway. His father cleared his throat and stepped closer to his son's stretcher. 'Good to have you back, my boy. We've set up a room for you. Matron Goodall and her excellent nursing staff will give you the best of care.'

'Why am I having a separate room?'

It was a genuine question from their son and without a hint of aggression. Pru waited for them to reply, swapping concerned glances with Milly and Jean. Neither of them dared move as they waited for Lord Ashbury to reply.

Lord Ashbury gave Matron a pointed look, clearly expecting her to explain.

'Master Montgomery, I'm Matron Goodall. Lord and Lady Ashbury thought that as Ashbury Manor is your home you might be more comfortable in a room by yourself so as to not to be disturbed by other patients. One of the downstairs rooms, a private sitting room, has been adapted into a small ward so that you will be as comfortable as possible during your recovery.'

'That's very kind of you all,' Montgomery said, 'but that won't do.'

It was a simple reply, Pru thought, but one with as much determination as she had ever heard. Montgomery Ashbury wasn't a man to be dictated to, she realised, unsure how he had found life in the forces.

Lady Ashbury winced. 'Darling Monty. It's for your own good. Once you've had a chance to settle in and rest after your tiring journey, I'm certain you'll agree with us.'

'Dearest Mother, I appreciate your sentiment, really I do,' he said, his voice gentle and filled with love. 'However, I really would much rather convalesce with other men than in a room by myself.' His mouth was set hard. 'I need the company of others right now. Please try to understand.'

Pru's heart ached for the poor man returning to his childhood home in such a reduced state. She waited nervously as Matron looked to his parents for their decision on what she should do next.

Lord and Lady Ashbury looked at one another and without speaking seemed to come to a mutual decision. Finally, Lady Ashbury spoke. 'If that's what will make you happy, Monty, darling, then that's what we'll do.' She addressed Matron with a forced smile. 'I'm sorry, Matron. Please do as my son asks and arrange for him to be taken to one of the wards.' She withdrew her hand from her husband's grasp and rested it on her son's shoulder. 'I'll come and speak with you properly once you're settled in.'

'Thank you, Mother.'

Lord and Lady Ashbury walked away. No doubt, Pru thought, with conflicting emotions: happy to be reunited with their son, yet sad to see him in such a bad way.

'Nurses Denton and Le Cuirot. Hurry ahead and arrange for a bed to be made up in Ward Two.'

'Yes, Matron,' they chorused.

'Nurse Le Riche, go and fetch Doctor Parslow. Explain to him that we'll be taking the patient to the private ward until a bed has been made up for him and that he can make his initial examination there.'

'Yes, Matron.'

'What if there isn't a free bed?' Milly asked frantically as they walked quickly to Ward Two. 'What will we do then?'

'I've no idea.' Pru was glad the poor man's parents had relented. He had more than enough to contend with without being left alone with his thoughts and memories of what he had experienced in the trenches.

Pru followed Milly into the ward and stopped next to her,

both scanning the room. 'Phew, there's a free bed over in that corner.' Pru sighed with relief. 'I'd forgotten that younger soldier had been taken to another convalescent home nearer to his family to be taught how to walk with a false leg.'

The bed had been stripped but not yet made up with fresh bedding. 'I'll go and fetch some linen. You'd better fill the carafe and bring over a screen for when Lord and Lady Ashbury come to see their son.'

'Good idea.'

The following morning, Pru spoke to the new arrival for the first time as she gave him a bed bath. She introduced herself and liked him instinctively. He didn't act at all as she had expected he might, being the son of a lord and lady. He seemed no different to most of the other patients despite his clipped voice and unmistakeably upper-class air.

'It must be a relief to be back home, I suppose?' she said, carefully wiping his chin and neck dry.

'It is,' he agreed, although he seemed a little hesitant. 'I wish I could see what they've done with the place now that the larger rooms are taken up by men like me.'

She hoped he would be able to soon. 'Do you know which room we're currently in?' she asked, squeezing out the excess water from the sponge she was using to wash his left arm.

'I'm not sure. Will you describe it to me?'

She stopped what she was doing and studied the area around them. 'There's panelling on the walls, and' – she looked over at the enormous fireplace on the opposite side of the room – 'there's a huge fireplace with a pale stone surround that's been carved with...' She tried to see what exactly it was to tell him. 'Um, I think they're lions facing each other, one either side of a crest?'

He smiled knowingly. 'Yes, that's right. In that case, we're in the Great Hall. I should have recognised the sound of people's feet on the tiled floor, now I come to think of it.'

Pru looked down at the squares of white marble with smaller black marble squares at each corner. 'The Great Hall,' she repeated in awe. She dried his arm and placed it gently on top of the sheet. She had never been in any other great halls and tried to imagine what happened in this room before the war. 'What was it used for before the war?' she asked, rinsing the sponge in the cooling water and wringing it out. As Pru waited for him to reminisce, she walked around the bed to his other side and began washing his other arm.

She wasn't sure if he had heard her, or if he was even still awake. When their eyes were bandaged, it was difficult sometimes to know how much the patient was paying attention to you.

'Balls were held in here,' he said eventually, a half-smile on his face as if lost in a happy memory. 'We always held a big party on New Year's Eve in here too each year. And...' He raised his clean arm and pointed over to the opposite side of the room. 'If I'm right about where I am in this room, over there is where a large Norway Spruce would be erected each Christmas. Father always enjoys being shown the tree that old man Stephens, his head gardener, cuts down for him each year. He's in his eighties and retired now and his son has taken over the role of head gardener to the estate, but it's a family tradition that old man Stephens chooses the manor's Christmas tree.'

Pru loved the thought that the old man was still valued by the family. She looked over at the corner on one side of the fireplace and tried to picture a decorated tree with presents neatly displayed underneath it. 'I'll bet it was magical,' she said dreamily.

'It was, Nurse Le Cuirot. And who knows, maybe after this interminable war comes to an end my parents might decide to throw another party. I'll make sure you receive an invitation.'

'Really? You'd invite me?'

'Yes. You and all the brilliant nursing staff and porters, and the patients who have spent time here.'

'I would love that,' she admitted.

'Nurse Le Cuirot!' Matron snapped from somewhere behind her.

Pru hadn't heard her coming into the ward and dropped the sponge in shock at the sound of the older woman's harsh voice. She bent to retrieve it from the sheet before it got damp. 'Sorry, Matron. Did you want me?'

'Why are you still washing this patient, Nurse? You should be onto the next one by now.'

Pru pulled an apologetic face. 'I'm sorry, Matron. I was—'

'You were talking. Now, do stop dawdling and get a move on.'

'Yes, Matron.' She focused on washing Monty's chest while listening out for Matron's retreating footsteps. 'I'm sorry about that,' she said, quietly. 'I should be concentrating.'

'Nonsense,' Monty said. 'I've enjoyed your company. I was chatting to Nurse Le Riche earlier. She said she was from

Jersey, hence the French-sounding name. I was wondering if you might also be from there?'

'That's right,' she said. 'We're old schoolfriends. We left the island together and were very excited to both be sent here to work.'

'I haven't been to Jersey since I was much younger. I think I'll have to make a point of visiting there once this is all over and done with.'

'You should, it's very beautiful with its golden sandy beaches and pretty lanes.'

'Do you miss it much?'

She nodded then remembered he couldn't see her. 'I do. But it's very beautiful here at the manor, and I'm enjoying my walks here when I'm off duty.'

'That's good to know.'

As Pru finished washing Monty she couldn't help thinking that one day he would be lord of Ashbury Manor. She felt certain the place and its staff would be in very good hands.

THREE

Pru

FEBRUARY 1917

Two weeks later, Pru was pushing a trolley away from the final patient whose dressings she needed to change when she collided with something solid.

'Oof.' She winced as the metal bar handle slammed into her hipbones and the bottles on the top tray rattled noisily. Please don't let them break, she thought, too tired to have to clear up a mess of glass and medicines.

'I'm dreadfully sorry, Nurse.' The person grabbed the trolley to stop it from falling on its side. 'I beg your pardon. I should have been looking where I was going.'

She ignored the deep voice and the accent she couldn't place as she focused on composing herself. You're not wrong there, she thought, fighting to keep from snapping at him. Finally composed, Pru looked upwards and into the bluest eyes she had ever seen. They were dark navy and the most piercing colour, she decided. Her breath caught in her throat and her mind went blank. She willed herself to speak. Then noticed the wing insignia on the left side of a khaki tunic. 'You're in the Royal Flying Corps?' she asked, for something to say. She had heard that some pilots came from places overseas and presumed this man must be one of them.

'I am,' he said, an unmissable note of pride in his voice.

She noticed a haunted look in his eyes as he stared down at her and she couldn't help wondering how many friends he must have lost in recent months.

Her right hipbone ached, reminding her that she had been annoyed with his clumsiness barging into her trolley with such force. She focused on his bravery, aware that pilots' lives tended to be short. She hated to think that this handsome man was putting his life at risk each time he flew his plane and she had no wish to be unkind to someone who was risking his life for her countryfolk. 'Might I ask what you're doing out here?'

He removed his cap and held it between both hands. 'I've come to visit one of my men.'

Pru was aware that Matron was dogged in her refusal to bend visiting times. 'I'm sorry but visitors aren't allowed into the wards for another' – she glanced up at the wall clock – 'three and a quarter hours.'

He muttered something she couldn't hear and seemed frustrated by this news.

'I'm sorry, but I have work I must be getting on with,' Pru said, not wishing to be caught chatting to someone who wasn't a patient while Matron was on duty. 'You'll be able to see him during the set visiting hours.'

He lowered his voice. 'I don't think I'll be able to come back later,' he said. 'Please, Nurse. I only wish to see him briefly. I need to see for myself that he's all right. Is that possible, do you think?'

Pru couldn't miss the concern in his eyes and wished she could help him but knew without asking that Matron would refuse. She shook her head, sorry for the pilot but unable to do anything about it. 'I'm sorry, but the doctor is doing his rounds. Visitors are not allowed to pop in willy nilly.'

His fair eyebrows pulled together in a frown. He seemed angry and she wished she could be more helpful. His eyes narrowed slightly and then the corners of his lips raised and drew back into a smile. 'Willy nilly? What does that mean?'

Realising he was amused by what she had said, Pru's cheeks flamed and any sympathy for him vanished. 'Are you mocking me?' Her previous irritation with him returned instantly.

His eyes widened and he reached out to rest his hand on her shoulder. Pru stepped backwards before he touched her. 'You're to leave. Now.'

He shook his head. 'I didn't mean to make fun of you, but I've never heard that expression before.'

She heard Matron's distinctive footsteps striding along a nearby ward and had no intention of being caught talking to him only to be reprimanded when she had done nothing to warrant it. 'You're going to have to leave,' she insisted. 'Immediately.'

His shoulders drooped slightly. 'I am sorry.'

'Now, sir.'

He gave her a nod and turned to walk away the way he had come, his long legs making short work of the distance between her and the door. It occurred to her that she hadn't thought to ask which friend he wanted to see and if she could have passed on a message to him. Pru felt mean. She wasn't usually so taken aback by a man but somehow this one got right under her skin in a way that no other had ever done before.

Seconds later, Matron walked out of the nearby ward doorway. 'Nurse Le Cuirot, what are you doing wasting time in the corridor? I'm certain you have much to occupy your time?'

Pru glanced in the direction of the pilot, who had reached the front door. He turned to briefly look back over his shoulder at her before stepping outside.

Relieved not to have been caught speaking to him, she began pushing her trolley. 'I was on my way to the sluice room with these dirty utensils.'

'Then don't let me detain you for a moment longer.' Matron flicked her hand a couple of times to hurry Pru along.

'Why is she such an old harridan?' Pru asked Milly and Jean as they sat in the sitting room a short while later. 'It doesn't seem to matter how hard I try, she always catches me when I'm not doing anything. I always look guilty too, whether I have reason to or not.'

Milly giggled. 'I had a teacher like that. He hated me and always caught me when I wasn't working or was staring out of the window daydreaming.'

'I think it's because you remind her of someone, Pru,' Jean

suggested before blowing on her steaming drink. 'I heard she was jilted only days before her wedding.'

'No!' Milly drew her chair closer to Jean's. 'Where did you hear that?'

'One of the orderlies.' Jean glanced around the room.

'Poor woman,' Milly said, nodding in the direction of two other nurses leaving the recreation room, where they spent most of their break times.

'That's horrible,' Pru said, hating to think of anyone being let down in such a cruel way.

'I know,' Jean said. 'He said that he'd heard Matron's fiancé had run off with her best friend – a beautiful dark-haired girl with blue eyes and dimples.'

Pru cringed, aware that she had dark hair, blue eyes and a dimple in her left cheek.

'It is dreadful,' Milly said, 'but that's no reason to be mean to Pru. Even if she does look like that woman, it's not as if she's done anything to warrant being picked on.'

'I agree,' Pru said.

Jean took a sip of her tea. 'Mind you, as much as she hounds poor Pru, I have to admit she keeps everything running brilliantly here.'

Pru knew Jean was right. And if she was honest with herself, Matron was someone she admired. The woman was certainly dedicated and ran her wards with a military precision Pru suspected some senior officers would appreciate.

That afternoon, a few minutes before visiting time began, Pru was rushing along a corridor on her way back from taking a bedpan to the sluice room when she glanced out of the window and spotted the pilot with the unusual accent standing with his hands behind his back as he waited to be let into the hospital with other visitors. She smiled to herself, glad to see he had returned to see his friend. She would have hated it if her turning him away earlier had meant that one of the patients went without a visitor. She wondered if he had been lying when he said he wouldn't be able to come back during visiting hours, or if something had altered to allow him to be here.

She joined Jean in the ward to check all the patients were settled and ready to greet their loved ones and friends who had made the journey to the manor to spend a little time with them.

'I'll go and let them in,' Pru said. She reached the ward door and opened it, immediately spotting the tall captain even though he was standing at the back of the group. His eyes twinkled in amused recognition although she couldn't miss a sadness behind them. He must have lost friends, she mused, sad for him and all the other pilots who took their lives in their hands each time their aircraft soared into the air.

The visitors made their way into the ward, but he stopped in front of her. 'You don't mind me speaking with my pal for a few minutes this time, do you?'

She couldn't help smiling. 'Seeing as you're here at the correct time, I'm happy to welcome you inside. Who were you hoping to see?' she asked, hoping he hadn't got the wrong impression of her earlier and wanting to show her kinder side.

'I've come to visit Major Monty Ashbury.' He held out his hand for her to take. 'I'm Captain Jack Garland. And may I know your name, Nurse?'

Pru swallowed, desperate not to show how his presence had taken her aback. 'I'm Nurse Le Cuirot,' Pru replied, instinctively taking his larger hand in hers and flinching when his touch sent some sort of shock through her.

He stared at her silently, a surprised look on his face.

Pru cleared her throat and shook his hand. What was wrong with her? 'The major is in this ward in the end bed on the right,' she said, her voice barely audible. 'I'll show you over to him.' She led the way, glad he was behind her and couldn't see the confusion on her face. She needed to gather herself. This was no way to behave, she told herself. She was supposed to be a professional. She dragged her thoughts back to her duties and why the captain was visiting. 'He's had a hard time of it,' she warned, relieved when her voice sounded almost normal.

'I know.' He increased his speed so he was at her side and she slowed to match his.

She wished he would stop staring at her like that – as if he could see into her very soul. His eyes seemed to hypnotise her. She tore her eyes from his and pretended to check the time. 'He should really be in one of the other wards with fewer men but he insisted on being here with the others. We have several pilots recuperating here at the manor right now.'

'I'm not surprised he wanted to be with everyone else,' the captain said. 'He's a good chap. I'm glad he made it out.' He stepped aside to let one of the orderlies pass. 'I'm pleased he's back at Ashbury Manor; he'll be happy to be home again.'

His beautiful accent and deep voice were mesmerising. 'Um, he's improving every day, but it's going to be a long time before he's well enough to be discharged, I gather.'

He mumbled something but Pru didn't catch what it was. As they walked, she gave him a quick glance, surprised to find him watching her. 'You're American, aren't you?' she asked, fetching a chair for him to sit on when she noticed that the one that usually stood by the major's bed had already been taken by another visitor.

'You have a visitor, Major,' she said, happy to see a bit more colour in Monty's slim face, his eyes still bandaged from his latest operation to try and restore his sight.

'Hello, Monty,' said the captain.

Monty grinned. 'I'd recognise that voice anywhere. Jack Garland. So, you're still around these parts then?' He turned his head in Pru's direction as she indicated for the captain to sit on the chair. 'He is American but he's very proud of his East End British roots, Nurse Le Cuirot. Aren't you, Jack?'

'I am.'

She was surprised to hear his parents were from London. 'Your parents are British?' She noticed the wings on Jack's uniform matched the ones she recalled seeing on the photo of Monty his parents had in pride of place in their sitting room, the few times she had been invited there to take afternoon tea with some of the other nurses. Pru was fascinated to find out more about this impressive man. She hadn't realised there were American pilots flying alongside British ones.

'Yes. They emigrated from London in 1890, four years before I was born,' Jack explained. 'My father is dead now but I know he'd be pleased that I've come back to support his country.' He cocked his head to one side. 'My mother not so much. She thinks planes are little more than death traps and wasn't impressed when I insisted on joining the Flying Corps.'

Pru hated to think of either of these men sitting in one of those machines and wasn't surprised to hear his mother felt the same way.

'Yes,' Monty interjected. 'We met at college when I was sent to stay in New York for a year when we were, what? Fifteen?'

'That's right,' the captain said. 'It was my family who put him up and then I was sent here the following year.'

'Gosh, you've known each other for a long time then,' she said, wishing she could feel as relaxed and natural with Jack as she did with Monty. She kept herself busy by filling Monty's glass half full of water in case he became thirsty.

Jack laughed. 'You make it sound like it was decades ago. We're only just twenty-two.'

These two men were clearly incredibly close. She couldn't imagine what they must have seen so far in their lives. How much they had all seen. Hadn't she witnessed more heartache and cruel injuries than she ever thought possible already? And she hadn't even set foot in Europe yet! 'Well, I think you're both very brave going up in those tiny machines.'

'Or maybe we're just too stupid to see the danger,' Monty joked.

She knew she should be moving on to one of the other patients but was fascinated to find out more about Monty's charismatic visitor. 'Are you pilots in the same squadron then?'

'Monty's my Squadron Commander,' Jack said.

'I see,' she said, not seeing at all.

'I might be his superior in the air,' Monty said, his voice

taking on a serious note. 'But if it wasn't for this man I wouldn't be lying here now.'

Pru watched as he gave Jack a thumbs up. It cheered her to see Monty in such good spirits. She had noticed it happening when the patient's combat colleagues visited. She had found it a little odd at first to note that some of these men appeared much happier to be in the company of fellow soldiers rather than their own family members but then it dawned on her that it was probably because of their shared experiences and not needing to explain their emotions to friends who had experienced the same traumas.

'I can see you'd like to chat, so I'll leave you in peace.' She straightened Monty's sheet. 'Don't let him overdo it,' she said automatically to the captain, raising her eyebrows at him and then feeling that attraction again when their eyes met and he smiled at her. She forced herself to continue. 'The major thinks he's invincible and although he might be, he still needs his rest.'

'I'm fine, Nurse Le Cuirot.' Monty laughed.

'I promise I won't tire him out,' Jack assured her. 'I can't be too long here anyway.'

Pru was sad to think of him leaving so soon. She saw Monty's smile vanish and realised she was being selfish. She had barely known this man for five minutes yet here she was yearning to spend more time with him.

'You're not going back there, Jack?'

Pru couldn't miss the fear in Monty's voice. She might not know where Jack was going or what he was about to face, but she hoped desperately he would keep safe. For some reason this man had lit emotions in her that she had never known before. 'You may stay for as long as everyone else does,' she said to Jack, trying her best to mimic Matron's efficiency.

'Thank you, Nurse Le Cuirot.' He smiled at her and Pru had to turn away before he saw how affected she was by his presence.

She walked over to the patient in the next bed. He was a young private and hadn't received any visitors so far since his arrival the week before. It broke her heart to see these injured men lying quietly, most likely pretending not to mind while others around them joked with friends and family.

'Is there anything I can fetch for you, Private Danby?' she asked, giving him her brightest smile. 'A warm drink, maybe? Or something to read?'

'No, thank you.' He motioned for her to come a little closer to him. 'I'm enjoying being entertained by these two next to me.'

'Ahh, I see. I'll leave you in peace then.'

She spotted a young, gaunt-faced woman in her early twenties looking around for something. Pru recalled seeing her arriving with an older woman as she was showing Jack to Monty's bedside. She had assumed she was with her mother. Now, though, noticing the lack of closeness between the women and the territorial way the older woman had taken the visitor's chair and was clasping the patient's right hand, Pru presumed that must be the girl's mother-in-law.

'May I help you with anything?' Pru asked.

'I, um … That is, could I have a chair, do you think?'

'I'll fetch one for you immediately.' Pru hurried from the timid girl to the other end of the room where two spare chairs had been placed in case they were needed, and carried one back to the patient's bedside. 'There you go. Call me if you need anything else.'

'Thank you, Nurse.'

The older woman glared at her. 'What are you bothering that nurse for? Can't you see she's busy working? You should be doing something useful like her to keep you from pacing around the house all the hours of the day.'

Pru's temper ignited hearing the older woman picking on her daughter-in-law.

'Leave 'er alone, Mam. 'Ere, Lil, bring your chair round this side and give us yer 'and to 'old.'

Pru calmed, relieved to hear the patient stick up for his wife. As she returned to the other end of the ward, she heard Monty chatting once more.

'Why would you go back there, Jack?'

'Shush, Monty. You know I have to.' Pru heard the silence so filled with meaning as to almost be tangible. 'I'm not here to talk about that. I'm here to see you and find out how you're doing.'

'I know I'll never be able to thank you for all that you risked to save me.'

'Monty. Enough,' he said, his voice low, clearly not wishing to be overheard. 'I only did what you'd do for me. Anyway, we've been over this too many times for me to want to hear it again.'

There was a brief silence. 'You weren't flirting with the nurse, were you, Jack?' Monty teased, a marked change in his tone.

Pru smiled to herself, glad that the men were not going to fall out. She noticed Private Danby lying slightly uncomfortably in his bed and plumped up his pillows. She began to walk away, relieved to hear Monty sounding more cheerful and unable to help wondering what it was that the captain had done for him. She looked at the captain from the corner of her eye to see his response.

'Me?' he said, pretending to be hurt by the accusation. 'You're the one who misbehaves. I was simply asking her a few questions.'

She saw one of the other nurses needed help with a patient's dressing and rushed to assist. Pru pulled the screen around the soldier's bed. He was another one without visitors today, she thought miserably, although it was probably because his family had yet to make their way to the countryside manor. She offered her services to the nurse and taking the kidney bowl from her colleague's hand, held it as she began undoing the patient's pyjama top to change his dressing. She heard Monty laughing and smiled when the captain said something she couldn't make out. The deep sound of the American's laughter made her and the patient she was helping smile.

'Those two are a tonic, don't you think, Nurse?' the soldier said, wincing as his recently stitched wound was inspected and re-dressed.

Pru nodded. 'They're a little too noisy though,' she said. 'If Matron hears them, she'll soon be sending the captain home.'

She hoped the captain continued coming to visit Monty and cheering him and the rest of the patients up as he was doing. Whatever her first impression of him had been when he'd crashed into her trolley, she couldn't help admitting she felt some sort of emotional pull towards him. Was it because he was different from any other man she had ever met? Or maybe it was how tall and handsome he was, or simply his larger-than-life charisma that people – including her – seemed drawn to? She had no idea. She couldn't miss the bond between him and Monty though. Whatever had happened between them, she sensed it was something dark that would connect them for ever.

FOUR

Pru
———
FEBRUARY 1917

T he following morning, Pru, Milly and Jean were on their way to Ward Two to assist the doctor on his rounds.

'You don't mind if I take the first lot of beds at the end of the room, do you?' Jean asked, sounding a little odd, Pru thought.

She and Milly exchanged glances. Pru knew that each of them favoured one or two of the more friendly, or shyer, patients, but they never asked to swap with the other nurses during the rounds.

'Yes, that's fine,' Pru said, not minding which patients she cared for.

'Is there any particular reason why?' Milly asked.

Pru wasn't surprised Milly's curiosity had been piqued; hers was too. She was stunned when Jean's cheeks reddened. 'No, no reason.'

Pru knew her friend well enough to know she was fibbing but had no idea why. She decided to act as if she hadn't noticed Jean's guilty reaction and instead look out for any signs that might reveal who or what was behind her request.

Doctor Parslow arrived to do his rounds and they followed him and Matron in silence as he called out his instructions for each patient. After the rounds were complete, Pru joined Milly near the station where one of the nurses was always on duty.

'Well, at least we now know for certain that I wasn't wrong,' Milly whispered.

Pru frowned in confusion. 'I know. I hope he's all right, poor man.' Milly cocked her head to one side and Pru realised she had misunderstood what her friend was trying to tell her. 'I'm sorry, I don't know what you mean.'

'The far bed. The one where Lord and Lady Ashbury's son is lying. Can't you see?'

Pru peered over in the direction of Monty's bed and saw Jean listening to something he was saying while pretending to be busy. Her friend's face was glowing and Pru realised with a jolt that Jean was in love with him. Her pulse quickened as she thought of all the things that could go wrong for her friend. He was upper-class and Jean, although kind, dedicated, and with a fresh-faced prettiness about her, was not the sort of woman Pru imagined his parents accepting into their aristocratic family, especially as the wife of their only remaining son.

'What's the matter?' Milly asked. 'You don't have a fancy for him yourself, do you?'

Pru was horrified that Milly had taken her reaction the wrong way. 'No, I don't.'

'That's a relief. Why the concerned look then?'

'Nurse Denton. Nurse Le Cuirot!'

Relieved for once to be interrupted by Matron, Pru stood up straighter, arms by her side, just as Milly was doing. 'Matron,' they choroused.

'If you have nothing better to do than stand and idly gossip while on duty, then I'm sure I can find ways to keep you busy.'

'Sorry, Matron,' Pru said.

'We were just about to, um…'

Pru saw her friend scanning the room looking for something to do. 'Change the water in the vases,' she said, finishing Milly's sentence for her.

'Good. Then why are you standing here dithering?' She waved them away in irritation as if they were a couple of annoying flies.

Pru smoothed down her apron and followed Milly over to a windowsill where several vases of greenery and flowers brightened the otherwise stately but subdued decor in the panelled room.

'That was quick thinking,' Milly said over her shoulder. 'Well done.' They picked up several of the vases and carried them out of the ward. 'You were about to tell me why you reacted like you did when you spotted Jean with Monty.'

'I don't think we should call him by that name, especially when Matron or Lord and Lady Ashbury are nearby. Do you?'

'None of them can hear us now, so stop trying to change the subject and tell me.'

Pru sighed. 'It's just that Jean is such a sweet girl.'

'Don't you think he's nice enough for her?'

They reached the sluice room where they were to wash out

the vases. 'It's not that. I'm sure he's lovely. It's just that, well, he's Lord and Lady Ashbury's heir now. Do you truly believe they'll be happy for him to become close to a middle-class girl like Jean? Or do you suppose they'd be more inclined to expect him to marry someone with a similar background to his own?'

'Ahh.' Milly set down the two vases she was carrying and placed her hands on her hips. 'I hadn't thought of that.'

'I wish I hadn't,' Pru said, lifting out the wilting flowers and dropping them into the nearby bin before returning to the sink and turning on the water to wash the vase. 'Maybe it might not come to that. After all, Jean hasn't said anything to us about her feelings for him, has she?'

Milly shook her head. 'No, but we both saw how she is around him.' She threw away her handful of wilting flowers. 'Or maybe we're wrong and she's just being friendly.'

Pru doubted it. Jean was friendly to all the patients and they'd both worked with her for long enough to know this was a first for her. 'Let's hope so.' She dried the vases. 'We'd better hurry up and get back to the ward in case we're needed for something else.'

They arrived back to see Jean looking concerned near the nurses' station. 'Are you all right?' Pru asked, concerned.

'Not really.' She took a deep breath. 'Doctor Parslow is having a few words with Matron about Monty. He's removing Monty's bandages later this morning.'

'It's today?' They all knew the importance of this event.

'Yes,' she said, her voice trembling and barely above a whisper. 'What will he do if he can't see, Pru? What if this latest operation on Monty's eyes wasn't as successful as we're all hoping?' She took a deep breath and clasped her hands.

Pru gave Jean a reassuring smile. 'Then we'll all have to do our best to help him come to terms with it. Let's try not to panic before we know though, Jean.'

Jean sighed. 'Yes, I'll do my best not to.' She brightened. 'Monty's asked me if I wouldn't mind being there to hold his hand when the dressings are removed and Doctor Parslow has agreed that I can be. Matron doesn't look very happy about it though, for some reason.'

'Don't take any notice of that miserable woman,' Pru said, irritated. 'If the doctor's happy then that's all that matters.'

'It is,' Milly agreed, reaching out to rest a hand on Jean's arm. 'He must like you if he's asked for you specifically.'

'We have become friendly since he arrived here,' Jean said shyly, lowering her gaze to the floor. 'Monty said that if he does still have his sight then he wants my face to be the first one after the doctor's that he sees.'

Pru's hand went to her chest. 'That's so sweet of him.'

Her heart ached for her friend and especially for Monty. She prayed that his eyesight had been restored and that his life could soon return to some semblance of normality. She had heard that nothing much more could be done for his damaged leg. At best he would always have a limp, but at worst he could end up having to use a wheelchair.

Milly nudged Jean. 'I think Doctor Parslow is wanting you to go over now.'

Jean looked from one to the other of them and seemed, Pru thought, close to tears. 'Wish me luck. Him luck. Oh, I don't know.'

'We will,' Pru said, giving her a gentle push. 'Go on. You

can do this. And remember, whatever the outcome, Monty will be holding your hand and that will be a comfort to him.'

'Yes,' Jean whispered, closing her eyes briefly before holding her head high and walking over to Monty's bed.

They watched as the doctor said something and then Jean pulled the screen around the bed, blocking their view.

Milly grimaced. 'I hope he's all right.'

'So do I.'

Pru kept herself busy for the next little while, assisting the patients and making up two beds. Why was the doctor taking so long, she wondered anxiously. Surely it didn't take ten minutes to take off a dressing and shine a light into someone's eyes? She peered over at the screen to see it was still in place blocking her view and said a silent prayer that all would be well.

She was about to turn away when the screen was rolled back and Pru saw that her friend was wiping tears from her cheek. Forgetting she was supposed to be keeping busy, Pru hurried over to her. Jean noticed her and smiled, then bit her lower lip. Had the surgery been successful, Pru wondered hopefully.

She got as close to Monty's bed as she dared and studied him. His bandages were off and he was staring up at Jean with a broad smile on his slim face. He looked happy.

Pru felt a lump form in her throat and knew she was in danger of crying. 'You can see?' she asked without thinking.

'I can,' Monty said. 'And you are?' he asked, before

immediately raising a hand to stop her from answering. 'Let me guess. I recognise your voice well. You're Nurse Le Cuirot, if I'm not mistaken.'

Pru laughed, delighted with the happy outcome. 'I am. I'm so thrilled for you.'

'It's all a bit blurry at the moment, but I can see more than I had expected to.' He gave a shuddering sigh. 'When that bomb exploded, I never imagined I'd be able to see again.'

'You were incredibly lucky that your optic nerves weren't cut. The heavy bruising to your left eye is slowly reducing and your sight in that eye will continue to improve, although we're not entirely sure by how much,' Doctor Parslow said, his hands in his pockets. 'The piece of shrapnel that I removed from near your right eye was trickier than I was hoping it would be but it seems that the operation was successful and the vision in that eye has been saved.'

'You're a hero, Doctor,' Monty said.

Pru watched the doctor shake his head. 'No, my boy. I just put you soldiers back together to the best of my abilities. It's men like you who are the heroes. I want you to rest now. Your vision will have improved a little more by tomorrow,' the doctor assured him, looking as relieved as the rest of them, Pru thought. 'Nurse Le Riche. Give the Major a few minutes to settle and then please apply a new dressing over his eyes. Only a light one this time.'

'Do I need to have it put back on again?' Monty asked, looking disappointed. 'It's been ages since I saw daylight and I've only just seen this delightful nurse for the first time.'

Doctor Parslow pushed his glasses further up the bridge of his nose. 'I'm very happy for you, Major Ashbury, but you need to take things slowly. You've been incredibly brave and you've done very well so far. Now, though, you need rest and to give those eyes of yours the best possible chance of healing. You'll have many other chances to see the nurses, but for now you need to follow my instructions closely.'

'What about my parents?' Monty asked suddenly. 'I'm certain they'll want to see for themselves that your brilliant methods to restore my sight have succeeded.'

The doctor nodded. 'You're right, they will.' He turned to Pru. 'Nurse, please fetch Lord and Lady Ashbury immediately and let them know their son has some excellent news for them.'

FIVE

Pru

FEBRUARY 1917

L ater that afternoon, Pru's stomach flipped over to see
Captain Garland waiting with the rest of the visitors to
be let into the ward. She was excited for him to discover
Monty's news, especially as she had discovered that he was the
one who had rescued Monty and taken him to a casualty
clearing station and that without him Lord and Lady Ashbury
might possibly be mourning the death of their third son.

Was it the war that brought out the hero in men like the
captain, she wondered, or were they always ready to put their
lives at risk to rescue those close to them? She didn't know but
imagined that Lord and Lady Ashbury must feel indebted to
this man for saving their son and heir.

She hoped that today the result of Monty's operation
would give him a reason to shed the lines of worry she had
witnessed on his face. She hated to think of the horrors that a
man like the captain must have witnessed.

'Nurse?'

Pru looked down at an elderly lady with a walking stick. 'Yes?'

The woman waved Pru down to her level and whispered in her ear. 'Is there a lavatory I can use? It was a long journey here and I'd like to spend a penny.'

Pru pointed her in the direction of the nearest lavatory. 'Just down the hall there,' she said. 'Do you need me to ask one of the other nurses to accompany you?'

'No thanks, dear,' she said. 'I'll be back in a jiffy.'

Pru smiled and watched her go. Then, drawing her attention back to the waiting visitors, she noticed the captain looking directly at her. Her breath shortened and she had to concentrate on not appearing as flustered as she felt. She realised he seemed concerned about something, as if he had bad news to impart to his friend. She hoped not. She didn't want anything to diminish Monty's newfound happiness.

Seeing that it was now visiting time, Pru pulled back the ward door and ushered the visitors inside.

Jack walked up to her, stepping aside to let others pass before speaking to her. 'Good afternoon, Nurse Le Cuirot.'

'Captain, it's good to see you again,' she said honestly as the other visitors filed into the ward before him.

He smiled at her, the skin near his navy-blue eyes crinkling slightly, causing her heart to pound rapidly. 'You didn't expect me to be here?'

She smiled politely, her hands clasped neatly in front of her skirts to keep them from trembling. 'I wasn't sure you'd be able to come back so soon. You did say, that first day here, that you wouldn't be able to return in the afternoon, but you did. I presumed your leave had been extended, or something of the sort.' She knew she was being nosy but was intrigued.

He watched her silently for a few seconds, then his eyes widened and he seemed surprised. 'You've been thinking about me?'

Pru was taken aback by his reaction and mortified to have admitted that she had given his whereabouts some thought. 'Only because I hoped you might be able to visit Major Ashbury again.'

'Right, of course.'

Pru hated to see him looking disappointed and wished she had thought before speaking.

'I was supposed to leave that afternoon but my departure was delayed. Everything's back on again now and I must tell Monty that after today I won't be able to visit him for a few weeks.'

Pru was taken aback by how much this news saddened her. 'You will be back again though, won't you?' she asked without thinking, wishing as soon as the words had left her mouth that she would learn when not to speak.

He looked startled. 'I, er … Yes.'

'Good.'

His lips drew back in a wide smile. 'Am I to take it that you'll miss me, Nurse Le Cuirot?'

Mortified at behaving in such a forward manner, Pru shook her head. 'No. I … I was simply thinking about Monty, er, Major Ashbury.' Recalling Monty's exciting news and wanting to divert the captain's attention from her being so foolish, she said, 'In fact, I think you should go in to see him right away. He has his own news he wishes to share with you.'

All amusement vanished from Jack's face. He reached out and took her hand in his. 'He's all right, isn't he?'

Hating herself for being so insensitive and giving him a fright, she forced a smile. 'I'm sorry, I didn't mean to give you the wrong impression. He's fine. Truly.' Her heart leapt. She had never felt such a strong attraction to a man before, and she realised how exciting it was. Was this what Jean felt when she was with Monty? She supposed it must be. She felt the heat from his fingers and thumb around hers, enjoying the sensation. She looked up at him and saw him gazing down at her. Had he felt the same spark of electricity pass through his skin as it touched hers?

She forced herself to speak. 'I'm sure he'll want to tell you himself.'

'I, er, had better go and see him then.'

'Yes.' She reluctantly withdrew her hand from his and returned the confused smile he gave her. 'If I don't see you before you go, Captain, I'd like to wish you good luck with whatever it is that you're being sent to do.'

'Thank you, Nurse Le Cuirot,' he said. 'I appreciate it.'

She watched him walk away, taking in for the first time his height and the breadth of his shoulders. She had noticed him standing head and sometimes shoulders above the other visitors, but they had been mostly women. Now, though, she saw he was at least a couple of inches over six feet. She wondered how he managed to fit comfortably in one of the planes he flew. With what she knew of him, Pru felt certain that he would find a solution to anything he turned his mind to. The Jack Garland she had seen so far was a thoughtful, caring and kind man and she knew from overhearing snippets of his conversations with Monty that he hid his deeper feelings from most people. She sensed that if she ever needed a friend, this man was someone who could be relied upon.

She heard the excitement in Jack's voice when he greeted Monty.

The upturn in the atmosphere in the ward – and, Pru mused, the rest of the manor and its occupants since Monty's results became common knowledge – was unmistakable. Everyone seemed to be invested in his recovery, not only because he was a thoroughly likeable man, but also because all the patients and staff at Ashbury Manor felt enormous gratitude to their hosts and longed for their happiness after the loss of their older two sons.

Pru was weary after almost two years of nursing badly injured men and grasped at anything positive that made her days more bearable. She wasn't sure how she would cope with peace now if it came. So much had happened around her. She groaned, irritated with herself for being downbeat at such a happy time. 'It will come,' she whispered. 'It has to.' Her parents expected her to return to Jersey when all the fighting had finished but now she had experienced life away from the island – and from the strict confines of her family – she knew she wanted to take time to discover more of the world.

She jumped when a hand rested on her shoulder. 'What?'

'Sorry, I didn't mean to alarm you,' Jean said. 'I was wondering when you're taking your break and thought we might go for a walk together in the gardens. I could do with some fresh air.'

Pru glanced out of the large window to her right and shuddered. 'It looks freezing out there,' she said, noticing how the earlier sunshine had disappeared behind thick, low steel-grey clouds. 'It looks like it's about to snow.'

'I know, which is why I thought now would be a good time for that walk.' Jean grinned. 'Before we get snowed in here and can't go outside for a few days.'

'You think that will happen?' Pru hoped not. She valued her daily walks; it was the one time she was usually alone and able to work through any troubling thoughts brought about by what she had witnessed during her shift.

'I've no idea.' Jean untied her apron and slipped it over her head. 'Will you be joining me, or not?'

Pru suspected her friend needed someone to confide in. She didn't often ask to join her, but simply left the building with her and walked next to her when she was free to do so. 'Yes, why not? We'll need to wrap up warm though.' She looked up at the wall clock. 'I should be finished soon. I only have a few small jobs to do. Why don't I meet you at the side door nearest the wooded area in fifteen minutes?'

'Perfect.'

Pru returned to the ward to check with Matron whether she was needed for anything else. Happy to be given leave to go, she rushed to the room she shared with Jean, Milly and one other new nurse and quickly changed into her ankle boots, coat, hat and thick scarf. She couldn't afford to catch a chill, especially not now they were so busy with new patients.

By the time she and Jean stepped outside, snow had begun falling. It didn't often snow in Jersey and seeing the delicate flakes billowing downwards made Pru feel like she was miles away from her everyday life.

'Isn't this perfect?' Jean asked, linking her arm through Pru's. 'In fact, I think life is pretty idyllic right now.'

Pru smiled at her friend as they walked down the stone path between neat hedging and bare flower borders. 'We're all certainly much happier since Monty's successful eye surgery,' she said, aware that her friend's happy mood was mostly due to him being able to see again. 'I thought it very romantic that he wanted yours to be the first face he saw. That must have been really emotional for you?' When Jean didn't react, she added, 'I know you've both become close recently.'

They walked on a few steps before Jean replied. 'We have.' She sighed. 'In fact, he's asked me to marry him.'

Stunned by her friend's unexpected announcement, Pru gasped. She stopped walking. 'He's what?'

Jean groaned. 'I know what you're thinking.'

'That you've only known him for a month?' Pru couldn't help herself. It all seemed far too quick.

'I know it sounds crazy. In fact, I wasn't sure whether or not to tell you yet, but I had to share my news with someone and who better than you?' Jean sighed. 'I had hoped you'd be happy for me.'

Pru wished she had managed to hide how shocked she was. Of course she was happy for her, but what if Monty had proposed as a reaction to his euphoria at having his sight restored? What if he changed his mind once he had time to think? She couldn't bear for her friend to be heartbroken. 'I'm just a little taken aback, that's all.'

Jean folded her arms. 'I understand. I have to admit I was

too, but Monty explained that losing his brothers and then being so badly hurt himself, well … he believes we should all grab happiness while we have the chance.' She shrugged. 'Let's face it, Pru, none of us know what might happen from one day to the next, do we?'

She was right, Pru mused. She reached out and rubbed Jean's upper arm gently. 'And he's right.' She gave Jean an encouraging smile, not wishing to ruin such a special time for her best friend. 'What did you say?'

Jean turned to her, tears in her eyes. 'At first I said that we should see how his surgery went before making any rash decisions.' She covered her mouth letting out a sob. 'Oh Pru, he thought I meant that I wanted to be certain he could see again. He didn't think I'd want to marry a blind man.'

'I hope you put him right.'

'I did. It took a little persuasion, but I insisted that wasn't the case.'

Pru pulled her friend into a tight hug.

'I eventually managed to persuade him I thought we should wait because I wanted to be certain that if he did get his sight back, he had seen me before he made up his mind.' She stepped back and looked away. 'I know I'm not the most beautiful woman, but I couldn't agree to let him marry me not knowing what I looked like. Imagine if we married and then his sight returned and he hated what he saw? It would break my heart.'

Pru was well aware that her friend had little confidence in her fresh-faced, rosy-cheeked looks. She wasn't glamorous in any way but she was pretty, as far as Pru was concerned. She was relieved that Monty obviously thought so too.

'You shouldn't be so hard on yourself. You're lovely and now you know that he thinks so, will you agree to marry him?'

Pru battled with her conflicted thoughts. As much as she wanted her closest friend to be happy, she couldn't help worrying about Lord and Lady Ashbury's reaction to discovering Monty wanted Jean as his wife. What if they had their own plans for their son's future and managed to convince Monty that Jean wasn't the woman for him? Her friend would be devastated. She struggled with her conscience, unsure whether to say as much.

'I know what you're thinking,' Jean said, narrowing her eyes at Pru.

'You do?'

'Of course. And you don't need to worry. I told Monty I couldn't think of anything I'd rather do but that maybe we should wait until we've had a chance to spend time with each other outside the hospital ward.'

Pru tried to hide her disappointment that Jean hadn't realised her true concerns about their marriage. She began to resume walking, but Jean held her back. 'What is it?'

'Nothing,' Pru fibbed, not wishing to hurt her friend.

'That wasn't what you were thinking, was it?' Jean asked, staring at her.

Pru held her friend's gaze as she tried to work out what to say. It was one thing for Jean and Monty to spend more time getting to know each other, but another entirely to have to contend with opposition like the difference in their class. It might be 1917, she mused, with the world taking enormous strides forward when class differences were forgotten between women working together while nursing or driving vehicles, and men fighting next to each other – but what about after the war ended? What then? Would everyone slip back into their class structures with their prejudices? She couldn't help worrying that they might and surely that would mean heartache for Jean.

Jean winced. 'I've been so stupid.'

'Don't say that,' Pru argued.

'But I have. How can I even consider a relationship with a man whose station in life is so far above my own?' She groaned. 'I've become used to us speaking to each other as equals while nursing him and I've forgotten who he is.' She shook her head. 'And who I am.'

And there it was, Pru thought miserably. 'I'm sure if Monty loves you, he'll find a way around it,' she said, not sure if he was strong enough to stand up to his formidable parents.

'You think so?'

Pru took her friend's hands in her own. 'I don't know,' she said honestly. 'But I do think that if you're aware of the difficulties that might await you, then it's something you and Monty can discuss.'

'I suppose you're right.'

Pru wished her friend's joy hadn't been so quickly eroded. She struggled to find the right words, and was relieved when a familiar figure waved to them from the side door and began walking over, his long strides making short work of the distance they had gone.

'That's Captain Garland, isn't it?' Jean asked, clutching Pru's arm. 'I hope nothing's wrong with Monty.'

'Captain? Is everything all right?' Pru asked, trying to hide her pleasure as he joined them.

He removed his cap and placed it under his arm.

'I'd keep that on if I were you,' Pru said, holding her hand out, palm up, to indicate the falling snow.

'Good idea.' He replaced his cap. 'Monty's fine, if that's what you mean. I was about to leave and saw you both out here on my way to the motor. I thought I'd say goodbye.'

'Goodbye?' Jean glanced at Pru. 'You're returning to France?'

'I am,' he said vaguely. 'I wanted to ask you to keep a close eye on my pal. He's in high spirits after discovering he can see again, but I worry that his focus has been on that happening and now worry that he might struggle when he discovers his leg is pretty badly damaged.'

He had a point, Pru realised. 'Don't worry. We'll take good care of him while you're away.'

'Thanks, I appreciate it.' He looked deep into her eyes and Pru couldn't think what else to say.

'You will be back though? Won't you?' Jean asked after a brief hesitation. Then, seeming to realise what she had just asked, her hand flew to her mouth and she mumbled an awkward apology.

'It's fine,' Jack assured her. 'I'll certainly do my best. I want to come and visit my friend again,' he said, glancing at Pru with an intensity that made her shiver.

'It really is cold out here,' he went on, mistaking her reaction, something she was very grateful for. 'I'd better let you carry on with your walk before your feet get too cold.'

'They're freezing already,' Pru said with a smile, desperate for something to say, and then realised that they actually were going numb.

'Don't you get cold in that plane of yours?' Jean asked.

He shook his head. 'Sometimes, but mostly I'm fine. I'm from New York, don't forget. I'm used to far lower temperatures than anything you'll find here or in Europe.'

He gave them a quick smile before turning and walking away.

'He's such a nice man, don't you think?' Jean asked, stamping her feet a couple of times. 'Monty said he'll never be able to repay him for saving his life like he did, and at a terrible risk to his own too.'

Pru watched Jack's retreating back, her breath catching in her throat when he suddenly turned and gave her a wave. Her heart pounded so loudly that she was surprised Jean didn't comment on it, but Pru realised her friend was too busy talking about Monty to notice.

'I'm glad Monty has a friend like him,' Jean said. 'You can see that the captain has hidden depths.'

Pru agreed, hoping that Jack would come back safely this time too.

SIX

Pru
___
JUNE 1917

Not much had changed in the months since Pru had first met Captain Jack Garland. She was relieved the United States had entered the war two months before and since the first of their infantry troops had arrived in Europe earlier that month, several American soldiers had come to Ashbury for treatment, and two were still recuperating at the manor.

Jack had been away since March; it was now June and Pru had been surprised by how often thoughts of him had invaded her free time. And she couldn't miss the concern on Monty's face when she quietly asked every so often whether he had heard from Jack. His mood always dipped when reminded of his absent friend, so much so that Pru eventually had to stop asking him. She might miss Jack but that didn't give her the right to worry Monty when he should be recuperating, or to put doubt in his mind about Jack's eventual return.

She still found herself looking up each time she heard a vehicle rolling down the gravelled driveway, or whenever she heard a deep voice with an American accent in one of the wards. Not that there were many of those, but it always threw her for a couple of seconds.

There had been new arrivals that morning but she hadn't been needed to help with them so made the most of her free time to catch up with a little mending.

'Pru, are you there?' There was a knock on her bedroom door as she was sewing up one end of a tie on her apron. She had caught it on a door handle the day before when she had nudged it shut with her elbow while her hands were full of clean dressings.

'Yes, come in.' She would have given a lot to have just a few more minutes' peace. It wasn't the poor Voluntary Aid Detachment volunteer's fault that she had been sent to find her though so she forced a welcoming smile onto her face. 'Matron is looking for me, no doubt?' she asked, pre-empting the girl's request.

'Yes, how did you know?' The girl's brown eyes widened in admiration.

Pru shook her head. Tying off the end of her sewing, she bit the thread and carefully put her needle into the tiny sewing basket she shared with her roommates. 'It was a guess. What does she want, do you know?' she asked, slipping her apron over her head and fastening it around her waist.

'She said there's a French patient, but that's all I know.'

'I'm on my way,' Pru said. 'You go ahead; I'll follow in a second.'

She couldn't have been more than two or three minutes arriving at the ward but Matron greeted her with her usual disappointed air. 'Where on earth were you, Nurse Le Cuirot? You're supposed to be on duty, not slacking.'

'I was sewing my apron, Matron,' she explained, aware that whatever she said would be greeted with annoyance.

'Follow me.'

Pru accompanied Matron to the bedside of a frightened young patient. His eyes were red-rimmed and she doubted he was even eighteen. He barely looked old enough to shave.

'This patient is French and can't speak any English.' Matron sounded as if the poor man had committed a terrible faux pas to be in England and unable to converse. 'Nurse Le Riche seems to think you can speak fluent French. Is that correct?'

'It is,' she replied, aware that Jean probably knew enough to be able to find out from the poor boy what was wrong with him.

Matron eyed her suspiciously and it took all Pru's efforts not to show her amusement that for once she knew something Matron did not. 'Good. Then you can explain that he's here for at least a few weeks until we can arrange for him to be sent back to France. Also, that he's not to worry. The usual things you would tell a new patient to calm them. I presume you can do that?'

Pru wondered if Matron ever found joy in anything. The older woman might spend her life looking after injured and scarred men but it seemed to Pru that she was as scarred as the worst of them – only her scars were in her mind and heart.

'Nurse! Did you hear me?' Matron glared at her. 'Wipe that soppy look off your face and move yourself.'

'Yes, Matron. I'll speak to him immediately.'

Relieved when Matron was distracted by another patient, she drew up a chair to sit next to the young private's bed and spoke in a friendly manner to him. He seemed stunned to discover that she could speak to him in his native language, and soon relaxed. After ten minutes chatting with him and writing down his address, with a promise to try and send a telegram to his family, Pru asked for one of the VADs to keep an eye on him.

She stood. 'Let me know if he becomes fractious at all, or if he needs something that any staff member can't understand.'

'Yes, Nurse Le Cuirot.'

Pru pushed the chair back and was about to leave the ward but noticed Monty waving and trying to get her attention. She smiled at him and went to see what he wanted.

'Is everything all right, Monty?'

'Yes.'

'Sorry,' she said, glancing behind her, confused. Had he been waving at someone else? 'I thought you wanted me for something.'

'I did.'

'Yes?'

'You were speaking French.'

It sounded more like a statement than a question. 'That's right, I was.'

'You sounded pretty fluent.' He frowned thoughtfully. 'Jean said the other day that she doesn't speak much French at all, when I asked her if the locals in Jersey spoke the language.' He shrugged. 'You know, because the island is so much closer to

France than England. She tells me that what she speaks is the local patois. I gather that's different.'

'It is.'

'You don't speak that?'

'The patois? A little.'

'May I ask why that is?'

Pru was used to patients being more interested in the nurses' and doctors' lives than they usually would be in people they came across, and knew it was down to the boredom of long days sitting in wards with little to do, so she didn't mind him asking.

'My grandmother is French and, despite moving to Jersey when she married my late grandfather years ago, refuses to speak English when we're alone as a family,' she explained enjoying reminiscing. 'She lives with my parents; they run a guesthouse.' She sighed. 'So, I've grown up speaking French at home, as well as some Jèrriais at friends' homes, which is how I know the languages.'

'Ahh, that makes sense.' He gave her an appreciative nod. 'Good for you, Nurse Le Cuirot. I'm sure that the matron has a lot to be grateful to you for, for once.' He winked.

Pru knew he was trying to make her feel better and it cheered her to know that others were aware of Matron picking on her. It helped reaffirm to her that she wasn't as useless as Matron sometimes liked to make out.

'Thanks very much, Monty. I appreciate you saying so, even if I doubt she'll ever openly admit I've done anything remotely well enough for her liking.'

A few days later, she helped Doctor Parslow with a patient who became distressed during visiting hours when blood from his wound seeped through the dressing on his shoulder. The doctor was examining it while Pru held the kidney bowl with the discarded dressing, when she heard Jack's voice asking to see Monty. She froze.

'Nurse?' the doctor said, snapping her out of her thoughts. 'The dressing?'

She looked down at her hands and saw that she was still holding the bowl. 'Sorry, Doctor,' she said placing the bowl noisily onto the trolley and lifting the fresh dressing for him to take.

'I think we're all pleased to hear the captain's voice again,' the doctor said without looking at her.

'No, I simply—'

'It's fine.' He smiled at her. 'Please try to concentrate.'

She focused on what the doctor was doing, not wanting to be caught acting unprofessionally again.

'Well, if it isn't the American Ace himself,' Monty teased noisily. 'I expected you back months ago. No doubt you'll have a good excuse for keeping me waiting all this time.'

'I do,' Jack replied. 'But not one I'll be sharing with your delicate English ears.'

They laughed and continued their conversation, each hurriedly saying what Pru supposed they had been waiting to during Jack's lengthy absence.

Eventually the doctor finished with the patient and left her to make the man comfortable by doing up his pyjama top, plumping up his pillows and straightening his sheets. She was anxious to look at Jack again. To see for herself that he was fine. She smoothed down her skirts and, picking up a clean kidney bowl, discreetly checked her reflection, hoping her cap was on straight and her hair still pinned back properly. Satisfied that she looked as neat as possible, Pru folded back the screen so that the patient could join in with everyone else in the ward.

One of the wheels on the screen squeaked as she pushed it back against the wall and she noticed Jack looking at her. His lips drew back in a long, slow smile, which she returned with one of her own. He looked thinner than before but seemed well enough and she was relieved.

'Good to see you again, Nurse Le Cuirot,' he said as she took hold of the trolley handle, intending to take it from the ward and dispose of the bloody dressing.

'Thank you, Captain. I'm glad to see you back here again.' She glanced at Monty and noticed he was giving Jack a questioning look. 'Major Ashbury is happy to have you back here again with us too, aren't you, Major?'

'I certainly am, Nurse. I was beginning to think he had forgotten me.'

Jack laughed. It was a deep baritone that made her pulse race. 'I can't imagine that ever happening, even if I wanted it to.'

She gave him one last smile and then wheeled the trolley out of the ward, leaving them to their reunion.

Later, as she was sorting clean kidney bowls in the sluice room, the door opened behind her. Thinking it was one of her fellow nurses, she joked, 'I spend so much time in here I'm beginning to think I should have chosen a different occupation as my contribution to the war effort.'

'And what might you have chosen instead?' Jack asked.

Shocked to hear his voice behind her, Pru dropped the bowl into the porcelain sink. The clatter was so loud she was frightened Matron or one of the nursing sisters might hear and feel the need to come in and check on her. She spun on her heels to face him.

'Captain? What are you doing here? This room is out of bounds to visitors.'

He stepped back into the hallway. 'I'm sorry, I should have realised. I didn't mean to startle you.' He raised his hands to calm her. 'I'll go.' He turned to leave.

Panicked that he might leave and be gone for another few months, Pru hurriedly wiped her hands on a nearby towel. 'No. Wait. Please don't go yet.'

He immediately stilled and turned back to her, eyebrows raised. 'You're happy for me to stay?'

She stepped past him and peered out into the hall, looking both ways. 'You'd better come in,' she said, taking hold of his sleeve and pulling him gently inside. Flustered to be alone with him, yet not daring to let him leave before he had shared what he had come to tell her, Pru worried that she had acted against her better judgement. Still, she closed the door quietly behind her.

He seemed bemused by her behaviour and she wasn't at all surprised. What was wrong with her? Ever since she had met this man, her mind seemed to falter when she was in his presence.

She cleared her throat and thought she'd better try to rectify the situation. 'You shouldn't be in here, but I'm curious to know what you've come to tell me.'

'I see.' He didn't speak for a few seconds and she wondered if maybe after witnessing her acting so foolishly he had changed his mind about talking to her.

'Captain?'

'Right. I, er, was hoping to speak to you alone.'

'You were?'

He opened his mouth to reply when Pru heard footsteps and voices and raised a finger to his mouth, instantly wishing she hadn't when the touch of his lips against her skin sent shivers through her. They were firm but soft and she was mesmerised by them. She realised she had startled him, and was again relieved when his expression softened and his eyes glinted in amusement.

They stood in a still, apprehensive silence. Pru listened, her finger still resting on his lips, and their eyes locked. She willed whoever was in the hallway to keep walking and not enter the room. She was aware that being alone in a small room like this with a man she barely knew, or even one she did know, simply wasn't something that would be tolerated. She would almost certainly lose her job if she was caught.

The footsteps kept going and Pru exhaled slowly. 'Thank heavens for that,' she said breathlessly as she lowered her hand from his face.

'Are you all right, Nurse?'

'I will be once I gather myself,' she said, aware that her erratic behaviour was brought about mostly by his presence rather than the thought of being in trouble. 'That was a bit scary.'

He frowned. 'I'm a fool for coming after you like this. I should have known it wasn't the way to go about things. I'm sorry for putting you in this difficult position.'

'It's perfectly fine,' she said, excited by the strange and unexpected experience of being alone with him. 'Now, maybe you should tell me what it is that's on your mind and I can check the hallway again to make sure it's completely clear before you go on your way.'

He rubbed his hands together and for the first time seemed unsure of himself. The difference in him made Pru want to smile, but she didn't dare put him off speaking. 'I was hoping to talk to you about something.'

'Go on.' She watched him as he thought through what he wanted to say.

'I wondered if you might agree to come out to dinner with me.' He looked down at his feet and then back into her eyes. 'Sometime soon.'

Delighted, she had to force herself to think. 'How soon exactly?'

'Tonight? Tomorrow, if you'd prefer?' He shrugged. 'Whenever suits you best, I guess.'

Her mind raced. He wanted her to go out with him? Alone? She would have loved to see him that night but knew it would be wrong to act too eager. 'I'm busy tonight,' she said, aware that the only thing she would be doing was washing her hair, finishing her mending or catching up with overdue correspondence to her parents. Not wishing to miss out on the opportunity or give him a chance to change his mind, she thought quickly. 'I can be free tomorrow evening though.'

His shoulders relaxed and for the first time she noticed he had been tense. Surely he wasn't as flustered in her presence as she was in his? Could he be? 'That's great. I have something I wish to discuss with you. Shall I collect you at seven?'

What could he possibly need to speak to her about, she wondered. She supposed she would have to wait and see. At least if he met her at seven she would have enough time after her shift to wash, change and do a little something with her hair. 'That's perfect,' she said, trying her best to sound as if this wasn't the enormous event that it was to her. She wished she had a newer dress to wear than the one hanging in her locker, but unfortunately she didn't have room for anything other than the essentials in her small sleeping area, and one dress was all they could reasonably fit in with their outer clothes and uniforms.

'Good.'

'Right.' She realised she should show him out of the small room. 'I'd better have a peek in the hallway so you can leave without anyone catching you. It would be more than my life is worth for Matron to catch you in here with me.'

'Yes, I'm sorry again about putting you in this predicament.'

'Please, don't worry.' She opened the door and seeing Milly and another nurse crossing from one room to the other to the right of her, stepped back and hurriedly closed the sluice room door as quietly as she could once again. 'The coast isn't quite clear yet.'

'This would be fun if there wasn't the chance you might get into trouble,' he whispered, smiling at her.

'It would,' she admitted, her body tingling with excitement. 'Do you have an idea where you'll be taking me tomorrow?' she whispered, unable to help herself.

He tapped the side of his nose with a finger. 'I'm not certain yet, but I have an idea.'

'That sounds delightful,' she said, knowing she would be happy with anywhere he chose. She opened the door to check the hallway a second time and leaned out slightly, unsure if she was relieved or not to find it was clear. 'It's fine,' she said, moving back slightly to give him space to leave. 'I'll see you tomorrow at seven.'

He gave her a brief smile. 'See you then.' He left the room with a backward glance and Pru closed the door quietly behind him.

She leaned against the closed door and willed her racing heart to calm down. What on earth had just happened? She rubbed her face with her hands. Then, remembering she was supposed to be washing out the kidney bowls, she reached out and turned on the hot tap to fill the sink. She lowered her hands into the warm water and exhaled sharply. She was going out on a date with Captain Garland. Could it be possible that he liked her as much as she did him? She certainly hoped so.

SEVEN

Pru

JUNE 1917

'Are you certain I look smart enough?' Pru asked, crouching slightly in front of the small mirror they had propped up on a bookcase and checking that her hair looked as neat as possible. Standing up straight again, she twisted to the left, looking over her shoulder at how the dress gathered at her lower back.

'Yes.' Jean handed Pru her jacket. 'Here, borrow this.'

'Are you sure? You love this jacket.' Pru draped the dark blue jacket over her bare shoulders.

'You look perfect. Anyway, where am I going to be able to wear this? One of us may as well get the benefit of it.'

Pru smoothed down the front of the thin woollen jacket. 'It's lovely, Jean. Thank you ever so much. I'll take very good care of it.'

Jean laughed as she picked up Pru's bag and handed it to her. 'You'd better. Now, get a move on otherwise he'll think you've changed your mind and aren't coming. I'll see you later.' She pointed at Pru. 'If I'm asleep, make sure you wake me. I want to know everything.'

Pru laughed. 'I'll do no such thing. You need your sleep. I'll speak to you in the morning.'

She was going to be late if she didn't do as Jean suggested and hurry. She leaned forward and gave Jean a kiss on the cheek. 'Thanks again for helping me get ready. I think my nerves would have got the better of me if I'd done it alone.'

'You look gorgeous and that's all you need to think about.' Jean opened their door. 'Now, go!'

Pru took a steadying breath as she hurried along the corridor and down the back stairs. Her excitement gave way to nerves as she wondered what she might talk to him about. Then she remembered he had said he wanted to speak to her about something. But what? Maybe it was something to do with Monty? Her stomach seemed filled with butterflies at the thought of running out of conversation and boring Jack. She would simply have to do her best.

Pru had forgotten just how long it took her to get from her dormitory to the opposite side of the large manor house, and when she reached the side door she stopped to let her breathing calm slightly. She patted her hair, which Jean had helped her put up with quite a few pins. Pru wished she had the courage to cut her long hair into a bob as Milly had recently done with her bright chestnut hair. Several other nurses had already copied her and Pru thought they all looked stunning. She was sure it must be easier to keep short hair; it would certainly be quicker to wash and dry it.

She stared at the door and tried to relax. Hopefully he was already waiting for her. The thought of being in his presence again excited her and unnerved her at the same time. He was unlike anyone else she had ever met and she couldn't help feeling a little shocked by the strength of her attraction to him. All she needed to do, she told herself, was to try and not show how daunted she was by him. She had spoken to Jack several times now and he had always been pleasant, but this time they were spending an entire evening alone. She took a calming breath, opened the door and stepped outside.

She had expected to have to walk round to the front of the house, where she presumed Jack would be waiting, but he was right in front of her near the side door steps. Seeing him took her aback slightly. 'Oh.'

'I didn't mean to surprise you,' he said apologetically. 'It's a dark night and I thought I'd do the gentlemanly thing and come to greet you and accompany you to the car.'

She stepped forward and immediately slipped on a small stone. Jack was next to her in a moment and, grabbing hold of her arm, stopped her from falling. 'Are you all right?'

'Yes, thank you.' She could sense her cheeks reddening at the embarrassing display, and was relieved it was too dark for him to notice. 'It seems you were right to come and fetch me. I haven't worn heels for such a long time, I think I must have lost the knack.'

'Then I'm glad I did.' They walked for a few steps. 'I have no idea how you ladies manage in those shoes; they can't be easy to get used to.'

'These aren't too high, thankfully,' she said, relaxing slightly. 'I think they're probably my limit though.'

Once they reached his car, he opened the door and, taking her hand, helped her up into the vehicle. Pru stroked the soft blood-red leather seat and pulled the collar of the jacket tighter around her neck. She hadn't expected it to be as cool as it was this evening after the warm day.

'This is a lovely motor car,' she said, starting to feel less intimidated by him now that their evening was underway.

'It's not mine, unfortunately. I've borrowed it from a friend,' he said from the front of the vehicle before bending to turn a handle and crank the motor. He quickly got into the driver's seat, let off the handbrake and they began moving down the driveway. 'Enjoying yourself yet?'

'Very much so.'

'I wasn't sure if you'd agree to accompany me tonight, but I'm glad you did.'

'Thank you. It's rather nice being out, for once,' she admitted. 'I usually spend my evenings with Jean and Milly. We share a room.'

'That sounds like fun.' He changed gears and smiled at her. 'Are you enjoying living and working at Ashbury Manor?'

'I am,' she admitted, wishing the vehicle was a little warmer. 'Very much. In fact, I think we all are.'

'I can sense a *but*.'

There was. 'It's exciting living away from home but I do miss my family sometimes.' She didn't want him to get the wrong impression and think she didn't appreciate Monty's family home. 'I love Ashbury Manor though. It's very beautiful, don't you think?'

'I know what you mean about missing family; I do too. I would love for my mother to be able to visit,' he said. 'I'm certain she'd be enchanted by Ashbury Manor. She's a huge fan of history and loves reading British historical fiction.'

'She is?' Pru pictured the row of Jane Austen novels lined up in her small bookcase in her bedroom at home. 'Does she have a favourite author?'

'She does.' He gave her question some thought. 'That's right, it's Jane Austen. She has all her books, and growing up I wasn't allowed to touch them. Not that I recall ever wishing to do so.'

Intrigued, Pru asked, 'Does she have a favourite?'

'Sorry?'

'A favourite Jane Austen novel.' Pru knew it probably wasn't the conversation he had imagined having when he had asked her out, but she was glad to have something to ask him that didn't show her ignorance about what he did. 'Which one does she like best, do you know? Mine is *Pride and Prejudice*, closely followed by *Sense and Sensibility*.'

He gave her a knowing smile. 'Ahh, yes. I gather there's something magical about those books, or so my mother insists each time one of us catches her re-reading one of them.'

Aware that he hadn't answered her question, and always intrigued to hear the favourites of other Austen fans, Pru asked again. 'And her favourite?'

'She does have one in particular.' He frowned thoughtfully. 'I can't recall what it is though. Name some other books by that author.'

'*Mansfield Park*.'

'Not that one.'

'*Northanger Abbey*, maybe?'

'Er, no.'

'I know. It has to be *Persuasion*.'

'No. I think it's a woman's name maybe.'

'*Emma*,' she said triumphantly, shivering in the cold. 'Is it *Emma*?'

He turned and gave her a beaming smile that made her insides clench and heart race. 'That's the one.'

'It's a wonderful book. Funny and clever.'

'I do miss her. My mother, that is.' He glanced at Pru briefly before turning his attention back to the road. 'I don't miss her reading passages from her books to me and my brother though.' He laughed. 'You two would get along.'

Pru was delighted he thought so, not that she could ever imagine meeting the woman, she thought sadly. 'We already have a shared taste in books,' she said, blushing slightly and thinking that they also both had feelings for Jack, albeit very different ones.

She was getting a little ahead of herself and was happy he didn't know what she was thinking. They were only going out for something to eat, after all. 'She must miss you very much,' she said, attempting to bring the conversation back to a less personal level.

'She does, but she has my older brother to keep her company. Although now the States has entered this war, I'm almost certain he'll enlist.' He slowed and turned into a small car park to the side of a Victorian country house. 'Here we go. I hope you like the restaurant. The food is superb; at least it was the last time I came here several years ago. I recall they have an excellent fireplace and I'm sure there'll be a decent fire tonight that should warm us up after that drive.'

'That sounds perfect,' she said, trying to keep her teeth from chattering. It was colder than she had expected for a June evening.

He parked the car and together they walked into the smart entrance with high ceilings and a sparkling chandelier.

Thankfully, they were close enough to the roaring fire to be slowly warmed up, and Pru smiled at Jack as they settled into their seats. Her heart skipped a beat and she knew she was in serious danger of falling deeply in love with this handsome man. 'Thank you for inviting me here tonight. It was very kind of you.'

'It's my pleasure,' he replied, his eyes boring into hers for a few seconds before he seemed to snap out of his reverie. 'Although,' he said, looking slightly uncomfortable, 'I did have a reason for doing so.' He grimaced, and Pru could see he had realised how insulting that sounded. 'That came out rather clumsily,' he said. 'I did want to take you out for dinner to spend time with you.'

'But you also had an ulterior motive,' she added, trying not to mind.

'I suppose so.' He closed his eyes and shook his head quickly. 'Sorry. That didn't sound how I meant it either.'

Pru wasn't in the least offended. In fact, his awkwardness calmed her. It reminded her that he might be devastatingly handsome with a deep voice that stirred emotions in her she never knew existed, but he was also only human. She struggled to contain her amusement. 'It's fine, truly. You did say you wanted to speak to me about something when we were in the sluice room.'

Pru suddenly noticed that a waiter standing near to them had a startled expression on his face. He must have heard what she had said. She glanced at Jack, willing him to say something.

'It wasn't how it sounds,' Jack explained to the man, his eyes twinkling in amusement.

'I'm sure it's none of my business, sir. Are you ready to look at the menu?' They nodded and took the leather-bound cards listing the limited menu. 'Would you care to peruse the wine list, sir?'

'Thank you, yes.'

The waiter walked away to get the list and Pru wasn't sure if she should be mortified or amused by his shock. She knew her mother would have been appalled to hear her coming out with such a thing.

'If you'll give us a few moments,' Jack said when the waiter returned, waiting for the man to leave before focusing his attention on Pru. 'I'm sorry about all this,' he said. 'I really should have thought before following you into that room at the manor.'

'Let's not worry about that,' she said, enjoying the evening far more than she had expected to. 'Anyway, the waiter was shocked by what I said, not you.'

'I imagine he's probably heard worse. I shouldn't worry too much.'

Pru giggled. 'I didn't see him walking over to us,' she admitted. 'I'll have to be a little more careful for the rest of the evening. I don't want to offend anyone else.'

Jack laughed. It was a deep, rolling laugh and the joyous sound made Pru want to join in. 'I can't imagine you'll ever offend me, Pru. You're a fun girl and I'm extremely glad that you accepted my dinner invitation.' The waiter returned. 'Any preference with the wine, sir?' Jack gave her a questioning look. Pru shook her head, and he ordered a bottle of something she didn't recognise.

'You said it was exciting living away from home for the first time,' Jack said once they were alone again.

'That's right.'

'And may I ask where home is?'

'Jersey. It's an island; part of the Channel Islands. They're about fifteen miles off the coast of France.'

'You're almost French then?'

'No, I'm British, but not English. If that makes sense.'

He frowned. 'I guess so. I'll have to make a plan to visit as soon as all this ruckus is over and done with.'

'I can show you around when you do,' she said without thinking. 'That is, if you wanted me to.'

His gaze made her heart tingle.

'I'd like that very much.'

Not wishing him to notice how flustered he was making her, Pru dug into the food the waiter had just delivered. She ate a mouthful of the chicken casserole savouring the delicious flavour enhanced by the potatoes, courgettes, and carrots and wondered how lonely he felt being so far from home. 'You must miss New York.'

'I do. Very much. I miss the excitement and noise of the city but most of all I miss my mother and brother.'

He hadn't mentioned a wife so he wasn't married, Pru thought, realising that she was pleased. 'They must miss you, too.'

'Yes, they do.' He drank some wine. 'I feel guilty about joining the RFC, but I felt compelled to do it. I've had a yearning to learn to fly for a couple of years and when the opportunity came to learn in the Royal Flying Corps then that's what I knew I must do.'

They continued eating and Pru studied his face. There was something anxious about him and it occurred to her that she still didn't know what it was that he wanted to ask her.

'Please feel free to talk to me about whatever it is that's bothering you,' she said. 'Is it about Monty?'

He looked at her. 'It is.' He lowered his cutlery, placing it neatly on his plate, and wiped his mouth with his napkin.

'Go on,' she said, before taking a sip of her wine.

He leaned forward. 'The thing is, he's told me he has asked your friend Jean to marry him.'

Pru's mood dipped. Is this where the two of them fell out? She hoped not. She told herself to wait to find out Jack's opinion of Monty's proposal before becoming defensive for her friend. 'He did.'

'May I ask what you think about it?' He laced his fingers together and waited for her to answer.

Pru didn't want to be disloyal to her friend but decided that hearing what Monty's closest friend had to say on the matter was something Jean would probably want her to find out. She wasn't sure how honest she should be though.

'I admit I was initially concerned.' She sighed. 'I still am if I'm honest. But not because I doubt Jean's love for Monty, or his for her,' she added, wanting to make the point.

'Is it because he's a pilot? Because I know Monty won't be flying again, not with his injuries.'

She shook her head and it occurred to her how fragile their happiness would be, should he fall for her as she was falling for him. 'No, although that would be a concern if he was still able to fly,' she admitted. 'I worry because I'm unsure how Lord and Lady Ashbury might take the news of the two of them wanting to marry.'

He seemed surprised and Pru wondered if it was because he was American and didn't realise quite how the British class system tried to keep people in their designated class. 'You think they might dissuade Monty from marrying her?'

'No,' she said, dabbing at the side of her mouth with her napkin and taking another sip of wine. 'That really is tasty.'

He smiled. 'I'm glad you like it.'

'I do.' She wasn't sure how to say it. 'I worry they might think her too middle-class to be a suitable wife for their son. Especially now he's also their heir.' She hoped she didn't sound pompous saying such things. 'Does that sound an unfair thing to accuse them of?'

He shook his head slowly. 'I'd like to say it was, but I think you've made a valid point. They love Monty very much. He's going to have a huge amount of responsibility once he inherits the estate and it's going to take a special kind of woman to cope with it all. Someone with a similar background, I imagine, who understands what life for the two of them would entail.' He stared at her, concern on his face. 'I don't suppose Jean has had that sort of upbringing, has she?'

Pru heard hope in his voice. She shook her head. 'Unfortunately not. Her family run a farm.' She tried to imagine having to relay this conversation to Jean. 'But surely if they love each other, he can teach her all she needs to know?'

'I imagine he'd be only too happy for the chance.' He reached across the table and took her right hand in his left one, the touch of his thumb gently stroking her skin on the back of her hand sending tiny electric currents through her entire body. 'I'm not trying to worry you, but I am concerned for Monty's sake. He's been through far more than he'll probably ever let on and he'll need a lot of support from the woman he marries.' He shook his head. 'I'm not saying Jean can't support him. She knows his injuries better than any other woman.' He looked away and she could see he was trying to find the right words to convey what he meant. 'I know them marrying probably sounds very romantic to Jean right now, but as well as the ongoing care that he'll need, she will have an enormous amount to learn where the running of the manor is concerned – dealing with the staff and the complications that go with that lifestyle.'

She wondered what experience Jack had of such a way of life and asked him.

Jack shrugged a shoulder. 'Very little experience personally, but I've been staying with them for summer holidays and that sort of thing for years. Monty always joked that he was the lucky one being the youngest brother of three because he'd never have to worry about taking charge of the manor.' He sighed. 'I've seen how busy Lord and Lady Ashbury constantly are, how heavily the manor weighs on their minds, especially since Charles and William were killed. Monty has never been prepared for the life he'll have to take on.'

Pru took another sip of wine to give herself time to think over what he had said. 'His parents aren't very old though, are they?' she said, trying to be positive.

'I don't see what that's got to do with our friends marrying.'

'I just mean that if Monty's parents don't die for another ten or twenty years, then Jean and Monty will have all the time they need for him to recover as well as he can, and for them to prepare themselves for what lies ahead. Don't you think?'

His face softened slightly and he seemed to relax. 'You're right. We'll just have to hope nothing happens to Monty's parents for the foreseeable future then, won't we?'

'Yes,' Pru said, feeling much better. 'And that Lord and Lady Ashbury don't disapprove of Monty's choice of a wife.'

He raised his eyebrows. 'I can't guarantee he won't have a fight on his hands, but I do know Monty and he's a determined chap. He'll get his own way if he loves Jean as much as I'm certain he does.'

Pru was relieved to hear it. 'Good. I like that he's stubborn and will push for what he wants.'

Jack was watching her thoughtfully. 'What?' she asked, intrigued.

He shook his head. 'You're a good friend to Jean. I know you'll be there for her whatever happens.'

'Of course. She's my best friend.'

He lifted her hand to his mouth. Pru couldn't take her eyes from his lips as they pressed lightly against her skin. Her breath was shallow.

His eyes locked with hers and for the first time she saw her longing reflected in them. 'I'm going to miss you, Pru,' he said, his voice gentle. He lowered her hand, resting it on the tablecloth.

'You're going away again?' she asked, her voice higher pitched than usual. 'When?'

'Soon.'

'Soon?' She wanted to cry, hating the thought of him

leaving again and not knowing when, or if, she would see him again.

'I don't know exactly when just yet, but probably next week. I know Monty's in good hands with you and Jean,' he said. 'At least I can be reassured he'll be well cared for.'

Pru felt a pang of fear at the thought of him returning to danger. 'I promise we'll continue to look after him as best we can.'

'Thank you.'

She watched him, trying to work out if the thought of returning to France frightened him. It didn't seem to. She wondered how people could be as brave as Jack and put their life in danger to save a friend. Could she ever do that, she wondered, unsure.

'Now.' Jack grinned, letting go of her hand. The coolness on her skin where his hand had been saddened her. 'What do you say to us choosing our desserts? They have a couple of sugary choices I'm dying to try.' He indicated a couple sitting at a table nearby having portions of chocolate mousse and Peach Melba.

Pru did her best to be cheerful. She didn't want Jack to think of her as a misery. 'I already know what I'm having.' She grinned, pointing discreetly to the peaches, raspberry sauce and vanilla ice-cream in a delicate glass. 'I haven't tasted something that looks that good for ages.'

When Jack dropped her back to the manor he insisted on walking Pru to the side door. Feeling happily full and sleepy, she was struggling not to yawn openly. 'I'm so sorry,' she said when he noticed her covering her mouth as she stopped by the door.

'I hadn't meant to bore you,' he said, his face serious.

Pru reached out to place a hand on his forearm. 'I wasn't bored, honestly. I'm just ever so tired, that's all. I had an early start this morning.'

He leaned forward and kissed her on the cheek. 'I'm joking. I shouldn't have kept you out so late. Thank you for agreeing to come out with me tonight.'

Relieved he wasn't offended, Pru gave in to a yawn that had been straining to get out. She covered her mouth. 'Gosh, I'm sorry.'

'Don't be. You go in. Hopefully we can go out again another time. Maybe on Friday evening? If you're free? I'm not sure what's on around here, but I can find out easily enough.'

She realised she would like that very much. 'Thank you,' she said. 'That would be lovely. Although can I ask that we don't go anywhere too smart?'

'No?'

She shook her head. 'I have to admit that this dress is the only smart outfit I have.'

'It's beautiful and suits you very well.' He opened the door for her. 'I'll hopefully see you during visiting hours. We can make more final arrangements then if that suits you?'

'Sounds perfect.'

He waited for her to step into the building. 'Good evening, Pru.'

His deep voice reverberated through her, making her close

her eyes briefly. 'Good evening, Jack. And thank you again for a lovely time.'

She stopped for a moment inside the hallway to gather her emotions. She stared at the back of her hand where his thumb had touched it and smiled. 'Jack,' she whispered, just to say his name.

Hearing a distant voice somewhere in the house, she hurried along the corridor, up the back stairs and to her bedroom, her mind racing with thoughts of Jack and how being with him made her feel. She was excited they had agreed to go out on another date. This time it was because he wanted to take her out and not because he wanted to ask her something. The thought made her smile. She couldn't wait to see him again.

Not wishing to wake either Jean or Milly, she slipped off her shoes and carried them from the top of the stairs along the corridor as she tiptoed into the bedroom.

'Good, you're back,' Jean said, turning on her bedside light and giving Pru such a shock she dropped one of her shoes with a clunk onto the wooden floorboards.

'Blast. I hope that doesn't wake anyone in the room below.'

'Never mind that,' Jean said. 'Tell me everything. I've been lying here waiting for you. I thought you'd be back an hour ago.'

Typical Jean to be impatient, Pru thought, amused. 'You'll have to wait for me to change and get into bed first.'

'Well, hurry up about it.'

Pru could barely contain her excitement as she told Jean, and then Milly, when she joined them after the end of her shift, all about her evening with Jack.

'He sounds as if he likes you,' Milly said, propping herself up on one elbow.

'I agree,' Jean said. 'I've noticed him looking at Pru a few times.'

'You never told me,' Pru said, wriggling her feet to warm them up. She knew she liked him but as charming as he was, Pru couldn't imagine a man as charismatic and handsome as the captain could possibly be attracted to an ordinary woman like her.

She thought guiltily at having spoken at length about Jean and Monty's relationship and wasn't sure if she should tell Jean what had been said. She looked at her gentle, sweet face and hated the thought of upsetting her closest friend in any way. No. She would have to keep her and Jack's thoughts to herself, at least for the time being.

'I'm going to get some sleep now,' Pru said, needing time to think. 'It's been a long day and we must be up early tomorrow.'

'It is tomorrow!' Milly giggled. 'Goodnight, girls.'

'Night, Milly,' they chorused.

EIGHT

Jack

Driving away from the manor, all Jack could think about was how much he had longed to take Pru in his arms and kiss her, but to do so would be unfair. He thought of her pretty smile and the dimple in her left cheek. She was such a sweet girl and seemed so unaffected by the countless injuries she must have been faced with during her work as a nurse. He wished he didn't have to leave England again so soon. He wished he could spend time getting to know her better.

Jack recalled his mother's fears about his Sopwith Camel being a death trap that might kill him and realised he was being selfish. He needed to put Pru first and do what was sensible. He mustn't encourage her to have feelings for him, he decided. If in fact she did. No, he must keep things between them merely friendly. Nothing more. As much as it pained him, Jack knew it was the right thing to do. He couldn't risk becoming involved with that beautiful, kind girl when he was endangering his life each time he flew. He had met too many widows and heartbroken fiancées to wish that on a woman he loved.

Loved? Did he love her? Jack was so distracted by the question that he almost missed the turning to the boarding house where he was staying.

And then it hit him. He did love her.

The realisation shocked him like a punch to his chest.

He would have to keep a check on himself when they went out together on Friday evening. He mustn't kiss her. Mustn't lead her to believe that he could be relied upon to stay alive long enough for them to have a relationship.

He parked the motor in front of the Victorian house and turned off the engine. At least Monty was safe now. He was in the best of hands and Jack knew that if Jean wasn't around to care for the man she loved, then Pru would be there to keep an eye on Monty while he was away. As much as he hated seeing Monty in his present damaged state, it was a relief to know his closest friend and confidant was out of the war for good now, and that he only had his own safety to worry about.

Monty would have the freedom to boldly move on with his life, find a wife and have the family he had always longed for. Ashbury Manor was a large home to fill, and Jack smiled, imagining his friend and a brood of aristocratic children running noisily through the halls as he and Monty had once done.

It also made Jack wonder when the time would come for him to settle down with the woman he loved. He reflected on what lay ahead of him and sensed that the thought was more of an *if* than a *when*.

NINE

Pru

JULY 1917

A few days later, Pru waited anxiously with Jean to hear the results of the latest surgery on Monty's damaged leg. Jean had been desperate to assist Doctor Parslow with the surgery but he wouldn't agree, instead choosing Milly.

'How do you think it's going?' Jean tugged on Pru's arm as they strolled through the formal gardens at the front of the house. 'Do you think he'll manage to save Monty's leg?' she asked without waiting for Pru's reaction. 'I couldn't bear it if Monty wasn't able to walk again. I know he'd be unable to cope.'

Pru had seen many times how badly patients took the news they had lost a limb, but she believed that Monty, especially with Jean's love, would find a way to move on with his life and learn to enjoy it fully.

'We've both witnessed Doctor Parslow's work enough times to know he is an excellent surgeon,' she said, trying her best to reassure her friend. 'If Monty's leg can be saved by anyone then it'll be him. Even if he can't save it, though, there are still choices that Monty can make.'

'A prosthetic, you mean?'

'Yes. We both know they're improving each year and aren't as cumbersome as they once were. They make aluminium ones now, don't forget. His parents can afford the best and will ensure he's fitted with the one that suits him best.'

They walked on in silence as Jean considered what Pru had said. 'I would marry him regardless of what happens today,' she said almost to herself.

Pru hugged her friend's arm tightly to her side. 'I know you would.' She thought of the fiancées and wives she had seen who had refused to return to visit their men after witnessing some of the more shocking injuries to faces, or missing limbs. Pru never understood their cruelty. How could you turn your back on someone you professed to love? It was unfathomable to her. Maybe, she reasoned, it was different if the future you had envisaged with that man wasn't to be. No, she thought. There was no excuse as far as she was concerned. 'I can't ever imagine not wanting to be with a man I loved, regardless of what happened to him.' She looked at Jean. 'Am I being naive?' She didn't think so.

'Let's talk about something else,' Jean suggested. 'I need to take my mind off this while I can.'

'That's understandable. What do you want to talk about?'

Jean reached down to pick a couple of daisies. 'I'd like to know about you and the captain.'

Pru groaned inwardly.

'I know you said you were on friendly terms with each

other, but I know you well enough to suspect there's more to your feelings for him.'

Pru had forgotten just how perceptive her friend could be. Then again, she mused, Jean had known her since kindergarten at their parish school in Jersey, so it was hardly surprising she saw through Pru's words.

'He's nice and I do like him,' Pru admitted, aware she was holding back from sharing her real feelings for him. 'I think he keeps a lot to himself.' She stopped walking and shrugged thoughtfully. 'I barely know him but I can't help thinking there's a haunted look about his eyes. Have you noticed it?'

'A lot of our patients have that look.'

Jean was right. 'I know, but this is different somehow. I'm not sure how exactly, but – oh, I don't know how to describe it.'

Jean looked at her. 'I'll have to see if I can spot it when he next visits Monty. Did you say you were going out with him again tonight?'

'I did.' Pru couldn't help grinning, and, not wishing to let her friend see, turned her head away as if finding the small lavender bush near her feet fascinating.

'Are you looking forward to seeing him again?'

Pru nodded. 'I am. I just wish I had something decent to wear,' she said, realising she wasn't prepared for her evening out. 'I did ask him not to take us anywhere too smart, but I hate the thought of being under-dressed for an occasion.'

Jean laughed. 'There isn't too much around here to take you to.' She gasped. 'Unless it's a private party,' she said. 'Do you think he'll know anyone else around here apart from Monty?'

'I think he probably does,' Pru said, worried. 'He's stayed

with Monty during past summers, apparently. Knowing how friendly Monty is, I'm sure he'd have introduced such a good friend to his social circle.' She watched Jean giving what she'd said some thought. 'Anyway do people still have those?'

'What?'

'Parties?' She couldn't imagine people had the money – or spare food – to hold them anymore. Bigger houses had much fewer staff since many had enlisted, and those that hadn't and were of fighting age had left the area when conscription had come into force the previous year.

'I've no idea.' Jean rubbed her gloves together. 'It's not as if either of us have ever had that sort of lifestyle to know, is it?'

'True.' Pru laughed.

'You won't be going anywhere at all if we don't find you something to wear.' Jean pulled Pru by the arm and they began walking again. 'Maybe Milly has a dress she might lend you for tonight?'

Pru pictured Milly's colourful outfits. 'I'm sure she will have something.'

———

'I've got just the thing,' Milly said cheerfully when Pru approached her later in their room. 'It's emerald green.' She went over to their tiny wardrobe and lifted a hanger out, showing the dress to the girls. 'What do you think?'

Pru covered her open mouth with her fingers. 'It's gorgeous.'

'I'm glad you like it.'

'How could she not?' Jean laughed, her hand going to her neck as she stared at the beautiful silk dress.

Milly tilted her head to one side and eyed first Pru and then the dress. 'It's going to look fabulous on you. I think it'll go perfectly with your dark hair, especially if you add a gold necklace or something.'

'I don't have anything like that.' Pru only had her silver St Christopher that her parents had presented to her before she left Jersey. It was her most precious piece of jewellery, even if it was her only piece.

'Then you can borrow mine,' Milly said, immediately going over to the small locker by her bed.

'No, I couldn't.' Pru was horrified at the thought of wearing something precious that didn't belong to her.

'Whyever not?'

'Because I'd spend the entire evening fretting about losing it. I'm already going to be worried enough that I don't spill something on your beautiful dress.'

Milly shook her head. 'I suppose I'd feel the same way if it was the other way around.'

Pru put on the dress, Milly helping her by doing up the tiny, hard-to-reach buttons at the back, then pulling her over to their small mirror. 'See how beautiful you look. The colour of the dress highlights your dark hair and pale skin.' She looked over her shoulder at Jean. 'Don't you think, Jean?'

'I do.'

Pru wondered what Jack might think of her turning up in such an exquisite frock. 'You don't think I look as if I'm trying too hard?'

Jean seemed confused. 'Too hard for what?'

'To get the handsome captain's attention,' Milly teased.

'Do you?' Pru stared her reflection, feeling embarrassed. If she was right and the captain was only asking her out because he needed someone for company while Monty was still recuperating, then how would it look if she dressed up like this? 'I don't want him to think I've misunderstood his reasons for taking me out tonight.'

Milly straightened one of the straps on Pru's shoulder. 'I think you're the one who's done the misunderstanding, Miss.'

'What do you mean?'

She felt Jean's hands on her shoulders. 'She means that he's asked you out because he likes you, not because he's looking for company and anyone will do.' Pru stared in the mirror and watched Jean smile at Milly. 'A man like the captain doesn't need others for company. I'm sure he's perfectly happy on his own. He wants to spend time with you, Pru. That's all Milly's saying and I happen to agree with her.'

Panic coursed through Pru. She spun round to face her friends. 'You really think so?' Could he possibly like her? Really? She looked from one friend to the other as they nodded. 'Oh dear.'

Milly laughed. 'What's the matter? Why are you looking so terrified?'

'Because I … That is, I…'

Milly went to the locker near her bed and took out a small evening bag that matched the dress perfectly. 'Don't think about it,' she soothed. 'Just try to enjoy every single moment. Here, take this.' She hung the bag's satin strap over Pru's hand and rested it in the crook of her arm.

'You'd better take this, too.' Jean opened the bag and placed a clean handkerchief inside. 'Now, deep breaths. Try to be calm.'

Pru wasn't sure she could manage that. She raised her arm and studied the bag. 'This is so pretty, Milly, but I can't borrow this as well.'

'You can.' She pointed a finger at her. 'And I'm not having any argument. It's the one condition I have for lending you my dress.' She frowned. 'And that you bring it back to me afterwards. I'm rather fond of this dress. It reminds me of the evening I met my Ronnie.'

Pru winced. 'I hadn't realised it was extra special.'

'It's fine,' Milly argued, her voice slightly quieter. 'It's not as if he's around anymore to remember it anyway.'

'Oh, Milly.' Pru sniffed to stop from crying. She put the bag on the nearest bed and went to unfasten the dress.

'What are you doing?' Milly shrieked.

'I can't wear this,' Pru said, struggling to undo the buttons at the back. 'I can wear my dress instead.'

'Nonsense,' Milly argued, slapping Pru's hands away from the fastenings. 'Honestly, I want you to. It makes me happy to think of this dress being part of a romantic evening, even if it can no longer be mine and Ronnie's.'

Pru swallowed back tears. She hadn't known Milly when Ronnie had been killed two years before but knew from what her friend told her that he had been gassed at Ypres and like so many other poor soldiers had taken days to die. It had been the reason Milly became a nurse – to help other soldiers like her Ronnie – but she suspected it was also her way of keeping busy while she grieved for a future they would never be able to enjoy.

'Fine, I'll wear it.' Pru leaned forward and hugged her friend, hating that someone so kind and generous had already suffered such a terrible loss.

They spent the next few minutes helping her arrange her hair. Finally satisfied she was ready, Pru draped Jean's jacket over her shoulders.

'You're both so kind,' she said, grateful to her friends and excited to be dressed so elegantly and wearing heels after being in sensible ankle boots all day. 'I hope the captain appreciates all your hard work,' she joked.

'He'll appreciate the effect far more if you get a move on and don't keep him waiting,' Milly teased.

Pru blew them kisses and hurried down to meet Jack. He was waiting outside the side door, as she knew he would be.

His eyes widened as she stepped out. 'My, you look stunning, Nurse Le Cuirot.'

Delighted with his reaction, she grinned and gave a little curtsy. 'Thank you.'

She saw the look of delight on his face and wondered if her friends might be right about him. Her heart raced at the possibility.

'I've brought along a blanket for your legs this time,' Jack said once they were settled in the motor. 'You looked so cold the last time we went out and I felt very guilty.'

'You needn't have,' she said politely, yet glad of the warmth when he draped the woollen blanket over her legs.

'We don't have too far to go but I thought you might enjoy a bit of dancing this time.' He gave her a questioning look. 'Do you like to dance?'

'I'll probably be a bit rusty but I love it,' she admitted. 'I can't recall the last time I went. Not properly. We've had a couple of dances at the manor for Christmas but that's about it.'

He took her hand gently in his and her skin tingled. 'I've been looking forward to seeing you again, Pru.'

Her breath caught in her throat and it took her a moment to gather herself enough to reply. 'So have I, Jack.'

He raised her hand to his lips and kissed it. She could get very used to moments like these, she decided. He lowered her hand and rested it on her thigh.

He stared at her in silence and then cleared his throat. 'I suppose I should start this thing so we can get going.' He took a metal handle, attached it to the front of the car and cranked it. The engine sprang into life and Jack got into the seat next to her and drove down the long driveway.

She had never imagined meeting someone as different as Jack Garland, let alone hearing him say he had been looking forward to seeing her again. It made her think that maybe Jean and Milly had been right after all. She hoped so. She thought of Milly and her loss, and the loss of other nurses, and that of Lord and Lady Ashbury, and it calmed her excitement. She didn't want to be one of those heartbroken women. Jack was in the Royal Flying Corps and she was well aware – and had been horrified to discover – that the life expectancy of new pilots was only about eleven days. Jack had already far exceeded that limit and she couldn't bear to let herself fall in love with him only to lose him.

She realised he was speaking. 'I'm sorry,' she said. 'I was miles away.'

He changed gear and slowed the car as they came to the end of the lane. 'Not too far, I hope?'

'No. Anyway, I'm back now.'

'I'm pleased to hear it.' He drove on a bit further. 'What were you thinking, Pru? Would you tell me?'

How could she?

'I'd rather not,' she said quietly. The last thing she wanted to do was put a damper on their evening before it had even really begun.

He reached out and took her hand in his. 'Was it about me being a pilot?'

Pru gasped. 'Er, yes. But…'

'It's fine,' he said, letting go of her hand to change gears. 'Meeting you has…' He hesitated. 'I like you, Pru.' He sighed heavily and glanced at her before returning his gaze to the lane ahead. 'It's more than that. I've never met a woman like you.'

Pru wasn't sure what he meant. 'Like me? How?'

He glanced at her again. 'A woman who makes me feel like I'm the happiest man alive when I'm with you. But I know that to fall in love with you would be the most selfish thing I could do.'

Pru's thoughts scrambled around in her head. 'You like me?'

He turned the car between two wide stone pillars and drove down a long driveway. He didn't speak and she panicked that she had misunderstood what he had meant. He parked the car and turned to her, taking her hand in his once more. 'I don't like you, Pru,' he said. 'I love you. I think I loved you from the moment I crashed into your trolley and you were so furious with me.'

What! What had he just said?

'You … you…?'

'I know. I'm being selfish telling you this.'

'Why?' She couldn't imagine hearing anything more perfect. Jack. Loved. Her. Pru Le Cuirot. She didn't know whether to shout it out or burst into tears. Instead she tried to calm her breathing and behave as a twenty-one-year-old professional nurse should.

'Because, darling Pru, what I do is dangerous. I never know if I'll come back from a mission, and if I do, what state this body or mind of mine will be in. I can't do that to a woman I love. It's too cruel.' He exhaled sharply.

Pru's temper flared. He was not going to do this to her. 'Jack Garland. Are you daring to tell me on one breath that you love me and in the next that we can't be together?' She glared at him. 'Well?'

His mouth moved but no words came out. He stared at her, his eyes wide. Then, when she was about to really lose her temper, his expression softened and he began to laugh.

'What's so funny?' She glared at him, her emotions conflicted – euphoric to discover he loved her, heartbroken that he couldn't be with her.

'Pru Le Cuirot, you are the most incredible woman I have ever had the good fortune to meet.'

Pru pictured how she must look at that moment and she felt a laugh rise through her chest. Seconds later, she began laughing.

She felt his hands go around her as he pulled her into his arms and kissed her. Without thinking, Pru gave into the sensations that his lips sent through her and kissed him back, lost in the moment.

Seconds later, or maybe minutes – she wasn't sure, neither did she care – Jack loosened his arms around her and moved back. He stared at her as if seeing her for the first time. 'I have a nagging feeling that you are going to be the first person to shatter my resolve not to become involved with anyone while this war is on.'

Pru could see he was caught between wanting to do what he believed to be the right thing and his feelings for her. She rested a hand on his knee. 'I know you think this is wrong and I admit that the thought of being in love with a pilot frightens me.'

'Frightens you?'

'Jack, I already have feelings for you that I've never imagined being capable of and…' She hesitated, feeling exposed to be so open.

'Please,' he whispered. 'Go on.'

She took a deep breath. 'I already look for you whenever I'm at work in case you've come to visit Monty. I listen out for your voice. When I see you, I don't quite know what to do. I'm worried I'll make a fool of myself, or say something silly and show you how much I like you.' She lowered her voice. 'Love you.'

'My darling girl. Every moment I spend with you I fall more deeply in love with you and it frightens me.'

'You? Frightened?' She was astounded to hear him say such a thing. This man who Monty looked up to and insisted to be the bravest man he knew.

'Yes. I want to be with you but in doing so I'm putting your happiness at risk because I have no control over whether or not I survive this blasted war.'

'What shall we do?' She wanted him to be sensible, to have the courage she wasn't sure she possessed and tell her that they should remain friends, but she also needed him to say he loved her again and that everything would be fine, that they could love each other.

He stared at her for a moment. 'I love you, Pru, you know that now, but I need to be fair to you.'

She bit her lower lip, waiting for him to say the words she didn't want to hear but knew she must. 'Go on.'

He sighed heavily and rested a hand on her cheek. 'I think that while this war is on, we need to remain friends.'

She hated to think that was all they might be but was grateful to him for having the courage to be the one to say it. 'I agree, Jack,' she said, having to swallow hard to stop herself from crying.

'It'll be fine, sweetheart,' he soothed. 'This war can't go on for ever and then we can be together, properly.'

'I know you're right,' she agreed miserably. 'But I wish things were different.'

'So do I, my love.' Someone laughed nearby. 'I suppose we should go in so I can introduce you to my friends.'

TEN

Pru

JULY 1917

Pru sat in the motor as Jack got out and walked around to open the passenger door for her. She wished she could sit quietly for a while and try to come to terms with what had happened between them. It was like being given a dream only to have it be snatched back immediately after.

'Are you all right?' he asked, taking the blanket from her legs and throwing it onto the driver's seat.

She wondered if he felt the same emotional conflict. She thought about what he had just said and knew that he did. 'I will be,' she said, trying to reassure him as she took his proffered hand and stepped down onto the gravel.

Pru looked up at the enormous property with a colonnade running the length of the front and wide stone steps leading up to a large front door.

'It's an impressive place,' she said, suddenly glad to have something to take her mind off what had just happened between them. 'A private party?' She hadn't expected that. Pru was relieved she had accepted Milly's offer of her dress now that she knew where they were going. She might feel a little out of her depth but at least she had the confidence to know she looked the part.

'It is, but they only use half of it now that most of the servants have either been conscripted or have left to work in munitions.' He gave her a reassuring smile. They each knew the other was putting on a brave face to get through the next few hours. 'It should be fun. You'll like Hugo and Verity, they're very welcoming. He's a friend of mine and Monty's. He, er, well, he was the first of us to be injured.' His forced smile vanished. 'He's more Monty's friend than mine, but as Monty couldn't be here tonight, he asked me to come and be there for both of us. It's Hugo's twenty-fifth birthday, you see, so I couldn't really refuse. None of us expected him to make it this far and I'm glad Verity insisted we all celebrate the event.'

Jack was clearly troubled by what had happened to his and Monty's friend, and Pru's interest was piqued to see for herself.

'We'd better not keep them waiting then,' she said.

Linking arms, they went inside.

Pru was surprised no one answered the door and that she and Jack were able to walk straight in. She took a moment to look around her. Pru had thought Ashbury Manor was glamorous but she had never seen anything like the inside of this place. She had to concentrate on closing her mouth a couple of times as she passed glittering chandeliers along the stone hallway. The sound of music met their ears as they walked further into the building and Pru gazed up at the display of huge paintings of people she presumed must be Hugo's ancestors.

Suddenly a beautiful woman with pale blonde hair ran out into the hall, almost crashing into Jack, and skidded to a halt. Pru couldn't imagine ever managing to look as regal and delicate as the woman did even after almost causing a collision.

'Jack! Darling, how splendid of you to come. We hoped you'd make it, but you're always here and there and no one ever seems to know when you'll reappear.'

Pru felt a pang of jealousy when the woman threw her arms around Jack's neck.

'Oh!' she exclaimed, noticing Pru for the first time. 'I'm dreadfully sorry. How unutterably rude of me.' She peered around Jack before stepping to the side to study Pru fully. 'And who is this exquisite creature, Jack Garland?' She gave Pru a beaming smile and instantly Pru's jealousy evaporated.

It felt a little odd to be under such scrutiny from the tall, ethereal blonde, but Pru couldn't help liking her immediately. They were complete opposites – this woman tall, fair and aristocratic while she was small, dark-haired and ordinary – but there was something rather appealing about the woman's child-like enthusiasm.

Jack let go of Pru's arm and slipped his arm around her waist instead, moving her a step forward. 'This is my good friend, Pru Le Cuirot.' He smiled at Pru. She felt a pang in her stomach at being described in such a casual way, especially after their intimacy in the motor a few minutes earlier. But, she reminded herself, that is what they had agreed upon. It was going to take some getting used to, she realised.

Jack continued, 'This is our hostess for the evening, Lady Verity Rivers.'

'Do call me Verity. I feel like people are addressing Hugo's mother when they call me Lady Rivers.' She pulled a face. 'And if you've ever met her, which I hope for your sake you haven't, you'd understand why that thought gives me the shivers.' She held out a dainty hand, which Pru took. 'I'm Hugo's better half. Welcome to Eastwell Hall.'

'Thank you. I'm delighted to be here,' Pru said. 'Jack mentioned it was your husband's birthday.'

Verity leaned forward and lowered her voice. 'It is. You caught me running to tell the staff when to bring in his birthday cake. I'd forgotten, you see.' She looked up at Jack. 'Hence me nearly careering into you, darling man.'

'Do you need me to do anything for you?' Jack asked, clearly used to Verity's casual affection for him.

'Absolutely not.' She waved her hand towards the sound of the laughter and music. 'You two go and find Hugo. He'll be delighted to see you.' She gave Pru a pointed look. 'And tickled pink to meet your guest.' Pru realised she must have looked confused at Verity's comment. 'Oh, don't mind me. It's just that Jack hasn't ever brought a female guest to one of our parties before, have you, Jack?'

Jack didn't seem very happy. 'I'm hoping I won't regret bringing Pru to this one,' he said finally, with a grin.

Jack took Pru's hand and led her into an enormous living room where couples were dancing and others grouped together, chatting and laughing in front of furniture that Pru suspected had been moved back for the evening. She tried to work out which person might be Hugo.

Suddenly, voices quietened and two men stepped aside to let another through. He was tall and wore an eye patch over his left eye. His mouth drew back into a smile on the right side, but the left side, she noticed with a tug to her heart, was a patchwork of messy scarring. He raised his right arm to welcome Jack, and it was then that she noticed his left arm was missing. She wondered if Jack might have been comfortable bringing her because as a nurse he knew he could be assured that she wouldn't react badly to Hugo's terrible injuries.

'Good grief,' Hugo bellowed. 'If it isn't old Jack Garland.' Jack let go of her hand and hugged his friend tightly. 'Verity never mentioned she'd invited you this evening.' Then he spotted Pru over Jack's shoulder and studied her, seemingly trying to get the measure of her before pushing Jack gently away. 'Hold on. Who is this exquisite creature you've brought with you? You've kept her well hidden.' He winked at Pru. 'Or have you two just met?'

'Stop bothering them, Hugo.' Verity laughed, appearing next to him and slipping her arm around her husband's waist. She kissed his scarred cheek. 'He's frightfully nosy, as you've probably guessed already. Hugo hates not knowing the gossip,' she said, giving Pru a theatrical wink. 'Isn't that right, Poochy?'

Pru grinned as 'Poochy' grumbled something in response. She could see he wasn't really offended by his wife's telling off, more amused. She liked them both very much and couldn't wait to tell Jean and Milly all about these fascinating friends of Jack and Monty's.

Verity stepped forward and linked her arm through Pru's. 'Come along. Let's leave the boys to catch up. They'll probably have lots of dull things to drone on about while we can get to know each other.'

Pru saw Jack give her a concerned glance and she smiled over her shoulder at him to reassure him she was fine as Verity led her to the other guests.

'Everyone, this is Jack Garland's friend, Pru.' There was a chorus of welcomes and Pru did her best to acknowledge most of them. 'I won't bother telling you all their names,' Verity murmured. 'It's always impossible to remember them when you're new to a group, don't you find?' Pru nodded in agreement, relieved not to have to try and put names to faces. 'You'll soon pick them up as you chat to each of them.'

'I'm sure I will.'

'Let's fetch you a drink. What would you like? Champagne?'

That sounded perfect. 'Yes, thank you.'

Verity motioned to a servant who brought over a tray of glasses. They took one each and then her hostess led her to one of the tall windows away from the worst of the music and chatter.

'I hope you don't mind me dragging you off like this,' Verity said, taking a sip of her drink.

'No, of course not.'

'It's just that I get terribly excited when someone new comes into our group.' She beamed at Pru. 'It can become rather dull when you see the same old faces day in and day out.' She lowered her voice. 'And Jack is such a private chap. I'm delighted to have been introduced to a lady friend of his.'

'Really?' Pru wasn't sure how to react to this information.

'Yes.' She looked astonished at Pru's reaction. 'I know Hugo's surprised to see you here, too. Don't get me wrong though, he'll be as excited as me. Do you mind telling me where you met?'

'At Ashbury Manor,' Pru said. 'I'm a nurse there.'

Verity's mouth opened in surprise. 'You know Monty then. How is he coming along? Pooch and I love Monty. We were terribly concerned when he was injured so badly. Poor darling.' She sighed heavily. 'We all owe Jack so much.'

Pru was puzzled. 'Jack? Why?'

'I'm told he saved darling Monty's life. Put his own life in danger when Monty's plane crashed in enemy territory, so Hugo told me. Landed his plane under enemy fire and somehow got Monty back behind British lines.' She shuddered. 'Hugo said Jack was worried that he had injured Monty more by moving him from his crashed airplane, but what else could the sweet man do?' She raised a finger to her lips. 'We'd better change the subject. They're coming over to speak to us and he hates it if we talk about it, for some reason. Doesn't think of himself as a hero, Hugo says. Insists anyone would have done the same thing, but I'm not sure I'd ever be that brave.'

Having seen how Verity was with her husband, Pru thought she was probably a much braver lady than she liked to let on.

Hugo had his arm around Jack's shoulders. 'My friend here tells me you're a nurse over at Ashbury.'

'That's right,' Pru said, struggling to come to terms with what Verity had just told her. She turned her attention to Jack. 'I was telling Verity how Monty is coming along.'

Verity glanced at her and Pru could tell she was giving her warning signs not to divulge anything else she'd said.

Pru had no intention of dropping her new friend in any trouble. 'I gather you're all friends of his.'

'Very good friends,' Hugo said. 'Monty and I grew up spending an awful lot of time together. Sent to the same school and all that. Good fellow, Monty. The best.' His eyes shifted up to look at Jack. 'Almost the best.'

Jack's look diverted instantly to Pru. She wasn't sure what he was thinking. 'Would you both mind very much if I asked Pru for a dance? She has to be back at the manor at a reasonable time and I would hate her not to have a few turns around the floor.'

Verity patted his arm and stepped away to stand next to her husband. 'You two enjoy yourselves. That's what you're here for.'

'Thank you,' Jack said, taking Pru's hand and leading her to the parquet flooring where other couples were dancing to the lively music coming from the gramophone. He took her in his arms and began to dance. 'I hope you're enjoying yourself and Verity didn't bombard you with too many questions?'

'Not at all. I like her,' Pru said honestly. 'She's made me feel very welcome.'

'She's a great girl. I'm happy for Hugo that he married her rather than the girl his parents were planning for him to marry.'

'Really? They don't approve of her?' Pru couldn't understand what Hugo's parents could possibly find to dislike.

'I think they were hoping for someone a little more reserved.' Jack laughed. 'More mouselike probably. In fact, the antithesis of Verity.'

Pru was stunned. 'How strange.' She would have thought

that as long as the two of them were from the same background his parents wouldn't have any issues. The thought made her even more concerned for Jean and Monty.

'After the way Verity's dealt with Hugo's injuries, his parents have finally conceded that maybe he wasn't so amiss in choosing her as his wife.'

'That's something, I suppose.' Pru was pleased for Hugo. He seemed such a kindly man. 'Verity's very vivacious and incredibly beautiful.'

'She is.' He looked down at her and stared at her as they moved. 'But not nearly as beautiful as you, Pru.'

She laughed. 'That's absurd,' she said, and was surprised to see hurt register on his face. 'I'm sorry, I didn't mean to be rude, but really you couldn't possibly compare me with Verity.'

His smile returned. 'It's fine. And I meant what I said.'

She didn't believe him. She could see for herself how stunning Verity was. Pru knew she was pretty, but in rather an ordinary girl-next-door kind of way. Verity looked like an angel with her exquisite features and white-blonde hair.

Pru soon forgot all about Verity as he held her against him and they moved to the music. She rested her head on his chest, enjoying the sensation of being in his arms. It felt like a safe place to be. Somewhere where she could make believe the world wasn't at war and sweet people like Hugo weren't being disfigured each day.

'I'm glad I met you, Pru,' Jack murmured.

'I'm glad you did, too,' she said, her voice barely audible above the music.

The evening flew by and before Pru knew it Jack was telling her it was past midnight, and he should be taking her back to Ashbury. She was disappointed to have to end their time at the beautiful stately home, but, not wishing to get into trouble with Matron, dutifully joined Jack in saying their goodbyes.

'It's been delightful to meet you,' Verity said.

'It has,' Hugo agreed. 'Jack, you must ensure you bring Pru to visit us again sometime.'

'I'll do my best.'

Jack drove her back in silence but Pru could sense him glancing at her every so often and caught his eye. She smiled. 'Thank you for inviting me tonight,' she said, wishing they could do it all again tomorrow. 'I've had a wonderful time.'

'I've enjoyed getting to know you a little better. Even if we can't be as free with our emotions as we'd both like to right now.'

She could hear an unmistakable sadness in his tone and wished she could comfort him and tell him everything would work out, but neither of them could possibly know that to be the case.

Jack drove up the manor driveway and parked the car to the side of the house. Then, turning to face her, he reached out and took a strand of hair that had come loose from one of the pins her friends had used to keep her hair in place. He let it run through his fingers.

'Will you come out somewhere with me again, Pru? Maybe for a walk tomorrow during your break, or when your shift is over? There's something I'd like to show you.'

Pru was intrigued to think what it might be. 'I'd like that,' she admitted, her breathing shallow.

He stared at her for a while and seemed to be trying to decide something. Then, leaning forward, he kissed her.

Pru melted into his kiss, letting him pull her closer to him as she slipped her arms around his neck. The only man she had kissed before Jack was Jean's older brother, Peter. He was sweet but his kisses never made her feel like she did right now.

'I know we agreed to try and stay just friends.'

'Friends who kiss,' Pru said, not wishing to stop having to kiss his perfect mouth.

Jack grinned. 'I like the idea of us being kissing friends.'

Pru nodded. 'Go on.'

He clenched his jaw. 'You know I'm going away again very soon,' he said quietly into her hair. Pru stiffened, hating the thought. 'I'd like to see you as much as I can before then, if you want to?'

'I'd like that very much.' She sat back and stared into his dark-blue eyes, trying to commit every detail of his handsome face to memory.

'What is it?' he whispered.

'I don't want to forget anything about you.'

He stared at her thoughtfully for a moment. 'Then would you be happy for me to arrange for us to have photographs taken of each of us?'

'You mean so that we can swap them to keep while you're away?'

'Yes.'

'I think it's an idea.'

'Then that's what I'll do.'

ELEVEN

Pru

AUGUST 1917

Jack had now been away for a couple of weeks and Pru was surprised by the physical ache she felt at missing him and recalled their snatched moments together before his departure. Love really could be painful, she thought as she finished filling Private Danby's water jug. He was still subdued, not entering into conversation with anyone, however many attempts were made, and the look of loathing she had caught him giving Monty the day before still shocked her.

She often went over her conversations with Jack. So far, they had kept to their promise to each other to be nothing more than kissing friends but Pru knew Jack was finding it as difficult as she was to keep things that way. She thought back to their last few moments together when their kisses had almost ended up with them going further, only for Jack to insist they stop.

'We mustn't,' he had said, his voice husky and low. 'Believe me, Pru, I want to more than anything, but it would be wrong for me to do so.'

She had tried and failed to hide her disappointment and frustration and thought that, as much as she missed him, maybe it would be good for them both to have a little time apart. If only he wasn't putting his life at risk in France.

She wiped her forehead, longing for her shift to end so she could take a cool walk in the woods. There was a slight breeze outside but it was coming from the wrong direction to give them any relief inside despite the windows being open in the ward.

'As soon as this interminable war is over,' Jack had whispered as they'd said goodbye, kissing away her disappointment, 'and I make it back in one piece, I promise you, Pru, we'll be married and never have to spend another night apart from each other.'

'Yes, Jack,' she had agreed, wondering if he realised how his casual proposal had made her heart leap.

Jean's gentle voice saying something to Monty in the next bed brought Pru back to the present and she crossed the ward to help a patient who was trying and failing to reach his empty glass. 'Here,' she said, filling it for him and placing it in his hand. 'There you go.'

She stopped to stare out of the window. It would soon be visiting time and she wondered if Jack might be there. Her heart leapt at the thought of seeing him again.

'When you've finished daydreaming, Nurse Le Cuirot,' Matron snapped, bringing her back to the present with a jolt, 'I want you to go and see Private Danby.'

'Yes, of course, Matron.'

'I've noticed he's a little more restless lately and would like you to spend some time with him before visiting begins,'

Matron went on. 'Maybe talk to him and find out about his family. I think it might help him if he were to receive a visitor so, if possible, we need to try and locate someone close to him. Then I will write to them and do my best to encourage a visit.'

'Yes, of course, Matron.'

Pru liked it on the odd occasion when Matron let her kinder side show. It saddened her to see the young private alone during each visiting time and she wished she knew why no one bothered to come to see him but Pru had noticed his expression being strangely odd at times and it unnerved her. She hoped it was simply a fear of what might happen to him once he was well enough to be discharged, which she assumed would be in the next few months.

Apart from Private Danby, most of the patients were in good spirits. She realised that it wasn't only personal visitors that he was missing, but also the friendship of any of the other patients.

She returned to the ward and collected the dressings she needed before going over to his bedside. 'Would you like me to take you outside for a walk, Private?'

'I can't walk. You know that.'

She did. 'I can help you with your crutches though. Or if your leg is too painful, I can bring a wheelchair for you to use.'

Out of all the patients Pru had to help, she had to admit, if only to herself, that this young man was her least favourite. The thought made her feel guilty. It wasn't his fault he was shy, but she wished he would at least try to make friends with some of the other men instead of skulking in his bed all day. She hoped Matron would manage to track down someone he knew, and the sooner the better.

'No. This leg is giving me a bit of gip.' He grimaced as if to emphasise his words. 'When do you think it'll start to heal properly?'

She placed the utensils she'd brought onto his bedside table and drew the screen around his bed. He never liked having his dressing changed and the fact that his injury was on his thigh seemed to add to his distress.

'Let me have a look.' She folded back his sheet and then, handing him a hand towel to cover his modesty, she undid his pyjama bottoms and helped him move to the side so she could pull down the material. Carefully removing the dressing, Pru focused on keeping her breathing level as she bent to examine his leg. She was relieved that other medical staff and even patients were only a screen away from her and able to assist her straightaway should she need them. There was something about him she didn't trust, although she felt unkind feeling that way, especially as he hadn't actually done anything threatening to her.

'It does look sore. I'll clean it and then apply a fresh dressing. Hopefully that'll bring you a little comfort.'

'I hope so.' He closed his eyes. 'I'm tired of always being in pain.'

There were men with far worse injuries who complained far less than he always did, but maybe he had a particularly low pain threshold? She knew the medication he was on and he certainly seemed to sleep as much as any of the other patients at night.

As she cleaned his wound, Pru remembered she was supposed to be finding out personal information for Matron. 'Do your family come from anywhere around here, Private?'

'Why?' he snapped in reply.

Determined not to let him unnerve her, she focused on what she was doing, relieved to have somewhere to look other than his face.

'I just wondered, that's all.'

'Because no bugger bothers to come and visit me, you mean?'

She knew better than to insult his intelligence by lying. 'I had noticed your family hadn't been to see you yet. I wondered if there was something I could do to help. Pass on a message from you to them maybe.'

'Don't waste your time worrying about the likes of me. I can see you're much happier spending time chatting to 'is lordship there.' He cocked his head in the direction of Monty's bed.

Pru could hear the hurt in his voice but also the anger. He clearly felt less worthy than the other patients and she wasn't about to let anyone feel that way. 'That's not true at all, Private Danby, whether you like to think it is or not. Anyway, you shouldn't speak about yourself in such a way.'

'Why shouldn't I?'

She looked him in the eye. 'Because you're as important as any other patient here.'

'Is that right?' he scoffed. 'Try telling that to his lordship's son and heir next to me.'

Pru finished applying the dressing and helped pull up his pyjama bottoms, taking the small towel from him as he did them up.

'I'm sure Major Ashbury would be the first to disagree with you.'

'Speaking for him now, are you?'

Pru was beginning to lose her temper. Private Danby might not have visitors but unlike Monty's his wounds were not life-changing and she wasn't about to let him get away with nastiness.

'I'm not speaking for anyone; I am giving you my opinion and you may accept it or not. But, Private, you are not the worst off in this hospital and I'll thank you to remember that fact.'

He glared at her. 'Have you finished now, Nurse?'

She realised she had gone too far. She was supposed to be gleaning information from him, not antagonising him. 'What do you mean?' she asked. Was he asking if she'd finished having a go at him, or doing her duty towards him?

'With this.' He pointed at his leg.

'Yes, I've finished.'

'Then you can leave me in peace.'

She drew back the screen and caught Monty's eye while her back was towards Private Danby. Monty winked at her to let her know he had heard her defending him and also, she assumed, to show he wasn't bothered by what the private had said.

She was relieved. Seeing that Monty wasn't fazed by what had just happened calmed her irritation slightly. It wasn't her place to lecture patients and if Matron had heard what she said, Pru suspected she might have been given a stern telling-off.

Spotting Jean passing the door, her face pale, Pru knew instinctively that something was wrong. She heard the sound of tyres on gravel and glancing out of the nearest window, saw the postman cycling away. Bad news. She shivered.

Pru picked up the utensils and discarded dressing and left the private to his own devices. She needed to find Jean and find out what had upset her. She quickly asked one of the VADs to take the things she was holding and hurried out of the ward.

She saw her friend disappearing through a door on her way outside and ran after her. 'Jean,' she called when she couldn't catch up with her friend's fast pace. 'Stop a moment, will you?'

Jean stopped walking but hesitated before turning to face her. Pru could see that her friend was gathering herself.

'What's happened?' she asked, reaching Jean. 'You're crying.' Monty was inside and Jean's parents were at their home in Jersey, so unless one of them had been taken ill, Pru thought, it must be news of Jean's brother causing her this pain. 'Is it Peter?' she asked, thinking about the handsome, quiet man who had always been fond of her.

'He's been shot, Pru,' Jean said quietly before clearing her throat. 'He's in a Netley Hospital in Southampton.'

'Oh, Jean.' Pru hated to think of Peter being hurt. She knew how close the siblings were. The fact that she hadn't reciprocated Peter's feelings when he had taken her out a couple of times and declared his love for her had been the one time in the history of their friendship that the two women had been at odds. 'I'm so sorry. He's back in England though, so that's something to be grateful for, don't you think?'

Jean shrugged. 'I need to know how badly hurt he is. I'm going to ask Matron for a couple of days' compassionate leave so that I can visit him and see for myself.'

DEBORAH CARR

'Good idea. I'm sure she'll agree to let you go,' Pru said, rubbing her friend's arm lightly in an effort to soothe her. 'Does the letter say where his injury is?'

'His left shoulder.' She held up the letter. 'It's from his commanding officer. Apparently, Peter wanted me to be the person contacted in case of any injury or, well, you know.'

Pru was grateful once again that her brother was too young to be conscripted. 'Yes.'

'I think I'll speak to Matron right away. The sooner I visit him the sooner my mind will be put at ease.'

'Good idea; you do that.'

Pru accompanied Jean back into the house. 'Do you want me to come with you?' she asked when they reached the door to Matron's tiny office.

'No, better not.' Jean smiled for the first time since receiving the letter. 'We both know how Matron will be only too happy to tell you off if she sees you here. I'll go by myself and let you know what she says.'

'Good luck.'

Pru raced back to the ward, shaky to think how close Peter had probably come to being killed.

'Nurse? Can you help me please?'

Pru turned to the fear-filled voice and saw one of the newer VADs struggling with a patient who seemed intent on trying to stand.

'No, Private, it's far too early in your recovery for you to attempt walking unaided yet,' Pru said, going over to calm the situation.

'What's wrong with Jean?' Milly said, arriving at Pru's side and grabbing her arm after she'd settled the private and returned to the nurses' station. 'I've just seen her going into Matron's office in floods of tears.'

Pru explained about Peter being hurt. 'Hopefully he isn't too bad,' Pru said. 'But Jean's pretty shaken up about it. They're very close.'

Milly shook her head. 'Poor Jean. I hope Matron gives her time to go and visit him.'

'So do I.'

Pru heard voices in the corridor. 'I think our patients' visitors are arriving. You give the ward a quick check and I'll go and get ready to open the door.' She glanced up at the wall clock. 'Two minutes.'

She left Milly straightening sheets and instructing the VADs to fill water jugs and remove trolleys and went outside into the corridor, instinctively looking over the waiting visitors' heads to see if she could spot Jack. Disappointed not to see him there again, she forced a smile and waited patiently.

Once visiting hours officially began, Pru pushed the door back and waited for the visitors to enter the ward. The chatter and excitement as those used to the place entered cheered her slightly. There were always a few who were visiting their sons or husbands for the first time who were more subdued, but thankfully today most people – apart from Private Danby, she noticed – seemed happy enough.

A hand rested on her shoulder. 'I was hoping you'd accompany me on a walk after your shift ends. I have something to show you.'

Hearing the familiar deep voice, Pru's heart raced and she spun around, forgetting for a moment that she was on duty. 'Jack!' Her arms went to hug him but she remembered herself and lowered them, giving him a pleading look. She heard Matron's footsteps coming down the corridor from her office and cleared her throat. 'Captain Garland, Major Ashbury will be delighted to see you're back with us again.'

His mouth drew back into a wide, knowing smile and he mouthed the words 'I love you' to her as Matron came up behind him.

'Captain Garland,' Matron said, stopping next to him with her hands clasped in front of the skirt of her uniform. 'Nurse Le Cuirot is indeed right. It's good to see you back here at Ashbury Manor again.' She gave Pru a disapproving look. 'Well, don't stand there, Nurse, accompany the captain to the major's bedside.'

'Yes, Matron.'

They walked to the other side of the room where Monty lay waving over at Jack. 'She's a bit of a battleaxe, isn't she?' he whispered. 'I seem to recall mentioning that I had something to show you.'

'You did,' Pru said, looking forward to discovering what it might be.

'Shall I wait for you after your shift? Outside the door of the west wing?'

'Perfect,' she agreed, barely able to contain her delight at seeing him again. 'I'll be finished when visiting is over.'

'I'll see you then.' He smiled at her and then, looking over at Monty, said, 'How the devil are you keeping? I hope you haven't been giving these poor nurses the run-around?'

She left Jack chatting to Monty and carried on with her work. Somehow the sun shone brighter and the birdsong seemed louder whenever Jack was around, she thought, fetching a chair for a patient. She smiled to herself knowing she was being fanciful but not caring. Everything seemed so much happier when he was at Ashbury. If only he didn't have to leave again.

———

At the end of her shift, Pru quickly ran to her room to freshen up before joining Jack for their walk. She was aware she was slipping into dangerous territory where Jack was concerned and, as always, she knew she was going to struggle to keep a tight rein on her feelings towards him. She wanted desperately to be able to go with her emotions and make the most of every single second they had left together. Maybe Jack was wrong to insist they wait. After all, she mused, if the worst was to happen then at least she would have memories of this special time with him.

He was waiting for her as she knew he would be. As soon as she stepped outside, he took her face in his hands and kissed her. 'I've been longing to see you,' he said, taking her hand as they began walking along the worn sandstone pathway. 'I don't know if it's better or worse to have to sit and watch you working, only able to pass the occasional comment to you while I'm visiting Monty.' He gave his question some thought. 'It's better, obviously, because at least I'm in the same room as you.'

'Albeit in a room with about twenty or thirty other people there at the same time.' She laughed, clutching his arm and kissing his shoulder. 'I've missed you so much.'

He bent his head and kissed her again. 'Not nearly as much

as I've missed kissing you and holding you in my arms.' He grinned at her with a mischievous expression on his handsome face before pulling her behind him as he ran the rest of the way into the woods.

Once hidden among the pines and oak trees, Jack took her in his arms and kissed her. Pru had been longing for this moment since his departure weeks before and kissed him back, abandoning all thoughts of anything but being with him.

His hands moved over her body and he groaned, kissing her neck and finding her lips again with his own. 'I love you so much, Pru. I wish we didn't have to wait but I know we must.'

Must we, she thought. Was it so wrong to act on their want for each other? Did they really have to be sensible? Her pulse raced. 'And I love you with all my heart, Jack. I wish we were married now and that you didn't have to leave me ever again.'

He ran his hands down her arms and took her hands in his. 'But we're not, sweetheart and we both know I must leave again. And…' He cleared his throat, looking more miserable than she could ever recall him being. 'Today is going to be the last time we see each other for a while.'

Pru's hand flew to her mouth but she was unable to stop a sob escaping. 'Please don't say that.'

He kissed her lightly. 'I probably shouldn't even have come here today. I only have a few hours before I have to go again. But I had to see you. Kiss you.' He kissed her tears away. 'I'd give anything not to have to leave you, but I'll be on a boat to France by this evening.' He pulled her tightly to him as she began to cry. 'I'm so sorry to do this to you yet again, darling girl.'

'It's not your fault, Jack.' Pru sobbed, desperately trying to calm herself, not wishing to make him feel badly when there was nothing he could do about it. She wished they could have met at another time in their lives when the urgency to make the most of every single second didn't continually haunt her. Each time he left she felt the sting of his departure more.

'I know I've mentioned marriage before,' he said quietly, his voice thick with emotion, 'but I've never proposed properly to you.' He bent down on one knee. 'Pru Le Cuirot, love of my life, I don't have a ring to offer you yet but I need to know, will you marry me?'

Pru took his beautiful face in her hands and, unable to stop tears streaming down her face, bent to kiss him. 'Yes, Jack. I'll marry you the first opportunity we get.' Her emotions overwhelming her, Pru lowered her face into her hands.

'Hey,' Jack soothed, taking her hands in his and gently lowering them. She felt his lips on hers and, wanting to cling to him, wrapped her arms around him and kissed him back. After a while they stopped and gazed at each other.

He grinned at her. 'You've made me the happiest man alive, Pru Le Cuirot, soon to be Pru Garland.'

She sighed happily. 'I love the sound of my new name.'

'Good, because it'll be yours for many, many years, God willing.'

They kissed again, then walked a little.

Jack bent to pick several daisies and handed them to her. 'Not much of a bouquet,' he said, smiling. 'But after this war is over, I'll make sure you have fresh flowers every day.'

'They're perfect.'

'Now,' he said, taking her hand in his. 'As I mentioned, I need to show you something.' He led her to the other side of the woods, through the huge wildflower meadow and down to a walled garden she hadn't noticed before.

'Is that where we're going?' she asked.

'Yes. I hope you're not disappointed by what I'm going to show you. It's not very exciting but it's something that has meant a lot to me since I first came to Ashbury.'

'Then I can't wait.'

They reached the garden and he pushed open the blue painted gate, stepping back to let her see inside. Pru gasped. 'It's beautiful in here. Why is it so far from the house though? I thought walled gardens were near kitchens.'

'They are,' he said. 'There's one at the back of the house. It's smaller than this one.'

'But why have two?' She was fascinated.

He led her inside and down one of the paths with neat beds on either side packed with flowers of every colour.

'It's magical.'

'I'm glad you think so.' He picked a strongly scented pale pink tea rose for her. 'You can add this to your bouquet but don't tell the head gardener if you see him.'

Pru shook her head. 'I wouldn't dare get you into trouble.'

'It was Monty's grandfather who had this garden built. He loved flowers and wanted somewhere special to keep his hives.'

'Hives?'

'Yes, that's what I've come to show you really. The beehives.'

They walked to the far corner of the garden where three stood peacefully. 'Did you ever help with them? Before the war, I mean?'

'Yes. Monty never understood my delight spending time down here with the head gardener, but he taught me most of what he knows about beekeeping. I loved helping him extract the honey from the hives and putting it in jars. If you haven't tried some yet, you should.' He raised an eyebrow. 'If you like honey, that is. I presume everyone does, which I shouldn't.'

'I love honey. My mother always buys jars from an old man who lives about half a mile away from our home. He says it's the flowers that give the honey its distinctive taste.'

'He's right.' He waved his arm across the expanse of the garden. 'It's why most of these flowers have been chosen for planting in this garden.'

'Really? But that's so clever.'

'I thought so too.'

He seemed pleased that she was keen to learn more and hear about the bees. It was good to see him smile and know she had made him happy.

TWELVE

Pru

AUGUST 1917

They left the walled garden and walked hand in hand through the woods towards the manor house, stopping every few minutes to kiss. Pru didn't think she had ever felt so loved or been so happy. She forced any thought of his leaving in a few hours from her mind, determined to make the most of their day.

Suddenly Jack stopped walking. Pru glanced up at him and saw he was listening for something.

'What's the matter?' she whispered, not wishing to alert anyone he might have heard somewhere near them.

'Something's wrong.' He began walking and pulled her along with him.

Concerned, Pru walked quicker to keep up with him. She heard a shout but couldn't make out what the person was saying. There was another shout and then another person calling to them. 'Jack? What do you think has happened?'

'I've no idea,' he replied. 'But I think we need to hurry.'

They broke into a run and Pru stumbled on a tree root,

grateful when Jack slowed to grab her so that she managed to right herself without falling.

'Fire!' a voice called out.

She gasped. 'Oh, Jack,' she said, barely able to stop a sob escaping.

He took her hand and they soon ran out from under the cover of the pine trees and stopped, staring upwards at the steel-grey smoke billowing from one of the upstairs windows.

'The patients!' she cried, picturing Jean and Milly who were still on duty. 'Jack, we have to save them.'

He let go of her hand and sprinted around to the front of the house with Pru following as closely behind as she could manage. The chaos that greeted them shocked her like a slap to her cheek. Orderlies carried out stretchers, and nurses pushed beds out of the front door one after the other. Lady Ashbury was pointing for her staff to push wheelchairs towards the lawn area in front of the house, the patients' faces ashen.

'The west wing is on fire, Jack,' Pru cried. 'That's where Ward Two is.'

'I know,' he replied, his voice low. 'I'm going in.' Jack raced into the building without a further word.

'Jack, no!' She reached out to grab his arm but he was too quick for her. Without giving herself a chance to think, Pru followed him inside. As she suspected he might, he immediately made himself useful, carrying a lighter patient outside, returning moments later as she was helping another patient with a broken ankle hobble out of the building.

She settled him near Lady Ashbury and ran back inside. She had looked around for Jean or Milly but couldn't see either of them looking after the patients who were already outside.

They must still be in the building, Pru thought, hurrying back inside. This time she could taste the smoke as it worked its way through the corridors. She covered her mouth with her forearm.

'Come along,' she urged when the patient she was helping stopped to get his breath, wincing in pain. 'We have to keep going. We'll be outside soon enough.' He grimaced as she pushed him gently sideways against the wall, out of the way of orderlies and nurses racing back inside. She noticed one was Jean and willed her friend to take care.

Pru passed the patient over to two of the housemaids and returned to the ward. Where was Jack? She helped a man into a wheelchair before pushing him outside to the lawn where she saw many of the servants setting down chairs and blankets ready for the patients.

Hearing glass shatter nearby, she spun around, staring in horror at the west wing of the manor, which was now almost entirely consumed by flames. Her heart pounded and panic coursed through her. She scanned the groups of nurses, doctors and patients desperately searching for Jack, Jean or Milly's faces but couldn't see any of them.

A bell rang frantically and she realised it was coming along the driveway towards them. Within moments firemen from the village began running into the building. Pru followed, determined to find those she loved, and just inside the front door she collided with Jack.

'Where the hell do you think you're going?' he shouted.

'I have to find Jean and Milly,' she explained, relieved to see he at least was safe.

'No, you don't.' He grabbed her, picked her up and carried her back outside, placing her on her feet near to the others.

'Jack, you don't understand, I have to go and help.'

'No. I don't want you back in there again,' he said, his face red from exertion. 'It's far too dangerous.'

'But Jack…'

'No, Pru. I can't let you.'

Frustrated with him for stopping her from doing what she needed to, she slammed her hand against his shoulder. 'You can't stop me. I work here, Jack. It's my duty to help. I can't stand here doing nothing,' she said, gasping as more firemen ran past them into the burning building.

'Then stay out here and look after the patients.' He took her by the shoulders and kissed her forehead. 'I can't let you go back in there. Anyway, I believe most of the patients are accounted for out here anyway.'

'They are?' Relief flooded through her.

'I think so.' He looked around them and she realised he was searching for something. Or someone.

'What's wrong?'

'Where's Monty?'

Fear grew inside her as she realised that she had not seen him since earlier that day.

'Surely someone will have helped him out by now,' she said desperately, yelping when a window shattered and razer-sharp needles spilled onto the gravel near where they stood.

Jack moved her further away from the building. 'You look for him over there,' Jack instructed. 'I'll check this group of men over here.'

They parted ways and both searched for him. Pru asked

each nurse whether they had seen him, but no one had. She felt sick and it dawned on her that she hadn't seen Jean either. Panic coursed through her and she struggled not to give in to tears. She couldn't leave her friend to die, not while she had breath left in her body. 'Jean Le Riche? Have you seen her?'

Nurses and orderlies shook their heads in a bewildered reaction. Pru spotted Matron and ran over to her. 'Matron, have you seen Nurse Le Riche anywhere?'

Matron stared at her blankly for a moment. Then, turning her gaze to the burning wing of the building, she stared for a second before looking back at Pru with a horrified expression on her face. 'No, I haven't,' she said, her usual formality forgotten. 'I haven't seen Montgomery Ashbury either.' Her face paled even further. 'Nurse Le Cuirot, you need to look for him. Lord and Lady Ashbury have suffered enough loss for one lifetime, they can't lose him too.' Someone called out for Matron. 'Do what you can.'

'Yes, Matron.'

'Nurse Le Cuirot.'

Pru turned back to her. 'Yes?'

'Don't do anything reckless. You mustn't put yourself in any danger.'

'No, Matron,' she agreed, happy to agree to anything if only she could go and find her friends.

Jack ran up to her. 'Anything?'

Pru shook her head, hysterics rising through her body. 'No, and Jean's missing too. Oh, Jack, I have a horrible feeling they're together in there somewhere.'

Without saying anything further she ran as fast as she could towards the front door. Just as Pru stepped into the entrance hall two arms took hold of her and lifted her backwards, taking her back outside.

'Damn it, Jack. Let me be. I have to look for them.' Pru writhed, desperate to be let go. 'We don't have time to waste arguing.' She had to find Jean and couldn't waste a minute, especially now the fire was spreading so quickly. 'Let go of me,' she demanded, taking hold of his hands and doing her best to prise them off her.

Jack put her down and turned her to face him.

'Please let me go,' she cried in frustration. 'I have to find Jean, Jack. No one's seen her since she went back inside. She's my best friend.'

He took her by the shoulders. 'You are not going back inside that building, Pru. I simply won't allow it.'

Enraged, she shrugged him off. 'Don't you dare tell me what to do. She's my friend, and if she needs my help, I'm going to go to her.'

'At the risk of your own life?' he shouted, his face puce with fury. 'You're not going in there. Arguing with me won't change my mind but it is wasting valuable time. Now, if you want to save your friend, and mine,' he added pointedly, 'you'll do as I say and let me go and look for them. Alone. I won't be able to concentrate if I'm worried about you too.'

Realising that she was hindering their friends being rescued, she gave in. 'Fine. Go find them, but for pity's sake be careful.'

His expression softened and he pulled her into his arms, kissing the top of her head. 'I love you far too much to chance you being hurt. Now go and help the men out here,' he said, indicating the distressed patients and harried nursing staff. 'I'll be as quick as I can.'

Before she could say another word, he turned and raced back inside the burning building.

'Jack,' she whimpered, willing him to be careful.

'Nurse Le Cuirot,' Matron called from somewhere behind her. 'Did you find her?'

'No, but the captain is in there looking for them now.' She knew Jack was a strong, capable man and if anyone could help their friends it was him. She spotted Milly busily trying to comfort a young private who was writhing in pain. Her heart soared to see her friend safely outside and she went to see what she could do to help her.

'He's burnt his hand,' Milly whispered.

Pru wasn't sure why her friend was behaving so oddly. Maybe it was the shock. 'Do you need me to fetch something for him?' she asked, confused.

Milly frowned. 'No.' She led Pru further away from him and busied herself sorting through blankets.

'What are you doing?' Pru asked. 'Is something the matter?'

Milly stilled, looked either side of them and then lowering her voice, whispered, 'I think it was the private who started the fire.'

'What?' Pru glanced at the soldier, whom she recognised now as Private Danby. He was muttering something to himself and trembling despite being covered with several blankets. He did have a wild expression in his eyes, Pru noticed, and he had been acting increasingly erratically over the past few weeks. 'Do you think he's capable of doing something like that?'

Milly shrugged. 'I would like to say no, but I can't in all honesty do that.'

'But why would he set fire to the manor?'

'I'm not sure. Maybe it had something to do with the visitor he had today.'

Pru was surprised. She had never known him to have anyone visit before today. 'We're going to have to report this.'

'I know, but to whom?'

They looked over at Matron, then to where Lady Ashbury was busily tending to another soldier, offering him calm words of reassurance.

Pru sighed. 'I think Matron is the right person.' She was their superior after all and always calm and authoritative in a crisis.

'I agree.'

Pru realised she hadn't seen Jack for a while. Surely he should have come back outside by now? She searched around her frantically. He wasn't anywhere. The manor was a large building, she reasoned, and there were many places where Jean and Monty could be. Why were they still in there? She hoped Jack would find them and soon.

'You all right?' Milly asked, interrupting her frantic thoughts. Pru told her about Jack going back inside to look for Jean and Monty. 'You didn't see them anywhere, did you?'

Milly gave her question some thought. 'No, actually. Not for some time now.' She stroked Pru's upper arm. 'Look, I'll go and speak to Matron. You stay here and keep an eye on the private. See if you can find out anything about the fire, or his visitor.'

'Will do.' Pru looked over at Private Danby and doubted

she could nurse someone who had consciously attempted to cause harm to those closest to her. She reminded herself that he was probably suffering from some form of shell shock and probably wasn't accountable for his actions – if he had in fact started the fire, which, she reminded herself, wasn't a certainty yet.

She took him a glass of water. 'How are you doing, Private Danby?' she asked, glancing over at the front door to see two orderlies carrying out one of their colleagues who seemed barely conscious. Her stomach contracted in fear. Where the hell were Jack, Jean and Monty?

'She's gone,' he said, his voice high-pitched and bordering on hysterical.

'Who?' She thought of his visitor.

'My mother.' His entire body shook and she grabbed a nearby blanket and laid it on top of the others about him.

'Tell me what happened.'

He stared at her, his eyes large. 'My cousin came earlier,' he said, staring at his burnt hands. 'He told me they didn't know I was here until the other day.' He stared into space, his teeth chattering.

'Go on,' she said, willing him to tell her everything before the shock got too much for him.

'There was a Zeppelin raid two months ago. My mother was killed when a fire consumed her house and the one next door.'

Pru was horrified. 'I'm so sorry.' She pulled a blanket higher up over his chest. 'Why did they take so long to break the news to you?'

'He said that the telegram notifying her I was here must have been burnt in the fire.' He shrugged. 'I don't really know.'

Pru thought about what Milly had told her. She needed to ask him now, before he had a chance to think through what he had done. 'Private?'

'Yes, Nurse?'

'Why did you start the fire?'

His eyes darted up to meet hers and for a second she thought he might deny what had happened, shout at her for accusing him of doing such a terrible deed.

'I've lost everything in a fire and don't see why these people' – he almost spat the words – 'with all their airs and graces should carry on as if nothing happened.'

'But they're not,' she argued. 'They've lost two sons and have turned their home over to help people like you.'

'That's what you say because you're one of them.'

Pru went to correct him then realised he didn't have full control of his faculties. At least now she knew what had caused this dreadful fire. She waved over an orderly. 'Please keep an eye on this man. Don't let him out of your sight.'

She made a mental note to speak to Matron and Milly about her conversation with the private. First, though, she needed to find Jack. He had been inside too long. She paced back and forth, staring at the burning building, watching smoke billowing out of the upstairs windows, willing him to come back outside.

More firemen had arrived from the next village and other locals were joining them to help bring the fire under control, lining up to pass buckets of water from the large fountain in front of the manor to the firemen inside.

Where was Jack? She swallowed the nausea as she stared at the front door, willing him to bring their friends outside to safety. 'Come on Jack,' she pleaded. 'Where are you?'

'We need help in here,' a husky, smoke-damaged voice yelled desperately from the entrance hall. Pru rushed forward, sensing Jack was one of those needing their help.

As she reached the door, she had to step back to make way for an orderly. She gasped to see he was carrying Jean. Pru covered her mouth to stifle a sob. Her friend was conscious but clearly in a bad way. Next, two orderlies made their way outside with Monty, half carrying him, his arms around their shoulders, his head drooping to his chest. They reached the grass and laid him down gently.

Pru knew there would be nurses taking care of her friends. But where was Jack? She clenched her fists, willing him to come out to her. She couldn't wait any longer. Unable to stop her tears, Pru ran in through the doorway. 'Jack!' she screamed, not caring that she sounded hysterical now. She was about to step further into the hall when a fireman stopped her. 'Move out of the way, please, Nurse,' he said, taking hold of her arm and pulling her aside just as Jack was carried out by two men. She could see he was unconscious and that his left hand was burnt and his clothes singed and torn.

'Bring him over here,' she ordered, leading the way to a shady spot under the trees.

Milly immediately appeared by her side carrying blankets and a pillow. She helped Pru set them down and waited for the orderlies to lower Jack onto them. 'I'm relieved the three of them are accounted for,' Milly said.

So was she. Pru knelt at Jack's side, her head pounding as

she assessed his injuries. She sighed with relief to find he was still alive. She took his uninjured hand in hers and held it gently between her own, bending down so that her lips were close to his ear. She wanted him to be able to hear her over the din that was all around them. 'Keep fighting for me, Jack,' she pleaded. 'I love you.' She kissed his forehead. 'You're going to be fine, Jack. I promise you. I'll make sure that you are.'

One of his fingers twitched. 'Did you see that, Milly?' she asked tearfully, desperate to know she hadn't imagined it.

'I'm not sure,' Milly said, giving her an apologetic smile. 'I'll fetch Doctor Parslow.' Milly handed Pru the dressings and saline solution she had fetched.

'Thank you.'

Pru shrieked as another of the windows exploded and instinctively covered Jack's head and chest with her body. Hearing screams, she glanced towards the building. Someone was still inside. Desperate cries for help filled the air and Pru watched in horror as a nurse began to run towards the burning building. She realised it was Milly.

'Milly, no! Milly!' she screamed after her friend. What was she thinking? Milly wasn't big or strong enough to carry anyone heavier than herself. 'Milly, come back.'

Pru looked around her hoping that someone would stop her brave, foolish friend from risking her life. 'Somebody, stop her,' she screamed.

A VAD brought over a bowl of water and two cloths. 'Matron thought you'd need these,' she said before rushing off again.

A couple of men ran to the building and Pru leaned to one

side to peer at the manor doorway, willing her friend to see sense and come back outside where she was needed.

'Try not to worry,' Doctor Parslow said breathlessly as he arrived at her side. It occurred to Pru that he meant Jack. The poor man probably hadn't stopped for a moment's break since the fire broke out. 'Focus on what you can do, not what you have no control over,' he said, his voice hoarse with exhaustion. 'This patient needs you more than anyone right now.'

Pru forced herself to focus on Jack, but each time she heard a cry or shout from inside the burning building, she glanced up, praying she would see Milly coming back unharmed. It wasn't like Milly to be reckless. Pru couldn't understand why she would have taken her life in her hands as she had done. It didn't make any sense.

'Nurse? Did you hear what I said?'

She realised the doctor was speaking to her. 'Sorry.'

'Clean this chap up as best you can while I examine this other patient. I'll check him over next.'

'Yes, Doctor.' Pru set about making Jack more comfortable and gently washed away the soot and grime from his face.

A couple of minutes later, the doctor returned.

'This is Captain Garland,' she explained. 'He's a regular visitor to the hospital; you might have seen him visiting Monty Ashbury? He went into the building and was injured trying to locate Monty and Nurse Le Riche.'

'Another brave soul,' the doctor said quietly.

She moved back to give the doctor space to examine Jack.

Pru remembered Jean and Monty and turned to try and see where they had been taken. She spotted her friend sipping at a glass of water. Relief flooded through her and she took advantage of Jack being tended to by the doctor to see if she could spot Milly anywhere. She noticed Monty being cared for by another nurse. He was conscious and explaining something to her. She was grateful to note that Jean and Monty seemed relatively unscathed. But why hadn't Milly come back yet? Pru swallowed to quell her rising panic.

'Come on, Milly,' she whispered. 'Get out of there, for pity's sake.'

She heard a moan and then coughing.

'Help raise his shoulders, Nurse,' the doctor said, taking a glass of water from a passing VAD. 'Drink this, Captain Garland. You'll feel much better.'

Jack's eyes snapped open and for a second Pru thought he might be delirious as he looked about him wildly. Then, seeing her, he calmed and closed his eyes briefly before trying to say something. 'What—'

'Don't try to speak,' the doctor said. 'Sip this water. Slowly.'

Pru held him by the shoulders, relieved to see he was coming round a little more. She sat slightly behind him, taking the weight of his upper body to keep him upright as she held the half-filled glass to his dry lips.

The doctor waited for Jack to take a few sips. 'Right, Captain Garland. Your left hand is burnt but it isn't too deep, thankfully. Your forearm is the same and both should heal fully with the right attention. Your leg also has a gash but isn't too bad. I'm going to leave Nurse Le Cuirot here to clean and dress your wounds. As soon as we've sorted out a new ward, we'll admit you and keep you in for at least a week or two.'

'You don't understand. I have to leave now,' he argued, his

voice croaky with smoke inhalation and exhaustion. He tried to sit.

Pru was relieved the doctor was having none of it. 'You are not going anywhere. If you have someone you'd like us to contact, then let the nurse know and she'll arrange for a message to be sent to them. Whether you like it or not, you will be here until I deem you recovered enough to be discharged.'

Jack frowned and looked up at Pru. 'Tell him, Pru.'

'Sorry, Jack.' She hated to defy him, but Doctor Parslow knew what he was doing and she trusted him enough to know that if he felt Jack should be kept in hospital then that's what must happen. 'The doctor's right. You have to be sensible.'

'But you don't understand,' he argued, before another coughing fit stopped him from arguing further.

'No, Captain,' the doctor said, standing and preparing to leave them. 'It's you who doesn't understand. We don't want the damaged areas to become infected because if they do your stay here will be far longer than the one I'm insisting upon now. Once the shock has worn off and you begin to feel the pain in your hand and leg, then I think you'll be happy that I took this decision from you. I'll leave him in your capable hands, Nurse Le Cuirot.'

Pru went to reply but a shout for help stopped her. Glancing in the direction of the voice, she saw one of the men she recognised as a footman struggling to carry a lifeless body out of the manor. Her throat constricted as she stared at the small, slim figure being taken from his arms by another man. There was no mistaking the wavy chestnut hair.

'Milly?' Pru whispered, wishing she was wrong. She rested

a hand on Jack's chest. 'I'll be back shortly,' she said without waiting for him to reply as she ran to her friend.

Matron reached her before Pru could get to her, and when Pru saw the caring way the older woman rested her hand against Milly's right cheek, she knew her friend was dead.

'No,' she whispered. 'Not Milly.'

She bent to check for herself that there was nothing to be done for her dear friend, only to feel hands taking hold of her upper arms and Jean's voice in her ear. 'She's gone, Pru.'

'She can't be! Not Milly.' She sobbed, collapsing in Jean's arms as the two of them mourned their sweet roommate who had suffered so much loss in her young life already. 'Why did she go in there, Jean? It's not as if she could carry anyone to safety. I don't understand.'

'Neither do I,' Jean whispered. 'Maybe she was caught up in the moment and just didn't think.'

Pru had no idea. All she knew was that she would never forgive herself for not managing to stop Milly from running into the burning building.

THIRTEEN

Jack
_____

AUGUST 1917

J ack heard Pru's sobs and his heart ached for her. He wished he had known to look for her nurse friend, then reminded himself that he had hardly been in any position to help anyone. She had been so happy when he had proposed and then when he'd introduced her to his beloved bees. He felt sad that their reunion had been shattered in such a traumatic way. He heard Jean's gentle voice and relaxed slightly, relieved Pru was with someone who could take care of her. Seeing the devastation on his darling girl's face, he attempted to stand. 'Pru,' he called. She needed him.

'No, you don't, Jack.' Monty's hands took him by the shoulders and pushed him back to being seated. 'I think the two of them need to be alone with each other right now, don't you? We can comfort them later when they're ready.'

He was right. He usually was, Jack mused. 'How are you feeling, old thing?'

Monty thanked a nurse who set a chair for him on the lawn next to where Jack was lying and helped him to sit. 'You're to take things easy,' she said, sounding, Jack thought, like a younger version of the stern matron who kept everyone in order.

Monty gave her an apologetic smile and then looked down at Jack. 'That's me told.'

'It is.' He looked at Pru and Jean once again, hugging each other, lost in their grief. 'It seems worse when it's not out in the field, doesn't it?'

Monty nodded slowly. 'Nurses shouldn't die,' he said wistfully. 'And especially not here.'

Jack remembered where they were and reached out his bandaged hand to rest it on his friend's foot. 'I know. Your parents are going to be devastated that this has happened.' He scanned the large group of people nearby. 'Do you think it was accidental?'

Monty's eyebrows shot up in surprise. 'Don't you?'

Jack didn't know and chided himself for adding to Monty's already heavy burden of concern. 'It's a possibility. Ignore me. I'm sure we'll find out soon enough.'

Monty looked around to check no one was nearby. 'Jack, we both know your instincts are rarely wrong. If you sense that someone did this on purpose then I believe that's what happened. There's something more, isn't there?'

'Monty, I found you locked in a room unable to escape,' he said. He looked about him, seeing doctors and nurses working on patients. 'The place is still ablaze.' He saw that Monty was deep in thought and knew that the two of them would be discussing this again very soon. Neither of them were known for letting things go, not when they believed there was an injustice to resolve. 'Let's focus on Jean and Pru for now,' he said. 'And your poor parents. There'll be time enough to look into this further.'

'Yes.' Monty winced and rubbed his bad leg lightly. 'Cursed thing is giving me the pip today.' He pressed his lips together for a moment. 'I know you're angry about being hurt,' he said. 'But at least you'll have something to focus on, apart from Pru, to keep you busy while you're here.'

'True.' Jack felt slightly appeased to think that he could do some good. He was determined to get to the bottom of who had started the blaze that had threatened to ruin his best friend's home and injure and kill decent, hardworking nurses. 'That poor nurse is not going to die in vain.'

FOURTEEN

Pru

AUGUST 1917

B y that evening the fire had been completely extinguished and the cleaning up had begun. Pru still couldn't come to terms with losing Milly. She and Jean had offered to clean Milly's body as a mark of respect but Pru had been secretly relieved when Matron insisted that two other nurses took care of their friend.

'I would like the pair of you, as Nurse Denton's closest friends and roommates, to pack up her things. We need to ensure they are returned to her family.'

'Yes, Matron,' she said. 'We'll see to it after our shift ends.'

Pru wasn't sure who Milly's closest relative might be as Milly had never spoken of any family, only a little of her late husband. Tears welled in Pru's eyes but she brushed them away. Now wasn't the time to give in to her emotions, and she wasn't the only one suffering loss right now, she reminded herself.

Pru helped make the patients comfortable as they prepared

for the move to the new wards, which were to be called Wards Three and Four, so that the fire-damaged Ward Two could be spoken about without anyone being confused. Pru was happy when Jack was placed in Ward Three, which had previously been used as a dining room. She loved the library, which was being converted into Ward Four, but knew Jack would enjoy the sunlight that streamed in through the dining room's huge, almost floor-to-ceiling windows.

'How are you doing, sweetheart?' he asked several hours later when she went to check on him before retiring to her own bed, where she hoped that her exhaustion would lead to a few hours' sleep. 'I'm so sorry about your friend Milly. She was a lovely girl.'

Pru nodded, barely able to speak. She took a deep breath. 'I'm fine,' she lied. 'Jean and I are supposed to pack up Milly's things tonight but I don't think I can face it yet. Maybe we can make believe, just for this evening, that she's still on duty and we'll see her again,' she said, her voice quivering with emotion.

Jack took her hand in his bandaged one. 'Today has been shocking for all of you.'

'It has,' she agreed, her voice catching. 'I just hope she didn't suffer too much.'

He nodded slowly. 'I spoke to the doctor earlier and he told me Milly died from smoke inhalation. I think that's probably better than the alternative if that's any consolation.'

'Thank you,' she said, loving him for caring enough to find out for her. 'It is.'

She noticed him wince. 'How are you feeling now?'

'Frustrated to still be here.' He must have noticed the hurt she tried and failed to hide. He reached out his good hand for hers. 'I'm sorry, sweetheart. It's not that I want to leave you. I don't. I wish we could be together all the time, you know that. But my squadron needs me. Things are so hectic over in France – we're short of pilots at the best of times and I'm not sure what they'll do now I'm stuck here for the next week or so.'

She understood his need to fly and be with his squadron but doubted he was going anywhere very soon. 'You won't be much help to anyone with a burnt hand, Jack. And if it's not treated and cared for correctly then it could become infected and that could be catastrophic for you.' She checked no one was watching and leaned forward to kiss him quickly on his mouth, surprising him and making him smile. 'You're just going to have to be patient, do what you're told for once and put up with seeing me every day until you're fit to leave again.'

He pretended to consider what she had just said. 'I suppose I don't have much choice, then, do I?'

'No. You don't.' She rested a hand on his cheek. 'I think the sight of you running back into that burning building will be seared on my brain for ever,' she said, her voice cracking with emotion. 'I can't lose you Jack. I simply can't.' The fear that he wouldn't come out of the building had terrified her and brought to light how precarious their lives were.

He pulled her closer. 'Hey, I'm a tough American. I can take whatever's thrown at me and I promise you I'll always come back for you.'

She hoped he would; the alternative was too terrifying. 'I hope so.'

'You'd better believe it, sweetheart.'

She looked over to Monty's bed, which sat between Jack's and the back wall of the panelled room and caught Monty's eye. 'How are you feeling?' she asked.

He propped himself up a little more and grinned. 'Grateful to still be alive,' he said. 'If it wasn't for this flying ace next to me then I'd be a goner.'

'You'd have found a way out,' Jack insisted. 'Anyway, we're all fine now, so let's not focus on what might have been.'

'I agree. It's too horrible to think about,' Pru said, hating to think what might have happened if Jack hadn't found Monty and Jean in the linen cupboard where they had been trapped by someone.

'Is something wrong?' Jack asked her. 'Something else?'

Pru stared at him, not wanting to cause alarm but aware that Jack was the best person to share what she knew about Private Danby who was behind the screen of a bed further down the ward.

'There's something I need to tell you both,' she whispered.

As she finished, she realised Jack's grip had tightened on her hand and he said 'I want you to come with me.'

'Where are you going?' Monty asked, clearly furious and a little in shock at hearing that the man who had lain not two feet away from him for months had attempted to murder him and Jean and burn down his ancestral home.

'Keep calm,' Jack said. 'Leave this to me.'

A shiver ran through her. 'Where are we going?' she asked, leaving the ward with him.

'That man needs to be arrested before he's tipped off that you've told anyone about his admission. He's clearly dangerous and we don't need him to realise that he's about to be caught.' He began leading the way out of the ward.

'Where are we going?' she asked, confused.

'To Matron's office.'

'What?'

He put his finger up to his mouth. 'Keep your voice down. I saw her talking to one of the VADs so I know she's not in her office. Quick, let's hurry.'

Pru didn't dare look back to see if anyone was watching them. Jack was right, they needed to call the police immediately while the private was oblivious to anything. 'But he admitted it was him,' she said thoughtfully. 'Won't he be suspicious that we've left the ward?'

Jack reached the office door and opened it, waiting for Pru to enter before closing the door quietly behind them. 'He probably thinks we're sneaking off for a quiet chat, or something. I don't know, or care. Listen out for anyone coming.'

Pru took a calming breath to steady herself and listened with her ear to the door. She heard Jack repeating what she'd told him to the officer on the other end of the line before quietly replacing the receiver on the hook.

'He's sending someone right now,' he said. 'Is there anywhere else you could be for a few minutes?'

'Why?'

'Because I don't want you there when they come for him. He'll know who's behind his arrest and I'd rather you're safely away from it all.'

She wished it was that easy. 'I'm on duty, Jack. I must go back.'

He tried to argue with her but she had no intention of listening to him. There were enough people in the ward to protect her should the private try to attack her. For a moment she felt a little light-headed and stopped in the hallway, reaching out to rest her hand on the panelling.

'You're unwell?'

She couldn't miss the panic in Jack's voice. 'No, just a little overwhelmed by everything that's happened today, I think. Come on, let's get back before anyone suspects there's something amiss.'

She was barely coping with losing one friend today, let alone knowing that Jean and Monty had almost died thanks to Private Danby's malevolence. Life was already fragile enough without someone purposely setting the place on fire and she was determined to see him arrested and removed from the manor. It was the only way she thought she might be able to sleep that night.

She saw Jack back to his bed next to Monty's. His friend coughed a few times and Pru went to pour him some water but he motioned for her to stay where she was.

'I can do it myself,' he said, picking up the small carafe and pouring water into a glass. 'You're very pale, Pru. Are you sure you should be working?'

'Not you as well, Monty,' she said. 'I'm just a little shaken by what's happened today, that's all.'

Monty gave her a sympathetic smile. 'Try not to be, dear girl. Jack will survive this and Jean and I are fine, if a little smoke-damaged.' He grinned. 'We need to look forward rather than backwards, Pru. All of us do.'

Pru forced a smile. 'You're right.' Where were the police? Surely they must be here soon, she thought restlessly.

'Why don't you go and get something to eat and try to catch a few hours' sleep? It's been a long day,' Jack suggested. 'Spending a little time with Jean chatting things through might make you both feel better.'

She could tell Jack was determined that she not be present when the police arrived. He was right, she supposed. Regardless of what happened when the private was arrested, she and Jean needed to be together to try and make sense of it all. 'I think I will.'

'I know she'll probably appreciate spending time with you right now,' Monty agreed. 'I'll speak to Matron and tell her I insisted you go and be with Jean. She won't argue with me. We'll see you in the morning.'

She realised her shoulders ached and her head was thumping. 'Thanks, both of you. I am a little worn out.'

She looked around her and when everyone's attention was elsewhere she bent to kiss Jack good night. 'I love you,' she whispered.

'Good, because I love you too.' He gave her hand a gentle squeeze. 'Now, get to bed.'

Pru had reached the bottom of the back stairs when she heard heavy footsteps running through the hallway into the makeshift ward. Shocked to hear the private's voice as he shouted and cursed, she sat heavily on one of the stairs, her legs unsteady. Jack had been right. What did she know of people being arrested? She was grateful to him and Monty for sending her from the room. And just in time, it seemed.

Having given herself a few minutes to calm down, Pru hurried upstairs to her bedroom. She opened the door as quietly as possible, not wishing to disturb Jean if she was already asleep. She peered around it and tiptoed inside.

'I'm awake,' Jean said, her voice thick from crying. 'No need to be quiet.' She sat up and they stared at each other miserably.

Pru stepped forward and sat on the side of Jean's bed before leaning forward and taking her friend in her arms. 'I'm so relieved you're unharmed.'

Jean began to cry. 'I can't believe we'll never see Milly again,' she sobbed. 'If Jack hadn't rescued us, I dread to think what might have happened.'

Pru held her tightly. 'But he did and you must try not to dwell on the *what ifs*. You're safe and so is dear Monty, thankfully.' She didn't admit that she was struggling not to give in to hysteria.

'But Milly.'

Pru groaned, feeling a physical pain in her heart. 'I can't quite believe she's not going to walk through that door any minute,' she whispered. 'Why did she run into the building like that, do you think?'

'I've no idea. None whatsoever.'

Pru picked at the skin on the side of her right thumb. 'Why didn't I move more quickly?' she said, angry with herself. 'I should have stopped her from going in.'

Jean shook her head. 'No. You couldn't have. Milly was a strong-minded woman and if she decided to do something then there's nothing you or I could have done to change her mind. You know that, don't you?'

Pru gave her friend's question some thought. She was right. Milly wasn't the sort of woman to be dissuaded from a cause. 'I suppose you're right.'

'Good. I'm glad you do. Today has been heartbreaking enough without having to watch you tormenting yourself.'

When Jean calmed slightly, Pru sat back. 'We both need a good night's sleep.'

'What about Milly's things?' she added, staring at the silver-framed photo of Milly's dead husband, which stood on her nightstand beside the book she had been reading. Pru noticed that Milly had been using the pretty leather bookmark she had bought her for Christmas the previous year and was pleased her friend had liked it.

'I think we should pretend she's on duty right now and not think about it until tomorrow morning,' Jean suggested. 'We might feel a little more able to go through her things then.'

'Good idea,' Pru said, relieved.

Jean sighed and lay back, resting her head on her pillows. 'I can't stop thinking about it though, Pru.'

Pru realised her friend needed to speak. 'Do you want to tell me what happened to you and Monty?'

'Please.'

Pru waited but when Jean didn't say anything she presumed her friend wasn't sure where to begin. 'Why were you and Monty in the linen cupboard, Jean?'

Jean groaned, her cheeks reddening. 'We wanted to be alone. We hadn't been able to kiss more than a couple of times and the lack of privacy was driving us both mad. If it wasn't other patients watching us, it was nurses, and I noticed his mother giving me a strange look the other day. Monty suggested we find somewhere where we wouldn't be seen. Hence the linen cupboard.'

Pru got up to change into her bed clothes. 'And was it nice?' she asked, grateful that she and Jack had been able to go out for evenings together and walks in the woods. She hadn't considered before how restricted Jean and Monty's relationship must have felt and thought how selfish that was of her.

'It was everything I imagined.' Jean smiled thoughtfully. 'He's a wonderful kisser.' She hesitated. 'I really love him, Pru. Very much.'

'I know you do. And I can tell from the way he gazes at you while you're working and watches the doorway when your shift is about to start that he loves you as much as you love him.'

Jean sat up, alert to what Pru was telling her. 'I know he does because he told me he's spoken to his parents and told them that he will be marrying me and that if they want him to take on Ashbury when his time comes then it will only be with me by his side.'

'Jean, I'm so happy for you both.' She hugged her friend tightly, delighted to know that she and Monty would have a future together. They might have different backgrounds but their personalities were well suited and she sensed that they would be very happy. She thought about Jack proposing to her earlier but decided now wasn't the time to share her news. Anyway, she reminded herself, the war had to end before Jack had any intention of making her his wife.

'What are you thinking?' Jean asked. 'You're very deep in thought. Has something happened I don't know about?' Jean frowned. 'You're trembling. Something has happened. What is it, Pru? Tell me.'

Hearing the panic in Jean's voice, Pru knew she had to tell her about Private Danby being arrested.

Jean pulled her bedsheet up to her chin. 'It was him? But why would he do something so callous to Monty and me?' Tears dripped down her face. 'To dear Milly? What have any of us ever done to him?'

Pru told her what Private Danby had said to her. 'Strangely enough, I don't think he intended hurting anyone, just the manor and all it represented to him.'

Pru sat with her arms around Jean until she calmed. 'It's been a terrible day, but we have to carry on. We can't let what one madman did ruin everything Milly and the rest of us here have been working hard for these last few years.'

'You're right.' Jean sniffed. 'I think we should try to get some sleep. It's been a long, terrifying day and we'll have to help with the rest of the cleaning up tomorrow. We're going to need to muster all our strength to sort through Milly's things at some point too.'

Pru went to her bedside table and taking out one of her handkerchiefs, blew her nose. 'You're right.'

'Get into bed and let's get to sleep. Hopefully we'll all feel a bit better in the morning.'

Pru doubted it but didn't argue. She washed her face and cleaned her teeth and as she wiped her mouth she heard Jean's soft snores. She hung up her towel and watched her friend for a moment. She had Jack to thank for saving her best friend's life. Jack was good and kind and incredibly brave. She shivered as she recalled him racing back into the burning building and risking his life for Monty and Jean, and she knew she would never be as grateful to anyone or love anyone as much as she loved Jack.

FIFTEEN

Pru

The following week, Pru was busy instructing two new VADs about a couple of the men who, due to thick dressings on their hands, were unable to feed themselves. 'Remember at all times to ensure you treat these patients with respect and don't undermine their dignity. It's difficult enough for them to have to require your assistance without being made to feel embarrassed in any way. Now, off you go. And if you have anything you wish to ask me, don't hesitate.'

She watched them go. It was strange to think that this time a week ago Milly had been busily working nearby. Now the only thing that remained of her friend were her and Jean's memories. They had discovered a distant cousin who had asked for Milly's belongings and that had been that. She took a moment to picture Milly walking in the rose garden to the side of the house. Then, when her throat constricted and she realised she was letting her emotions get the better of her, she cleared her throat to try and gather herself.

Earlier that morning a new nurse, Gladys Newton, had

moved her things into their room and taken over Milly's bed. It wasn't going to be easy getting used to having to share with someone she didn't know, but from what she had seen so far of Gladys the girl was hardworking, if a little gruff.

Pru was distracted by loud voices emanating from the hallway. She recognised one of them and after a moment trying to place where she had heard it before, smiled as she realised it was Hugo. She supposed he must have heard about the fire and wanted to check up on the family.

'Pru?' He peered at her before a smile lit his damaged face. 'Heavens, you do suit that uniform of yours very well.'

She blushed. 'Lord Rivers,' she said, enjoying the cheeriness he had brought into the building. 'How lovely to see you again.'

'It's Hugo, dear girl.' He rested a hand on her cheek. 'I can see why our American friend is so taken with you. Can't you, Verity?'

'Stop flirting with the poor girl, Hugo,' Verity said, moving to stand next to him. 'We heard about that horrible fire and your dear friend.' She reached out and rested a hand on Pru's upper arm. 'How are you holding up?'

'I've been kept very busy, which helps. It's lovely to see you both again.'

Verity kissed Pru on both cheeks. 'We simply had to come and see if there was anything we could do. We popped around last week but were told that our help wasn't needed but I simply couldn't keep away, not when such a terrible thing has happened in Monty's home. I hope no one minds.'

'I'm sure Monty and Jack will be delighted to see you,' Pru replied, imagining their happy faces.

'We've brought food and...' Hugo seemed at a loss for words. 'And things Verity thought might be needed.'

Verity took Hugo's hand, raised it to her lips and kissed it. 'He means blankets, food hampers, drinks, that sort of thing. We weren't sure whether the kitchens were damaged at all. If you need anything else at all please let me know, won't you? I'm happy to send out for anything you might need at Ashbury. We have stacks of linen and, well, everything you might possibly need.'

'That's very kind of you both. I'll pass on your offer to Matron; she's the one in charge of the supplies,' Pru said, thinking again how happy it made her to see this couple so much in love and yet so thoughtful of others. 'I'll arrange for someone to bring it in from your car.'

'No need, it's already been done,' Verity said. 'Let's go and find those naughty boys. If I know them, they've been up to all sorts of scrapes since the party.'

'Of course.' Pru smiled, wondering if this was Verity's way of dealing with difficult incidents – by keeping things light. Pru decided she rather liked it. It was preferable at least to the dour way some of the orderlies and manor staff had been acting. 'Let me show you through. If you'll follow me.'

She listened, amused, as Hugo related in his typically enthusiastic way how he, Jack and Monty had spent many happy hours at parties in London and competing with each other racing the horses across his father's land during school holidays. 'They are both utterly fearless,' he said. 'As soon as I heard about the fire, I knew both of them would be involved in some way and no doubt putting themselves in danger.'

'You obviously know them very well,' Pru said, pushing

thoughts of Milly's selflessness from her mind as she stopped at the ward door. She opened it and indicated for them to enter ahead of her. 'I'll let them explain everything, including why Jack's also now in one of the hospital beds.'

She saw Jack look up as the door opened. His obvious delight to see his friend and his wife cheered her.

'I might have guessed you couldn't stay away from drama for very long, Hugo,' Jack teased. 'At least we can't blame you for this one.'

Hugo threw his head back as he guffawed. 'That was supposed to be our secret.'

Monty pushed himself up further in his bed. 'Everyone knew you blew up the chemistry laboratory, Hugo Rivers. There's nothing secret about it.'

Verity leaned her head closer to Pru. 'He might sound jocular but Hugo was terribly concerned when we heard about the fire,' she said quietly. 'He insisted we came straight over but Lord Ashbury's butler sent us away, insisting that our help wasn't needed. Hugo was furious but I told him that the poor Ashburys had more than enough to deal with, having their house rearranged yet again to find rooms to replace the damaged wards in the wing.'

Pru wasn't surprised Verity was well informed about everything. She imagined the incident and the private's arrest had probably been the gossip of the nearby villages and supposed it made a change from hearing sad news from the Front.

'Hugo's supposed to be taking things easy after a bit of a setback last week, but when he heard that people had been hurt, he refused to keep away. I hope our being here isn't too disruptive.'

'Not at all,' Pru said, aware that Matron would have something to say when she discovered visitors in the wards out of visiting hours. 'I think Hugo's exuberance is exactly what we all need right now. It's been a bit heavy here since the fire and I'm sure you can imagine how well Jack's taken to being admitted to the ward.'

Verity giggled. 'Not very well at all, I imagine.' She studied him. 'Is he badly hurt?'

Pru shook her head. 'Not really, but he has burnt his arm and hand a bit. He also has cuts and bruising and some smoke damage to his lungs.'

'Will it stop him returning to do his duty? He'd hate not being able to fly.'

'No, it's only temporary.' She was thankful he was still able to do what he loved and should be back to full strength in a week or so, although dreading him leaving to return to his unit again. She wasn't sure how she was going to face his departure from her, especially after the shock of losing Milly, and was aware she was feeling fragile emotionally. 'He's a bit impatient about being restricted here though, so any distraction Hugo can provide will give him something else to focus on and that can only be a good thing.'

She realised Verity was watching her closely. 'Would you be able to take a few minutes to walk with me?' Verity asked. 'I've been cooped up for days with Hugo and would love a little fresh air and someone different to talk to for a bit.'

Pru knew Matron was busy elsewhere and liked the thought of getting to know Verity a little better. It felt only right that she do her best to be friends with those closest to the man she loved.

'I'd like that,' she said honestly. She looked over at the men and seeing they were oblivious to whether she and Verity were there anyway, happily left them to their conversation. 'Let's go this way. We're less likely to be seen.'

'How thrilling.'

Pru hurried through the passage to the back door, unsure if a lady like Verity had ever passed through this way before. 'You don't mind, do you?'

'No, silly. I'm loving this. It's the most excitement I've had for weeks.'

They laughed. Pru wasn't sure if Verity was teasing or telling the truth. As they reached the back door and made their way around the house to the formal terraced gardens, she couldn't help thinking that most people probably imagined upper-class women like Verity, married to men with magnificent estates, probably spent all their time partying and entertaining – when in reality that seemed not to be the case at all.

'What are you thinking?' Verity asked as they walked leisurely. Pru couldn't think how to reply. 'Are you thinking that my life isn't how you imagined it might be?'

Stunned to hear Verity put her thoughts into words, Pru stopped walking. She knew she needed to be honest if she wanted to be friends with this woman. 'I was. Is that dreadfully rude of me?'

Verity grinned. 'No. It's honest of you and I appreciate that. There aren't many people, apart from Hugo and those adorable men in there, who are truthful with me.'

Encouraged by Verity's reply, Pru decided to ask about her relationship with Hugo. 'How long have you known them all?'

Verity gave her a wistful smile. 'Hugo was friends with my older brother, Will.'

Pru couldn't recall meeting him. 'Was he at the party?'

Verity shook her head slowly. 'I wish he had been. No, he was killed early in the war.'

'I'm so sorry. I didn't know.'

Verity's perfectly erect shoulders drooped slightly. 'The men don't talk about it much. We all loved him enormously, and then one day he was gone. I think we all grieved deeply for a long time in our own ways.' She shrugged. 'But *what ifs* and *wishing* don't bring a person back to life, do they? Somehow you have to find a way to keep going.'

Pru felt a pang of fear. Was that what she would have to do if Jack didn't return? 'You do,' she agreed quietly.

'I'm grateful he lived long enough to attend my and Hugo's wedding. He was thrilled when we fell in love, bless him.'

Pru could see how much Verity needed to confide in her and wondered how many close female friends she might have. She listened quietly as the woman spoke.

'He always said we were perfect for each other.' She beamed at Pru. 'Yes, I know I'm taller than him and we do look a little odd as a couple, but he understands me and knows me better than anyone ever has, including Will. I can't imagine loving anyone more than I do Hugo.'

Pru felt a rush of love for the woman who, like so many others, had suffered so deeply. First the loss of her beloved brother and then her husband being terribly injured. 'It must have been terrifying to learn that Hugo had been hurt.'

Verity's right hand went to her chest and she stopped walking for a moment. 'I thought I would give up and die if Hugo didn't survive. When they told me about his injuries, I think that a lot of people expected a flighty woman like me to walk away from our marriage, but that was never an option.'

'I don't know you very well at all,' Pru said thoughtfully, 'but even I can tell that your love for each other is incredibly deep. You have the sort of bond that most people would give up everything to experience, even for a short time.'

Verity looked as if she was about to cry. 'Thank you, dearest Pru. I'm not sure if you're right about people thinking that, but I'm grateful to hear you say it. I love him. I love his character, his funny ways and most of all I love that I'm the most important person in his life. He is devoted to me and I would walk away from everything in my life in a heartbeat if it meant keeping Hugo.'

Pru swallowed away the lump in her throat. This vile war had a lot to answer for, but one thing it had shown her, time and again, was that it not only brought out the worst in people but also the very best. She felt Verity's delicate hand on her forearm.

'Please don't cry, Pru. I never meant to upset you.'

'You haven't, I promise. I'm happy for you both that you found each other.' She placed her hand on Verity's. 'I'm very grateful Jack took me to your home that night.'

Verity pulled her into a hug, her delicate flowery perfume filling the air. 'I'm jolly glad I met you too, Pru. You're an extraordinarily kind and giving girl. Jack is very lucky to have found you.'

'Thank you, but I feel like I'm the lucky one.'

Verity's arms dropped away and they began walking again. 'We were told what Jack did, racing back into the building when he realised that Monty and your friend were trapped inside. I worry sometimes that he's too brave for his own good. He was lucky this time, as he has been several times before.' She went silent and Pru could tell Verity was leaving many things unsaid. 'We just have to hope he doesn't put his own safety aside again. I worry that Jack Garland's like a cat and always landing on his feet but at some point he's going to use up all of his nine lives.'

Pru shivered. 'Let's hope this war ends before that happens.'

SIXTEEN

Jack

SEPTEMBER 1917

By the end of the first week in the ward Jack was irritable and by the second he threatened to discharge himself if Doctor Parslow didn't allow him to spend time doing what he chose. He loved seeing Pru each day but the frustration of being near her and keeping things sensible between them while also wanting to take their romance to another level and risk leaving her a widow was getting to him.

'I'm going crazy stuck here,' he moaned, not wishing to admit how hard he found it, being near to her each day and having to act as if there was nothing between them; having to contend with snatched smiles across the ward and her hand grazing his whenever she tended to his dressings. 'I need to fly again.'

He didn't miss the hurt expression on her face and tried to soften his words. 'I at least need to be let out of this place to go for a walk. It's my hand and arm that are burnt, not my feet.'

'I'll speak to Doctor Parslow and see what he says.'

'It's fine. I'll do it.' He checked no one was listening. 'I need to be busy, Pru. I can't be stuck in there any longer.'

'I imagine you need some privacy, too,' she said, bandaging his arm, having changed the dressing. 'I think I'd go a bit mad being in here night and day without a little time away.'

He reached out and took her hand, keeping it below the level of the bed so no one could see he was holding it. 'I'm sorry. I don't mean to be grouchy and I have loved being able to see you for longer, but I'd rather we were alone and able to talk freely.' He lowered his voice. 'I need to kiss you.'

He saw the sides of her mouth turn up in a smile and her dimple appear in her left cheek and was glad he had cheered her up again after snapping at her earlier.

What was he doing saying such things to her? He felt irritated with himself. He needed to hold back. He might be stuck in this place now but soon he would be returning to fly and that meant risking his life once again. He needed to be sensible, and telling the woman he loved that he wanted to kiss her was hardly that.

'It's probably a good thing that I am stuck in here and you're busy working.' He smiled to soften his words. She slipped her hand from his and continued finishing what she was doing. He watched her concentrating on pinning the end of the bandage neatly and didn't think he could love her more than he did now. She was so caring, thoughtful and loyal and he couldn't be the one to chance ruining her life by encouraging her love for him.

'There,' she said, taking the scissors and the bowl with his old dressing in it. 'You'll do for now.' She smiled at him and they stared at each other. He could see how much she longed to be alone with him. 'I'd better be running along. Speak to the doctor and maybe we can take a walk to see your beehives a bit later?'

He nodded then watched her walk away. She was even happy to go with him to watch the bees, though he doubted she really had any interest in them. Maybe in time, he mused.

———————

Having put his foot down with Doctor Parslow, Jack waited for Pru at the end of her shift.

'This is what we all need,' he said, holding her hand as they walked along the path and into the shade of the woods. 'Fresh air, and plenty of it.'

'I don't care where we are as long as I'm with you,' she admitted. 'I wish you didn't have to leave me behind again.'

He put his arm around her shoulder and bent to kiss her. 'I feel the same way, sweetheart. But you're safer here, I can assure you.'

Her frown made him want to kick himself. Why didn't he think before speaking when he was around her? 'I'll be fine though,' he said, wondering why he was giving her false hope. 'I'll do my best to stay out of danger. Hopefully this war will end soon.'

'We keep saying that,' she answered, her voice hollow as if she was losing hope of that happening.

He stopped walking and gave her a pointed stare. 'It will, Pru. Believe it. Then all this will be over and...' He hesitated, wishing he knew for a fact that he would be around when the fighting came to its conclusion. 'And then we'll be together. We have to be positive, my darling.'

'I know, but it doesn't make it any easier.'

He tucked a loose strand of hair behind her left ear. 'When we're married, we'll only have ourselves to please. Where would you like to live?' he asked, determined to take her mind off all that had happened recently. He knew it was wrong to give her false hope but they could dream, couldn't they? What was life without dreams?

She sighed happily. 'I'd like to live in a cottage near the sea somewhere.'

He pictured a stone cottage on the shores of an isolated beach where they could live peacefully alone. 'How would it look?'

'Um, it'll have a pale-blue painted door with a window with blue shutters either side, which we'll close during storms.'

He pulled her closer picturing their imaginary home. 'There will be storms?'

'Or course!' She laughed. 'But we'll be tucked up safely inside in front of a roaring fire while the wind is howling all around us and the waves are crashing against the beach.'

Her words conjured up images of the two of them waking in their bedroom the morning after a storm, the sunshine streaming through the slats in the closed shutters and nothing for them to do all day but lie in each other's arms. 'It can't come soon enough for me.' He kissed her neck, making her shiver.

'Nor me,' she said dreamily. 'I think about it every day.'

'I'll picture this when I'm back flying,' he said. 'It'll be the thought of you and me in our cottage that will keep me going.'

She turned to him and wrapped her arms around his waist, clinging on to him. 'I wish with all my heart that you didn't have to leave me again,' she whispered. 'I'm sorry.'

'What for?' he asked, kissing the top of her head as it rested against his chest. 'I feel the same way you do.'

'But it's not your fault you have to leave,' she said, not looking at him. 'I'm sorry. I'm being selfish.'

Putting a finger under her chin, he raised it so she had no option but to look up at him. 'You're no more selfish than me. I promise I'll do whatever it takes to come back to you. Never doubt that for a moment, my darling. While there's a breath in my body, I'll fight my way back to you. Remember that.'

'Oh, Jack, I love you so very much it hurts.' She stood on tiptoes and slipping her arms around his neck, pulled him down to her so their lips met. 'I never knew love could be this wonderful, or this painful.'

He held her tightly, never wanting to let her go. 'I was thinking the same thing.' He sighed heavily. 'We're lucky to have met each other, if a little unfortunate with our timing, I guess.'

'I know you say you don't want to leave me, but whenever you return to flying there's always an excitement in your voice,' she said, taking him aback.

'What do you mean?' He knew full well what she was alluding to but hated her to think that it was because he did want to leave her.

He moved back slightly and looked her in the eye. 'It's not so much excitement as determination to go and do what I can to pay back those responsible for killing Verity's brother Will and so many of my men who never made it home. Even Monty and Hugo, who are back where they belong, are shadows of their former selves. It's that anger and determination that stops me from being afraid.'

Pru looked aghast at his words. 'You? Afraid?'

He grinned at her. 'I might have done a few things that some people, like Monty, consider brave, but believe me when I say I'm only human and I feel fear like everyone else. I probably just hide it better than most.' He hugged her to him. 'Don't look so shocked.'

'Actually that makes me feel much better.'

Confused, he frowned at her. 'How?'

Pru laughed. 'Because, Jack, if you feel fear then it means you'll take time to consider whether or not the danger you're putting yourself in is worth it.'

'It does?' Now he was the one feeling bemused.

'Yes, because fear makes you stop and think, if only for a second.'

'If you say so, then I'll have to take your word for it.'

She slapped him playfully on his arm and he yelled in pain, grabbing it with his other hand.

Pru gasped. 'Jack, oh heavens. I'm sorry. I didn't mean to hurt you.'

He let go of his arm and pulled a face at her. 'I'm only teasing.'

'You brute,' she said, slapping him harder. This time it did hurt a little but he had no intention of upsetting her further by letting her know.

'Let's go and see your beehives now.'

He took her hand and they walked through the woods, then the wildflower meadow, each lost in their own thoughts. This was all he needed, he reflected, breathing in the sweet summer air. His hand in hers, a summer's day and peace and quiet. Would they be lucky enough to experience this together after the war?

They stood in the walled garden near the beehives, his arm around her slender shoulders and hers around his waist. 'Would you mind if we had a couple of beehives behind our cottage?'

Pru smiled up at him. 'You can have whatever you want.'

'It's going to be perfect, isn't it?' he said, allowing himself the luxury of dreaming about their future again.

'Make love to me,' she said, her voice quiet.

Jack froze. Had he misheard? 'Pardon?'

'I think you heard me.'

He didn't know what to do. 'I, er…' His mind raced. If he agreed, which he desperately wanted to, then he was going against all he had promised himself where Pru was concerned. If he said no then she would feel rejected. Hurt. He couldn't do that do her.

SEVENTEEN

Pru

SEPTEMBER 1917

Pru wasn't sure it he was stunned or horrified by what she had said. She felt him tense and braced herself for his rejection. Now that she had said the words aloud, she realised she needed him to show her what it would be like to be loved by him, just in case. She forced the thought away but it bounced right back. What if, despite Jack's best efforts, something did happen to part them and he was unable to come back to her? Would she regret never making love to him? Yes, she thought.

'Jack, you're going away soon.' She took a deep breath to muster the strength to say what she needed to share with him. 'I'll hope and pray with all my heart that you come back to me.'

'You don't believe I will?' He looked unsettled at her suggestion.

Pru held him closer, staring up at his shocked, handsome face, sensing that they might not have the future together they both craved. 'No,' she fibbed. 'I believe you will. But what if you can't, for some reason?'

'Don't say that, Pru.'

She could see she had hit a nerve. Had he been dreaming about their future and had she just burst that bubble? Pru hated herself for upsetting him but her instincts had unsettled her. 'Jack, we've no idea how this war is going, or where you'll be sent next. I believe I'll see you again,' she said, hoping her instincts were wrong and it was merely her dread induced by Milly's unexpected death that had caused her to think in such a negative way. 'But we don't know what's going to happen.'

He went to speak, but she put a finger against his lips to stop him. If she didn't say what she needed to right now then she would lose her nerve and this was too important to her to risk that.

'I love you, Jack, more than I ever imagined possible.'

'Sweetheart.'

'Please, I must say this while I have the courage. I know I've shocked you by what I've said, and I don't mean to, but if the worst were to happen then I want to have no regrets. I want to know what it feels like to be loved by you.'

She felt his body tense and then slowly relax in her arms. Relieved, she calmed slightly as she waited for him to respond.

'When?' he asked, his voice husky.

'Now?'

He stared at her silently and she sensed he was conflicted about how to answer. She was about to lose her nerve and tell him everything was fine as it was, that he didn't have to do this if it worried him, when he spoke.

'The folly,' Jack said.

'Sorry?' Pru wasn't sure she had heard him correctly.

'There's a folly not far from this garden. They used it for hunting parties before the war.'

Pru was stunned. She hadn't ever seen a folly. 'What about it?'

He moved his arms from behind his back and taking her hands in his, brought them forward. 'If I'm to make love to you for the first time it's going to be somewhere romantic.' He smiled, sounding unsure of himself. 'Or at least as romantic as I can make it in the circumstances.'

How typical of Jack to want to make things perfect. Pru relaxed, realising that his hesitation wasn't because he didn't want to love her but because he was frightened that it was the wrong thing for them to do. 'The folly it is then. I've never seen a folly before,' she said, thinking it was turning out to be a day of firsts.

He began leading her away, breaking into a jog. 'I wish it was mine. Ours.'

'It can be our special place,' she said breathlessly as they exited the walled garden. They walked to a copse of trees that thinned out onto a hilly open area. Jack stopped and pointed towards what to Pru seemed like a cross between a doll's house and a fairy-tale castle.

She gazed in awe at the beautiful round building with a domed roof and stone steps leading up from the grass. 'It's like nothing I've ever seen before.' She stepped forward. 'Are you sure we can go inside?'

'It's where Monty and I used to spend time away from the

endless stream of guests that always seemed to be staying at the manor.' He began walking again, leading her towards the unusual building. 'We used to sneak into the kitchen and pack up enough food and drink to keep us going for the day – and if there was a larger house party and we were less likely to be missed, the night – and come here to talk and fish in the stream that's out back.'

'It sounds blissful.' She tried to picture the men as boys, playing and having fun. Carefree, never imagining what lay ahead of them.

'It was. I missed all of this when I returned each time to my folks in the States.' He smiled. 'It's good to be back here, especially with you.'

Her pulse raced a little faster at the thought of why they were here.

'Right, enough reminiscing,' he said, leading her towards the folly. 'I want to focus all my attention on you.'

They ran up the few steps leading to the round building and Jack shouldered the door, holding it open for her to step inside. 'My queen.' He grinned. 'What do you think of your castle?'

She stared up at the ceiling, surprised to see a finely painted array of gold stars and colourful planets on a midnight-blue background. There was a small fireplace with a basket of logs next to it. A worn-looking sofa stood in front of it, in the middle of the circular room, with a rug on the floor between them. There was a small mahogany table with two chairs on either side in front of a curved window, and two fishing rods leaning against the wall behind the door as if he and Monty had only just spent time there.

'Doesn't anyone come here anymore?'

'No. It's very much Monty's place. Or it was before he was injured. I'm not so sure what he'll do about it now he can't get here easily.'

'It's magical,' she said honestly. 'Thank you for bringing me here. I've never been in a place remotely like this one, and I can't imagine I ever will again.'

'You never know.' He walked over to the fire. 'Would you like me to light this? It's a little chilly in here and it'll warm the place up quickly.'

Pru loved the thought of making love by a roaring fire. 'It'll be just like our cottage that we've dreamt of living in after the war.'

Jack smiled and bent to kiss her. 'I like that. As if we'll be living our dream, if only for this afternoon.'

She watched while he set and lit the fire, stepping into his arms when he stood to watch it catch. 'This is perfect, Jack.'

'I'm glad.'

Her stomach flipped as he turned and took her face lightly in his hands.

'Are you certain you want this, Pru?' He kissed her lightly on her lips. 'I'll be happy for us to lie in each other's arms in front of the fire if that's what you'd rather do.'

'No,' she said, without a second's hesitation. She couldn't imagine a more perfect moment for them to make love for the first time. 'I meant what I said.'

'I want to so badly,' he said, his voice gruff, 'but I told myself we should wait. I still think we should.'

'What?' she asked, confused by his hesitation.

He gazed down at her. 'Don't get me wrong, I don't want to

wait. I just feel guilty taking what we have to a more intimate level and then going away to France.'

'I know you have a point,' she said thoughtfully, 'but since Milly died most things seem of little importance to me.' She closed her eyes and took a calming breath. 'Losing you, for whatever reason, and not having experienced being loved by you frightens me much more than anything else.'

She didn't care that her cheeks were flaming at her admission until it occurred to her how forward she must sound to him. 'Do I shock you by what I'm saying?'

He stared at her and she wasn't sure if he was judging her or considering her words. He kissed her again. 'How can I think badly of you when I want the same as you do?'

She slipped her arms around his waist and pressed herself against him, kissing his neck.

Jack groaned as he took her in his arms and lowered her to the rug.

———

Pru kissed Jack's bare chest, her hand resting on his heart. She hadn't expected their lovemaking to be so all-consuming.

'Are you all right?' he asked, stroking her hair, his voice tender. 'You're very quiet.'

'I'm happier than I could ever dare hope to be.' She shivered slightly despite the fire near to them. Jack pulled his coat from the sofa to cover her. 'I love you so much, Jack.'

'I love you too, my darling girl.' He smoothed back her hair from her face and bending his head closer to hers pressed his lips against her hair. 'I've wanted to do this for so long but never imagined it would happen before we were married.'

'Do you mind that we didn't wait?' She hoped she hadn't ruined his expectations of her. She heard a gentle laugh come from his throat and looked up into his navy-blue eyes.

'What do you think? You've made me the happiest man alive, Pru Le Cuirot.'

Relieved to hear him say it, she mustered up the confidence to ask another question. 'Do you think we'll be able to do this again before you leave?'

She felt his laughter in his chest. 'I certainly hope so.'

They lay in blissful contentment for a while longer, his muscular arms around her keeping her warm and feeling safer than she had ever felt before. Pru wished they could stay there for ever. 'Wouldn't it be perfect if this was our home?'

Jack cleared his throat. 'I think we would miss having a bathroom and kitchen.' She could hear the amusement in his voice. 'Maybe a bedroom?'

'Will you want to return to New York after the war, Jack?' She knew she was risking ruining their moment but couldn't stop herself from asking him.

He sighed. 'I always thought I would, but that was before I fell in love with a girl from a small island just off the coast of France.' He kissed her shoulder. 'I'll be happy living wherever you wish.'

She thought of the pretty beaches and headlands in Jersey and how much she wanted to show them to Jack. She had no idea what New York would be like and pictured a vast, bustling, noisy metropolis. 'We could spend a year in Jersey and the next in the United States,' she suggested dreamily. 'Or the other way round, I don't mind which.'

He put his hands under her arms and drew her up his body until her lips met his. 'Let's worry about that later, shall we? Right now, I need to show you how much I love you.'

'Again?' She giggled.

'Yes, again.'

EIGHTEEN

Pru

NOVEMBER 1917

Pru sat on her bed staring at Jack's photograph, thinking back to lying naked on top of him by the fire and losing herself in his kiss. She would give anything to be in his arms again, or even to see him from a distance. He had been called back to his unit only two days after they had made love and as much as she hoped Doctor Parslow would insist he wasn't ready, it wasn't to be. Although Jack had promised to send word to her as soon as possible, it had been two months since he'd left and still she hadn't heard anything from him. Pru was struggling to contain her panic.

'Is anything the matter, Pru?' Gladys asked joining her in their room. 'You're looking ever so peaky.'

Pru held up her photo of Jack. 'It's been two months now, Gladys.'

'Well, that's not so long, is it? Not with times being as they are.' She unbuttoned her dress and stepped out of it.

'I suppose not,' Pru relented, a familiar ache in her heart. 'I can't... No, it's nothing.'

Gladys slipped a hanger through the neck of her dress. 'Go on. What's wrong?'

Pru hoped she was overtired and giving in to her imagination. 'I just can't help worrying that something's happened to him. I know I'm probably being silly.'

Gladys hooked the hanger on their small wardrobe door and sat on Pru's bed next to her. 'Look, I know it probably sounds odd coming from me,' she said, not adding anything about her missing fiancé, whom no one had heard from since the start of the Battle of Loos. 'But even I can see that Jack's different to most men.'

Pru wasn't sure what her friend was insinuating. 'I ... I don't understand. Different in what way?'

Gladys shrugged. 'Well, he's tougher than most men I've ever met,' she said thoughtfully. 'I'm not sure what it is about him, but there's a worldliness you don't often come across. He gives me the feeling he can deal with anything life throws at him.'

If only that were true, Pru thought, hoping Gladys was right. 'He does have a certain something,' she said wistfully. 'Maybe I'm overtired. I haven't been sleeping too well lately.'

'That's the ticket. No point in getting yourself worked up about him if there's no way of knowing where he is, or what he's doing, is there?'

'I suppose there isn't.' Pru realised she hadn't asked after Gladys's fiancé for a couple of weeks. 'Still no news?'

'Not a dicky bird. But, as my old mum likes to say, "No news is good news". I know that's probably not the case but it's what I intend focusing on until I hear otherwise.'

'Good for you, Gladys,' Pru said, not sure if she could be as pragmatic as her roommate.

Gladys stood. 'Right, I'm going to try and catch forty winks before my next shift.'

'Thanks, Gladys. I appreciate you listening to me fretting. I feel a bit better now,' she said, wishing that really was the case but aware that her friend had waited for over a year to hear anything from her fiancé so she had a long way to go until that point. 'I'm going to try and go to bed earlier tonight and hope that helps a bit.' She slipped Jack's photo underneath her pillow and stood. 'I'd better hurry or I'll be late for my shift. Sleep well.'

She checked her hair was neat and hurried out of their room. As she walked quickly along the corridor towards the wards, terrifying scenarios about Jack's whereabouts threaded through her mind, tormenting her. Unable to stand not knowing a moment longer, she decided enough time had elapsed since she had last questioned Monty. If anyone would know something it would be him. He loved Jack almost as much as she did, and she could tell he was worried too.

Typically, Matron was on the warpath. Something had upset her, that much was clear to the rest of them on duty. Pru would have to wait until Matron's attention was taken before she dared chance approaching him.

'Good morning, Monty,' she said, eventually having found a quiet moment to approach him. She forced a smile. 'How are you feeling today?'

He studied her face before replying. 'Pretty much the same as you, I presume.'

'I look that bad?' she asked, recalling Gladys's comment.

He sighed. 'You'll always be pretty, Pru, but you do look a little, how should I put it … washed out.'

'Thanks,' she said without smiling.

'Worrying about Jack, I shouldn't wonder?'

'You, too?'

He sighed heavily. 'I wish I could say I wasn't but I'd be lying. I have this niggling feeling I can't shift that something's wrong.'

Pru's was surprised. So, she wasn't the only one. 'Me, too.' Nausea rose through her. 'I've never been frightened for him before. Well, not like I am this time.'

Pru noticed a fleeting expression cross Monty's face. If she had glanced away she would have missed it, but she hadn't. 'You know something, don't you?' she asked, moving closer to him and lowering her voice. 'You must tell me, Monty. I need to know.'

He frowned, clearly conflicted. 'Pru, you know it's not allowed.'

'Who've you been speaking to?' She needed to know and had no intention of letting him keep any information to himself.

'One of the men from our unit popped in to see me during visiting hours.'

'And he told you confidential information?' She was shocked but pleased she might be about to hear some news for herself.

'I was their Squadron Commander, and Jack's,' he explained. 'It's precarious out there and we're all close.' He stared at his hands thoughtfully. 'You can't help but be when you face something your family couldn't possibly understand.'

Pru could understand why. She bent forward. 'Who's going to know apart from you and me? I won't tell a soul, but I need to know. Please, Monty.'

He gritted his teeth and seemed conflicted for a few seconds. 'Fine. But I hope that includes not telling Jean, because if she thinks I've been instrumental in upsetting you she'll kill me.'

Pru made a cross with her index finger across her chest. 'Cross my heart.'

He scanned the room. 'I'll keep this brief because I don't know much, but what I do know is...' He grimaced. 'Are you sure you're ready to hear this?' he whispered. 'I can't have you running off in hysterics and alerting the entire ward that I've upset you.'

Frustrated and furious with him for not telling her immediately, she glared at him. 'I promise I'll be the picture of calm. Now tell me before I do something we'll both regret.' It was an empty promise and they both knew it.

'He's been captured.' He stared at her, gauging her reaction.

Her breath caught. Not wishing to give him an excuse to stop confiding in her, Pru cleared her throat, suspecting there was more. 'Go on,' she urged, her voice tight. She pressed a fingernail deep into the pad of her thumb, hoping the pain she was inflicting on herself was enough to keep her from passing out. 'Tell me everything.' Hearing Matron's heavy footsteps, she quelled her panic. 'Quickly, Monty.' Before he had a chance to reply, she added. 'Is he with any of his own men?'

He shook his head. 'Maybe one other.'

'Why, what happened?'

Monty seemed angry with himself suddenly. 'When my plane was shot down and Jack landed and rescued me from German lines, we both knew it had been little more than a miracle that we survived his plane being shot down too. He wasn't so lucky this time. A couple of the chaps witnessed one of ours with engine trouble. He had to land on enemy soil. They said his plane didn't seem smashed up like mine was, so he probably wasn't injured when he went down, but another saw Jack go down after him and land. Another later reported that he saw several Germans running for them. They don't know what happened next but that's why we presume they were captured. That's all I know. Truly, Pru.'

'He promised me he would be careful,' she hissed. 'Why does he take these chances, Monty?'

Monty stared at her and she sensed his guilt at Jack's part in his rescue. 'I don't know, dear girl, but I can't say I'm not glad he came back for me.' He shook his head. 'I just hope he hasn't just run out of his ninth life.'

She snatched her hand back from him, stung by his words. 'Don't ever say that! Jack will come back, I know it.'

'You don't though, dear girl.' He glanced past her. 'We need to be realistic. Neither of us know what's really happening to him, but I can imagine it far better than you. I've been in scrapes with him before.' He rested his hand lightly on his damaged leg. 'I've seen him in the field and the man is impressive.'

'He is?' she asked, clinging on to anything positive Monty had to say.

'We have to remember though, Pru, that regardless of his

toughness, Jack is only human. He can only face so much and come away unscathed.'

She tensed, her breath shallow. 'You might have given up on him, Monty but I never shall. Jack will come back, I know it. I trust him with all my heart. He won't leave me here.' She swallowed away tears, barely able to continue. 'He won't leave me.' Was she trying to persuade Monty or herself?

Monty looked close to tears himself. He reached out and took her hand in both of his. 'I believe he will never intentionally leave you, Pru. He loves you more than anyone, but as impressive as he is, he is still just a man.'

'Nurse Le Cuirot, is there a reason you're bothering Major Ashbury?'

Damn, Matron had seen her. How typical was that? Pru withdrew her hand from Monty's hold. 'I'm sorry for getting upset, Monty,' she whispered. 'Truly. I know you're only trying to prepare me and I'm grateful. Thank you.'

'I was asking her something, Matron,' Monty said, sounding very much like the aristocrat he was, Pru thought, watching Matron frown in her direction before walking away.

Pru turned away, cross with herself for giving in to her emotions when all Monty had tried to do was answer her questions. She would apologise to him later. She needed to get back to work and noticing one of the younger VADs struggling, went to help her settle a patient in a wheelchair. Once done, she picked up two kidney bowls with discarded dressings from a trolley, surprised when the familiar smell of iron in them made her gag. Returning them to the trolley and needing an excuse to leave the ward, Pru was relieved to notice a small pile of clean bedding that must be surplus to requirements. She grabbed it and made her way to the linen cupboard. She needed to be alone to gather her wits before she lost all semblance of control and wept for Jack in front of the entire ward.

Pru stood in the darkened room, the only light inside filtering through the small window that was partially blocked by drying clothes hanging from a raised airer. Memories of stolen moments with Jack hit her and unable to help herself, she gave in to her tears.

Where was he? Was he even still alive? The fear that he might not be brought on a wave of fresh sobs until, unable to stand any longer, Pru's knees gave way and she slumped to a crouch on the floor. She couldn't face being without him, not when they had grown so close. Not when... She forced away the memory of them lying naked in front of the fire. The thought of never being able to love him, to be loved by him again, was too terrifying to contemplate.

Hearing footsteps drawing closer to the door, Pru got to her feet. She wiped her eyes with the backs of her fingers and pinched her cheeks. She hated the thought of anyone seeing her like this. She stood in front of the sink and turned on the tap, relieved for once that the water was cold, and dabbed her eyes, hoping that they weren't as puffy as they felt.

The door opened and Pru felt the person's presence but acted as if she was too involved with her cleaning to notice.

'There you are,' Jean said. 'I wondered where you'd gone.' Pru struggled to answer. 'Pru?'

Pru was aware that Jean wouldn't leave until she had replied. 'Did you need me for something?' she asked without turning to face her.

'What's wrong with your voice?' Jean didn't say anything for a few seconds. 'Is anything the matter?'

'Yes. Why?'

'I've just spoken to Monty and he's very upset.' She stepped closer. 'Pru? What's the matter? Is it Jack? Monty said there hasn't been any news but have you heard something?' Jean took her by the shoulder and pulled her around to face her. 'What is it? Are you sick?'

Pru shook her head slowly, feeling the heat of tears as they ran down her cheeks. She took her handkerchief from her sleeve and wiped her eyes. 'I'm fine. But I was horrible to Monty before. I didn't mean to be, but when I spoke to him about Jack he said ... well, he said things.'

Jean pulled her into her embrace and Pru welcomed the comforting pressure of her friend's arms around her back. 'Oh, Pru. He won't have meant to hurt you. He's upset that he did.'

Pru sniffed. 'I know. I'll speak to him when I've gathered myself. I'm going to have to wait until Matron isn't around though. She's already told me off for spending time talking to him.'

'There now,' Jean said, patting her on the back. 'Don't upset yourself. Monty's fine. He's a tough old stick on the quiet and knows how you and Jack feel about each other.'

She sniffed. 'I know he does.' She gave a noisy sob. 'Poor Monty. It's unforgivable of me to snap at him. It's not his fault Jack's missing.'

Jean's arms fell away. 'He's missing? Monty didn't say.'

'Missing is wrong,' she said, recalling Monty asking her not to say anything to Jean. Pru chose her words more carefully. 'I think Jack's been captured.'

'You do?'

'Yes.' She could feel herself losing control again. 'If only there was something I could do to help him.'

Jean crossed her arms in front of her chest. 'Now you listen to me. Upsetting yourself like this isn't going to help Jack, is it?'

Pru shook her head and sniffed. 'No.'

'The best thing you can do is carry on looking after Monty and most of all yourself for when he does come back.'

Pru brightened at her friend's words. Jean was right. 'You think he'll be home again then?'

Jean stared at her thoughtfully. 'Honestly, I don't know. I do trust Jack to come back if at all possible though, and he wouldn't want you to give up on him, now would he?'

He wouldn't, Pru mused guiltily. She took a deep breath and exhaled sharply. 'You're right. I have to focus on him coming back.'

'Good girl. You do that. Now, I'm going to go and tell Monty that you're not cross with him and that you'll be fine.' She placed her hands on Pru's shoulders. 'Will you mind if I leave you now?'

'Of course not.'

'Promise?'

Pru nodded. 'I promise.'

'Good.' Jean opened the door and Pru grabbed it to stop her from closing it. 'Jean?'

'Yes?'

'Please tell Monty I'm sorry and that I'll speak to him later.'

Jean smiled. 'I will. You gather yourself and come back to the ward when you're ready.'

Pru watched her friend leave. Jean was right. She needed to focus on Jack's return and banish all other thoughts. She patted her hair and checked her cap was on straight. Smoothing down her skirt and apron, she took a few calming breaths and left the peace of the room to return to the ward.

NINETEEN

Jack

DECEMBER 1917, BELGIUM

J ack pressed his hand over the corporal's mouth. 'Shush,'
he hissed, desperate for the man to keep quiet in their
hiding place behind the bomb-trashed pigsty, which was
all that was left of a farmhouse they had used to screen them
since the previous morning. He raised a bleeding finger and
held it in front of the man's face. How he was supposed to get
this soldier home when both of them were in such a lousy state
and had no plane to fly, he had no idea.

Why hadn't he looked to see how near the German soldiers
were before landing to help the corporal? He was irritated with
his foolishness. He reminded himself that he would have still
tried to rescue him somehow. It had been clear from his own
cockpit that Falkner was alive and unhurt when he saw him
stepping from his plane immediately after his landing. If only
the poor chap had managed to fix his engine and if only he had
had the time to help him, they might both be back home again
instead of hiding from the bastards who had spent three
months interrogating them before they managed to escape

from the chateau somewhere on the Belgian border where they had been kept.

He tried to swallow but the lack of saliva made his tongue and throat feel like someone had taken a sheet of sandpaper to it. How could they be surrounded by so much water and have nothing to drink? The putrid mud all around them had made their escape slow going. The only thing it had proved good for was to camouflage their clothes, though they were now soaked through and he wasn't sure if they would be shot or freeze to death first.

The sound of several more German voices made Jack duck even lower than before. He grimaced as his left calf muscle began to cramp, the spasms becoming more intense by the second. He gritted his teeth and closed his eyes, trying to block out the searing pain.

Slowly the voices retreated and Jack relaxed enough to massage his calf. 'Darn leg.' He felt the soldier next to him move and saw him attempting to sit up. 'You coping, Falkner?'

'Yes, sir. Doing my best to.'

'Good man.' Jack checked the makeshift sling he had created from his shirt to support the soldier's bleeding arm. 'You're lucky the bullet went straight through,' he said, not sure if that was the case and hoping that they could get back behind the British lines before infection set in. His mind drifted to his difficult escape with Monty and he was relieved that Falkner was able to at least stand on his own and hopefully make a run for it.

Jack's side ached where he had been nicked by a bullet and the scar from the burn on his arm was giving him a bit of trouble; he suspected it might be infected. Now he just needed luck to be on their side so they could make a dash for it when no one was looking. He needed to find a way to get back to Blighty.

He had been away from his beautiful Pru for far too long already and ached to hold her in his arms and kiss her beautiful mouth. He realised Falkner was whispering something to him.

'What's that?' he asked, wondering if he had heard the soldiers moving further away.

'I said, Happy Christmas, sir.'

Jack stared at the haggard man, who looked almost forty but whom he knew to be a couple of years younger than himself, and tried to take in what he was saying. Did he mention Christmas? 'What?'

'It's Christmas Day, sir.'

'No. Is it?' His mood dipped even lower. He should be exchanging gifts with his darling Pru, singing Christmas carols with her, holding her in his arms as they made plans and promised to love each other for ever. Not slouched in this freezing mud, praying he wasn't about to die. He could see Falkner was waiting for him to say something. 'Ah, yes, Merry Christmas to you, Falkner.' He closed his eyes and braced himself. 'I've had enough of this dump. What do you say to us making a run for it? If we're lucky we might find our way back to our lot before the day's over.'

Faulkner gritted his teeth. 'I'd like that very much, sir.'

'Good lad. After my count of three, run as fast as your legs can carry you to that copse of trees over there. Don't wait for me.' When the younger solder frowned, Jack grinned. 'I'll probably be way ahead of you,' he teased, having no intention of letting the man fall behind. 'Once you're there, keep going.' Jack knew they were taking a big chance, but it was so cold that if they didn't move soon hypothermia would get them before the damned Hun did. He pointed in the direction of the trees. 'That way.'

'Yes, sir.'

'Good. Now, let me help you to your feet. Stay crouching until I say.'

'Yes, sir.'

Jack had no idea if what they were about to do was the right thing, or suicidal, but they were running out of time and he had no intention of dying there. Now seemed as good a time as any. He helped Falkner to his feet. 'You ready?'

'I am, sir.'

'Good man. Right. One. Two. Three!'

Jack gave Falkner a split second to get going and then took off after him. Within seconds guns began firing at them. If you can hear them, Jack kept thinking as his feet pounded on the wet, slippery ground, they haven't hit you. 'Keep going, Falkner,' he yelled. 'We're almost there.'

TWENTY

Pru

'*Deck the halls with boughs of holly…*'

It was almost Christmas – and it looked as if her first Christmas with Jack wasn't going to be this one after all. There still hadn't been any news from him. Each day she entered Monty's ward she caught his eye and was given a subtle shake of his head. Her throat constricted by sadness, and unable to sing, she mimed instead as the other nurses' singing rang out through the large room.

Pru felt that even the sunshine seemed duller since Jack's departure. She still walked in the woods each day when the weather wasn't too miserable. She had only walked as far as the folly once since he had left, as it had upset her so much to think how happy they had been there together that she dared not go back again. Not until Jack's with me, she decided.

It took all her effort to concentrate on her work and when she was off duty all she wanted to do was be outside walking. For the past week she had woken feeling sick and found that the fresh air helped her keep her nausea at bay. She hoped she wasn't coming down with anything. She needed to keep busy and the thought of being confined to her bed with her fretful mind for a couple of days terrified her. She was probably just run down, she thought, unsurprised. The intake of men had increased dramatically since the terrible third battle of Ypres on the Western Front, which had reached its climax the month before at a village called Passchendaele. Another two rooms at the back of the hall had been taken over by the nursing staff and converted into small wards to make room for them. They were hoping that the work on the fire-damaged wing of the house would be finished fairly soon but the lack of building materials had caused delays, which, according to Monty, Lord Ashbury was finding more and more frustrating. She wasn't surprised. The poor Ashburys had probably never thought that such a huge part of their home would be taken over by wounded soldiers and nursing staff.

To keep connected with Jack, she had begun to make notes in a small diary her mother had sent her the previous Christmas so she didn't forget any anecdotes he might find amusing or interesting. When he did come back to her, she wanted him to know she had never for one second lost faith that he would, even if it wasn't quite true. Since her brief upset with Monty the previous month, she had managed to keep her emotions in check at least when on duty and most of the time when in her room. It didn't help on days like these though, when others were celebrating the festive season and especially now she felt particularly unwell.

Someone dug their elbow into her side. 'You're not singing.'

It was Brenda, one of the nurses who had started a couple of months after her and Jean. She wasn't one of Pru's friends, mostly because the girl was dour and quick to snitch on anyone she felt was receiving more favourable treatment than her.

'I have a sore throat,' Pru whispered.

'If you say so.'

Pru didn't care that the girl thought she was lying. She moved slightly away from her and continued to mouth the rest of the words. She spotted Monty sitting in the first row next to his mother, who was holding one of his hands and resting it on her lap. He was watching Jean intently, the love in his gaze clear for anyone to see. Pru wondered if his parents had got used to the idea of their son and Jean marrying. At least Lady Ashbury wasn't holding it against her son, to judge by the way she was acting with him now. How much of a relief it must be for his parents to know he was safe, albeit injured, and at home with them. His injuries were slowly repairing though they all now knew that he wouldn't be able to walk again unaided. He would have to use a wheelchair or crutches, maybe progressing to a walking stick at some point if he was lucky.

The carol ended and they went straight on to sing 'God Rest Ye Merry Gentlemen'. Pru tried to picture Jack and where he might be. She hoped he wasn't somewhere dreadful. Maybe he had escaped, she thought hopefully. He'd done it before and that time he had somehow brought himself and Monty, injured and in a terrible state, back to safety. She prayed silently that he survived whatever he was facing now and would come home soon.

Pru realised the singing had stopped and the local vicar was giving a short sermon. She tried her best to focus on what he was saying, but it was difficult not to drift off and think of Jack again.

Her gaze fell on the paper chains hanging from one corner of the room diagonally to the opposite corner. The patients had been given the coloured strips of paper and a small pot of glue to make the chains the previous week. Since the weather had become cold and wet, they had needed something to take their minds off not being allowed outside for fresh air. Some hadn't been enthusiastic but Monty and the rest of them gave it their all and now the wards looked cheerful and festive.

The decorations reminded Pru of home. Her parents would have a small fir tree sitting in the bay window of their living room by now. It would be decorated with the pretty ornaments her mother had collected over the decades and no doubt their slightly worn angel would have pride of place on the top of the tree. Several presents would be wrapped, probably in paper that her mother had kept from the year before and the year before that. Picturing home made her long to be back there, sitting in their small living room in front of a roaring fire, listening to her father sharing his news about the people he had spoken to that day while her mother caught up on darning socks, or putting the finishing touches to a cardigan she might be knitting for one of the neighbour's grandchildren.

She realised she hadn't replied to her mother's most recent letter. She would have to do so as soon as her shift ended. Her mother would expect a swift reply despite there being very little to tell her apart from the new decorations and the carol service. Her mother would enjoy reading about that though.

Lord Ashbury was standing and thanking them for all their hard work during the year. 'And that leads me to wish you all a very happy Christmas,' he said, smiling down at Lady Ashbury and then Monty. 'And invite you all to partake in the buffet we have laid out for everyone to enjoy in the entrance hallway. Those of you who are unable to help yourselves will, I have no doubt, be well catered for by our dedicated nursing staff.'

The patients clapped politely and as soon as Lord and Lady Ashbury left the room, noisy chatter and laughter began.

'That's awfully kind of Lord and Lady Ashbury, don't you think?' Gladys asked.

'It is.'

'I was speaking to one of the housemaids earlier,' she said. 'Apparently Cook has been saving rations and making preparations for today and the Christmas lunch tomorrow for weeks and weeks.'

'How will the food have kept that long though?' Pru asked, unsure how anyone could cater for so many people during wartime and especially when there wasn't an abundance of food anywhere.

Gladys shrugged. 'I suppose they have tinned foods. That keeps for ever, doesn't it? Then they'll have been pickling fruit and veg harvested from the gardens in summertime, don't forget.'

'I suppose so.' Pru thought of the two walled gardens. The smaller one near the kitchen and the larger one she and Jack had liked to visit. It must be bare there now that most of the flowers will have died back, she imagined. She wondered what happened to the bees Jack loved so much during the winter. Did they hibernate? She realised she had no idea.

Pru helped serve food to the grateful patients and it

cheered her to be surrounded by so many smiling faces. She was serving the patient next to Monty's bed when Jean came over and she realised the two of them were whispering about something. Pru tried not to listen and kept her attention on helping the man on the bed in front of her.

'No, Monty. It's not that easy,' she heard Jean say, her voice very low. She hoped they weren't falling out and that it was simply a lovers' tiff. 'We'll have to wait until we know what's happened to Jack.'

Jack?

Why were they arguing about Jack? She asked the patient if he was happy with the choice of food she had brought to him, so that Jean wouldn't think she could hear their conversation, and then listened to what Jean was saying as the patient replied.

'I can't, Monty. It wouldn't be fair, not when she's so worried about him. No, it'll have to wait and that's all there is to it.' Jean marched off to the other side of the ward and Pru tried to fathom what her friend had been referring to. What wouldn't be fair? What was she insisting they wait to do? It didn't make much sense. *Serves me right for eavesdropping,* she mused.

The following morning, Pru woke to Jean giving her forearm a gentle shake.

'Happy Christmas, Pru,' she said.

Pru rubbed her bleary eyes and pushed herself up against the metal headboard of her bed. She had taken a long time to fall asleep the previous night, unable to still her mind after what she had heard. 'What time is it?'

'Seven o'clock. I know it's a little early for us to get ready for our shift but I wanted to give you this first.'

Pru yawned. Then, seeing the small, neatly wrapped packet in her friend's hand, she smiled. 'I have something for you, too.' She leaned across to her small bedside table, opened the cupboard door and took out two packets, one for Jean and the other for Gladys. Gladys was still on duty so she would have to hand hers to her later.

'Here's yours,' Pru said. 'I hope you like it.'

'Likewise.' Jean placed her gift in Pru's hands.

They both opened their gifts carefully, untying the ribbon and unfolding the valuable paper that they would each use for the next birthday or special occasion.

Pru waited for Jean to look at the polished wood picture frame she had bought her from the village the previous week. 'I thought you could keep a photograph of Monty in it.'

Jean held the frame to her chest and beamed at Pru. 'Thank you. I love it.' She pointed to Pru's gift. 'I hope you like what I've bought you. I had no idea what to buy, when there's so little to choose from near here.'

Pru folded back the last piece of paper and picked up the delicate grey leather gloves. 'They're beautiful,' she said, stroking them. 'And so much smarter than my knitted ones.'

Jean smiled. 'I hoped you might like them.'

'I love them.' She leaned forward and kissed Jean's cheek. 'Thank you.'

They put their gifts away and Pru caught her friend watching her. 'Is anything the matter, Jean?'

Jean frowned. 'I was hoping you'd tell me.'

Confused, Pru tried to imagine what her friend meant. 'I'm sorry, I'm not sure…'

Jean glanced at the bedroom door, then taking Pru's hands in her own, leaned forward and lowered her voice. 'Are you pregnant?'

Pru snatched her hands back and gasped. 'What?'

Pru watched an apologetic look cross Jean's face. Then, shaking her head, Jean narrowed her eyes. 'No. I won't be sorry,' she said almost to herself. 'I've noticed you're unwell and have been for a few days, even maybe weeks now. You're eating far less than you usually do and I can't ignore how pale you go when dealing with blood.'

'What do you mean?' Pru asked.

Jean narrowed her eyes. 'I saw how you blanched and changed your mind about taking out those bloody dressings in those kidney bowls.'

Jean was right. Now that she thought about it, the smell of blood agitated her and had done for weeks now.

'I remembered my mother saying how sensitive her sense of smell was when she was pregnant with me,' Jean said, giving Pru a pleading look.

Surely she couldn't be carrying a baby? She thought back to when she and Jack had made love in the folly. Everything around her stilled. She couldn't recall when she had had her most recent monthly. Her heart raced. Jean was right. Her mouth dropped open in horror. How had she not realised? What was wrong with her? Her eyes filled with tears and her breath became shallow in her mounting panic. 'What am I going to do?'

Jean wrapped her arms around Pru and held her tightly. 'Firstly, you're not going to work yourself into a state.'

'I've been so focused on Jack and what might be happening to him,' she said. 'And then we've been working overtime caring for the new intake of soldiers,' she said, trying to think why she hadn't even considered the possibility. She began to panic. 'I've no idea where Jack is and when' – she gulped, sobbing – 'or if he's ever coming back.' She grabbed a hankie from her bedside table and blew her nose. 'I can't stay here if I'm to have a baby. They won't let me.' She pictured her parents' horrified reactions if she returned unmarried and pregnant. 'And I daren't go home like this. Jean, what am I going to do?'

Her heart pounded frantically and for a few seconds she thought she might pass out. If only Jack was here.

Jean placed her cool hands either side of Pru's cheeks and wiped away her tears with her thumbs. Resting her hands lightly on Pru's shoulders, she leaned in close. 'We will find a way to deal with this, Pru,' she said calmly. 'I promise you.' The conviction in her voice took away some of Pru's panic. 'You're not alone. Don't ever forget that. Jack might not be here with you but I am. Now, take a few deep breaths.' Pru did as she suggested, unable to think what else she could do.

'I can't bear to think that I'm pregnant. Not like this. I'm not married.' Her breath caught in her throat as a thought occurred to her. 'What if Jack doesn't come back?'

Jean looked away.

Pru sensed that her friend had a plan. *Already?* She bit back an angry retort and then when she felt she had enough control over her emotions, said, 'You may as well tell me what you're thinking.'

Jean didn't look at her, but instead focused on her fingers as she clasped them together on her lap. 'I have thought of a way to solve this for you, but you're not going to like it.'

If it didn't involve Jack then of course she wouldn't like it. Then again, she thought miserably, it wasn't as if she had many choices. 'Tell me,' she whispered.

Jean turned to her slowly and looked her in the eye. Pru could feel the intensity of her friend's gaze on her and knew she wasn't ready to consider the option she was about to hear.

'You could marry Peter.'

Peter? Peter! Was Jean losing her mind? Pru struggled to imagine why she would even consider doing such a thing. She loved Jack and he was the only man she had any intention of marrying; surely Jean knew that. 'Your brother Peter?'

'Yes.' Jean rested a hand on her chest and looked away. 'I know it's not what you want to hear. But whether you like it or not, you're going to have to make some decisions now.' She looked nervously at Pru. 'We both know he's always been in love with you,' Jean said, her voice softening.

'That's as may be,' Pru snapped. 'But I don't love him! You know I don't.'

'I do. So does he. But you like him though, and you know he's a fine, decent man. He'd give you the world if he could.'

So would Jack, Pru thought, determined not to cry. She raised her hand to stop Jean from saying anything further. 'Stop it. Please.' She glared angrily at her friend. 'How could you even think I would consider being with another man, Jean? I thought you knew me better than that.'

Jean took Pru's hand in hers. 'I know that's how you feel, of course I do. But Pru, when was the last time you heard from Jack? You're running out of time and have to make a decision before you start to show. After that your reputation will be ruined and then where will you go?' She sighed, her sadness obvious on her face. 'Please don't think I'm being unfeeling suggesting this to you. I can only imagine how devastated I would be if I was in your position right now and it was Monty who was missing.' Pru felt Jean's hand tighten around hers. 'I know it's not what you would choose for your future. It's not what I would choose for you either. But what other choice do you realistically have?'

Pru felt tears run down her cheeks. 'I don't know,' she cried, feeling sick and terrified and more alone than she ever had before.

'Which is why, as your closest friend, I need to help you make the right decision for you.' She rested a hand on Pru's stomach. 'And for this little baby you're carrying.'

Pru wanted to push Jean's hand away and shout at her for even thinking she might marry another man, but what reason she had left told her that Jean was trying her best to be there for her.

'You can't stay here,' Jean whispered.

'I know that.' Her words came out in a sob. She was a nurse. She should know better. She had let her need to love Jack blind her to the repercussions. How utterly stupid of her.

'Do you think your mother will welcome you home unmarried and carrying a child?' Jean added.

Pru winced. Her mother's guesthouse would lose most if not all of its visitors if an unmarried mother lived and worked there. 'I don't see how she can even if she wanted to.' Pru doubted she would want to and felt certain her father too wouldn't entertain the idea of her returning to their home in this state.

'Exactly. This why you need to be sensible and think with your head, not with your heart. You know you and your baby will be well looked after by Peter and marrying him would ensure your reputation is spared.' Pru hated to agree that Jean did have a point. 'If you married Peter, you'd be able to return home to Jersey, have your baby and hold your head up high.'

Pru's legs gave way and she reached out to grab the nearby table.

Jean grabbed a chair and dragged it over to her, helping her to sit. 'You'll be fine,' she soothed. 'I promise you.' She pushed Pru's head lower. 'Take a few deep breaths and try to calm down.'

Pru felt sick and this time it wasn't because of the baby. How could she be calm when her life was crashing around her? 'I need to find Jack.'

Jean's hand stilled on her back for a few seconds. 'I know.'

Pru couldn't mistake the sadness in Jean's voice and knew her friend was trying to do her best for her. She took a few more deep breaths and slowly sat up again. She needed to try and think straight and stop attacking the one person on her side. 'You've spoken to Peter about this already?' she asked, hating to think anyone else knew or that her friend was making plans behind her back.

Jean came round and knelt in front of Pru, resting her hands on the arms of the chair. 'No. I wouldn't do that without speaking to you and finding out if you were happy for me to do so.'

Pru was glad to hear it and felt slightly more in control of the situation. 'Then how do you know he'd agree to marry a woman who…' She hesitated, trying to form the words. 'A woman who was carrying another man's baby? A woman he knows isn't in love with him?' Or ever would be, Pru thought, picturing Peter's gentle face. 'He deserves so much better than this.'

Pru watched as Jean lowered her face into her hands. She knew Jean wanted to help her at all costs and was willing to offer up her own brother to save her reputation. Pru also knew she needed to at least attempt to consider her friend's proposition. It was, after all, a sensible one. Although she had not given up on Jack yet.

Eventually, Jean raised her head and looked at her. 'This will be harder for you than for Peter, I imagine. We both know how much he cares for you. He's always been open with me about loving you, so I don't doubt for a second that he would agree. You don't have to decide now though,' she said, giving Pru a tight smile. 'But you really can't leave it too much longer.'

Pru rested both hands on her stomach, glad their uniform and petticoats would hide what was soon to be showing underneath. 'I need to think,' Pru said, trying not to let the panic in her chest at the thought of a future without Jack overwhelm her once again. 'I'll … I'll let you know when I've considered everything you've said.'

Jean sighed and Pru saw the sorrow etched on her face. She could tell her friend felt guilty for being so happy with Monty while Pru was facing the hardest decision of her life. 'You're a good friend, Jean, and I appreciate you trying to help me.'

Jean wrapped her arms around Pru, but instead of her friend's hug comforting her it made her feel claustrophobic and she had to battle with herself not to push her away.

'I'll wait for you to decide what you wish to do,' Jean said. 'If you need me to write to Peter, I will. I'm sure he'll be happy to go along with this unless he's met someone he loves more than you, which I doubt because he's never said anything to that effect in any of his letters. If he's in agreement with this plan, then he can apply for a special licence and you can give in your notice, or maybe request compassionate leave for some reason or another and go to meet him in Southampton. You can be married there.'

Jean really had given this a lot of thought, Pru mused, knowing she should be grateful to her friend for trying to help rather than angry with her.

'Will you consider it for me, Pru?'

What choice did she have? 'I will,' she said, close to fresh tears. It was the least she could do. But first, she thought, she was going to write to Jack and hope that somehow her letter found its way to him before she was forced to make a decision that would change both their lives for ever.

TWENTY-ONE

Pru

JANUARY 1918

Pru woke with a start. She had dreamt that Jack had returned to collect her and that they were on their way to be married. As soon as she opened her eyes and saw she was still in her shared bedroom with Jean and Gladys snoring lightly nearby, she knew it was nothing but a dream and her heart plummeted. He wasn't coming back, she thought, aching to see him again.

It was a brand-new year and a week since she had promised to give Jean an answer. She had written several times to Jack but there had been no reply to her letters so far. If she couldn't make contact with Jack, then maybe Monty could try some other way to do so on her behalf.

She still wasn't ready to ask her friend to arrange things with Peter. The thought made her feel sick and it would mean admitting she had given up on Jack. To leave things as they were though meant she was taking a chance she might lose the only option left open to her. Her head ached. She massaged her temples, praying for Jack to come back to her.

She imagined the last time they had lain together in the folly. The warmth of his skin next to hers, his arms around her body and his kisses. Her heart ached to think that she might never experience that joy with him again.

'Pru?' Jean whispered. 'Is everything all right?'

It took a moment before Pru managed to speak. 'Yes.' She hesitated, aware that once she put things in motion she would not be able to stop them. 'I'm just going for a walk to get some fresh air,' she said.

Pru got out of bed, washed and dressed quickly, and made her way down to the ward. She needed to speak to Monty as soon as possible. She had to give it one more try. If Monty couldn't help her then she would have no choice but to seriously consider Jean's suggestion.

She reached the ward and crept up to his bed. 'Monty?' she whispered, hoping the nurse covering the early shift was too busy dealing with a patient who had upset his water carafe over his sheets to notice she was in the ward.

Monty opened his eyes briefly then rubbed them and tried to sit up. 'Pru? Is something wrong?'

She put a finger up to her lips to keep him from being too noisy. 'I need you to help me.'

'Whatever you want, just let me know.'

She gave him a grateful smile. 'Thank you. I've written to Jack countless times but haven't received any reply from him at all. I know you ask after him when you can, when you speak to the other men in your squadron, but I need you to try again. Maybe there's some other way to contact him. Today, if you can?'

Monty frowned. 'Pru, I don't know how I can do that.'

'You must try, Monty. I know I'm probably asking the impossible, but I have to know as soon as humanly possible if he's ... if he's alive.' Her voice broke with emotion. She cleared her throat. 'Can you do that for me? Please?'

Monty nodded. 'I'll do my best for you.' He studied her. 'Is there a particular reason you need to speak to him? Is there a particular message you need me to send?'

She gave his question some thought but didn't feel able to tell him the real reason behind her urgency. 'No. I simply need him to know that I must speak with him soon. Today or tomorrow if I can.'

'I'll do what I can.' Monty took her hand in his and gave it a gentle squeeze.

'Thank you, Monty. I know I'm asking a lot of you.'

'I'm happy to try.'

———

Pru somehow managed to keep going by putting all her energy into her work.

Three days after she had asked for Monty's help, he waved her over when she was about to end her shift. He had had a couple of officers visiting him that day but that wasn't unusual.

'You have news?' she asked, plumping his pillows to seem busy. She was about to place the second pillow behind his head when she noticed the strain on his face. 'Monty?'

'Pull the screen around, will you, Pru?'

He asked without looking her in the eye and her heart

plummeted. This was bad news, she sensed it with every instinct.

'Sit down, please.'

She did as he asked and waited. Monty wrung his hands together for a few seconds. He seemed to be struggling to find the right words.

Eventually he looked at her and she saw unshed tears in his eyes. 'Monty?' she whispered, her throat tight with tension. 'Is Jack…? Is he…?' She couldn't say the words. Couldn't even think the words.

Monty pinched the top of his nose and took one of her hands in his. 'Dear Pru, I…'

'Just tell me any way you can. The message will have the same impact, whatever it is.'

She needed to know but willed him not to say what she sensed he was about to.

'Dear girl,' he said, gulping back a sob before clearing his throat impatiently. 'Jack is … is dead.'

Pru heard the words as they echoed around her brain. 'Dead?' she murmured, her voice tight.

Monty nodded. 'Do you wish to know the details?'

'Yes,' she said, not knowing if she could bear to hear what he had to say.

'It seems that Jack and the other chap he tried to rescue escaped from where they had been held. Unfortunately, it appears it was only Falkner who managed to get back to safety. He's in a hospital in France and badly injured.' He took a deep breath. 'I'm so very sorry, Pru. I would have given anything not to have to give you this news.'

'I know you would, Monty.' She felt strangely calm, even though all the colour had drained from her world and any joy she felt with it. 'We both love him. We'll both always miss him.'

'We will.' His voice quavered. 'Will you be all right, Pru?'

'I will have to be,' she said, resigned to a future without the only man she had ever loved. 'We'll both have to be, won't we?'

He nodded slowly and closed his eyes. She noticed he was struggling to contain his emotions and, not wishing to embarrass him, she leaned forward and kissed his cheek before leaving him to his grief.

As she left the ward, she heard laughter and wondered how the world could carry on when she had lost Jack. Her vision swam and she reached out for something to hold on to. Clutching a door handle and turning it, she pushed open the door and found herself in the sluice room. This was where she had been alone with Jack for the first time. How could someone as larger than life as Jack be dead? Unable to keep her legs from giving way a second longer, Pru slumped to the floor. She grabbed a handful of her skirt and pressed it to her mouth to muffle her screams as she gave in to the terror of having to live in a world where Jack no longer existed.

Pru had no idea how she managed to return to her bedroom, or how long she had sat on the side of her bed. She seemed to recall Jean popping her head around the door some time before and then leaving without saying a word. She still couldn't believe that Jack was dead. Yet, in her heart, she knew that if he was alive, he would have found a way to contact her. She felt a strange fluttering in her stomach like tiny bubbles. Was that the baby moving? Their baby?

Pru wondered if people died from a broken heart. Right now she wished she could close her eyes and drift away to nothingness. She had thought that losing Milly was heartbreaking but somehow losing Jack was another level of grief entirely.

There was a light rap on the door before it opened and Jean walked in. 'Monty told me about Jack,' she said. 'I'm so sorry, Pru.'

Pru swallowed away tears. 'Thank you.'

'Is there anything I can do for you?'

Pru took a breath, determined to force out the words before her courage failed her. Whether she liked it or not, Monty's information had shown her that her time had finally run out. She had no choice now but to marry Peter. 'Jean?'

'Yes?'

'Please write to Peter for me.'

Jean didn't reply immediately and Pru could almost feel her friend's shock. 'I'll do it today,' Jean said eventually.

'Thank you,' Pru whispered, her voice tight with emotion. What had she done? She closed her eyes, desperate to calm herself before hysteria took over. She needed to be calm. To be strong. This wasn't about her anymore. This was about her doing her best for Jack's baby.

TWENTY-TWO

Pru

JANUARY 1918

Pru stood in front of the small, family-run hotel where Peter had booked rooms for them for her first night in Southampton. He had sent her a note to let her know where to meet him and that he would be waiting for her inside. All she needed to do was put one step in front of the other and go to him.

Pru took out the letter he had sent to her as she built up the courage to enter the building. The paper wavered in her trembling hands as she re-read it, knowing she should be relieved – grateful, even – and not heavy-hearted. This sweet man was doing a selfless and generous thing by marrying her and she must always remember that.

Dearest Pru, my friend,

I will keep this letter short but wanted you to know that I have always loved you and although this situation might not be as I had imagined things between us, I have no hesitation in accepting my sister's suggestion. I will do my best to make you as happy as I possibly can.

I suppose I should ask you formally. So, dearest Pru, will you marry me?

If you wish to accept my offer of marriage, which I hope you will do, please send word to me letting me know when you are to leave Ashbury Manor to travel to meet me in Southampton. I will then apply for a special licence for us to be married and reserve places for us to travel back to Jersey on the mailboat a day or so after that.

I am to be discharged from the hospital in a couple of days and will have to return to Jersey as I have been pensioned out of the army due to my injury.

Please don't worry that the damage to my shoulder will incapacitate me in any way, I might not be able to hold a heavy rifle any longer but I will still be able to work for my father at his printing works and support you and our family.

I am afraid that I do have one stipulation though, Pru. I've given this a lot of thought and hope you understand why I wish to put this in place between us. I would like you to promise never to reveal the name, or any other information about the father of the baby you are carrying. I would like the true parentage of our baby to be kept between ourselves, and Jean, of course. Will you be able to do that, do you think?

I look forward to us meeting again and renewing our friendship, and hope that one day you will love me at least half as deeply as I have always loved you.

Sincerely yours,

Peter

She stared at the immaculate white-fronted building, unable to force her feet to move. By stepping inside she was committing herself to Peter. Her heart pounded and she breathed deeply to calm her rising panic. This was her future now, she reminded herself.

She pictured the beautiful manor house and all the joy it had brought to her. Meeting and falling in love with Jack, sharing a room with Jean and dear Milly, laughing with them when they should be going to sleep. How had so much changed in such a short time? How was Milly no longer alive, or darling Jack? How was it possible she was here, standing on a pavement in Southampton trying to muster the courage to walk to a new life? A now familiar flutter in her stomach reminded her why she must have the courage to see this through.

Bracing herself to meet her future husband, Pru straightened her shoulders, forced a smile onto her face and walked shakily up the stone steps to the front door and into the reception area.

'May I help you, Miss?' a young, fresh-faced man asked.

'Yes, please. My name is Miss Le Cuirot. I believe my fiancé has reserved a room for me. Sergeant Le Riche. He's already staying here.'

The man's eyebrows shot up when he heard Peter's name. 'Yes. Good man, the sergeant. You're in Room Three. I'll show you the way.' He lifted a key from a hook above a row of cubbyholes on the wall behind him and stepped around the counter. He looked down at her case and reached to take it from her. 'I'll carry this for you, Miss.'

Pru thanked him and followed him upstairs, unsure when or where she should meet Peter. 'Do you know which room my fiancé is occupying?'

'I do, Miss, but we have a policy whereby unmarried couples aren't allowed in the same bedroom together.' He looked over his shoulder as he stopped at a painted door with the number three on it. 'I'm sorry,' he said, slipping the key into the keyhole and turning it. He pushed the door open and waited for her to walk inside. 'My mother's a bit of a stickler about these things.'

Pru was hoping to be able to speak to Peter privately about their plans, but it seemed that they would have to take a walk to do so. 'Not at all. I completely understand.'

She gazed at the sparse but clean furnishings in the small front bedroom. 'It's lovely and light in here,' she said, hoping the bed was softer than it appeared.

He placed her case onto the floor and smiled. 'I hope you're happy here at Whitehaven. I gather you'll be moving to a different room for a few days from tomorrow.'

'Yes,' Pru said, wishing she had longer before her wedding day. She took a penny's tip from her coin purse and handed it to him.

'Thanks, Miss. You must be very excited.'

'I am,' she lied.

'If there's anything else, Miss?'

She was about to say no but then had a thought. 'If you might let my fiancé know I've arrived, that would be very kind. Please tell him I'll meet him in the downstairs lounge area in ten minutes.'

'Of course, Miss.'

'Thank you.'

She watched him leave and stood in the middle of the room, trying to come to terms with finally being in Southampton. Well, this is it, she mused. This time tomorrow she would be a married woman. 'Mrs Le Riche,' she whispered, trying to get used to the thought that she and Jean would soon be sharing the same surname. Her heart ached painfully at the reminder that she would now never be Mrs Jack Garland.

Feeling a little wobbly about what was in store for her, Pru decided to sit and write a quick note to post to her parents. She needed to take her mind off what she was losing by marrying Peter and focus on her and Jack's baby to keep from backing out of her agreement with Peter.

She took off her coat and hung it on the hook on the back of the door. Sitting at the small dressing table, she opened the drawer and was pleased to find a couple of sheets of paper and an envelope. So far, her parents were unaware of any changes in her life and she needed to give them warning that something had happened before she turned up on Peter's arm on their doorstep.

Dearest Mum and Dad,

This is a quick note to let you know that I will be returning home to Jersey in the next few days. Things have changed for me and I have a surprise for you. One that I hope you will be very pleased to welcome.

Please don't worry about me. I am extremely happy and looking forward very much to seeing both you and beautiful Jersey again, and sharing my wonderful news with you.

My love, as ever,

Pru x

She stared at the words and wished with all her heart that she was about to introduce them to Jack. *Stop it.* She folded the sheet of paper, slipped it into an envelope and wrote her home address on the front, deciding to stop at reception and ask to buy a stamp on her way to meet Peter.

After washing her face and hands, she brushed her hair and, feeling slightly fresher and a little calmer, left her room.

Pru walked down the stairs with butterflies doing a manic dance in her stomach. It was only Peter, she reminded herself. The same man she'd known most of her life. She took a deep breath at the bottom of the stairs, then, holding her letter, walked over to the reception desk.

Having bought the stamp and stuck it onto her envelope, she crossed the hall and opened the door to the living room, where she was relieved to find Peter waiting for her alone. She stared at him, watching him turn. He wasn't as tall or as well-built as Jack, but when he smiled his sweet face lit up, clearly delighted to see her. In that instant, Pru's nerves vanished. She needed to be brave. To put her feelings aside and at least try to behave as she imagined a soon-to-be married woman might behave. She might not be in love with this man but she would be forever grateful to him for his unselfish act.

'Peter.'

He walked over to her and took her left hand in his right. She noticed he didn't move his other arm and presumed it was due to the damage he had received to that shoulder. 'Pru. It's good to see you again.' He looked her up and down. 'My, you're looking extremely well.'

'Thank you.' She smiled, aware that he was being kind. She had lost weight since discovering her shocking situation and the dark circles under her eyes belied her sleepless nights and many days crying. 'I could say the same about you.' She looked at his shoulder. 'How is your shoulder healing?'

'More slowly than I'd prefer but it's much better than it was.'

He saw the envelope in her hand. 'Shall we go for a walk so you can post that? Unless you'd rather stay here and have a chat about things?'

She shook her head, preferring not to have to face him when they discussed their wedding plans in case she gave away her true feelings. 'Let's go for a stroll, it's such a lovely day.'

He held out his elbow and Pru slipped her hand through his arm before they made their way outside. 'It is a little nippy,' she said when they were standing on the pavement, glad her coat was warm enough for the cool weather. 'If we can find a post box then I'll pop this letter into it. I want Mum and Dad to have a little warning about us being married.'

She felt Peter's step hesitate slightly, so stopped. 'If you've changed your mind I will understand,' she said, praying he would do no such thing.

Peter faced her. 'Pru, you know I've been in love with you for years. The only reason our wedding will not go ahead is if you decide you'd rather not marry me.'

Pru had to clear her throat to be able to speak. If only she had that option, she thought miserably. 'I'm ever so grateful to you for doing this for me, Peter. I hope you know that.'

He didn't seem to know what to say. Then, pointing across the road, he said, 'Look, there's a post box. Let's send your letter off and then we can have a proper chat.'

They ran across the road as soon as there was space in between the carriages, omnibuses and military vehicles.

'Gosh, it's very busy here today, isn't it?' she said

'There's a ship at the quayside and I have a feeling a lot of these vehicles are probably bringing soldiers for embarkation. Poor devils.'

How many of them would return in one piece? Pru thought sadly. 'I do wonder when this terrible war might end,' she told him. 'It's not only the soldiers I worry about, but also their families and all the widows and orphaned children who will have to find a way to make ends meet after the fighting ends.' She thought of Jack and her mood dipped.

Realising Peter was replying to what she'd said, Pru guiltily pushed her thoughts of Jack from her mind. She had made her decision and needed to find a way to make the best of things for the baby's sake, and for Peter's, she reminded herself.

'There,' she said, pushing the envelope into the red post box. 'That's done. Right. Let's go and have that talk.'

Peter led her to a grassy parkland and stopped at a bench near a copse of trees. 'Shall we sit here for a bit?'

Pru did as he asked and waited for him to speak. She hoped the conversation wouldn't get tricky for either of them.

He twisted around to half face her and took her left hand in his. 'Pru, firstly I need to know you've thought everything through.' She went to reassure him but he gave a shake of his head and continued speaking. 'I need to say what's been on my mind. I want to know that if we do this it's for good and that you're aware of what I'll expect from you.'

'That sounds ominous,' she said, trying to make light of the concerns his words conjured in her mind.

'I don't mean it to, but I do need to know you're certain about us.'

'Us?' His hand twitched and she realised what he was referring to. She and Peter were the couple now. The thought was like a knife into her heart.

'Yes, Pru,' he said, lowering his voice when a couple walked nearby. He waited for them to move out of earshot before continuing. 'I love you, Pru. You know that. I also know that you don't love me.' She went to argue, but he shook his head again. 'No. Please don't deny it.' He stared at her intently. 'I need to know you'll always be completely honest with me.' He waited for her to respond.

'I promise you I will, Peter. Always.'

'Thank you.' He gave her a tight smile. 'I know I said I want this baby.' He tilted his head to one side. 'Our baby. To grow up believing I'm his, or her, father.'

'Yes.'

'I hope that someday we'll be blessed with other children, but I promise I will treat this child the same as any others we might have.'

'Thank you.' She wasn't surprised to hear him say such a thing; he had always been kind.

'I, er...'

'Please carry on. I want you to tell me all your concerns and hopes for us, Peter. We need to understand each other fully before we commit to a marriage.'

'We do.' He gave her hand a gentle squeeze. 'I don't know anything about the man you're in love with, although I sense Jean knows.'

'She does.'

'I don't wish to hear his name, Pru. Nor anything about him. Ever.' A pained look crossed his face. 'Does that sound odd?'

'No.' She wasn't sure she could live with not knowing such a thing about her spouse, but everyone was different, Pru knew that much. 'If that's what you wish, then I will never mention him.'

'Thank you.' He took a deep breath. 'As I said, I know you don't love me and of course I won't expect…' He hesitated before continuing. 'Um, marital relations between us, to begin with.' Pru hid her relief at hearing this. 'But I do hope that at some point in the future you will learn to love me and maybe then we might be able to, er, live like a proper married couple.'

Pru reached out and rested a hand on his cheek. 'Thank you, Peter. You truly are a generous man.' She sensed that by being married to this handsome, kind man she was far luckier than she probably had a right to be. He was giving up any chance of meeting the love of his life, someone whom he could slowly get to know, fall in love with and marry. If she was truly going to give this marriage her all then she needed to commit to him fully. It was the least he deserved. 'But no.'

'No?' His gaze fell from hers and she could almost feel his disappointment. Pru realised he had misunderstood her reply.

'I'm saying *no* to your proposition that we wait.' What difference did it make, she thought, hating to imagine being intimate with someone other than Jack. The sooner she got the act over with and forced herself to commit to this man the sooner she hoped to get used to how her new life was going to be.

He closed his eyes, clearly trying to take in what she had just said. 'That's sweet of you, Pru, but I don't want you to do anything that doesn't come naturally to you. I want you to want me. Do you understand? Not to be grateful to me. That won't make me happy at all.' He sighed. 'I'm hoping that at some point you will learn to love me.'

She understood his reasoning. 'I already love you, Peter,' she argued. *But as a friend*.

'But you're not in love with me.' He gave her a gentle, sad smile. 'I know I'm asking a lot and I'll completely understand if that never happens. And,' he said, when she went to speak, 'I'd rather that we never discussed this again.'

'Then that's what we'll do.'

He leaned forward and kissed her on the forehead. 'Even with the reasons behind why we're here now,' he said, 'I still feel I'm a very lucky man.'

Pru took him by the shoulders and pulled him to her, pressing her lips against his mouth in a rushed kiss. 'I'm the lucky one, Peter.' He went to argue but she shook her head. 'Don't you dare say anything to the contrary.'

His face lit up. 'Now that we understand each other, I believe it's time for the next step in our relationship.'

What was that, Pru wondered, watching Peter stand then drop to one knee. Someone gasped and Pru noticed two nurses out of the corner of her eye, but she didn't dare speak and ruin the moment for Peter. He pulled off his gloves before taking a small, dark-green leather box from his right-hand pocket.

Pru saw Peter's damaged left hand for the first time.

He noticed her doing so. 'Does it bother you?'

'Don't be silly.' She had seen far worse while nursing.

'Prudence Le Cuirot,' he said, his voice slightly shaky. 'Will you do me the honour of marrying me?'

She forced away an image of Jack. 'Yes, Peter. I will.'

The nurses cheered and Pru glanced over at them to see they had been joined by two soldiers, one with a cast on his arm. They shouted their congratulations as Peter, now smiling, raised the lid of the leather box and lifted the ring from it. He held his hand out to take hers and when Pru gave him her left hand, he smiled.

'Would you mind removing your glove? My hands are a bit full here.'

Pru bit her lower lip, embarrassed. 'Sorry, I didn't think.' She removed her glove and slipped it into her pocket. Willing her hands to stop trembling, she held out her left hand for him once more.

He took it and slipped the ring onto her wedding finger.

'I'm relieved it fits,' he said, although it was slightly too large.

Pru wanted to give the ring back, to tell Peter she had made a terrible mistake and couldn't marry him after all. But instead she studied the small sapphire with two diamond chips either side and, knowing he was waiting to see if she liked the ring, forced a smile. This sweet man didn't need to know her anguish. He was to be her husband. However much she wanted to reassure him, she couldn't help thinking how strange it was to be wearing a ring on the finger she had always presumed would proudly display Jack's token of love to her.

'I hope you like it,' he said, rising to his feet, not taking his eyes from her.

'It's very pretty, Peter. I love it.' She smiled up at him, hoping he believed her.

'You do?'

She looked at his dear slim face, so desperate to please her, and her heart ached for them both. She nodded. 'I really do.'

'The gems aren't as large as I would have liked them to be,' he said, taking her hand and pointing to the small jewels.

She leaned forward and kissed him lightly on the lips, imagining that was the right thing to do in these circumstances. She knew that if Jack was in front of her now she wouldn't have to think what to do; she would act on instinct. 'It's a beautiful ring and I'll treasure it.'

'I'm glad you like it.'

Pru realised she was getting a little cold and withdrew her hand from his. 'Shall we start walking again?' she suggested, taking her glove from her pocket and slipping her hand into it to try and warm it slightly.

'Good idea.' He held out his arm for Pru to slip her hand through it and they resumed their walk. 'I forgot to mention that I have our special licence. I've booked the Registry Office for ten-fifteen in the morning. Does that suit you?'

'Yes,' she said, wanting everything finalised sooner rather than later so that they could return home. She hoped that once they were back in Jersey it might be easier to avoid being tormented by thoughts of Jack all the time by helping out around the guesthouse.

'I wish you could have had a proper church wedding,' he said quietly after a few minutes.

'Why?'

He laughed. 'I don't know. Isn't that what all women want for themselves?'

Pru shook her head. 'Not all.' She thought of the wedding she might have had with Jack if things had been different. Jean and dear Milly could have been her bridesmaids.

Stop it, she thought, angry with herself for allowing those images into her head.

'You're very thoughtful,' he said, looking concerned. 'Would you like to return to the hotel now? I know it's a little bitter out here now the sun has disappeared behind the clouds.'

Pru gave his arm a gentle squeeze against her side. 'Stop fretting about me, Peter,' she said, reverting to the friendly Pru of their youth. 'I'm fine.'

It wasn't a lie. Not really. She was deeply fond of him and comfortable in his company. If she had to be with anyone now she no longer had darling Jack at her side, she might as well be with someone she liked as a person.

The sky darkened as they walked and Pru was certain a drop of rain had fallen onto her cheek. She wondered if the rain might mask the tears she was trying hard to contain.

'It's raining,' Peter said. 'I think we should make for that café in the pavilion over there.'

Pru spotted the wooden construction to their right and nodded. They broke into a run as the rain grew heavier and

Peter, holding her right hand tightly in his, pulled her along. They reached the front door, grateful for the overhang of the roof for shelter. He opened the door and waited for her to enter.

'A table for two, please,' he said to the tired-looking waitress.

'That one do, sir?' she asked, indicating a small table towards the back of the room.

'Perfect.'

They followed her over and took off their coats before making themselves comfortable. 'A table in the kitchen would have done for me,' Pru said with a smile, trying her best to seem cheerful for Peter's sake. 'As long as there's a roof over it.'

They ordered bowls of vegetable soup and bread with a pot of tea and as they waited for their early lunch to be served to them, Pru took off her gloves and looked at her ring. 'This is one way to celebrate our short engagement.'

Peter laughed. 'It could have been a little more glamorous. I'd have preferred a bit of a get-together rather than getting soaked to the skin in a downpour.'

Pru was relieved she didn't have to pretend to be happy at an engagement party. She shook her head. 'We're not quite that wet, thankfully.'

As they ate, it dawned on her that she had no idea where he was expecting them to live when they returned to Jersey, so she asked him.

'I thought we could move into my parents' home. Though if you prefer, and of course if your parents offer, maybe you might feel happier living back at the guesthouse.'

'I think the guesthouse might be the better idea,' Pru said, relieved to hear his suggestion. 'Mum and Dad will have vacant rooms now it's wintertime and I know Mum will want to help me when the baby comes along.'

'She knows about the baby?' he whispered, his hand stopping halfway to his mouth, causing him to spill his soup from his spoon back into the bowl.

'Heavens, no.' She placed her spoon in her bowl and picked up a piece of bread. 'I haven't even decided when best to tell her.'

'Would she be too shocked if you let her know we married so soon because of the baby?'

Pru supposed it would only be a half-truth. She liked the idea. Lying wasn't something she was comfortable with and it would be a relief not to have to pretend she fell deeply in love with Peter and felt compelled to marry him in haste. Her mother would be surprised enough to discover they were together as a couple as it was, after years hoping they would get together and Pru insisting she didn't see Peter that way. She knew how much her mother had looked forward to the role of mother of the bride at her wedding and hated to think she had cheated her out of her dream.

'She's going to be disappointed that I didn't wait until I was married,' she said, keeping her voice low. 'But I'm hoping she'll be too excited about us and that we're having a baby to be too concerned about what we've done and her missing out on preparing a wedding.'

'Good.' He thought for a moment. 'Why don't we go to your parents' home as soon as we disembark from the ferry? We can speak to them straightaway and then, when we see my parents, we can hopefully tell them that everything has been settled and it'll be a fait accompli.'

'Good idea.'

Pru pictured the pretty garden at the back of her parents' home where she tried to imagine herself reading by one of the colourful flower borders and rocking the baby to sleep as the birds sang in the trees overhead. Yes, she thought, she would be happiest there.

TWENTY-THREE

Jack

JULY 1918

J ack thought back to his brief chat with Monty the previous day. It had been a shock to discover that Pru no longer worked at the manor.

'What do you mean she's no longer here?' he'd asked, stunned. His damaged cheek itched under the bandage in the warm ward. He had been happy to discover Monty had arranged for him to be brought to the manor to convalesce after his latest operation in Amiens. He had been unconscious for weeks and apparently not expected to survive as he had been so weak from starvation and everything he had suffered at the chateau with Falkner. He thought of the following three months when he had been so drugged up to keep the pain from his damaged face and leg at bay that he'd barely known his own name; and then the weeks of recovery in hospital he'd endured after that before he had felt capable of putting his emotions into words and writing to her.

It seemed like years since he had last been here but he had imagined Pru's surprise and delight to see him on her ward.

DEBORAH CARR

The first time he had seen his face in the mirror he'd been horrified, wondering if Pru could ever love him with half his face looking more like one of his mother's patchwork quilts than a cheek. Then he had remembered her reaction to Hugo and trusted that she would love him regardless of any injuries he might have.

'But I wrote to her here. Several times,' he said. 'Why weren't my letters sent on to wherever she is now?'

Standing next to Monty's chair in the manor gardens, Jack now realised he had been selfish and rather cowardly not travelling back to Ashbury Manor to see her. 'Where is she?'

'She's, um, she's gone back to Jersey,' Monty mumbled.

'What? When?'

Why was Monty looking so evasive? It wasn't like his friend to keep things from him but he sensed he was doing so now. 'Monty?'

'Listen, Jack,' Monty said. 'We need to have a chat about something.'

'Whatever it is, tell me.' A terrible thought occurred to him. 'She's not hurt, is she?'

'She's married, Jack.' Monty said without looking him in the eyes. 'She married Jean's brother Peter back in January.'

Jack could see Monty's mouth moving but couldn't keep up with what he was saying. The disbelief faded and Monty's words hit him like a punch in the gut. 'Married? To Jean's brother?' It made no sense. None at all. 'I don't understand. Why would she do that?'

Monty didn't reply. Jack could see he was struggling but wished he would spit out what he was holding back from him.

'Surely there can't be anything else.'

Monty clenched his teeth before taking a deep breath. 'She's had a baby, Jack.'

Jack stared at him. Was it the medication making him imagine these words? 'What? But she loved me. I know she did.' Did he? Yes, he reminded himself. She did love him; he was certain of it.

Monty looked him in the eye for the first time. 'She was pregnant when you left, Jack. The baby she had last month is yours.'

Jack stared at his friend. He had thought that being shot down, captured and tortured with Falkner in that hell-hole was the worst thing to ever happen to him. Then, when he hadn't been able to save Falkner from those bastards, he thought that might be the lowest he could feel. But this was worse than anything he could have ever imagined.

'She's married and this other guy is bringing up my baby?'

Monty's face reddened and Jack could see his friend's temper rising. 'Bloody hell, Jack, what would you have had her do? She had little choice but to marry the man. Thank heavens he has feelings for her and was willing to go along with Jean's suggestion.'

'This is Jean's fault? How could she have done this?

'Damn it, Jack. This is your bloody fault. You're the one who left her in that state. What the hell were you both thinking?'

Jack opened his mouth to speak but found there were no words.

They sat in angry silence for a while. Monty was right, Jack realised. It was his fault that this had happened. He had been the one to make love to her; he had chosen to circle to try and see if Falkner had survived his crash landing, only to be spotted and shot down. Why did he always feel like he had to play the hero? And now this had happened.

'I have to see her.'

'No, Jack.' Monty glared at him. 'Be sensible.'

'Sensible?' Had Monty lost all feeling?

'Yes. You have no idea how difficult it was for Pru. You didn't see how desperate that poor girl was when you didn't come back and we thought you had died. All the reports said Falkner was the only one of the two of you to survive so I had to tell her you were gone. She believes you're dead, Jack. The kindest thing to do is to leave her be.' He groaned. 'Look, we both know Pru's a loyal girl. If she sees your injuries, as a nurse and someone who loves you, we both know she would wish to come back and help you recover.'

That didn't seem such a terrible thing, Jack thought, aware he was being selfish.

Monty glared at him. 'I know what you're thinking but if you really love her, you will put her needs and those of your baby before your own happiness. Do you want her to see you and be caught between you and the man who helped her when she had nowhere to turn?'

He hated Monty at that moment.

'But my baby won't know I'm its father.'

Monty sighed heavily and Jack sensed there was something more he had to tell him. 'What is it?'

'I'm sorry, Jack, but Pru's promised Peter not to ever tell the child that he isn't her biological father. He doesn't want to know anything about you and as far as everyone apart from you, me, Jean, Peter and Pru are concerned, he *is* that child's father.' He rubbed his bad leg and winced. 'Jack, you have to let her be and get on with her life.'

He stared at Monty, knowing he was right and that it was the kindest thing to do to let Pru go. The thought of never seeing her again almost got the better of him, but he was determined to hold it together, for now at least. He had no right to mess up her life a second time. To do so would be far too selfish and cruel. Although he had no idea how he would find a way to live without her, he loved her too much to hurt her again.

'Fine, I won't make contact with her,' he said, hearing his voice tremble. 'But I am going to go to Jersey and see her for myself.'

'Jack, don't. Please.'

'I have to, Monty. I promise she'll never know I've been there.'

He sat back on the leather seat as the taxi drove him down grass-banked lanes. He had spotted the sea at the end of one of them and breathed in the salty air. Jack studied the piece of paper in his hand. Pru had mentioned her parents' guesthouse a few times to him and he remembered the name. Now he had the address and he couldn't believe he might be able to see her in only a few minutes. His shock at discovering her marriage and that he would never know his child still hurt. He doubted he would ever recover.

His pulse raced as the taxi took him past fields dotted with Jersey cows. She hadn't been kidding when she told him how pretty this little island was. He reached out to open the window a little wider and winced when the pain in his damaged ribs made him catch his breath. At least she wouldn't know how badly he had been hurt or see his face all torn up and put back together like an uneven puzzle. It was only a small mercy but it was something.

'This is where you're wanting to go, sir,' the driver said, slowing the vehicle to a stop and pointing to granite pillars either side of an entrance drive. 'Are you sure you don't want me to drive you up to the house?'

Jack shook his head. 'No, thank you. If you wouldn't mind waiting for me a little way down the road though, I'd be grateful. I'm unsure whether my friend is at home, and I might need to find somewhere else to stay.' It was a lie, but the driver didn't need to know more about his plans.

'Fair enough.'

Jack paid the fare so far then walked slowly down the long driveway, breathing in the warm, salty air and smiling at the colourful flowers dotted round the feet of the tall pine trees on either side. A horse neighed somewhere in a distant field.

He reached the house but there was no movement anywhere and it didn't seem as if anyone was home. Deciding they might be outside in the garden, he took the path around the side of the house, hoping to see if he could find anyone.

He reached a neat garden area surrounded by a wall, a colourful array of roses and lavender interspersed with towering hollyhocks filling the borders and the air with their delicate perfume. He breathed in the scents, enjoying smelling the same thing that Pru did each time she walked in her garden or opened a window. Being so close to her made all his struggles to get home again worthwhile.

He was about to turn and leave when the sound of a door opening alerted him. Barely daring to breathe, he stopped, glad to be standing behind a large pink rose bush when he heard a man's voice.

'Pru, sweetheart, where are you?'

'Out here, Peter, in the garden.'

The sound of her voice so close caused him to hold his breath. He peered through the bush and saw her standing in the shade of a gnarled apple tree. He wished he could savour the moment for longer. Go to her. Take her in his arms. Slipping his right hand into his jacket pocket, Jack's fingertips brushed against the small box holding the engagement ring he'd bought for her after leaving Ashbury for that last mission.

'There you are, dear,' Peter asked, his voice nearing. 'I've brought Emma out to you. She's been crying and I wasn't sure if she needed feeding again.'

She'd named the baby Emma? Monty had omitted to tell him the baby's name, probably on purpose so Jack wouldn't feel so connected to the little girl. Was it after his mother's favourite book? He liked to think so. It was a tentative connection but made him think that there was a possibility she still loved him.

Unable to help himself, Jack stepped sideways to get a better look at the woman he loved with all his heart. His breath caught as she turned to speak to the man and took the baby from his arms. Jack didn't think he had ever seen anything more beautiful, or more heartbreaking. He should be standing there with his arm around her shoulders, not this Peter fellow.

[""]

Jack's heart splintered into fragments as he stared at her. His darling, precious Pru. She was a mother now. He was desperate to leave but unable to make his feet move and so was forced to watch as Pru's husband began leading her towards the house. He wanted to shout for her to stop, tell her he was there and loved her still – would always love her – but he had promised Monty not to cause her pain. He had already been the cause of far too much of that.

Pru walked a couple of steps, then stopped and glanced in Jack's direction. Horrified to think she might catch him watching them and intruding on their private moments, he ducked behind the large bush.

'What is it, my love?' the man asked.

Pru gave a gentle shudder. 'It's nothing. I thought I felt something. Like someone was watching me.'

Jack's heart broke. She can feel me here, he thought.

Peter kissed her cheek. 'You're imagining things. There's no one here but us. All the guests are out for the day and your parents are visiting their friends in town, remember?'

'It was the strangest feeling,' she said, her voice filled with an unmistakable sadness.

Jack struggled to keep his composure. He waited a few seconds to be certain they couldn't hear him, before hurrying back down the side of the house and out onto the lane. He spotted the taxi parked nearby and went to it. His life was never going to be the same again. And it was his own fault. For the first time he wished he had died alongside Falkner. At least then he wouldn't have to keep living knowing the only woman he had ever loved would never be his again.

Part Two

TWENTY-FOUR

Pru

JUNE 1940

'Mum, I hate leaving on bad terms.' Emma wiped a stray tear from her cheek. 'I wish I'd never found that box at the back of your wardrobe now.'

So did Pru. Now her daughter knew that the man who had loved and cared for her since she was born wasn't her father. Why had she stupidly kept that letter from 1918 for all these years? Wasn't she supposed to have kept the truth about Emma's true parentage a secret? Pru suspected she might have hoped that one day she would be able to open up to her daughter about Jack. At least Emma hadn't found it and confronted her until after Peter's death.

The damage was done now though, she thought, wishing she wasn't the only family Emma had to turn to in Jersey now that Pru's parents had died and her brother had moved away. Pru doubted her daughter would ever see her in the same light again. She looked across the kitchen at Emma's face, blotchy from crying, unable to miss the disappointment in her precious daughter's eyes. She would give anything to be able to go back in time and destroy Peter's letter.

'Mum, did you hear what I said?'

Pru realised she hadn't. 'Sorry, darling, I was miles away.'

Emma gave her a suspicious look. 'You haven't changed your mind then?'

Pru tensed. Was Emma referring to Pru's refusal to share her birth father's identity? Her daughter was grieving for a darling dad who had died five months before; telling her now that the biological father she had only just discovered was also dead was too much for her to chance. Emma was already having to leave her home, now that the German army looked as if it could arrive in the Channel Islands at any time.

'Mum!'

'Sorry, I'm not sure what you're asking me.'

Emma gritted her teeth and groaned. 'I was wondering if you're sure you don't mind me going to Winchester to stay with Aunty Jean and Uncle Monty?'

'You know I don't mind. I'd rather know you're safe with them than stuck here on the island when we've no idea what's going to happen.'

'That doesn't make me feel better about you remaining here.'

Pru could have bitten her tongue. She really needed to think before speaking but she was upset. She and Emma had always got along so well. Pru sensed that their parting was going to be all the more painful since they wouldn't have time to talk though all that had happened over the past three days. The pain their confrontation had caused was too raw for them both right now.

'I still don't understand why you won't come with me.'

Pru couldn't miss the accusing tone in Emma's voice. She supposed it did seem odd, choosing to stay in Jersey when she had somewhere as beautiful and welcoming to go to as Ashbury Manor.

'I need to stay behind and look after this guesthouse. You know that.'

'I don't though, Mum. That's the point.' Emma glared at her. 'Other people are leaving their homes, walking away with nothing but a small suitcase. Thousands of them. There's nothing to stop you coming with me, and you know it.'

She did, and she wished she could explain her reluctance, but being reminded of Jack as she would be at Ashbury Manor wasn't something she felt emotionally capable of facing, so soon after losing Peter – and certainly not with Emma to witness any reaction she might have.

'I'm sorry, darling, truly I am, but I simply don't feel I can leave this place. It was your grandparents' home and I'd feel badly if it fell into enemy hands.' It wasn't a lie, not really, she told herself guiltily.

'But it's not as if they're here any longer.'

Pru winced at the reminder. She missed her parents but for once she was relieved they weren't still alive to know what might happen next to their beautiful island. 'I don't feel like I should be leaving the island right now,' Pru said, trying her best to keep a determined tone in her voice. 'Not when things are so worrying in France.'

'I wish I hadn't arranged to leave you now,' Emma said. Furious with Pru after discovering her mother had lied to her for all these years, Emma had contacted her aunt and uncle to ask if she could go and stay with them. 'It's been almost six months since Dad died. I think about him and miss him every day and I know you're probably still not over the shock of him going in that way. Don't you think it would do you good to get away from here? Not having to be in the same house where you both lived for the past twenty-two years?'

'You're probably right,' Pru agreed, thinking back to the moment she had found Peter lying on the pathway in the garden a few days after they had celebrated New Year. The doctor said he had suffered a massive heart attack and probably wouldn't have known very much pain. Pru still had nightmares though that he might have been calling for her and she hadn't heard him. She took a calming breath. She needed to focus on persuading Emma to leave without her. 'I'm not ready to leave yet,' she said honestly. 'But I can always follow you.'

'You won't come even for a holiday?' Emma asked. 'I'm sure you'd enjoy seeing the manor again; I know I'm looking forward to it.'

Pru sighed. 'Jean's always been the one to come to us, hasn't she?'

'When was the last time you were there?' Emma asked, picking up one of the sheets and helping Pru fold the freshly laundered bedlinen she had been working through when their conversation began.

Pru didn't have to think; she remembered the day she left the manor more clearly than most memories. Reeling from the pain of hearing Monty tell her Jack was dead. Desperate to see Jack again and refusing to give up hope that it might happen. Her guilt that Peter was pushing aside any hope of marrying for love by committing to marrying her and bringing up her baby. 'January 1918.'

Emma frowned. 'But that's back when you were a nurse there, wasn't it?'

Pru nodded, taking the folded sheet and placing it neatly on the pile next to her. She knew what was coming next.

'You mean you've never been back since the Great War?'

Pru forced a smile. 'You make it sound terrible. There just wasn't any need to visit before,' she added before Emma could say anything further. 'Jean always insisted on coming here to see me whenever she visited her parents. You remember, she used to bring Sam sometimes too.'

'Yes, he was horrible. I remember him putting woodlice in my hair when I was about four. I was terrified.'

Pru recalled Emma's hysteria and Jean being furious with Sam. 'Aww, he was better behaved after that,' she said. 'Just a little mischievous perhaps.'

Emma scowled and folded a pillow sham, smoothing down the cotton before placing it neatly on top of the other linen in the basket. 'He's probably grown up to be a nasty piece of work too. Anyway, that still doesn't explain why you never went back to the manor. I'd have thought you'd want to see the place again. Just think, I'll be able to have more of that delicious honey Aunty Jean always brings over for us. I've missed eating it on my toast since we ran out of it last week.'

Pru stilled. The honey. She wondered if Jean knew the significance of it each time she brought a jar over when she came to visit the island, or did she just bring it for its goodness and as a souvenir of Ashbury Manor?

'Mum, you're away with the fairies again. Did you hear what I said?'

Pru wasn't sure what to say and, when she didn't answer, Emma added, 'Ignore me, Mum. I don't mean to be nosy.'

Pru shook her head. 'No, it's perfectly understandable that you would be curious. I would have loved to return, if only to visit Jean and see how different things are since she and Monty took over the estate after his parents died.' She hugged the bedsheet to her chest. 'Jean knew how I'd promised your dad never to mention your real father and we both knew he'd associate the manor with me meeting him, so it didn't really seem fair to Dad to even consider returning.'

Emma surprised her by taking the bedsheet from her hands and pulling her into a hug. 'Do you want to help me try and find out what happened to him?'

Pru knew they were stepping on dangerous ground. She shook her head. 'It's too soon after your father's death for me to think about him.' She felt guilty for the half-truth. She was slowly recovering from the shock of Peter's death, but mostly she didn't think Emma was ready to hear everything. She and Peter had always been close and Pru knew her daughter needed time to grieve him and also come to terms with the shocking news that he wasn't her biological father.

'I've upset you, Mum,' Emma whispered.

Pru kissed her daughter's soft cheek. 'You haven't. We've had a strange few months and it seems that the next few months at least will be ones filled with changes. I love you more than anything or anyone and there's nothing you could do to truly upset me, Emma.'

Emma hugged her again.

'What are you thinking?' Pru asked.

'That you've gone through so much in your life and I never had a clue about it. I feel badly about looking in that box and bringing up painful things from your past. It was wrong of me.'

'Well, there's no need. You had to know sometime and this clearly was the time you were meant to find out.' She watched a range of emotions cross Emma's face. 'I am sorry for lying to you but I was carrying out Dad's wishes and needed to consider his feelings. If I hadn't married him your life and mine would have been tainted by the stigma of me being unmarried and I couldn't do that to you, not when I had the choice to be married and respectable.'

'It's fine, Mum. I'll probably take a little time to get used to the idea that someone else was my father, but Dad will always be my dad.'

Pru was relieved to hear her say as much. 'I'm glad. Your dad was a special man and he loved you deeply.'

'I know he did.' Emma sighed. 'I wish you'd been able to share your feelings with me, but I understand why you kept this a secret.' She tilted her head to one side thoughtfully. 'Did Granny Le Cuirot never ask you about me?'

Pru shuddered. 'She had no idea, thankfully. She would have been devastated to know the truth.' She explained how she and Peter made out that they had been courting for much longer than the short time they actually had. 'So, you see, there really was no one to speak to about it.' She smiled, aware how lucky she had been all these years with no one ever knowing her secret apart from Peter, Jean and Monty. 'And now I can share these things with you.'

Pru had been hoping that would be the end of their conversation. As much as she was acting fine, she felt exhausted by it and by keeping her emotions firmly in check for Emma's sake.

'That's all very well,' Emma retorted, 'but you must have loved my biological father very much at some point. How did you cope when you lost him?'

Pru had no intention of discussing Jack or anything about him. Not yet. 'I had you to focus on and bring up. Loving you gave me everything I needed to keep going.' She rested a hand on Emma's cheek.

Emma leaned into it. 'It's so sad.'

Pru shook her head and smiled. 'It's fine. I believe in fate and all this was meant to happen for some reason. I've had a very happy life with your dad. He was the sweetest, kindest man and the best father you could have asked for. We both loved every moment bringing you up and witnessing you becoming the clever, beautiful girl you are today.'

Emma's eyes filled with tears and Pru knew she had been right not to discuss Jack just yet. Like her, Emma always put on a brave face, wanting people to think she could manage when a lot of the time she was crying inside. 'Sweetheart, I know this is difficult.'

Emma wiped her eyes with a handkerchief. 'I wish I'd had a chance to say goodbye to Dad.'

'Me, too.' Pru sighed. 'I'm sad he's gone but I'm relieved he won't be alive to have to deal with whatever is coming our way with this rotten war. He was an honourable man and would have protected us with everything he had and that would have made me incredibly anxious.'

'I think you're probably right.' She chewed her lower lip thoughtfully and Pru sensed Emma had more to say. 'What did my father look like?' Emma asked, touching her fair hair. 'Was he fair, like me?'

Pru tried and failed to push away the image of Jack that she always seemed to have in her mind. 'Yes.'

Emma smiled. 'The only thing I ever thought strange,' she said, a wistful tone to her voice, 'was that you and Dad both had dark hair and I was so fair. It seemed odd.'

Pru pictured Jack, so handsome and like no one else she had ever met. 'He was tall, broad-shouldered and fair-haired,' she said, sighing. 'He had the bluest eyes I'd ever seen and he was the bravest man according to his friends. I loved him very much. I never imagined it was possible to love anyone as much as I did him.' She shook her head, laughing. 'Until you came along, that is.'

'Oh, Mum.' She could see Emma was only just managing not to cry again. 'Please consider coming with me to England. I'm sure Aunty Jean would love you to visit her finally.'

'I will think about it and I'll contact you immediately if I change my mind. I'm not ready yet though. Maybe in a month or so.' Pru straightened the flowerpot on the windowsill, unable to look her daughter in the eye. 'Don't forget that your aunt and uncle might be a little sensitive when it comes to speaking about your biological father, so tread very carefully if you do mention anything. Aunty Jean is still grieving for her brother and we must remember that.'

'Don't worry, Mum. I'll be careful not to upset her. I'll take this lot up and put them in the airing cupboard for you.' She picked up the basket of folded laundry.

'Thank you, sweetheart.' Pru took Emma by the shoulders and turned her around to face the stairs. 'Hurry now. You don't want to be late and miss that boat.'

Emma reached the door and stopped. 'Are you really certain you don't mind me going, Mum?' she asked over her left shoulder.

Pru put her hands on her hips. 'I'm fine, sweetheart. You mustn't worry about me. I'll follow you immediately if I don't feel safe here.'

'Promise?'

'Yes. Now, go.'

Pru watched her daughter walk upstairs and braced herself for the farewell that they would both soon be facing. As painful as it had been saying goodbye to Jack that last time, Emma's departure from the island, and not knowing when they would be together again, was breaking her heart.

TWENTY-FIVE

Emma

JUNE 1940, ENGLAND

Emma stared out of the taxi window as it swept up the long, tree-lined driveway, determined not to miss a single moment. Her mother had told her how magnificent the manor house and grounds were but nothing prepared her for her first view of the place. It was strange to imagine her mother as a young woman her own age working here. Emma knew from what little Pru had said that her time here had been precious and it was strange to think that her own aunt and uncle lived in such splendour.

The taxi stopped and a footman immediately hurried out of the huge double front doors. He opened the taxi's rear door and waited for her to step out.

'Thank you,' Emma said, feeling a little disconcerted, as if she were still a little girl playing 'grown-ups'. She stared up at the imposing Jacobean house and waited for him to take her case from the back of the car.

'Emma, darling!'

'Aunty Jean,' she cried, delighted to see her godmother striding towards her with arms outstretched.

'I can't believe you're finally here,' her aunt said, studying her face. 'You look beautiful as ever. If a little peaky.'

Emma patted her hair, unsure whether she was making it tidier or not. 'It was a rather rougher trip on the ferry than I'd have liked.'

Her aunt put an arm around Emma's shoulders and led her inside. 'Come along. Stephens will take your case to your room while we go and find Monty. He's dying to see you again, poppet. Although,' she lowered her voice, 'he's a little under the weather at the moment.'

Emma hated to hear that her darling uncle wasn't well. 'It's nothing too bad, I hope?'

'His leg is playing up a bit. It drives him crazy and makes him insufferably grumpy but having you here will cheer him enormously.'

'I do hope so,' Emma said, happy to feel so welcomed. 'Ashbury Manor is even more beautiful than the photos you showed us last year,' she said. 'I've never been anywhere this grand before. I can't believe I'll be staying here.'

'Please think of it as your home as much as ours while you're with us.'

Emma gazed around her at the splendour of the high-ceilinged, tiled hallway and its huge fireplace with carved surround. Gilt-framed portraits hung from the walls and drew the eye up the cantilever staircase to the floor above. She stopped walking and gazed up at the magnificence of the intricate strapwork ceiling, wondering how the master craftsmen managed to create something that impressive in plaster so that it lasted hundreds of years.

'It's rather ornate, isn't it?' Aunty Jean's hand went to her chest and rested there. 'I was in awe of this place, just as you are, when I first arrived here. It took a while after Monty and I were married before I was able to feel truly at home.' She straightened the right side of her cardigan, which had become creased from her embrace with Emma. 'It was rather a shock to move from the attic, where I shared a room with your mum and one other nurse, down to the bedroom Monty and I sleep in now.'

Emma wasn't surprised it had taken her aunt a while to think of this place as her home. She had visited her paternal grandparents' home many times and the simple, sparse house and attached printing studio were worlds away from a property like this.

'Is that little Emma?' Monty bellowed from a room to their left.

Jean laughed. 'There's clearly nothing wrong with his hearing when he wants to hear something.'

Emma followed her uncle's voice. 'Uncle Monty,' she called, delighted to see him.

He tapped his right cheek. 'And am I to be given a kiss from my favourite niece?'

She giggled, thrilled to see that although he was using a wheelchair now and clearly wasn't as fit as the last time she had seen him in Jersey, his humour was still the same. She ran up to him and bent to hug him, kissing him firmly on his cheek as he had instructed. 'It's wonderful to see you again.'

'Good to see you too, young lady.' He grinned. 'Now stand there and let me have a good look at you.'

Jean followed Emma into the smart living room and gave her a knowing look. 'As you can see, I'm not the only one who's thrilled to see you again.'

'You've grown up so much in the past two years, young lady.' He shook his head, grinning. 'How old are you now?'

'I was twenty-two a couple of weeks ago.'

He shook his head at Jean. 'Can you believe it, Jeanie? Twenty-two already.'

'I know,' Jean said, her voice wistful. 'Where have those years gone?'

'Our Sam is twenty-two in December. He promised to come home for the weekend, but we haven't seen hide nor hair of him yet.'

'Sam?' Emma tried to hide her disappointment to think that she would have to share her time here with their ghastly son. 'Gosh, I haven't seen him for over ten years.'

'Well,' Monty said. 'You can catch up with him when he arrives.'

Emma excused herself to go and wash her hands and then sat with them to enjoy a refreshing cup of tea and finger sandwiches.

'This is delicious.'

She finished eating her sandwich while answering her aunt and uncle's questions about her dad's funeral and thanking them for the large wreath they sent over for it.

'I was heartbroken not to be there,' Jean said, dabbing her eyes with a handkerchief she pulled from her cardigan sleeve.

'I'm sorry, my dear,' Monty said, taking her hand in his and patting it with his other one. 'It was my fault your aunt was unable to be there,' he explained miserably. 'I was rather unwell for a time and ended up in hospital and your dear aunt refused to leave me.'

'That's perfectly understandable,' Emma said, certain she would have done the same thing. 'I know Mum understood completely.'

'She did? Are you certain?' her aunt asked.

'Yes, I am. Mum would never have expected you to leave Uncle Monty behind when he was in hospital.'

'You're quite right, she wouldn't.' Her aunt seemed to relax slightly.

'It's so pretty here,' Emma said, wanting to change the subject so that she didn't let her emotions get the better of her. 'I'm so excited to finally be here. I can't believe it's my first time.'

Was it her imagination or did her aunt shift uncomfortably in her chair? Her uncle cleared his throat. 'I must admit we were a little taken aback that you chose now to visit,' he said. 'Especially with things as uncertain as they are with the Channel Islands being so close to the French coast. Your aunt thought that maybe you were coming here with Pru.'

'That was my plan,' she said, recalling her conversations with her mother about how her aunt and uncle might feel to discover she was searching for her long-lost father. 'Unfortunately she didn't feel ready to leave the guesthouse and couldn't be persuaded. I'm hoping to do something useful for the war effort though. I thought I'd go into the village on Monday and try to find somewhere for me to sign up.'

'Good girl,' her uncle cheered. 'That's the ticket.'

'As long as it's not anything dangerous.' Jean frowned. 'Your mother's been through enough in her lifetime without you putting yourself in danger.'

Emma agreed. 'I don't intend doing anything silly, just my duty, Aunty Jean. Please don't worry about me.'

Jean finished her tea and placed her cup and saucer onto the small occasional table in front of them. 'When you're ready I'll take you for a good look around the place. Then you can rest for a while before supper.'

'Thank you. I can't wait to see everything. I want to explore every part of this magnificent place.'

'Not everything,' Monty said, looking, Emma thought, rather agitated for some reason.

Emma looked from him to her aunt. Had she said something wrong?

Her aunt gave her a stilted smile, which Emma noticed didn't quite reach her eyes. For some reason the look in them was rather distant and very different from how it had been since her arrival. 'What your uncle means, dear, is that you're to stay away from the folly.'

'The folly?' She had never seen a folly and hadn't known there was one at the manor. 'I didn't know you had a folly. How thrilling.'

'Maybe you can see it at some point in the future,' Monty said, giving her aunt a quick glance. 'For now, though, it's pretty derelict. I couldn't live with myself if anything happened to you.'

'Monty's right, dear,' Jean agreed. 'Hopefully we'll be able to find the right craftsmen to fix it but I doubt that'll be until after the war, now that so many men have enlisted.'

'Never mind,' Emma said, wanting to placate them. 'I'll just have to wait then, won't I?'

'There's plenty more places for you to explore,' her aunt said more cheerfully. 'But do stay away from it if you see it in the distance, just in case.'

'Will do,' Emma said. She finished drinking her tea and smiled at her aunt. 'I'm ready for that look around the manor now if you wish.'

'Come along then.' Jean looked at Monty. 'You're sure you don't mind us leaving you for a bit?'

He lifted the book that sat on the table next to him. 'More than happy, my love. I have a lot of reading to look forward to today with everything happening in France.'

They left Monty, and Emma listened in awe as her aunt walked her through the different rooms. 'This was Ward Two where I first met Monty,' she explained. A little further along one of the corridors, she opened a door. 'In there is where we washed up pans and things. We called it the "sluice room" and next door was our linen cupboard.'

Emma peeked inside. 'It's more of a room than a cupboard,' she exclaimed. 'This place must be a constant reminder of your nursing days, I suppose?'

'It is,' she said, her voice quiet. 'I think of your mum often and of all the fun and sadness we shared together.' They walked up two flights of back stairs that were wooden and not carpeted like the main, grander staircase. 'In here,' she said, reaching to open the door and waiting for Emma to step inside the small room, 'is where your mum and I slept. Initially, we shared the room with a lovely girl called Milly.' She didn't speak for a few seconds and Emma recognised the same expression as she had seen on her mother's face a few times when she was reminiscing, making her wonder what had happened. 'She was replaced with someone else whom we liked but it was never really the same.'

Emma studied the small room, finding it almost impossible to imagine three single beds being able to fit in. 'You didn't have much room, did you?'

Jean shook her head and smiled. 'No, but it didn't seem to matter to us. Your mum and I didn't have many belongings. We had lockers and small bedside cabinets for our private things.'

'I don't think Mum has ever mentioned a Milly to me. Did she leave the hospital?' Emma asked, her curiosity getting the better of her. She supposed the nurse had met someone and left to marry.

'She died,' Jean said quietly. 'It was terribly sad and we both missed her very much.'

Emma stared at her aunt. 'Died? Was she ill?'

Jean shook her head. 'No.' She cleared her throat. 'There was a fire here.'

'There was?' It seemed that she still had a lot to discover about her mother's time at Ashbury Manor.

'Milly ran in to try and save someone and died of smoke inhalation. It was a miracle more people didn't perish that day. Monty and I were rescued by—' She suddenly stopped speaking and looked from Emma to the window and seemed conflicted about continuing with her story.

'Please go on.'

Jean crossed her arms. 'By a very brave man. We were trapped inside.'

'You were trapped?' Emma covered her mouth, shocked to think that her gentle aunt had come so close to death herself.

'Yes. It was terrifying. I was with Monty and someone locked us in the linen cupboard.'

'Did you ever discover who it was?'

'One of the patients. A troubled man who started the fire. He was arrested and I believe he ended up in a psychiatric ward. It's strange to think that you can see someone each day and know so little about what's going on in their mind.'

Emma thought of her mother and all the secrets she probably still had to discover. 'I agree.'

'He was a very troubled soul.'

Emma bit her lower lip, distressed to think of such a terrible thing happening. 'I'm so sorry, Aunty Jean. That's so sad.'

'It was. Poor Milly had dealt with terrible heartache before your mother and I met her. We were all very shocked by what happened to her.'

Emma sensed that Milly's untimely death had affected her mother and Jean more than either of them would ever let on.

———————

The following day, her aunt and uncle left their home for an appointment in the village and Emma was excited to be alone at the manor. She loved them both dearly but was relieved to have time to herself, and decided to go for a long walk. Her aunt had explained that they were down to three gardeners now and that they had been tasked with keeping the rose garden neat and only dealing with the larger areas when they had time. Their most important job apparently was the kitchen garden but a lot of other things at the manor had changed. Apart from that, Emma imagined that her aunt and uncle's lives probably weren't all that different to how they were prior to the war.

Emma turned left, walking around the house and down a pathway into some pretty woods. The shade of the huge trees was welcoming on such a warm day. The pathway meandered through the trees and eventually she came out into the sunlight once more on the other side of the woods, stepping out into a huge wildflower meadow dotted with daisies, cornflowers, buttercups and poppies whose pretty red heads bobbed in the slight breeze.

It was magical.

She kept walking, unsure exactly where she was going. Passing another copse of trees she picked a posy of wildflowers to take to her bedroom after her walk. She wished her mother had agreed to accompany her. Mum would have loved this, she thought. She would have to find a way to persuade her to come and visit, even if only for a couple of days. Emma was sure that if her mum did come to the manor again, she would be able to find a way to put to rest some the memories that still haunted her.

Not wishing to go where she shouldn't, Emma decided to ask someone so that she could avoid the folly. She spotted a walled area to her right with a painted wooden door, so she doubled back on herself and went to look inside. It was slightly open so she entered, relieved to see someone working at the far corner. It was a beekeeper. He would know where the folly was, surely.

'Hello?' Emma called. He didn't seem to hear her as he stood pointing a metal container with smoke coming out of it at one of the hives. She walked closer to him and called out to him once again. 'Excuse me?'

The next thing she knew, she was being pushed roughly from behind. Emma shrieked as she fell forward, landing hard on the stone pathway. She gritted her teeth as pain shot through her right knee, and, sitting up, she turned to see who had attacked her.

'Buddy!' the man bellowed. 'Get down, now!'

Emma saw a large bouncy dog that looked like a cross between a Labrador and something else.

The man tapped his thigh and the dog loped over to him. 'Are you hurt?' he asked, hurrying over to her.

Emma raised her hand. 'I'm fine,' she insisted, not sure that she was, and rubbed her sore knee. She got to her feet.

The man stared at her. At least she presumed he was staring at her. It was a little difficult to see though the beekeeper's hat with the black mesh obscuring his face.

'Did you want something?' He didn't seem all that friendly all of a sudden, which was odd, seeing as it was his dog that had pushed her over. Maybe he was simply surprised to see a stranger in the garden.

'Um, I was wondering if you could help me.'

'Should you be in here?'

'Yes.' She realised that entering the walled garden hadn't been the clever idea she had imagined it to be.

'Really?'

She wasn't sure what business it was of his but, wanting his help locating the folly, decided to appeal to his friendlier side. If indeed he possessed one.

She smiled. 'I'm Emma,' she said.

The man dropped the smoking canister and instead of bending to pick it up just kept staring at her. What on earth was wrong with him, she wondered, starting to feel a little uncomfortable.

'I'm a guest at the manor.' When he didn't reply, she thought she should repeat what she had just said. 'I said, my name—'

'I heard you,' he said, his voice a little softer.

She heard the catch in his voice and wondered if maybe his wife's name had been Emma. 'I didn't mean to upset you.'

'You didn't. It's a beautiful name.'

TWENTY-SIX

Jack

JUNE 1940

That dimple was so like Pru's. Jack stared at the girl, her fair hair the same colour as his, nothing like Pru's raven locks. So this was Pru's daughter. *His* daughter. He knew it beyond question. How he had longed for this day, dreamt about it, yet never imagined it might actually happen. He knew he should move, pick up the canister, at least try to act as if he hadn't been hit by a bolt of emotional lightning.

He should act like he didn't know who she was. He peered at her, trying to guess whether she had come to look for him. Would Pru have told her about him after her vow to keep his identity a secret? The memory of what Pru had needed to do to save her reputation still stung. Did she even know he was still alive? He hadn't dared try to contact her, though so many times he had almost given in and written to her. Monty had been right that she deserved to be left to live the life she had chosen.

He bent to pick up the canister.

'I'm sorry if I gave you a shock,' she said, her voice gentle though a little higher pitched than he recalled Pru's being. 'I hadn't meant to.'

'Were you looking for me?' Had someone told her of his existence? Would she be disappointed to discover he was her biological father?

'You?'

He realised she was shocked by his question. So she wasn't looking for him then, he thought, disappointed. 'Is there something I can do for you or are you just wanting to look around the garden?'

She leaned to look past him and he saw that she had noticed the beehives. 'Is that where the delicious honey comes from that Aunty Jean brings to Jersey for Mum and me each visit?'

He couldn't speak for a moment. They had eaten his honey. Enjoyed it. Jack couldn't recall the last time he had felt so happy. Felt anything much at all. 'It will be.'

'We always look forward to it every time she comes to the island.'

'You do?' He thought back to the first time he had asked Jean to take a jar with her to Jersey. She had been shocked, but they had agreed that she would simply let Pru and Emma believe the honey was from the estate gardens, and hide the fact that it was Jack's way of giving them something he valued. It was a joy to hear his own child telling him how she had looked forward to and enjoyed his gift, even if she was oblivious to the love behind the simple jar of honey. Jack almost had to pinch himself to reassure himself that this was actually happening and not one of his fantasies.

'Love it. It's the one thing we both look forward to.'

'It is?' He noticed she was holding a small posy of wildflowers like the ones he had given Pru on the day he had proposed to her.

She nodded. 'Very much so.'

'Lady Ashbury is your aunt then?' He knew he was probing to find out more about Pru but couldn't help himself. It wasn't as if he was telling the girl who he was, so what was the harm?

'Yes. She's my mum's oldest friend, as well as her sister-in-law. Isn't that lovely?' Emma said. 'They both worked here during the Great War.'

He reached down and stroked the dog's head. 'Are your parents staying at the manor with you then?'

The smile left her pretty face then and he wished he'd had the sense not to have asked her.

'No.'

Something was very wrong. 'Nothing's happened, has it?' The words were out of his mouth before he had time to think. He could see by her expression that he had shocked her and wished he hadn't been so stupid.

'It depends on what you mean,' she said. 'My father died recently.'

'I'm sorry, losing a parent is hard to deal with.'

She nodded slowly. 'Thank you, it is.' She looked around the garden silently for a few seconds. 'I wish Mum had agreed to come here with me. I know she would love it here. Especially this garden. She loves her garden.' She pointed to the hives. 'And I'm sure she'd enjoy seeing where the honey comes from.' She looked straight at him and for a moment he felt like she could see through the mesh and had spotted his tear-filled eyes. 'You wouldn't mind showing her the bees, would you?'

He had to swallow to be able to speak but, unable to find the words, nodded instead.

'That's kind of you, thank you.'

Recalling reading that the British government had demilitarised Jersey, Jack suddenly felt concern for Pru. 'Isn't your mother worried about remaining in Jersey with the threat of the Nazis moving ever closer to the islands?'

Emma looked as if she was becoming upset and he felt mean having asked such a cruel question. 'I tried to persuade her to come with me, but she insisted she was needed at home to run our family guesthouse. But I think it's more to do with her still grieving for Dad.'

Then Pru had loved him, he mused, glad for her that her marriage appeared to have been a happy one but stung to think that she had loved another man deeply.

'Although now the Germans seem to be getting very close to the islands, I can't see how anyone will want to go there for a holiday, can you?'

'What? Um, no. No, I can't.'

She shrugged. 'Enough about me and my troubles,' she said, seemingly trying to appear cheerful. 'Mum did promise that if it got too dangerous there she would come here to stay. I'll just have to hope she keeps to her word.' She pointed to the canister in his hand. 'What are you burning in there? It's such a gentle smell.'

'Hay and thyme,' he said absentmindedly as he tried to push away a thought that was nagging at him.

'Why are you trying to smoke them out?' she asked,

evidently hoping to engage him in further conversation.

'To calm them.'

'I'm sorry,' Emma said suddenly. 'I can see you'd rather be working.'

'No, it's fine,' he said, hating to think he had given her the impression that he wanted her to go.

'You wanted to know what I was doing here.' She looked about her as if to check they were still alone. 'I was told to stay away from the folly but I'm a little lost and not really sure where it is. I saw you and thought you might tell me so that I can avoid it. Would you mind?'

So they hadn't told her anything, Jack thought. He wasn't surprised. Knowing Jean, she would quite rightly want to check with Pru first before telling Emma their secret.

'Not at all.' He explained about the copse of trees to the right of the garden. 'It's beyond there. If you keep to this side of the copse you should be fine.'

'Thank you,' she said, giving him the sweetest smile, which reminded him so much of Pru it took his breath away. 'I'll leave you in peace with your bees, but I'd love to come back to the garden again if you wouldn't mind me doing so?'

'I'd like that very much,' he said honestly.

Jack watched the girl leave, unable to unscramble his thoughts. She was taller and fairer than Pru and didn't look much like her at all, apart from when she smiled, showcasing that dimple of hers that was so reminiscent of her mother

The girl clearly thought him a little odd and he couldn't blame her for that. He hadn't been very gracious but, he mused, the shock of seeing a stranger in what he had come to think of as his own private space had taken him aback. He was glad he had been wearing his hat so she couldn't see his face. His scars were no longer the livid red they had once been but they still stretched in a patchwork across his cheek.

He recalled the way Emma said her name and thought how much his mother would have loved to know one of her sons had a grandchild named after her. It still pained him to think that she had died not knowing he had survived the Great War. How she must have suffered to lose his brother as well just before her death.

He shook his head. England was his home now and had been ever since he had returned after settling his mother and brother's affairs in New York following the end of the war. There had been no one in his homeland to live there for. He thought back to Monty's insistence that he must stay with them at Ashbury Manor, when he had returned crushed and broken, having lost those closest to him in such quick succession. It had taken him years to learn to live without anyone in his life, but he hadn't wanted another woman after Pru, and moving into the folly – after Monty had allowed him to pay for a bathroom and small kitchenette to be installed – had been an ideal solution. Now he had met Emma. What a charming, sweet girl.

Pru was still in Jersey. He wished desperately that this wasn't the case, though not entirely because he wanted her for himself. He read Monty's day-old papers and had been unsure that the prime minister was right to hope that if the people of the islands were left without weapons to defend themselves they might be left alone by the enemy. They were in a precarious position now and Jack couldn't extinguish his fear that by making that choice the British government had left the islanders to the mercy of the German army. He hoped he was wrong.

To discover his beloved Pru was now a widow and alone on an island only – what was it? Fifteen miles off the coast of France? Something like that? He remembered her saying how she could see the French beach clearly from her bedroom window. That was far too close for his liking, especially now the Nazis were pretty much on Jersey's doorstep.

He tried to calm his rising panic. How could he stay here wandering around his walled garden, calmly taking care of his bees and keeping himself to himself, while Pru's life was possibly in danger?

Jack's thoughts began to race. Was there a way he could help Pru? Would she even accept his help after all that he'd put her through? Buddy nuzzled Jack's leg and he reached down and stroked him. Pru might have refused Emma's request to come to the manor by saying she had to look after the guesthouse, but he sensed there was more to Pru's reasoning than that. Was it because she didn't want to be reminded of what they had shared together here? Could it be that? Jack wondered.

Now Peter had passed on, it was time to let her know that he had survived and find out whether she still loved him or not. Because Jack knew that the most important thing he needed to focus on right now was rescuing Pru from whatever she might soon be facing, for their daughter's sake.

TWENTY-SEVEN

Emma

JUNE 1940

A s she neared the house Emma heard the sound of tyres on gravel. Someone was driving pretty quickly up the driveway and she quickened her pace, wondering if it was her aunt and uncle arriving home earlier than expected.

It wasn't.

'Well, hello there, little cousin.' An extraordinarily handsome RAF pilot waved to her as he jumped out of the driver's seat of a green sports car. 'What's the matter?' he asked, a wide grin on his face as he marched purposefully in her direction. 'Don't you recognise me?'

'Not immediately, no,' she said, her mood dropping when she realised it was her horrible cousin Samuel. 'You've changed rather a lot.'

'You haven't.' He laughed, taking her in his arms and swinging her around in a circle.

'Put me down.' He might look much better than he had as a child, but he was still noisy and a little over-enthusiastic for her liking.

'Sorry. Ma's always telling me off for being too exuberant. Shall we go and see if Cook has any treats for us?'

Did he still think he was twelve, she mused, unimpressed. How was she going to put up with him for the next few days? She reminded herself that this was his home, not hers, and she needed to be polite however much he irritated her.

'Fine.' She nodded. 'Don't forget your bag,' she said, noticing one on his passenger seat.

'I was going to leave that until later, but you're probably right.' He leaned into the car and picked it up, slinging it on to his shoulder as if it weighed nothing more than a bag of carrots, despite it bulging at the sides. 'Come along then, cous.' He laughed to himself.

'Something amusing you?'

'Only that you seem pretty unimpressed to see me.' He pulled a face at her. 'And I was so looking forward to meeting up with you again.'

'To torment me, no doubt.'

He roared with laughter. 'I'm not the same kid you remember. I've changed a lot since then, I hope you'll find, and I intend making sure that by the time I leave you and I will be the best of friends.'

She didn't hold up much hope for his chances. 'There's really no need.'

He laughed again.

'What's so funny now?' she asked as they reached the front door and Stephens, who she presumed had been waiting for them, opened it.

'Good afternoon, Captain Ashbury.'

'Stephens, good to see you.' He patted the footman on the shoulder. 'Still haven't escaped my father's clutches, I see.'

Emma was horrified by Sam's comment, but Stephens seemed amused by it.

'Not yet, but soon, hopefully.'

She accompanied her cousin through the house, surprised when he didn't go to the living room but pushed open the baize door separating the family from the staff and waved for her to follow.

'Should we be going this way?' she asked, almost having to run to keep up with him.

'I thought you might want to choose a small vase for those,' he said, indicating the posy she had forgotten she was carrying.

'Really?'

He stopped walking and gave her a wink. 'And to say *hello* to Cook. She'd never forgive me if I didn't go to see her as soon as I arrived.'

Emma wasn't sure if he was deluded or if the cook did expect to see him in her kitchen.

They entered the large, busy room with pans bubbling away on the huge range. Sam stopped, hands on hips, waiting, Emma presumed, for someone to notice his arrival.

A scullery maid hurried into the room from a smaller back room and gasped. 'Master Samuel!'

Cook turned, the scowl on her face immediately vanishing when she saw that Sam was indeed standing waiting for her. 'Master Samuel. You are here. Well, well, well,' she said, beaming at him and waving the poor maid away. 'It does my soul good to see you back here again.'

'Thank you, Mrs B,' he said. 'It's wonderful to be here again. I've been missing your delicious food and longing to come back and eat properly.'

Clearly delighted by his compliment, the cook tilted her head to one side. 'You'll be wanting some of my strawberry tarts, no doubt?'

'You know me only too well,' he said, grinning. 'I was telling my cousin here how heavenly they are and she's desperate to try one. If you have enough,' he said, raising an eyebrow. 'If not, I'll have to eat alone.'

He winked at Emma to show he was teasing.

Emma shook her head, trying to look unimpressed but unable to help smiling. Maybe he wasn't so bad after all. The servants clearly adored him.

'How was your day?' Uncle Monty asked Emma, joining them after having disappeared into his study for half an hour. Emma loved the pretty drawing room and felt sleepy and content after enjoying a delicious supper of chicken pie accompanied by tasty vegetables from the kitchen garden.

'I had a lovely walk,' Emma told them. 'I went through the woods. Your grounds are so open and pretty.'

'And you didn't go near the folly?' Jean asked.

'No. Not at all,' Emma said. 'I did get a little lost, but I saw one of your gardeners and asked him where the folly was so that I could avoid it.'

'Which one?' Sam asked.

'Sorry?' Were there more follies that she didn't know about?

'Which gardener? Did you catch his name?'

'No. Does it matter?' Before he could answer, she added, 'I'm afraid I can't describe him either because he was wearing a beekeeper's outfit.'

'Beekeeper?' Sam grinned. 'That'll be Jack. He's not really a gardener.'

'Sam, that's enough,' Jean snapped. 'He does look after the walled garden.' She smiled at Emma. 'I'm glad he was helpful.' She looked at Monty. 'What?'

He shook his head. 'I told you Emma would be perfectly fine.' He rolled his eyes. 'Your aunt wasn't happy about leaving you here so soon after your arrival, but I told her you'd find things to keep yourself occupied.'

'I did. I was absolutely fine,' Emma said, rubbing her aching knee absentmindedly and hoping to reassure her aunt. 'And no sooner was I back at the house than Sam arrived.'

'I don't understand,' Sam said, clearly confused about something, but Emma had no idea what it might be.

His father waved for him to be quiet. 'Enough, Sam. Don't witter on. Your mother and I would rather hear how've you been getting along since we last saw you, my boy.'

Sam raised his eyebrows and gave Emma an apologetic look. 'We can all sense something is about to begin,' Sam said, looking serious for the first time. 'Especially since France called for an armistice on June the sixteenth and then a couple of days later the prime minister gave his speech saying...' He thought for a couple of seconds. 'What was it? Oh yes, something like "The Battle of France is over. The Battle of

Britain is about to begin." I think things are going to heat up and get interesting very soon.'

Jean shuddered. 'Don't say such things, Sam. I've enough to worry about with your father not taking things easy, and losing staff here, without worrying more than I already do about you.'

'It's fine, Mother. Please don't fret about me. I'm like a cat, I have at least nine lives.'

'Sam!'

'What have I said now?' He reached out to take his mother's hand. 'Is something the matter? You don't seem yourself today.'

'It's nothing, my boy,' Monty said. 'We're all a little anxious these days what with one thing and another.'

Emma wondered if maybe they were concerned about her mother still being in Jersey. She wouldn't be surprised if it was that and what Sam had said about things heating up for the RAF.

'I wish you'd consider your words, especially when speaking to your mother,' Monty admonished, as if affirming her suspicions. 'You know how she worries about you flying. Remember she knew pilots in the Great War.'

'Weren't you one of them, Uncle Monty?' Emma asked, recalling her mother once mentioning something about him being in the Royal Flying Corps.

'That's right, my dear. Thrilling it was, too.'

'Monty, please.'

Emma watched her aunt give Uncle Monty a pointed glare and wondered how many patients she and her mother must have lost. She supposed they must have seen terrible injuries during their nursing days and it was little wonder Aunty Jean was concerned for her only child's welfare.

'I was wondering if you've written to your mother, Emma, to let her know you've arrived here safely. I think you should.' Her aunt slipped her hand from Sam's and folded it neatly with the other one on her lap. 'It's a shame she doesn't have a telephone but I know how Peter didn't like the things. If you'd like to post a letter there's a post box at the end of our drive.'

'I hadn't realised. Thank you. I'll excuse myself now, if you don't mind, and write to her immediately.'

TWENTY-EIGHT

Jack

JUNE 1940

J ack rose early the following morning and went to speak
to Monty. He hadn't been able to sleep since meeting
Emma and had been planning how best to travel to
Jersey. Pru needed him, whether she knew it or not, and this
time he had no intention of letting her down.

He found his friend sitting at his desk reading a broadsheet
while he puffed languorously on a cigar. 'Isn't it a bit early for
that, old chap?' Jack asked, walking in without bothering to
knock. He noticed the window was open and made himself
comfortable on the leather armchair beneath it.

Monty jumped and a large piece of ash dropped from the
end of his cigar onto his desk. 'It's not often you grace us with
your presence, Jack,' he said, swiping the ash onto the polished
floorboards with the back of his hand.

'I need your help,' Jack said. He looked to one side and
stared into the fire that one of the servants would have lit
earlier. It might be getting warmer now but Monty's study was
on the north side of the manor, out of the sun, and ever since

the war he had tended to feel the cold. 'I met Emma,' he said quietly.

'So I gathered.'

Jack looked at him, surprised. 'You know?'

'She told us yesterday.'

'About me?' What had she said, he wondered?

Monty raised his hand, causing more ash to drop. 'She doesn't know who you are, Jack, but she told us about the beekeeper who told her where the folly could be found.'

Why did he feel so disappointed? He had known yesterday from her reaction to him that she had no idea who he was. 'Of course.'

'Would you like me to ring for coffee?'

'No, thanks. I was hoping you'd let me have the use of your car.'

Monty seemed shocked and Jack wasn't surprised. He rarely asked his friend for anything.

'You're going to Jersey to fetch Pru, aren't you?'

Jack nodded. 'I might have guessed you'd know.' When Monty didn't speak, Jack went on. 'I can't leave her there alone, Monty. We both know how brutal war can be.' His hand went up to his cheek but stopped before his fingers touched the scarring. He hated to touch the uneven skin, even all these years later. 'I can't sit here knowing she's all alone there on that island. How would she defend herself?'

Monty struggled to stand and walked the few steps to a nearby table. He removed the crystal stopper from one of the decanters in the tantalus, poured large measures into two glasses and handed one to his friend. 'I know it's early but I think we both need one of these, don't you?'

Jack could see his friend was unnerved so took the drink despite the early hour. He raised his glass and Monty mirrored his action. 'Good health, my friend.' He knocked it back in one. 'You do understand why I have to go to her, don't you?'

'I do.' He stared at Jack for a few seconds. 'If it was Jean alone on that island facing such a threat, I'd do exactly the same thing.' Monty took his half-smoked cigar from where he had left it resting on the side of the ashtray and went to sit by the fireplace. 'Emma told you about Peter dying, didn't she?'

'She did.' He knew what was coming next.

'But you swore you never wanted her to see you again.' Monty touched the side of his face. 'After what happened.'

Jack recalled his dark years after first returning to the manor. 'That was before I'd come to terms with her marrying another man.' He shook his head. 'Yes, I know why she did it and I understood, but that didn't mean it hurt any less. I also still had to come to terms with looking so different.' He shrugged. 'Anyway, that was when she had a husband and a good life. Now she's a widow and alone. Her daughter is here and clearly concerned for her mother. Monty, I have a terrible feeling the German army will invade the islands and I can't sit here and not at least try to rescue Pru.' He waited for Monty to speak, unsure what was troubling him.

'Has it occurred to you she might not react well to seeing you again?' He took a puff from his cigar. 'And I don't mean because of your scars. She still thinks you're dead, Jack. She's not going to be pleased to know we've all lied to her for the past twenty-two years.'

Jack hadn't thought of that.

'And maybe,' Monty continued, 'she doesn't need or want to be rescued, Jack? Have you considered that?'

Jack hadn't thought that far. His only waking thought had been to find her and bring her back to safety in England before it was too late. 'I've no idea, but I can't sit idly by and do nothing.'

'I agree, but I also know how much you still love her.' He raised his hand to stop Jack from arguing. 'We both know it's true otherwise you would have moved on with your life. As much as you think living here at the folly and looking after your bees is moving on, we both know that really you've isolated yourself from the rest of the world as much as possible because you haven't recovered from losing Pru. And Emma,' he added.

Jack felt the sting of his friend's words. They held a lot of truth and he didn't bother to deny it. Monty knew him far too well to be fobbed off with any feeble argument. 'Go on, Monty. I can tell there's more.'

Monty took a sip from his lead crystal glass. 'It's just that you've survived two close calls during the last war, Jack, and I'm frightened that your luck might have run out for this one. You're much older now.'

Jack laughed. 'I'm in my mid-forties, Monty, as are you,' he argued. 'I'm hardly in my dotage yet.'

'Maybe.' Monty grimaced. 'I'm such a mess now that I feel much older. Bloody legs.' He picked up his glass again and drained it in one gulp. 'That's better. Right, I need to know that if you get into any difficulty, you'll send word to me. I don't know what I could do to help but I'd certainly give it my best shot.'

'I promise you I will,' Jack said, reassured to have his friend's backing.

Before Jack had a chance to say anything, Monty spoke again. 'What if the Nazis have reached the island by the time you get there, Jack?'

'I'll worry about that if I need to. I'm aware I can't waste any time. So, will you give Stephens permission to drive me to Weymouth this morning?'

'Of course.' Jack stood and waited for Monty to struggle to his feet. He knew better than to offer him help. Monty held out his hand for Jack to shake it. 'Then I wish you all the luck in the world. I have a feeling you're going to need it.'

'Let's hope not,' Jack said, pulling his friend into a brief hug. 'I have to admit that I feel alive for the first time in twenty years.'

'I can see that,' Monty said. 'It's good to have you back, old thing.'

'It's good to be here.' He thought of the woman he loved. 'And when I bring Pru back here, and I have every intention of doing so, then I hope that she and I can start to work things out between us.'

'I wouldn't get ahead of yourself,' Monty said, the warning clear in his tone. 'Just get her safely back here and then worry about whatever happens after that.'

'I will.'

TWENTY-NINE

Emma

JUNE 1940

E mma heard her uncle's car going down the drive. It was still early but after a restless night's sleep fretting about her mum back in Jersey she decided to stop wallowing. Her mum had promised she would follow her if things back there got too sticky and she had to trust that she would do so.

What was it that her mother always said to her? *If in doubt, keep yourself busy.* Emma had always thought it an odd thing to say, but right now it seemed like the most sensible option. She needed a job. That's it. And, she decided, she needed to move on and find rooms for herself. She loved her aunt and uncle but hearing Sam talking rapturously about being an RAF pilot made her realise how ineffectual her life was right now. Sam was leaving the following day and Emma didn't fancy the idea of rattling around in the manor house trying her best to not get in her aunt and uncle's way. She loved being here but there was little for her to do.

She needed to take control of her life now, but how? What job could she possibly do? She worked in a dress shop at home but as much as she enjoyed that work, it wasn't exactly doing much for the war effort. She supposed she would simply have to see what vacancies there were nearby.

Getting up, she washed and dressed. Calmer and longing to move on from feeling inadequate, Emma brushed her hair, pinched her cheeks to give them a little colour and made her way downstairs to speak to her relatives.

'You're looking tired,' her aunt said, concerned.

'Just a bit of a restless night,' she admitted.

'It must be rather unsettling for you being away from home with so much going on,' Monty said. 'We recall only too well how many changes there were during the last war. This one might be different in many ways but people will still have to come to terms with their lives altering drastically, more's the pity.'

'I agree,' Emma said. 'Which is why I've decided to find a job and somewhere to live.'

'You're wanting to leave us? To go to work?' her aunt asked, glancing from Emma to Monty. 'But there's no need, Emma. You're more than welcome to stay here with us for the duration of the war.'

Emma was grateful to her aunt for her kindness, but she had made up her mind and had no intention of being dissuaded.

'Thank you, Aunty Jean, but I've listened to Sam talking about his flying, and know how you and Mum felt about your nursing in the last war, and I simply must do something. I'd make a dreadful nurse, so I won't try to do anything like that, but I need to do my bit in some way. I want to feel like I'm contributing.'

She caught Sam's eye. 'I think it's a brilliant idea,' he said.

'Sam, really,' his mother admonished. 'I hope you've not been putting ideas into Emma's head?'

'Sam hasn't done anything other than be extremely supportive of me, Aunty Jean.'

He seemed pleased to hear her say so. 'Mother, Emma is twenty-two and if she wants to find work then I say good for her.'

'He's right, Jean,' Monty said quietly. 'You and I wouldn't be dissuaded when our parents tried to keep us from what we insisted on doing during the Great War. How can we expect the youngsters today to think differently to how we did back then?'

Jean rested the tips of her fingers against her forehead for a few seconds. 'I suppose you're right. Although I wish I could disagree.' She sighed. 'Where will you look for work though, Emma?'

Sam smiled. 'I might be able to help,' he said. 'Do you have any problem with factory work?'

'The girl can't work in a factory, Sam!' Her aunt seemed horrified.

'I can't see why not. Many women and men are doing exactly that so why not Emma?'

'He's right, Aunty Jean. I'd be delighted to work anywhere, but if it's somewhere helping the war effort then all the better as far as I'm concerned.' She smiled at her cousin. 'Thank you.' Emma couldn't hide her excitement. 'Any suggestions you might have will be very welcome.'

'I do have a suggestion, as a matter of fact,' he said.

'Sam, you don't mean that Spitfire factory? The large one in

Southampton?' her aunt asked, a horrified expression on her face. 'It's such a noisy, not to mention dirty and dangerous, place.'

Was it? Emma wondered.

'I doubt it's dirty, Mother,' he argued. 'Unless you've been listening to the maids gossiping again. It will be noisy though,' he said to Emma. 'But that can't be helped.'

'It's fine, truly.' Emma understood her aunt's concern for her but had no intention of letting anyone hold her back from feeling useful.

'I have a contact there,' Sam added. 'I'll give him a call and try to set up an interview for you.'

'That would be incredible. Thank you ever so much.'

Jean pursed her lips. 'If anything were to happen to you, Emma ... well, your mother would never forgive me.'

'I'll be fine,' Emma promised, certain her aunt was over-reacting.

'Then Monty and I will go and leave the pair of you to your plans.' She gave a tired smile and they left the room.

Sam pulled a face and Emma struggled not to laugh at his expression.

'Why don't we go for lunch in the village first?' he said. 'I think we could both do with getting away from here for a bit.'

She liked the idea of going into the village and seeing what it was like. Making the planes would be the next best thing to flying the things, she decided.

'I'd love that,' Emma said, feeling much better. 'Maybe I'll also find a room to rent.'

'You're not happy staying here?'

He seemed slightly disappointed, and she hoped she hadn't

offended him. 'Don't get me wrong, it's beautiful and your parents have been extremely welcoming, but I don't feel like I'm doing anything worthwhile staying here. It feels odd being waited on, too. I'm not used to the sort of lifestyle that you've grown up experiencing, and although it's exciting for a holiday, it would feel a little strange to live like this for a long period.'

'I understand you wanting to be busy,' he said. 'I'm also not one for sitting around doing nothing. We'll leave soon.'

'Wonderful,' she said.

'Is that a spring in your step?' Sam teased.

'It might be.' She liked this new, kinder, Sam. He was thoughtful and easy to get along with. 'Thanks, Sam, I appreciate your help.'

'My pleasure,' he said, taking her hand in his and giving it a gentle squeeze. 'You'll be fine. We'll sort something out for you, I promise.'

She wanted to believe him and knew that with Sam in her corner she stood a much better chance. She realised for the first time that she was going to miss his company when he returned to his squadron.

THIRTY

Jack

JUNE 1940, JERSEY

J ack was relieved the ferry trip was over with quickly. He could cope with most weathers in a plane but boats really weren't his favourite mode of transport. He was glad there weren't many people onboard so that he could disembark quickly but was shocked to see hundreds of people waiting to board, mostly women with children and some older men. He was going to have to move himself if he intended leaving the island with Pru in tow.

He rarely felt nervous but although he had been determined to come and rescue her, the hours it had taken to get here had given him far too much time to think of all that might stop that happening. Mostly that Pru might refuse to leave. If Emma couldn't persuade her to go with her, then what hope did he have? Jack manoeuvred his way through the crowd, relieved when he spotted several taxis waiting to collect visitors.

He spoke to the nearest one and gave the driver Pru's address. Sitting in the back of the vehicle, he reminisced about the last time he had come here. He still recalled the crushing pain of seeing Pru holding baby Emma, with another man's arm around her shoulder. He knew he should be grateful to Peter for looking after these two precious women but he couldn't help wishing that it had been him bringing up his daughter and him loving Pru all these years. He turned his attention to look out of the window, determined to focus on the present.

'Not many folk coming to the island these days,' the driver said.

'I won't be here for very long,' Jack said. 'Just visiting an old friend briefly.'

It didn't take long for them to reach the guesthouse and this time he let the driver take him to the front door. 'If you'll wait here? I'm hoping I won't be too long but I'll cover any time I take up so that you're not out of pocket.'

'As you wish.'

Jack paid the driver to cover the journey to the guesthouse and then got out of the car and walked up to the front door.

He was nervous as he rang the doorbell, desperate to get their initial meeting over with. What if she fainted on seeing him so unexpectedly, he mused, aware that to her he had been dead these past twenty years. He should have thought more about how he was going to approach her. He heard footsteps coming down the hallway. It was too late to come up with anything now.

The door opened and she stared at him as if she was seeing an apparition, which he supposed wasn't a surprise. He didn't know whether to say something or let her shock dissipate. Eventually, when she drew her fingers up to the side of her forehead in confusion, Jack realised he had to take charge of the moment.

He reached out and took her hand in his. 'Pru,' he said, trying to keep the tremble in his voice to a minimum. 'You aren't seeing things. It is me. Jack.' When she still didn't say anything, he gently led her inside and closed the door behind them, not wishing the taxi driver or any neighbours who might be watching to witness what was happening.

'Jack?' She reached out and touched his damaged cheek. 'Your face?'

He tried not to recoil from her touching his scars, not wishing to cause her any more upset than he clearly already had.

'You're alive.' She looked him up and down, her eyes wild as she tried to process what she was seeing.

'I am.'

'Does Monty know?'

'Monty?'

She still didn't move. 'Yes,' she said, still obviously confused by what she was seeing. 'He will be so happy to know you weren't killed.'

'Monty knows. So does Jean.' Jack wondered if maybe seeing him on top of the trauma she had experienced recently – with her husband dying so suddenly, Emma leaving and the threat of invasion – might have sent her mind into freefall.

'Let's go through and sit down. I'll make you something hot to drink if you like. Something sweet.'

He began leading her through the house to the back where he assumed the kitchen might be when she suddenly stopped and spun round to face him. 'You're alive?'

Jack smiled at her sweet face. 'Yes, sweetheart. I am,' he said gently. 'I've come back to fetch you and take you to Ashbury Manor.'

She slammed both her palms against his chest and pushed him away from her with such force that he stumbled backwards, only just stopping himself from falling by grabbing hold of one of the bannisters on the nearby stairs.

'How dare you come back from the dead like nothing's happened and tell me you're rescuing me.' She marched through to the kitchen and turned, glaring at him with her hands on her slim hips. She shook her head and crossed her arms. He could see she didn't know what to do with herself. This was not the happy reunion he had hoped for. Pru was furious.

'How long have they known you're alive?'

He cringed inside, aware that to tell her was going to open a floodgate of fury. 'Since July 1918.'

She stared open-mouthed at him, her face reddening in temper. 'Twenty-two years?' She paced back and forth, glaring at him. 'What is this? Some sort of joke? You've all kept this secret from me?'

'Pru, please let me explain.' He reached out to take her hand in his but she slapped it away.

'Don't you dare touch me. Do you know how I mourned for you? I had to keep my grief to myself so I was forced to do it in secret. Do you know how that feels, Jack?'

'Pru, listen.'

'No, Jack. You listen.' She told him how Peter had been the one to rescue her and their daughter. How Peter had loved them and given them a good life. 'And where were you while all this was going on?'

'I moved back to Ashbury and lived in the folly.'

She shook her head and gritted her teeth, holding on to the top of the table next to her. He watched her compose herself and take a few deep breaths, as she used to tell patients to do when they were in a state, back when she was nursing.

She didn't look up at him. 'Go.'

'Pardon?'

She raised her eyes to his. 'I said go.' He didn't know what was worse, her fury or her cold calm.

He stared at her, trying to take in her face, now with tiny lines at the sides of her eyes. Her hair was still almost black and she was still very beautiful. He had no intention of leaving her here to the mercy of the damn Nazis. 'No.'

She narrowed her eyes. 'How dare you? If I ask you to leave my house you will do so, do you understand?'

Jack pressed his palms together, aware that he had to think quickly if he had any hope of her listening to him before he had to leave. The first thing he needed to do was apologise. 'I am sorrier than you will ever know that I didn't make it back to Ashbury until six months after you married Peter,' he said without taking his eyes from hers. 'I wanted to tell you that I was alive but Monty persuaded me that it would be selfish of me to do so. That you were making a new life for yourself and for Emma.'

'It's easy to say that now, after all this time. Did you ever think about us?'

He could see her anger was dissipating slightly and being replaced by sadness. 'Every single day,' he admitted. 'I promised Monty never to try and see you or contact you or Emma. He told me about the promise you had to make to Peter.'

She looked down then back at him. 'He was a good man.'

'So I'm told.' Jack pushed his hand into his pocket and felt the small leather box. Now wasn't the time to show it to her. He only hoped that she would one day give him the chance.

'We were happy enough.'

'I know.'

'How do you know, Jack? It's not as if you ever saw us when you were secreted away at Ashbury.'

'I came here.'

She looked stunned. 'When?'

He told her about his trip to Jersey and how he had needed to see for himself that she was safe and well. He watched her face soften as he spoke, relieved. 'I've met Emma. She came to the walled garden and was telling me how she enjoyed the honey I sent to you both.'

'That was from you?' Pru's voice was barely a whisper and he hoped that he might have a chance of persuading her to go with him.

'She's frightened for you, Pru,' he said, aware that the only form of persuasion he had was to try and get Pru to go with him for Emma's sake. 'She's safe enough with Jean and Monty, but she misses you.'

'She told you this?'

'Yes.' Pru seemed surprised. 'Why are you really still here, Pru? Is it because it was your parents' home, or is it Peter?' Then it dawned on him. 'Good grief. It's neither of those things, is it?'

She pursed her lips. 'Isn't it?'

He was right. 'No. You're still here because you couldn't bear to return to Ashbury and all the memories the place still holds for you. Isn't that right?'

She folded her arms across her chest. 'I see that I was misguided to feel that way though, wasn't I, Jack?' He winced as she practically spit out his name.

He noticed the clock on the wall and knew that if they were to leave the island that day, he had to try harder.

'I have a taxi waiting outside for us and Emma is on the other side of the Channel waiting for you.'

'She knows you're here?' She gasped. 'You told her who you are?'

He shook his head and held out his hands to stop her losing her temper again. 'No. I didn't say a word to her, I promise. She thinks I'm the beekeeper from the estate, nothing more.' She saw Pru's shoulders relax slightly. 'Please, Pru. I'll help you pack. Come with me. While there's still time.'

For the first time he saw her waver. So she *was* frightened to stay. He had been right. 'What have you got to lose by going back to Ashbury?'

She stared at him, clearly unsure of the answer.

He moved his hands up to point to his scars. 'These are from men like the ones on their way to this island, Pru. Despite what you might think of me – and believe me, I am truly sorry for how things panned out – if there's any way at all that I can persuade you to come with me, I will. I'll agree to anything. Anything at all. You cannot stay here on this island, as pretty as it is. You need to be with your daughter. Safe.'

She stared at him silently. The seconds turned to minutes

and Jack was beginning to wonder if she would ever speak again when she nodded gently.

'I will come with you Jack, for Emma's sake. You stay here and I'll pack a suitcase and speak to my neighbour. How long do I have?'

'We're on the first boat out in the morning.'

She walked past him, stopping to glare at him one last time before walking slowly up the stairs.

Jack leaned against the wall and almost wept with relief.

THIRTY-ONE

Emma

JUNE 1940

Emma ate her toast and honey as Sam told her he had arranged for her to have an interview at the factory at ten o'clock. Excited and a little nervous, she thanked him and finished her tea before running upstairs to change into something she felt more suited to an interview.

'It's a factory, Emma. They won't expect you to be too smart,' Sam called after her.

They drove down to the factory and Sam pointed out the Itchen. 'This is Woolston,' he said as they drove through the town. 'And that' – he pointed to a vast factory which Emma took to be on the banks of the river – 'is Woolston Works, which is where we're going.'

Her confidence waned. She wasn't used to places that enormous. Hundreds of people must work there, she decided, unsure if she hadn't been a little hasty in her determination to interview with the Air Ministry.

Sam patted her hand. 'It's fine. You'll be fine. Trust yourself.'

'Are you sure?' She could hear the tell-tale wobble in her voice. 'We don't have anywhere nearly as big as this in Jersey.'

He gave her a reassuring smile. 'Just remember that everyone working inside this enormous place is wanting to do their bit for the war effort, just like you and me. They're no better than you are and you have as much right to be there as anyone else.' He turned the car towards a parking area. 'If you decide you really don't want to work there after your interview then you don't have to. We can always look for other work for you instead.'

'Yes, that's true.' His reassurances made her feel much calmer and her panic slowly receded.

'I'll come in with you to introduce you and then wait outside to drive you back to the village afterwards.'

'Thank you, I'd appreciate it.'

———

'Well, that wasn't so bad, judging by the grin on your face,' Sam said as she returned to his car. 'What's the verdict, then? Did he offer you the job?'

'He did,' Emma squealed as soon as they were inside the car and out of everyone's hearing. 'Thank you for bringing me and arranging that,' she said, grabbing hold of him and hugging him.

'Oof.' He laughed, caught off guard. 'Hey, steady on. I only made a telephone call, nothing much.'

She let go of him and giggled. 'Sorry, I didn't mean to bowl you over like that. Anyway, you brought me here and if it wasn't for you calming me down before I went in, I probably would have chickened out.'

'No, you wouldn't,' he disagreed as they settled into the MG.

'You don't know that.'

'I do. You're too determined and I'm guessing too brave to let much put you off something you want to do.'

Was she? She hoped he was right, but she wasn't altogether sure that he knew her as well as he obviously thought he did. Not wishing to disillusion him, she decided not to argue.

'Did you accept the job?'

She nodded and pursed her lips thoughtfully.

'What's the matter?' he asked before starting the engine. 'Something wrong?'

She shook her head. 'No. I was just thinking that I can't believe it was that simple. Where are we going now?'

'Back to Ashbury Village for some lunch. I think you could probably do with something to eat and drink by now,' Sam said as he pulled out of the parking lot.

She realised she was a little thirsty. 'I only want something light like a toasted teacake,' Emma said, too excited to have an appetite.

'Then that's what you'll have.' He smiled at her. 'I'm glad you're settling in here already.'

'So am I,' she said, relaxing and enjoying being with him.

'Where are we going?' she asked a while later as they entered the village.

'I thought in there might be good,' he said, pointing to a pretty, double-fronted place with 'Dolly's Tearoom' painted in dark pink across the top of the two windows. 'I've eaten here once or twice and it was pleasant enough.'

'It looks lovely to me.'

They parked and walked inside and were shown a table near to the window. Having ordered their teacakes and a pot of tea for two, Sam smiled at her. 'This is going to be a cheaper lunch than I expected,' he teased.

'I'm the one who should be buying you lunch,' Emma said. 'Not the other way around.'

Sam looked indignant. 'I've never heard such a thing, nor met a gentleman who would allow a lady to pay for their meal.'

Emma pulled a face. 'How very old-fashioned of you, Samuel Ashbury.'

'I'm pleased you're happy with the job.'

'I am – very.' It dawned on her that Sam would be leaving to return to his unit later that day. 'I've just realised that I have to work tomorrow night. I suppose I should really walk back to the manor today so that I know how long it will take me to get from there to this village in time to catch my bus to the factory.'

Sam shook his head. 'No, it's fine. I could ask Stephens to give you a lift and pick you up later? I'm sure he wouldn't mind.'

'Are you sure? I'd hate to put him out.'

Sam leaned forward. 'I'll ask him. If he does mind, I'm sure he'll tell me. Anyway, if we find you somewhere to stay in the village then you won't need to worry about the journey between the manor and the village each day, will you?'

'No.' She smiled at him. 'You're really kind, do you know that? You've been so helpful to me and all I've done is taken you away from valuable leave time with your parents and asked you to drive me somewhere.'

'It wasn't that far and anyway I've enjoyed myself. I was expecting to have a couple of very quiet days but spending time with you has been...' He took a second to think. 'Interesting.' He laughed and Emma joined in, aware that to anyone else she would have been rather trying.

'Then you have a strange way of having fun,' she teased.

The waitress brought over a tray with their order. 'Did I overhear you saying you were looking for rooms?'

'That's right,' Emma said. 'Why, do you know of any nearby?'

'I do, as a matter of fact. There's little cottage nearby that has a room available to rent.'

'Oh, thank you. I'm Emma,' she said, thinking that if she was to live in the village then she should really make some friends. 'And you are?' Emma waited for the waitress to introduce herself.

'Maisie.' She pointed out of one of the small windows. 'Can you see the little lane going up the side of the hardware store?' Emma nodded. 'It's up there. A pretty little cottage with a sweet front garden. It's a little rundown and the sisters who live there are...' She stopped to think. 'I'm not sure how to describe them.'

The owner of the café, who Emma soon discovered was Maisie's mum, joined them, resting her hands on the back of her and Sam's chairs and bending slightly so they could hear her quiet words. 'They're a little eccentric, is what my Maisie is trying to say. Tiz and Terry Healy. Salt of the earth, but a bit barmy.'

Emma bit her lower lip to stop herself laughing. She caught Sam's eye and he immediately looked away and out of the window before clearing his throat.

'Do you know them, Sam?' Emma asked.

'I think I know the ladies you're referring to. They're decent types, but I can see why you'd say they were a little eccentric.'

The owner straightened. 'You could do worse than staying with them. Tell them that Janice told you to go and see them.'

'Thank you, I'll do that.'

'Are you new to the area?' Maisie asked, the tray hanging by her side. 'We don't often have new people coming to live here in Ashbury Village. It can be a little quiet most of the time.'

'Don't put her off, love,' Janice said. 'Don't mind my daughter. It's a lovely place to live, isn't it, Captain Ashbury?'

Emma was initially surprised that the woman recognised Sam and realised that as he was from the manor house most people in the village must know who he was. 'I am new around here,' she said. 'My mother worked at the manor during the last war. She was a nurse.'

'Is that right? I wanted to be a nurse,' Janice said. 'But my parents had this place and insisted I stay and help them out.' She looked around her to check no one was listening to their conversation then leaned forward, lowering her voice again. 'I think they were frightened I might fall for one of the patients or doctors and run off with him.' She chuckled to herself.

'Chance would have been a fine thing. Ended up marrying her father.' She puffed out her cheeks as she gestured towards Maisie. 'Should have ignored my parents.'

She walked back to the kitchen looking amused by her own joke and Emma grinned at Sam. 'I think I'm going to like it here.'

'Good, I'm pleased. Right, drink up,' Sam said. 'We may as well go and speak to the sisters as soon as we're finished here.'

Emma wasn't sure what to expect, but the anticipation of starting a new life in the English countryside was exciting.

They stood across the lane from the slightly tumbledown cottage with its wisteria-covered walls in need of a fresh coat of paint and a lazy ginger cat slowly licking one of its back legs.

'What do you think?' Sam asked quietly. 'We don't have to go in if you'd rather not. I can help you find somewhere else.'

'No, it's fine.' Emma hadn't been to the village before but it wasn't that big and she doubted there would be much choice when it came to finding available lodgings. 'Let's go and knock on the door and see if someone's inside.'

They crossed over to the garden gate, which squeaked loudly when Emma pushed it open. 'Well, if anyone's in they'll have certainly heard that they have visitors.'

Sam opened his mouth to speak when something caught his attention. Emma heard a window being pushed open and followed Sam's gaze up to see a red-haired woman wearing a silk turban and holding an artist's palette and paintbrush. She smiled down at Sam and without stepping away from the window shouted over her shoulder at someone, 'Tiz, open the door, will you? There's a jolly handsome RAF pilot walking up the garden path.'

She leaned out of the window. 'My sister will be with you presently.'

Seconds later, a platinum-blonde – looking, Emma thought, like a cross between Jean Harlow and Greta Garbo – opened the door. Unlike her sister, she didn't seem very happy at all to have been disturbed.

'Yes?' she asked, giving Emma a searching look before taking a long drag from her Bakelite cigarette holder.

'Um, my name is Emma Le Riche and I was told you might have a vacant room.'

Tiz looked from Emma to Sam and didn't seem to appreciate his looks nearly as much as her sister had done.

The sound of footsteps neared, and the door was opened wider by the redhead. She stepped forward. 'Please don't mind my sister,' she said, her clipped tone friendly. 'Do come inside so we can discuss this further without the neighbours eavesdropping.'

Emma glanced up at Sam and he tilted his head, motioning for her to follow the artist.

'I'm Terry,' she said, indicating that they take a seat in the neat little living room. It was packed full of ornaments and cushions and every spare inch of wall displayed paintings that she presumed must have been done by Terry. 'You're looking for accommodation then?'

'That's right,' Emma said. 'I was offered a job at the Spitfire factory this morning and the lady at the tearoom down the road – um, Janice – suggested I might come here and speak to you about a room.'

'What do you think, Tiz?' Terry asked without taking her eyes off Sam. 'You're not married, I take it?'

'No,' Sam said. 'Emma's my cousin. My mother and her father are siblings.'

Emma opened her mouth to put him straight but realised just in time that now was not the time.

'We only have the one room,' Tiz said. 'I'll show you up now if you want to have a look. There's no point in wasting time if you decide it's not for you.'

Emma thought she might as well look at it. At least then, if she didn't like it, she could ask Sam to go with her to try and find somewhere else.

'You follow Tiz, Miss Le Riche,' Terry said. 'I'll stay down here and entertain your cousin.'

Emma noticed Tiz give her sister an unimpressed glare before leading the way back into the hall and up the stairs. 'There's only three bedrooms here and at the moment Terry's taken one over as her studio, but she can move her easel and paints back into her own bedroom easy enough.' She stopped at the top of the stairs for a breather. 'It's this way,' she said, leading Emma to a door at the front of the house, to the room where Terry had been painting when they arrived.

Emma stood just inside the door and gazed at the sun-filled room.

'What do you think?'

The faded wallpaper was covered in flowers that seemed to be pink and blue hydrangeas. A worn rug lay over most of the polished floorboards and had splatters of paint covering one corner where the newspaper she guessed Terry had placed under her easel to protect the flooring had folded back. There was an old washstand with porcelain ewer and bowl, and, unlike the room downstairs, the only ornaments in the room were two wooden-framed photographs, one on either side of a pair of brown and white dogs, their backs to each other like a pair of bookends.

'It's very nice,' Emma said, thinking that with a good clean the room could certainly be comfortable. Unable to help herself, she went and sat on the bed to test it. 'If I can afford to stay here, I would like to.'

'Oh, right?' Tiz looked a little taken aback to hear she liked it. 'Well, I'll have to check with my sister about how much rent we'll need to charge you, but you'll be given a cooked breakfast and an evening meal. We eat at six-thirty every night. And no gentlemen callers will be allowed upstairs.'

Emma could feel her face reddening. 'That won't be an issue, I can assure you.'

'I think we should go back downstairs and consult my sister. I don't think I should make decisions without her agreement.'

They rejoined Terry, who, Emma noticed, was sitting closer to Sam than she had been when they'd left the room. Sam seemed amused by something Terry had just whispered to him.

Terry mentioned the amount that she and her sister would expect Emma to pay for the room and board.

'That's fine with me. Thank you.' She smiled at Sam, happy to have sorted everything out before returning to the manor. 'How soon would I be able to move in?'

'Give us a day or two to clean the room and then you can move in to Oak Cottage.'

'Oak?' Sam asked.

Emma hadn't noticed any oaks of any kind near the place.

'Yes, centuries ago there was a beautiful wood behind here but it was cut down to build the rest of the village. Such a shame,' Terry said, shrugging one shoulder.

It was, Emma agreed. They said their goodbyes and Emma arranged to return in a few days' time.

'Happy?' Sam asked as they walked back to his MG.

'Very, and it's all down to you.' He smiled at Emma and her stomach did a little flip, taking her by surprise. Oh no, she thought, horrified. She couldn't fall for Sam now, even if the truth of her parentage meant they had never been related by blood. It would be far too awkward.

'What's the matter?' he asked as they crossed the road to his parked car.

Emma felt her face redden. Why did her cheeks have to let her down right now? She had to think quickly. 'I was thinking how little I have to pack to take to the cottage.'

Sam frowned. 'I'm sure you'll accumulate bits and bobs in time. Although,' he added, 'when the war is over, you'll most likely want to return to Jersey and won't want to be encumbered with boxes of stuff.'

He had a point but Emma liked the idea of adding a touch of her personality to her new room. She would have to wait and see what came her way. For some reason she thought of the beekeeper.

'Did you know that your mother always brought Mum and me a jar of honey whenever she came to visit us?'

Sam laughed. 'What a strange thing to think about now.'

It probably was, Emma agreed. 'I never thought about where the honey had come from. Now I've met the beekeeper I feel a touch honoured that all his hard work produced something so delicious and special to Mum and me. We always loved eating it on our toast each morning.' Her voice quavered.

Sam stopped and held her by her upper arms lightly. 'I suppose it was Mum's way of bringing some of Ashbury Manor to your mum.'

Emma liked the idea. 'I've never thought of it like that. What a sweet thing to do.' She recalled telling the beekeeper how much they had enjoyed it and wished she could have seen his face to see his reaction. She hoped he was pleased. She told Sam what had happened when she met him.

'Jack will have appreciated that, I'm sure. He's always been a solitary man and I've always sensed there was something sad about him. My father confided in me once that he had lost the woman he loved and never got over it.'

Emma was saddened to hear such a thing. 'The poor man.'

'I think it's his love of his bees, and latterly Buddy, that have kept him going.'

Emma hated to think of someone suffering in such a way and decided she would make a point of going to visit him again to try to get to know him a little.

Sam's hands fell away from her arms. 'Don't look so sad, little cous. Jack has survived this long and I know he loves living at Ashbury because he told me so when I asked him years ago why he never left.' The clock in the church tower chimed the hour and Sam frowned. 'We'd better get a move on. Mother will never forgive me if I dash back to base without spending a little time with her first.'

Emma realised how she had taken up yet more of the time he should have spent at home with his parents and smiled guiltily. 'I feel very selfish taking you from your parents so much yesterday and today. You're supposed to be relaxing and having fun with your family, not running around the countryside trying to sort out my problems.'

'You are my family and I'm happy to do whatever you need me to.' They reached the car and he opened the passenger door for her.

Emma went to climb into the car and tilted her head up to kiss his cheek just as he turned to check she was inside. Her lips grazed his and for a second neither moved. Then Emma gave a sharp intake of breath and sat down.

'I'm sorry, I didn't mean to do that.'

Sam stared at her, a bemused expression on his handsome face. 'Don't apologise.'

'No, really, that was a clumsy thing to do.'

He stared at her for a few seconds before shaking his head. 'It's fine. Don't worry about it.' Rushing to the other side of the car he leapt over the door and into his seat. 'Right, unless you want to kiss me again, I think we should hurry up and get home.'

Emma laughed, more in shock than embarrassment, and slapped his arm. 'Stop teasing me.'

'I'm not teasing you.' Sam laughed, mimicking her voice.

Relieved that once again Sam had saved the moment, Emma relaxed. She had found a job and a place to live that she instinctively knew she was going to like and also spent a fun time with her cousin. Today was turning out to be much better than she had expected.

THIRTY-TWO

Emma

JUNE 1940

Saying goodbye to Sam that afternoon was far harder than Emma had ever imagined it might be. How had he gone from being her childhood tormentor to such a fun-loving, supportive friend?

'I've asked my father to see that you are taken to and from the village until you've moved into the cottage, isn't that right, Father?' Sam said as he bid farewell to everyone.

Monty nodded. 'Yes.'

Emma watched as Sam kissed his mother's cheek and then shook his father's hand. He then took her by the shoulders and pulled a face.

She watched him step into his car and close the door. 'Well, I'll be off then. I'll see you all again on my next leave. TTFN.'

Emma forced a smile. Sam had been the best fun and she longed for him to return to the manor and for the opportunity to be able to spend time with him again. For now, though, she decided as she stood next to her aunt and uncle waving at his retreating car, she would focus on making the best of things and settling down in her new room and learning her new job so that when Sam did next come home she would be able to make him proud to see how much she had achieved.

'Come along inside, dear,' her aunt said. 'We have guests coming for dinner this evening – two very good friends – and you're to join us. I gather from Sam that you've found a room to stay in so that you're closer to your new job and you should know as many people as possible in the area, don't you think?'

'Yes, I suppose so.' Emma would have rather eaten a light supper and gone to bed with her thoughts. It had been a long and exciting day, but one that also filled her with mixed emotions. Was she ready to leave the manor? She wasn't sure. She shrugged off the conflicting thoughts. 'I don't know if I have anything suitable to wear.'

'I'll find something for you in my wardrobe,' her aunt said. 'I'll have it taken to your room. We're about the same size so I'm sure I won't have a problem finding something to suit you.'

———

Later, after Emma had taken a bath, she returned to her room to find that her aunt had kindly left a pretty green satin dress on her bed.

Having done her best with her unruly hair, she arrived in the drawing room a little later and saw a beautifully ethereal woman with the palest hair and bright, mesmerising blue eyes standing with an unattractive man who by the sounds of things had a jolly good sense of humour.

'Ahh, Emma, there you are,' her uncle said, motioning for

her to join them. 'These are our dearest friends, Lord and Lady Rivers. They don't live far from here and I believe your mother—'

'Thank you, Monty,' Jean cut in rudely.

It wasn't like her aunt to be anything other than charming, especially in company, and her reaction shocked Emma.

The pretty woman stepped forward and held out her hand. 'Please, we're Hugo and Verity,' she said. 'And it's a delight to meet you.'

A footman Emma didn't recognise entered the room. 'Lord Ashbury, there's a call for you in your study.'

'For pity's sake, Monty,' her aunt said. 'Surely you don't need to take every phone call that comes in? We have guests.'

Hugo stepped forward. 'He's a busy man, Jean. Verity and I understand. Please, Monty, don't worry about us.'

Emma saw her uncle give Lord Rivers a grateful smile but by the set look on his face she suspected that he had no intention of not taking the telephone call.

'I shan't be long. Carry on without me for now, please.'

Emma took the glass of sherry from the tray that Stephens was holding out for her. 'Thank you,' she said, noticing that he didn't look as cheerful as he had when Sam was around. She didn't blame him. Some of the joy had vanished from the manor since his departure.

'Your aunt and uncle tell me that you're Pru's daughter,' Verity said. 'I don't think I've seen your mother since, what was it, do you think, Hugo? Twenty years now?'

'Must have been 1917,' Jean said.

'Ahh, of course it must,' Verity said, her bright blue eyes

sparkling with amusement. 'I never was the best with figures. How is the darling girl?'

'I'm not sure,' Emma said, trying to control her emotions. She explained why her mother was staying behind in Jersey.

'You poor, sweet child,' Verity said. 'How frightening for you.'

'Thank you, but I'm fine. It's my mum I'm worried about.'

'I remember Pru well enough to know she's resilient. I'm sure she'll be fine.'

Emma wasn't sure how anyone could know anything of the sort but didn't like to be bad-mannered enough to share her thoughts so she listened politely as Verity and Hugo chattered about the deteriorating situation in France and what might happen to the Channel Islands, relieved when Monty rejoined them in the drawing room. His face was very pale and she hoped his call hadn't been bad news. She prayed he might change the subject to lighter matters so that she could at least try to imagine that her mother was safe somewhere.

'What's the matter, Monty?' Hugo asked, walking over to his friend. 'Bad news?'

Monty didn't reply but slowly walked over to Emma. Her mind raced and her breath became shallow as it dawned on her that he had news specifically for her.

'What is it?' She took a deep breath, trying to keep control of her rising panic. 'Please tell me it's not bad news about Mum.'

'No, dear girl,' he said.

'Emma, you're looking very pale,' her aunt said.

'Sit down, dear,' Verity suggested as she and Jean came to

stand either side of Emma and the three of them sat on the sofa.

'I'm so sorry,' Emma said. 'I thought for a moment then that you had bad news about Mum. I must be more frightened for her than I had thought.'

'Here,' her aunt said, taking her glass from her hand and holding it to her lips. 'Drink this. Stephens, please send for some hot sweet tea.' When he didn't move, she shouted, 'Immediately!'

'Maybe we ought to go,' Verity said.

Emma didn't like the idea of her aunt and uncle sitting with her for hours trying to calm her. More than anything she needed to be alone, and she assumed that she was more likely to have that chance sooner if Lord and Lady Rivers remained at the manor for dinner.

'Please don't go,' Emma said. 'Not on my account. I'll be fine.' She took another sip of the sweet liquid that she disliked so much. 'I'd rather everyone carry on as normal.' She breathed in deeply and exhaled as slowly as she could manage. 'It's not as if I can do anything to change things, is it?'

'No, dear,' Monty said. 'I'm afraid there isn't.'

Later that evening, after a tense dinner where everyone seemed determined to talk about everything other than the current situation in Europe, Lord and Lady Rivers left and her aunt went to leave the room. 'I think you should turn in now too, Emma,' she said. 'Sleep, if you can manage to. It's the best thing for you right now.'

'Thank you, Aunty Jean. I'll just take a brief stroll in the garden before turning in.'

'Good girl. I'll see you in the morning.'

Emma watched her leave and walked out of the double doors to the garden as her uncle spoke, reminding her that he was still there.

'Emma, please try not to worry about your mother, I'm sure she'll be fine,' he said, following her outside.

Confused, she turned to him. 'It's kind of you to say, but how can you be certain?'

'Please trust me on this. All will become clear soon.'

Emma hoped he was right but couldn't understand why her uncle was being so mysterious. She realised he had taken hold of her arm and was leaning heavily on it.

'Uncle Monty, you shouldn't be trying to walk if it's so painful. Let's get you back inside and I'll promise to try and not worry about Mum.' The short walk had taken a lot out of him. 'I hope Aunty Jean doesn't wake up and see you this tired.'

'You're not the only one.'

It took a few minutes to return to the house even though they hadn't gone far into the garden. Emma helped him to the first-floor landing and then let her arm slip from his back.

'I'd better go to my room,' she whispered. 'I'll see you in the morning.'

He stared at her silently for a moment. 'You know, you're brave just like your mother and … and your aunt. Your mother will be very proud of you.'

She liked to think he was right. 'Good night, Uncle.'

'Good night, dear girl.'

THIRTY-THREE

Pru

JUNE 1940

'Pru, you can't ignore me for ever,' she heard Jack say. 'We're going to have to talk about this at some point.'

She had watched the harbour as the ferry moved away, crossing St Aubin's Bay and rounding Noirmont Point, although the view was blurred by the tears in her eyes. When would she and Emma be able to return? And when they did, would their home still be there? What was going to happen to her beautiful island, she wondered, and all the people left on it?

She heard Jack trying his best to coax her to speak but she couldn't find the words to reply. Too much had happened too quickly. Her head ached to think that he had been alive all these years and she had not known. She was struggling to comprehend how Jack and her two closest friends had kept something of this magnitude from her. None of them had ever said a word. Not a single word to cause her to suspect he wasn't dead. What would they have done if she had decided on a whim to visit Ashbury Manor? She leaned on the metal

319

railing and stared down at the almost black sea as the ferry raced through it.

'It's cold out here,' Jack said. 'You should come inside and sit for a while. It's going to be at least another four hours before we dock at Weymouth.' He rested a hand on her shoulder but Pru shrugged him off.

Now that he had mentioned it though, she realised she was trembling. 'Fine, I'll come and sit but I have nothing to say to you, so please don't try to talk to me.'

They made their way inside the noisy vessel and found somewhere to sit in the busy seating area filled with sad and frightened people. How much heartache could they all endure? Pru recognised a couple of women who were talking quietly and watching her and Jack, no doubt wondering what this man must be to her. She was glad they didn't ask because she would have had no idea how to answer them.

They sat for a while without speaking but Pru could feel the heat of his leg against her own. She hated the sudden proximity to this man she had spent half her life grieving for. What a lot of wasted emotion, she mused, trying her best not to let her anger get the better of her. She was embarrassed about her reaction to seeing him again, but what had he expected?

THIRTY-FOUR

Emma

JUNE 1940

Emma packed her case, ready to leave the manor and move into Oak Cottage, and walked downstairs to say her goodbyes to her aunt and uncle.

'I do wish you wouldn't leave so soon,' her aunt said. 'You will return for Sunday lunch, or when Sam is on leave, I hope?'

Emma had already explained about the bus that ran between Ashbury Village and the factory. 'It makes more sense for me to take a room in the village, but I'd love to come back on Sunday,' she confirmed. 'I'm not sure when my day off will be, or if I'll be working nights,' she explained, 'but I'll let you know as soon as I do.'

'Good girl.' Her aunt pulled her into a hug. 'We'd love that.'

Emma returned her uncle's smile over her aunt's shoulder, happy that neither had been too upset about her decision to move out.

'You'd better ring for Stephens, Jean,' he suggested. Once her aunt had walked to the other side of the large room to take hold of the bell pull at the side of the fireplace, he pulled Emma into a hug, and whispered. 'I know you want your independence, Emma, but please don't be a stranger. You've only been here a few days but already we've become very used to your lively presence in the house and will miss it.'

Emma was touched by his comment. 'Thanks, Uncle Monty, I promise I'll be back to see you soon and often.' She saw her aunt turn and watch them. 'I'm very grateful to you both for making me so welcome here.'

Jean returned to stand by Monty and took his hand in her own. 'And we've loved having you here, Emma. It's been a joy. We will miss you terribly.'

'She's only moving to the village, dear,' Monty said.

Stephens appeared at the living room door. 'The car is ready, your lordship.'

'Thank you, Stephens.'

It was time for her to leave and now that she was about to go Emma couldn't help feeling sad that her stay at the manor had come to an end. She was torn about leaving and would have loved to spend longer at Ashbury Manor with its beautiful land and kind people, but she needed to be useful and moving to the village did make sense.

Emma smiled. 'I'll see you both very soon.'

She followed Stephens out to the car and stepped into the back seat when he opened the door for her.

'When do you begin work at the factory?' Stephens asked as he drove down the driveway.

'Tomorrow,' she said, aware she was a little more anxious about her new job than she had imagined she might be.

'I wouldn't mind flying spitfires like Master Samuel,' he said after a while.

'Then why don't you enlist?' As soon as she had asked the question Emma wondered if maybe there was a medical reason why the footman wasn't able to realise his ambition. 'I'm sorry, that came out wrong. I meant—'

'It's fine. Please don't concern yourself,' he said, turning onto the main road and accelerating. 'My father has forbidden me leaving the manor. I'm hoping conscription comes in soon, then he won't be able to stop me.'

Emma understood his father's reluctance for his son to enlist but wondered if he knew that it was only a matter of time before Stephens left anyway. 'Well, good luck when you do go off to war,' she said. 'It's frightening to think that this is happening after our parents were involved in the war that was supposed to end all wars, isn't it?' she said thoughtfully.

'I heard your mother lives in Jersey. You must miss her.'

Emma felt the familiar lump form in her throat at the thought of her mother and what she might be going through. 'I do, but I have to trust that she's safe; there's little else I can do.'

He drove on for a short while. 'You probably won't have too much time to think when you're working shifts in Southampton.'

'That's what I'm hoping.' She was banking on him being right. The thought of her mother's impossible situation and knowing Sam was flying about defending the country terrified her.

A short while later he drew up to Oak Cottage and stopped the car. Then, turning to face Emma, he leaned his arm on the back of his seat. 'I've heard people talking about these ladies.'

'Oh?' she asked, hoping that he wasn't about to share anything too shocking. It was too late for her to return to her aunt and uncle's home.

Stephens grinned at her. 'They're right characters. I've met them several times. Well, not so much as met them but come across them in shops and in the street.'

Emma grimaced. 'I hope you're not trying to tell me that I've made a terrible mistake taking a room with them.'

'Nothing like that.' He laughed. 'I do think you'll have a more interesting time staying here with them than away from it all at Ashbury Manor though.'

'You're probably right.' Movement from the house caught her eye. 'We're being watched from the upstairs window,' she said quietly out of the side of her mouth.

Stephens laughed. 'Then I'd better help you out of the motor and take your things inside for you.'

He stepped out of the driver's seat and opened her door.

'Please don't worry. I'll take my own case inside.'

'You're sure?' he asked, taking it out of the boot.

'Absolutely.' She took her bag from him and smiled. 'Thanks for the lift, Stephens. And, if I don't see you before, good luck with whatever you end up doing.'

'Thanks, Miss Le Riche.'

'Emma. Please.'

'Emma … Are you sure you're happy for me to leave you here?' he asked with a twinkle in his eye.

'Yes, thank you.' She lifted her case in one hand and taking her handbag in the other, carried them up the short tiled pathway to the front door. She didn't look up, not wishing Terry to realise she had seen her watching. 'Well, here goes,'

Emma whispered to herself, hoping she had made the right decision to come here after all.

She smoothed down her skirt and raised her hand to knock when the front door swung open and Tiz stood in front of her, holding the door in one hand and a cigarette holder and a glass of something that appeared to be whisky in the other.

The older woman's eyes followed Emma's gaze. 'Ginger beer,' she said, as if reading her thoughts. 'You didn't change your mind then,' she said, giving Emma space to enter. 'I wasn't sure if you might.'

'No,' Emma replied, embarrassed to think Tiz had picked up her brief uncertainty. She carried her case inside. 'I've been looking forward to coming here, as a matter of fact.'

Tiz sniffed as if she didn't believe a word of what Emma had just said. 'You can take your things upstairs if you wish, or maybe join us for a glass of something refreshing first. We don't stand on ceremony here at Oak Cottage.'

Emma was relieved to hear it. She had found it strangely tense living in a house where so many servants' lives revolved around the few members of the family living above stairs. Emma supposed it wouldn't have seemed odd if she had grown up there as Sam had done. She wondered how he coped now that he was in the RAF and having to look after himself. He seemed to manage perfectly well.

Tiz coughed.

'Sorry,' Emma said, realising that she had been daydreaming in the hallway. 'I think I'll go upstairs and unpack first, if you don't mind?'

'Entirely up to you.'

Emma gave what she hoped was a grateful smile and

carried her case up the stairs and into the front bedroom that she had been shown on her last visit. She closed the door behind her, lowered her case to the floor and leaned back against the door. It was good to be here. She walked over to the window and sat on the cushioned window seat, listening to the happy young voices of two girls about her age as they chatted and pushed prams along the lane. A car drove past them slowly, the male driver returning the women's waves. This was more like it, she thought. This was life happening in front of her eyes.

She unclipped her suitcase and lifting out one of her dresses, walked to the walnut wardrobe and opened the double doors. Taking a hanger from the rail, she hung up her dress. Soon all her clothes were put away and then she noticed a small bookcase filled with hardbacks and paperbacks and wondered how long it would take her to read through them all. The thought of her tiny library made her happy.

She decided to make the most of the pleasant weather and take a walk around the village before getting too settled. If she was going to live here then she wanted to become familiar with the place as soon as possible. She supposed she should speak to the sisters before going out though, so picking up a cardigan and her bag she went downstairs to see them.

'Ahh, you're here, sweetie,' Terry said, floating into the room with a long, brightly coloured silk housecoat over what looked like silk pyjamas. She seemed terribly elegant and being fairly tall, carried the look off very well. She was carrying a bunch of flowers that she might have just picked from the garden, and in her other hand was a green mottled jug. Emma was expecting her to take her time arranging the colourful blooms but instead Terry simply plonked the flowers into the jug and placed it unceremoniously on the mantelpiece.

'I keep my creative side for my paintings,' she explained, clearly amused by Emma's surprised reaction. 'Tiz can make them look pretty whenever she chooses.' She raised an arched eyebrow at Emma. 'I might be the most heavenly artist, but arranging flowers simply isn't my forte. My sister, on the other hand, can't paint for toffee but is the one responsible for making the cottage the cosy place it is.'

'I see,' Emma replied, unsure what else to say.

'All settled into your bedroom then?'

'I am, thank you.' She glanced out of the window. 'I thought I'd make the most of the fine weather and go for a stroll through the village.'

Terry followed Emma's gaze and spotted one of the local youths leaning over the low metal railings at the end of their garden and picking two of the flowers. She glowered at him and marched forward, leaning out of the window to bellow, 'Leave those dahlias alone, you little snot. Touch another and I'll tell your mother what you've done.'

His eyes widened in horror and he stood upright before sticking out his tongue and running away.

'Little beast. Why people choose to have children is beyond me.'

Emma hid her amusement at the little boy's reaction. She estimated he must be around eight or nine and either very brave or silly, she wasn't sure which. 'I'll get a move on then,' she said. 'Do you need me to pick anything up for you in one of the shops while I'm out?'

Tiz entered the room. 'Don't you worry yourself about

that.' She noticed the vase of flowers. 'I see you've been picking my damn flowers again. I do wish you'd leave that sort of thing to me. I was saving those.'

Terry glared at her sister. 'I was only trying to help.'

'I'm sure you were,' Tiz said, looking exasperated. 'Don't do it again.'

Emma had to move out of the way quickly so Terry didn't barge into her as she stormed out of the living room. 'I think she's upset,' she said as Terry flounced up the stairs to her studio, her silky coat flying out behind her.

'She isn't,' Tiz said, taking the jug off the mantelpiece and tidying up the flowers. 'She just loves to create drama when she's meant to be painting. She must be at a tricky bit, which will be why she's been wasting time picking my flowers.'

Not wishing to be caught up in their quarrel, Emma decided to get going. 'I'll see you later,' she said, hurriedly leaving the house.

It was hotter outside than she had realised on her arrival and there wasn't a cloud in the sky. She strolled to the end of Oak Cottage's pathway and looking both ways, tried to decide which way to go first. To the left were houses leading, it seemed, to a pretty church. To the right, more houses, and shops and the café where Sam had taken her to lunch. Deciding that it would be nice to look in a few shops, Emma turned right.

She knew Sam had not long finished his training and wondered what he was doing at that moment. Whatever it was, she hoped he was safe. Maybe he was enjoying the sunshine with the other pilots. She hoped so.

'Hello.'

A girl's voice snapped her out of her thoughts. She recognised her as the waitress from the café. 'Hello. Maisie, isn't it?'

The girl gave her a beaming smile and seemed delighted that Emma had remembered her. 'I'm finished for the day now. If you'd like someone to show you around then I'm more than happy to do so.'

Emma had been hoping to spend a little time quietly wandering around the village and was about to turn down Maisie's offer but noticed the girl seemed anxious for her to accept. 'That would be lovely. If you're sure you don't have anything else you should be doing.'

'Not at all.' She gave Emma a friendly smile.

Emma was relieved to have made the kindly girl happy. 'Where shall we start?'

'Let's keep going this way,' Maisie suggested, turning to walk back the way she had come towards the shops. 'I was going to suggest showing you our little library but as you're staying with the sisters, I'm sure you'll have more than enough books to keep you busy in their cottage.'

'You've been inside then?'

Maisie nodded enthusiastically. 'Only the once, but I loved it. It's such an interesting place, with all the paintings hanging over every surface in the hallway and living room, and all the furniture and ornaments. You have to wonder where it all came from.' She batted a pesky fly from her arm. 'Obviously the paintings are Terry's, but everything else probably came from the major.'

'The major?' Emma asked, intrigued.

'Their father. He had a big house about a mile away When

he died it was sold to pay off death taxes and I remember Mum saying that the sisters kept what they could of his.' She lowered her voice and leaned in closer to Emma. 'Mum told me that the night before the sisters were to move out of the big house, some of the villagers, including my mum, went there in the middle of the night to help Tiz and Terry remove ornaments and smaller pieces of furniture they wanted to keep. They were handing them out of the window. She said it was great fun and very exciting. Everything was brought back to the village and hidden in people's homes and a couple of the back rooms at the pub until after the major's house had been sold at auction. The sisters then moved into Oak Cottage and all the bits the villagers had hidden for them were returned as soon as the auctioneer and the man from the tax office had left the area.'

Emma was astounded. 'How incredible to think they got away with doing such a thing.' She couldn't imagine her mother being involved in anything like that but admired the sisters for their determination.

'My mum said it was scary for a time, but the villagers agreed that too many of them had helped take the bits and bobs for the local Justice of the Peace to bother prosecuting them all.'

'Good for them. I think I'm going to like living here very much.'

They began walking towards the shops.

'Have you always lived here?' Emma asked

'I have.' Maisie sounded embarrassed. 'But I hope to leave and find work elsewhere.'

'Why?'

Maisie's step faltered. 'Because it's dull living here. Nothing much ever happens.'

Emma understood how the girl felt – hadn't she thought the same thing about Jersey? Now she would give anything to be back there. 'Enjoy it while you can,' she said sagely, thinking about her home and friends in Jersey and how quickly everything seemed to have changed for them all.

'What do you mean?'

She realised she had frightened Maisie. 'Only that you never know when things might change. It's a pretty village and the people I've met so far seem lovely.'

'I suppose you're right.'

They stopped to look in some of the shop windows, though it turned out that neither of them had any money to spare. 'I have to keep what I have now for my rent,' Emma explained. 'I'd love a new coat for winter but I doubt my wages will be enough to let me save for one.'

'Mine is a hand-me-down from Mum,' Maisie grumbled. 'I'd love a new summer dress, even though Mum insists that the two dresses I have are fine for now.' She frowned. 'When I bring up the subject of new clothes she now says, "Don't you know there's a war on?"' Maisie shook her head. 'As if any of us could ever forget.'

'If only,' Emma said, walking on to the next shop and seeing that there was a greengrocer up ahead. 'I could do with a couple of apples,' she said, thinking of the pretty apple tree in their garden and missing the juicy fruit all of a sudden.

'Come along then, let's get some.'

Emma went straight to the barrel of apples and picked one up in each hand, breathing in the sweet scent. They smelt slightly different to the Cox's Orange Pippins they grew at home. 'I'll have these two, please,' she said, handing them to a man wearing an apron, his shirt sleeves rolled back to his elbows.

He popped them into a brown paper bag and Emma paid for them.

THIRTY-FIVE

Emma

JUNE 1940

The following morning, Emma woke with a start. Thinking about her new job instantly filled her stomach with butterflies and she felt slightly sick. She heard Tiz clashing about in the kitchen and realised she was making breakfast, though the last thing Emma felt like doing was eating. She got up and taking her towel from the end of her bed, went to the bathroom, washed and cleaned her teeth.

Ten minutes later she was downstairs seated at the small kitchen table with a bowl of porridge. Emma didn't much like porridge but did her best to eat it.

'That's right,' Tiz said. 'Get it down you otherwise come lunchtime you'll be starving and you won't want that.' She patted a sandwich wrapped in greaseproof paper and tied with a piece of string. 'I've made you a ham sandwich. There's little ham, to be honest with you, but it's better than nothing and you'll probably be glad of it by the time you eat it.'

Emma thanked her and finished her breakfast. She was about to take her bowl to the sink to wash it, but Tiz took it from her. 'Leave that with me. Nervous?' she asked as Emma went to leave the room.

'I am, a bit.' She wished she wasn't, but the thought of spending the day with strangers in such an enormous factory terrified her. 'I hope I don't mess anything up.'

'You won't. You'll be fine if you pay attention to what they tell you, and I'm sure you can do that well enough.' Tiz snatched something from the worktop. 'I forgot. This came for you in yesterday's post while you were out. Terry didn't think to check through to see if any of the mail was addressed to you.' She frowned in Emma's direction. 'I hope it's not important.'

Emma thanked her and took the envelope, hoping it was a letter from her mother. It wasn't. She realised it must be Sam's writing.

Dear Emma,

I hope you're settling in well at Oak Cottage. I wanted to wish you well for your first day at work. I imagine you might be a bit nervous but know that you'll do sterling work there once you find your feet. I'm hoping to get back home for a couple of days soon and will stop off at the factory on my way back. Maybe I'll be able to give you a lift home?

I can't help wondering if you've heard anything from Aunty Pru. I do hope so and if not that you're not worrying too much about her. I know from Mother that she is a strong lady and feel certain she'll be fine.

I'm looking forward to seeing you again and hearing all your news.

With kindest regards, your cousin, Sam

Emma folded Sam's letter and slid it back into the envelope. She noticed Tiz taking her time washing her bowl and realised she was probably waiting to hear any news.

'That was from my cousin Sam,' Emma said. 'He seems fine and is hoping to come home on leave sometime soon. Only a couple of days, but it'll be lovely to catch up with him again.'

'That's good to know. He's a good lad, that Sam. He doesn't have any of the airs and graces some youngsters who've grown up as he has display and I like him far better for it.'

So do I, thought Emma.

Tiz leaned forward and peered out of the window. 'That chauffeur bloke is parked outside. I suppose he's taking you to work on your first day?'

Emma had been hoping to catch the bus and not be driven in her uncle's Rolls Royce. She didn't want the other workers imagining she was anything other than a normal girl just like them. 'I'd better go then,' she said, slipping on her cardigan and picking up her bag. 'I'll see you later. Have a lovely day.'

She went outside. 'Why are you here?'

Stephens grimaced. 'I can see you're not pleased to see me.'

'It's nothing personal,' Emma said, explaining that she would have rather caught the bus with any other factory workers from the village. 'After all, it was the main reason I moved to live at Oak Cottage.'

'I thought you might say that,' he said, holding the door open for her before getting in the driver's seat. 'Your uncle insisted and you know I'm not exactly in a position to refuse to collect you when he's sent me here.'

'No, I suppose not.'

He drove out of the village and Emma settled back, trying to focus on the beautiful countryside.

'Nervous?'

'A little.' She couldn't wait to finish her first day, or even her first week, and hoped that by then she might have an idea about what she was doing and would have proved herself to be worth employing. She was also looking forward to making new friends and hoped that the women she was working next to were friendly.

They arrived at the factory and Stephens went to get out of the car.

'Do not open my door for me,' she said before he had a chance to do so. 'I don't need these women to get the wrong idea about me.' She spotted a small group of women chatting and cringed when one pointed to the car and the others turned to stare. 'Damn, they've seen me.'

'You'll be fine,' he said. 'Good luck.'

Emma groaned and got out of the car. She saw that the women were waiting by the entrance and wished she didn't have to pass them. Ah well, she thought nervously, there was nothing for it but to act friendly and hope for the best.

'Good morning,' she said, reaching them.

'Ooh, look,' said an older woman with a scarf tied around her hair like several of the others. 'It's Miss La-Di-Dah and she's talkin' to us.'

'It's not my car,' Emma explained.

'Nah?' the woman scoffed as her friends laughed and nudged each other. 'Whose is it then?'

Emma's mood dipped further. 'My uncle's.'

They doubled over laughing and jeering at her. 'Come to 'ave a look at how the other half live then, have yer?'

'No. I've come to do my bit for the war effort.'

One of them mimicked her and they all began laughing again.

She felt an arm slip through hers. 'Ignore the old bags,' a friendly voice said, leading Emma towards the door.

'I think they've got the wrong idea about me.' She looked at the woman and saw someone not much older than her. 'Thank you for helping me,' she said. 'I'm Emma Le Cuirot.'

'Strange name that. I'm Aida Gordon. Your first day, I suppose?'

'Yes,' Emma said, relieved she had found a friend. It was a start, she supposed.

THIRTY-SIX

Pru

JUNE 1940, WEYMOUTH

Eventually, what seemed like an eternity later, the boat docked and they were able to disembark.

'This way,' he said, insisting on carrying her case when she tried to grab it from him.

She followed him out to find a smart Rolls Royce waiting for them. 'Monty?'

'Yes,' Jack said. 'He insisted.'

She wasn't surprised. If he thought that sending his fancy car to collect her was going to calm her before she arrived at his house, he was very much mistaken.

The driver, a friendly young man called Stephens, '... opened the doors for them and whispered something to Jack as Pru got into the car.

'I'll be coming back this way in a couple of hours,' Stephens said as he drove them to the manor.

'For Emma?' Pru heard Jack ask.

'Yes. His lordship said I was to collect her, but she's not going to be happy about it.'

Pru didn't like to think of Emma being unhappy. 'Why?'

'Because she told me off for dropping her off at the factory there this morning, Madam. It was her first day and she's going to be extremely angry when she sees me waiting for her after her shift ends.'

'She has a job?' Pru couldn't hide her surprise.

'Sorry, yes, Madam. I probably shouldn't have said.'

'It's fine, please don't worry. I'm glad she's finding her way here.'

Pru felt herself calming slightly. However shocked and upset she was with Jack, Monty and Jean, it would be a relief to see her beautiful daughter again.

She sensed Jack tense next to her. 'I should probably mention that she's also moved out of the manor house.'

She could hear the reluctance in his voice to have to impart this message. 'What? Already?'

'It was her choice.'

'Seriously, Jack! Is there anything else you've kept from me?' She glared at him and saw him struggling to reply. 'Never mind. Where is she staying?'

'Stephens knows,' Jack said. 'He only just told me about Emma leaving Ashbury. He dropped her off at her new lodgings yesterday.'

'That's right, Madam,' Stephens said. 'She's staying in a room at Oak Cottage in the village. With two sisters. They're very, er … nice.'

Pru could sense an undertone but decided to wait to speak to her daughter and hear from her exactly what had happened and how she was finding her new home.

As the car drew almost silently up the long driveway, Pru

gazed out of the window waiting for the manor house to come into view. It hadn't changed at all, she thought, sighing instinctively at her happy memories of the place. Seconds later, she remembered all that had happened in the past twenty-four hours and her mood dropped. Now she had to confront Monty and Jean.

Pru entered the hallway and was greeted by Jean and Monty. She looked from one to the other and noticed their unsmiling faces. Good, she thought. At least they had the sense not to expect her to be happy to see them. 'We need to talk,' Pru said.

'We do.' Jean indicated the room to their right and Pru followed her through to a beautiful pale yellow living room that had clearly been redecorated since she had left. 'Please, take a seat.'

Pru did while Monty and Jack followed them inside and Jean rang for tea.

They sat in silence for a few seconds.

'Pru,' Jean said, her hands clasped together on her lap. 'I can imagine how you're feeling right now after—'

Furious but determined not to lose her temper as she had done with Jack, Pru interrupted her friend. 'I very much doubt you have any idea how I'm feeling right now, Jean. I'm still trying to come to terms with the discovery that the three of you chose to lie to me for twenty-two years.' She looked from one to the other of them, each of them lowering their gaze under her scrutiny. 'I've promised myself I won't lose my temper, not because I don't think each one of you deserves that but because I refuse to upset myself again like I did yesterday.' Monty and Jean looked at Jack then back at her. 'I don't want my daughter to come here and see me upset. It'll be shock enough for her that I'm here at all.'

A servant brought in the tea and Jean poured each of them a cup.

'Stephens has left to fetch Emma,' Jack said, his deep voice sending sensations through her.

Pru wanted to be angry with him for being a party to the lies and wished he didn't still have such an effect on her. Damn him, she thought angrily, taking the cup of tea that Jean was holding out for her.

'I think in the circumstances,' Jack said, 'that I should drink this and return to the folly. I don't think it's fair for Emma to find out who I am while I'm sitting here.'

'You don't want to face her?' Pru asked, surprised. Jack had never to her knowledge been cowardly before.

He stared at her. 'I want you to decide when she's to be told who I am, Pru. It's evident that matters were taken out of your hands by our decisions in the past and that can no longer happen.'

'Oh dear,' Monty said. 'I've been waiting for this.'

Pru's head whipped to her right to look at him. 'Is that right, Monty?' She narrowed her eyes at the man she had thought a trusted friend. 'What, I wonder, have you been waiting for? The time to tell me that Jack is alive and well?' She heard Jean gasp but ignored her, determined to continue. 'That not only is he alive, but he's been living here, at your home, for the past twenty years?'

'Now, Pru,' he said, clearly trying to reason with her.

She slammed her hand down onto the highly polished mahogany coffee table in front of her. 'Don't you dare "Now,

Pru" me, Monty. I thought you' – she shot a glare at Jean – 'especially you, were my friends. My trusted friends. And now I discover that the most heart-breaking thing to have happened to me – the devastating loss of the man I loved – was fiction. How could you have let me believe he was dead? How?'

'Pru, please,' Jean began.

Monty raised his hand. 'No, Jean. Pru's right. We've hurt her and I for one am sorry from the bottom of my heart.'

Pru was happy to hear him acknowledge that what they had been a party to was wrong. She noticed Jean's expression. 'You want to say something, Jean, I can tell. You may as well say it before Emma gets here.'

'I will then.' Jean took a sip of her tea and placed her cup and saucer on a table near to her. Pru noticed her hand was shaking and realised that this was also difficult for her friend. 'Firstly, I want to apologise for us all keeping Jack's presence from you. Monty's right. It probably was the wrong thing to do, but we did it with the best of intentions, I promise you that.'

Pru wanted to believe her.

'At first, Monty and I thought it was the right thing to do because to tell you would have surely added to your difficulties.'

'Difficulties?'

'Yes,' Jean said. 'Being pregnant and alone, and having to make the decision to marry my brother. If you weren't already married when Jack returned, of course we would have told you.'

'We would,' Monty agreed.

'*I* would have told you,' Jack insisted. 'I *wanted* to tell you, Pru.'

Monty tapped his walking stick on the floor. 'That was my fault, Pru. I persuaded Jack that telling you was the most selfish thing he could do and that if he loved you, he would leave you to your marriage with Peter and let him bring up Emma.'

Pru swallowed the lump in her throat. She looked at Jack and gave Monty's words some thought.

'Was I wrong to do as he suggested?' Jack asked, his face solemn.

She considered what she had just heard and shook her head, admitting that he wasn't. 'No. I can see how it made sense to you.' She sighed.

He closed his eyes for a few seconds. 'I'm relieved to hear you say that, Pru. Thank you for your understanding.' He put down his cup and saucer and stood. 'I think I should make myself scarce now. I've left Buddy for long enough. Stephens was looking after him but I think it's time I went and took him for his walk.' He stared at Pru. 'I might see you later then?'

'Maybe.'

Pru watched Jack leave the room and noticed for the first time that he had a slight limp. It occurred to her that apart from the obvious damage to his face she had no idea what other permanent damage his injuries had left him with.

'Pru,' Jean said quietly, drawing Pru's attention back from the living room door. 'I know it seems to you that we've been disloyal.'

'A little,' Pru admitted.

'I promise you that was never our intention. Whether

rightly or wrongly, our only hope was to save you from further pain. We were both shocked when Jack returned. Weren't we, Monty?'

'Jean's right. I don't think anything has shocked me as much as seeing him walking through the front door.' He looked down as if reliving the memory. 'We love you, Pru. What else would you realistically have had us do?'

Jean fiddled with the cuff of her cardigan sleeve before looking at Pru again. 'You were so fragile when you left the manor to marry Peter,' she said. 'I worried that if you discovered that Jack had returned only a month after Emma's birth, it might be too much for you to bear. Was I wrong?'

Pru gave her question serious thought. Emma's birth had been a difficult one. She had been in labour for three days and it had taken her months to recover. 'I want to argue with you,' she said, 'but I can understand why you made that decision. And maybe in time, when I feel less emotional about seeing Jack again and what's happened, I might even agree with you. But it's still too raw right now for me to think dispassionately about it just yet.'

Monty cleared his throat. 'Jack really did want to come and fight for you, Pru,' he assured her. 'Did he tell you that he went to Jersey and saw you and Peter with Emma?'

She nodded. 'He did.'

'I was terrified at the time that you might see him and be caught between the two men in your life.' He sat back in his chair and groaned.

'Are you quite well, dear?' Jean asked, leaning forward and reaching out to rest her hand on his arm.

He smiled. 'Just a bit achy, nothing too bad.'

Pru watched, wondering if all this confrontation might be a bit too much for him. She could see clearly that he wasn't as well as he had been the last time she saw him, when he visited Jersey two years previously. 'Maybe I should go up to my room and freshen up,' she suggested.

'Please wait,' Monty said. 'While Jack isn't here, I'd like to explain a little more about how it was for him.'

Pru decided to have the good grace to listen to what Monty had to tell her. She was staying in his house, after all, and maybe she did need to hear Jack's point of view. She hoped it would help her understand why he had never contacted her, or even tried to after that one secret visit. 'Go on.'

'Thank you.' He accidentally knocked his walking stick from where it was leaning against the arm of his chair and motioned for Jean to leave it when she went to retrieve it for him. 'You should know that when Jack returned to the manor he had assumed he would be reunited with you. To say he was devastated to learn you were gone would be an understatement. He barely spoke to anyone and then when he heard that his brother had died, followed shortly thereafter by his mother, he left for New York as soon as he was able to travel and we thought we might never see him again.'

'But he came back,' Pru said. 'Jack told me he's been living in the folly all these years.'

'That's right,' Monty said. 'I wrote to him in New York, Pru. I know him better than I knew my own two brothers and I was frightened that he might do something reckless. I begged him to come back to Ashbury and stay with us, to give himself time to think and heal.' His voice quavered and Pru saw how difficult it was for such a private, contained man to share this with her.

'Please, go on,' she said, needing to hear everything.

'He did eventually return to us but found it too difficult being here so persuaded me to let him move to the folly.' Monty shook his head. 'He needed solitude more than anything. So I let him make changes to the folly – adding a kitchen and a bathroom, that sort of thing – and then I suggested he take over the care of the walled garden and the bees so that he would have some purpose again.'

Jean sat forward in her chair. 'It was those bees and the creation of the jars of honey I brought with me each time I visited that kept him going for those first few years, Pru. I'm certain of it.' She gave Pru a pleading look and Pru didn't think she could take much more. 'We've all made choices that might not be right,' she said quietly, 'but ultimately none of us would ever choose to hurt the other on purpose. Don't you agree?'

Pru barely knew what to think anymore. 'I suppose so.' She stood. 'If you wouldn't mind, I think I need a little time alone to gather myself before Emma's arrival. I don't think I can take too much more emotion today.'

Jean went to stand. 'Of course, Pru. You do what you feel is right.'

Like you did, Pru thought. 'Thank you. I'll come down when I hear the car bringing Emma.'

She felt like her head had been put in a vice and squeezed for hours. Leaving the room in a daze, she went upstairs and washed her face with cold water before lying on her bed and bursting into tears.

Jean had said that this had been Emma's room until

yesterday. It had been a shock to discover that Emma was staying at a house in the village and already had a job in Southampton. Pru smiled. How typical of her daughter not to take it easy but to be so organised. She was grateful to Monty for sending his driver to collect her and bring her to the manor. She pictured Emma's face when she discovered her there.

Pru closed her eyes. She still couldn't believe Jack was alive.

THIRTY-SEVEN

Pru

JUNE 1940

Pru went down to join Jean and Monty a little later. She felt a bit calmer now she'd had time to rest and think through what they and Jack had said. She was glad when Jean simply asked her if she would like a sherry while they waited for Emma to arrive.

'How did you find your room?' Jean asked. 'A little different to sharing the attic room?'

Pru took a sip of her sherry, enjoying the sweet taste. 'Very. It's a beautiful bedroom, so bright and sunny.' She heard tyres crunching on grave and stood. 'Emma's here.'

Within seconds, Emma's voice could be heard as she hurried into the living room. 'I really must ask that Stephens —' Her voice caught in her throat when she saw Pru.

'Hello, darling,' Pru said, walking over to her statue-still daughter, whose mouth was open in shock.

'Mum?' Emma murmured, staring at her. 'How?'

Pru couldn't wait a moment longer to hug her child and opened her arms for Emma to step into them. They held each other tightly and Pru breathed in the faint smell of oil and something else that she thought might be metal. 'It's good to see you again, sweetheart.' She heard Emma breathe in deeply and knew she was taking in Pru's scent: Guerlain's L'Heure Bleue.

'I can't believe you're here.' Emma leaned back and stared at her. 'You look a bit tired but well. I'm so relieved.'

'Shall we sit down?' Pru asked, taking Emma's hand in hers and leading her to the sofa. 'I'm fine. A little stunned to be here after all these years. I only arrived a couple of hours ago.'

'You're here for good?' Emma asked.

'I am, darling. Your aunt and uncle have very kindly invited me to stay at the manor.' She looked around the room. 'I have to say it's surreal being here again for the first time in over twenty years.'

Emma frowned. 'Did Aunty Jean and Uncle Monty tell you I'm no longer staying here?'

'They did.' She could tell Emma was upset not to be here with her but didn't want her to feel badly on her account. 'I'm impressed you've found a room and already have a job. Well done, darling. You must be happy to be working.'

'I am.' She seemed unsure.

As if Jean had picked up on Emma's thoughts, she said, 'You're welcome back here anytime though, Emma, I hope you know that.'

Emma gave her a grateful smile. 'I do. Thank you. I wish I was still staying here though so I could spend time with Mum now she's here.' She scowled. 'But I've got to go to work tomorrow and can't take time off so soon after starting.'

'I think your mother needs time to settle in and recharge

her batteries anyway,' Jean suggested. 'Now she's here you'll both have plenty of time to catch up. You can see her whenever you're not working and then maybe come to stay at the weekend?'

'I like that idea,' Emma said.

Pru gave Jean a grateful smile. 'So do I.'

The drawing room door opened again and in walked Sam. 'I see you've found each other then.' He walked over to where Emma and Pru were seated.

'When did you arrive?' Monty asked. 'We didn't hear your motor.'

'Just after Emma.' He gave Emma a kiss on her cheek. 'It's good to see you again, little cousin.'

Pru studied the handsome young man and was surprised at how comfortable Emma seemed to be with him.

'Hello, Aunty Pru,' Sam said, stepping forward and giving Pru a hug.

'I would say you've grown since I last saw you, Sam,' Pru said, trying to keep the atmosphere light for Emma's sake, 'but seeing as the last time I saw you was when you were ten that's not really surprising.'

Sam laughed. It was a jolly, deep laugh and Pru instantly liked the man her nephew had become. 'I'm glad you approve.' He cocked his head in Emma's direction. 'I'm not so sure your daughter would agree.'

'Stop teasing Emma,' Jean said, giving him an adoring look. 'Leave Emma to talk with her mother.'

Pru realised her daughter was contemplating something by the thoughtful look on her face. 'What is it?'

'What happened to change your mind about leaving Jersey? Nothing's happened, has it?'

So much had happened, Pru mused. Too much to share with Emma straightaway, though she knew she had to start to let her daughter in on more of her life. 'Jack came to get me.'

She watched as Emma processed her words. 'Jack?'

Pru supposed Emma didn't know him well. 'The beekeeper.'

Emma didn't speak but kept staring at her mother as if she had said something incomprehensible. 'Pardon? Why would he go all the way to Jersey? For you?' Her eyes narrowed and Pru left Emma to work through what had happened. 'How did he persuade you when I couldn't?' Emma gasped. 'Is Jack...?' Pru felt like a fist was clutching her heart as Emma gave first her and then Jean and Monty a questioning look. She locked eyes with Pru once more. 'Is Jack my father?'

'What?' Sam gazed at Pru, shock and confusion on his face.

Pru couldn't speak for a few seconds. 'Yes, darling. He is.' She was relieved that Emma didn't withdraw her hand but kept holding hers. 'Do you mind?'

Emma shrugged. 'How can I mind? He persuaded you to come here, which is all that I've been hoping and praying would happen since I left Jersey.' She puffed out her cheeks. 'I can't quite believe that I know who my real father is now.'

It occurred to Pru that Emma probably hadn't had much contact with Jack, especially if he spent most of his time away from the house, down in the walled garden. 'I'll introduce you both properly when we've all had time to gather ourselves.'

'I'd like that.' Emma lifted Pru's hand to her lips and kissed it. 'Maybe when I come to stay here at the weekend.'

'You don't mind waiting?' Pru asked

Emma shook her head. 'No. I'm a little nervous to meet him and I think I need a couple of days to prepare myself. Maybe you might need some time to speak to him before then too.' She gave Pru's hand a gentle squeeze. 'I'm happy to know who he is though,' she said. 'Please don't think that I'm not.'

Pru marvelled at her daughter's perception.

'Does he know who I am yet?'

Pru smiled. 'He told me that as soon as you smiled at him in the walled garden that day and he saw your dimple you reminded him so much of me despite your fair hair that he knew instantly who you were.'

Emma seemed happy to hear it. 'Good. At least he won't be shocked to meet me properly for the first time this weekend.'

'I'm sure he can't wait.' Pru didn't think she could ever be happier. She was back with her daughter, who, it seemed, didn't mind learning that Jack was her father. It was all she needed to know right now. She blinked away tears to be able to see her clearly.

'I can't quite believe you're here,' Emma said, her voice barely above a whisper. 'I don't think I have the words to tell you how much this means to me.'

'I was thinking the same thing,' Pru admitted, pulling Emma into a hug and holding her tightly.

THIRTY-EIGHT

Pru

JUNE 1940

Pru had spent the morning quietly walking around the nearby gardens, aware that through a wood and across a wildflower meadow Jack was getting on with his life and probably wondering what she might do next. She wanted to see him but wasn't quite ready yet. She might understand much better why her friends and Jack had made the choices that had altered her and Jack's lives but it still took a little getting used to, so she was glad that Jack had been thoughtful enough to give her the space to come to terms with everything. Or at least attempt to do so.

She was looking forward to seeing Emma again and couldn't wait for Sam to collect her from the cottage and bring her to Ashbury for the weekend. She was anxious about introducing Emma and Jack properly and wanted them to like each other and not just for her sake. They all had a lot to get used to in their lives, she mused, bending to sniff one of Jean's pretty yellow roses.

It was lunchtime and as she had agreed to spend it with

Monty and Jean, she realised she had better hurry if she wasn't going to keep them waiting.

———

Pru lowered her spoon onto the plate under the empty soup bowl. 'It was incredibly sad watching islanders queuing up for the boats,' she said when Jean asked her what it had been like to leave the island. 'It wasn't so hard for me because now that Maman is no longer with us and Emma was here I didn't have the same dreadful fear of having to leave loved ones behind.'

'What about the guesthouse?' Monty asked. 'Do you have someone looking after it?'

Pru shrugged. 'Of sorts. My closest neighbour promised to keep an eye on the place, but as we have no idea what the Germans intend doing with the vacant properties, or how long they will end up being on the island, I have to trust that it will still be there when I return and all the things I couldn't bring in my single suitcase are still intact. I doubt it somehow, but it's the choice I made and I know I'd rather be where I am right now.'

'Things can be replaced though, can't they?' Monty said thoughtfully.

Pru agreed, mostly. Unfortunately, it was the sentimental items from her parents, such as their letters, photographs and so many memories caught up in little gifts they had given her over the years, that she wouldn't be able to replace if the house was looted. She had managed to bring a few baby photos of Emma, her favourite photos of herself and Peter and some of her parents and brother, but not very much at all in the one case she had been allowed to travel with, since she needed to be practical and bring clothes and her most important personal papers. She closed her eyes to block out the thought.

'It must have been devastating for people to leave loved ones,' Sam said.

Pru sighed heavily. 'Quite a few of the men, especially farmers, were unable to leave and had to be parted from their wives and children, although I think the most frightened must be mothers having to leave elderly parents so they could be evacuated with their children. And then there were those with pets. So many were taking them to be euthanised before leaving.' She covered her eyes momentarily. 'I was one of the luckier ones, not having to make difficult choices.'

'You've had such a dreadful few days,' Jean said quietly. 'And after everything we did to you ... I'm not quite sure how you're holding up right now.'

'It has knocked me a bit,' Pru admitted. 'But I am with Emma here and we're both safe and that's all that matters.' She saw the strain on Jean's face and realised that as much as she had been furious with her friend, Jean had done what she thought best – just as Pru had when she decided to marry Peter and unintentionally broke Jack's heart. 'You did what you thought was right, Jean. I can't hold that against you; I realise that now.'

Jean gave a sob and lifted up her napkin to dab at her eyes. 'I'm sorry.' She gulped. 'I'm not the one who has suffered. I have no right to cry like this.'

Pru shook her head. 'Please don't, Jean. I will be fine and we'll all find our way through this strange situation. There is too much horror going on in Europe at the moment and we need to be kind to each other, nothing else.'

'Thank you,' Jean said with a sniff. 'You're very generous to say that.'

There was a brief silence and everyone focused on the food in front of them.

'I suppose you've found the manor rather different,' Sam said.

Pru was grateful to him for changing the subject to a less emotional topic. 'It's comforting to see the west wing returned to its former glory,' she said, thinking back to the terrible fire. 'I'm looking forward to taking a few walks and familiarising myself with the place again.' She noticed Jean looking concerned. 'Everything is so much prettier now that the rooms are back to being used for their original purpose.'

'I forget you've never seen the house as it was intended,' Monty said, giving an approving nod when the footman came to remove the used crockery. 'I'm sure Jean will enjoy giving you a guided tour of the place, won't you, dear?'

'Sorry? Yes, of course.'

'So, Sam,' Pru said, wanting to divert attention from herself. 'How are you finding the flying? Is the RAF all that you imagined it would be?'

Sam's face lit up. 'I'm loving every second, Aunt Pru. Things are getting busier now for us, which is good. I'm looking forward to being useful and putting all my training into action.'

Pru listened as her handsome nephew spoke. She hadn't failed to notice the way his face had lit up when Emma addressed him during her visit the other day, and thinking back to how her daughter had reacted to him, Pru realised that the two youngsters had feelings for each other. Her heart sank. She loved Sam, but she adored her daughter. Emma was clever and sociable but her life in Jersey had been very protected, unlike Sam, who had been sent to boarding school and learnt to fend for himself from the age of seven. She hated to think that he might end up breaking Emma's heart as Jack had broken hers. If only he hadn't become a pilot.

'How did you manage to get permission to come back so soon?' Jean asked her son, interrupting Pru's musings.

'Compassionate leave,' he said. 'I told him that my aunt had been rescued from the Channel Islands before it fell.' He looked at Pru. 'I'm sorry, I'm supposing that it will, although I probably shouldn't say such a thing in front of you.'

'It's fine,' she said. 'I have a horrible feeling you're right.'

'Shall we go for that tour of the house, Jean?' Pru suggested when they finished eating.

'I'd like that.' She turned to Sam. 'We'll see you later when you bring Emma back. Don't be too long though, I'm sure she'll be hoping to spend time with her mother.'

'Thanks for fetching her, Sam,' Pru said, sensing he was looking forward to seeing her daughter almost as much as she had been. 'Shall we go now?' She smiled at Monty. 'I feel a little badly taking Jean off and leaving you all alone.'

Monty shook his head. 'Don't. I'm happy to sit here enjoying one of my cigars and quietly contemplating life.'

'Come along, Pru,' Jean said, pulling a face at her husband. 'I've never known Monty to do anything quietly, have you?'

Pru admitted that she hadn't and walked over to her friend and linked arms with her. 'Where shall we begin?'

Jean nudged her. 'I know just the place.'

They went out to the hall.

'Wasn't the drawing room a ward when we worked here?' Pru asked, trying to picture it as it had been without the comfortable sofas and elegant soft furnishings.

'That's right.'

They crossed to the double doors that Pru remembered as the entry to Ward Two and walked in. Pru stood just inside the room and stared around her. Where once there had been plain curtains, now hung heavy velvet material. Where the patients' beds, their visitor chairs and the screens had been, now had nothing apart from polished flooring lit by the many wall sconces and three chandeliers, an enormous one in the middle of the rectangular room and two smaller ones on either side of it.

'This room seems so much bigger.'

Jean looked around her thoughtfully. 'I always thought it seemed bigger with the beds and paraphernalia inside.'

Pru gazed to the end of the room on the right where Monty's bed had been and pictured him lying there, his cheeky retorts and Jean's shyness around him. 'Monty was over there, wasn't he?'

'He was. Those were such...' She hesitated. 'I want to say special days, but so many terrible things happened that it would seem wrong to describe it that way.'

Pru understood Jean's sentiment. 'And the young private

whose bed was next to Monty's,' she said. 'I felt sorry for him not having any visitors – until he started the fire that caused so much damage and killed dear, sweet Milly.'

Sadness swept through her as she thought of her lovely friend who had already suffered so much in her young life by the time she and Jean had met her. 'I think of her sometimes,' she admitted. 'I wonder what sort of life she might have enjoyed if that young chap hadn't ended her life so tragically.'

'So do I.'

They gazed silently into the room, Pru not seeing it as it was now but as she remembered it.

She suddenly felt the heat from Jean's hands as she gently rubbed Pru's upper arms. 'Let's go somewhere else. I think we've been here long enough.'

Pru was happy to stay and try to recall more. It had been such a strange time during the last war, but had also been her first taste of freedom, and passion.

'Where to now?' she asked trying to sound a little playful.

'You'll have to wait and see.' Jean grinned at her. 'Come along.'

Jean left the room and Pru followed, giving the ballroom one last glance before closing the door and hurrying down the corridor to catch up with her friend.

She noticed Jean's footsteps slow slightly as they neared a cupboard door and Pru's heart raced as memories flooded back. 'The sluice room.'

'Do you want to look inside?' Jean asked. 'We use it as a boot room now, but it used to be the sluice room back then.'

'Yes, please.' Pru took hold of the handle and turned, holding her breath as she pushed the door open and saw the small window and the racks either side of the room that had once held pots and bedpans. This was where Jack had asked her out to dinner that first time. She had loved him so much. She closed her eyes, glad that Jean was standing behind her and couldn't see how deeply affected she was by being there. It might be used for different things now but the atmosphere was still the same. She breathed in, happy there was still a slight hint of the smell she found so familiar.

Pru wrapped her arms around herself. 'I'm sorry, Jean.'

'What for?'

She seemed genuinely surprised, Pru realised. 'For being insensitive. You've lost Peter and I'm spending my time upset about Jack and all that happened between us.'

Jean wrapped her arms around Pru and hugged her before letting go and smiling at her. 'You've been through an awful lot these past few months,' she said. 'I'm the one who should be apologising, not you.'

Pru laughed. 'What a pair we are.' She was relieved that the tension between them had evaporated as quickly as it had appeared.

'A pair of what exactly?' Jean grinned, leading Pru out of the room and closing the door.

'I don't know...' Pru racked her mind for something amusing. 'Nitwits.'

Jean laughed loudly. 'Hah, that's typical of you. Nitwits.' She giggled again. 'Isn't that what Matron called us once?'

Pru thought back and realised that Jean was right. 'Yes, she did.' She frowned. 'I wonder whatever happened to the old bat?'

'Went to live with a cousin a few years after the war, or so Monty told me. Though how he knew, I've no idea.'

'I'm sure Monty knows everyone.' Or he always seemed to, Pru thought.

Jean took her to a few more of the rooms. 'Shall we go to the attic where we shared a room with Milly now, or wait until another day?'

Pru didn't fancy going back to where they had spent so many happy times with their friend. She suspected that if she did see it tonight then her sleep would be filled with dreams of Milly and she wasn't ready for that, not yet. 'Maybe another time.'

'Yes, I agree.' Jean linked arms with her again. 'We could probably both do with a drink. Shall we go and see what Monty's up to?'

'Probably on his second cigar by now, don't you think?' Pru had no idea but had noticed the look of delight on his face when they had decided to leave him and look around the house.

'He'd better not be,' Jean said. She leaned in slightly closer to Pru despite them being alone. 'He's not as well as he'd like everyone to believe,' she confided. 'It's his heart. But typically Monty won't take any notice.'

'Has his doctor told him to cut down on the cigars?'

Jean rolled her eyes. 'Supposedly. He's only smoking one a day now,' she said, 'but it's the size of the three that he used to smoke, so he's not really doing what he's told.'

Pru couldn't help feeling amused at her old friend. 'He's always been such a character, Jean. I'm so glad that you two were married.'

They reached the drawing room just as Pru heard the tyres of Sam's sports car crunching on the gravel driveway. 'The children are back,' she said happily. 'I'm looking forward to spending the weekend with Emma.'

'I'm sure you are,' Jean said. 'I'll give you some time alone with her. We'll continue with our tour of the manor house another time?'

'That would be wonderful.'

'Now, I'll leave you to go and see your lovely daughter. You must have so much to talk about. I've put you both in the same bedroom. That way you can chat with each other to your hearts' content. I do hope that's okay.'

'Thank you, Jean,' Pru said, touched by her friend's thoughtfulness. 'That's such a kind thing to do.'

That night, after she and Emma had bathed and were lying in their beds, Pru thought how grateful she was to be with her daughter once again.

'Has it been really horrible for you, Mum?' Emma asked into the darkness.

'A little,' she admitted, not wishing to go into detail.

'Do you mind telling me a little about how it was?' she asked. 'I don't know what's worse,' she said, her voice low and emotional, 'having to leave your home and friends behind with nothing more than a suitcase or staying on the islands and having to face the unknown. It's incredibly frightening, all this, don't you think?'

Pru did. 'It is, darling. We're living in uncertain times, but we must stay strong and remember we're luckier than most evacuees. At least we have relatives who have offered us somewhere safe to stay. And most of all, I'm grateful that we're back together again. I don't know how I would have coped if I hadn't been able to leave.'

Pru cleared her throat to stop herself from crying. The thought of having to spend heaven knows how long apart from her daughter was too much to cope with. And suddenly she realised that it if hadn't been for Jack it might have happened. 'That didn't happen, thankfully and we mustn't torment ourselves with what ifs.' She had done that for far too long in her life already, she thought.

'I agree.'

Pru heard the wobble in her daughter's voice and got out of bed, wanting to comfort her. 'Move over,' she said, lifting the sheets and blanket up on one side of her daughter's bed and sliding in next to her. Pru rested her arm on one of the pillows and felt as if all was well in her world when her daughter rested her head on it and snuggled in beside her.

'It's good to be with you again, Mum,' Emma said, sniffing.

'It's perfectly understandable if you want to cry, darling,' Pru soothed as Emma's tears dampened her chest. 'Everything will be fine. You mustn't worry.'

She knew from experience that she had no idea how things would be, but right now, she had more than enough to be thankful for.

THIRTY-NINE

Pru

JUNE 1940

Pru woke just before five in the morning. It was a treat to slowly come round after a proper night's sleep and lie in the peaceful bedroom, alone with her thoughts for a while. The previous few days had been exhausting and it was a joy to know that she was back together with her darling daughter.

She stretched languorously and turned on her side to watch Emma's sweet face as she slept. Pru didn't want to disturb her and so got out of bed, walking over to the window and peeking through a tiny gap in the curtains. The sky was lightening and it was almost sunrise so she wrote a note letting Emma know she had gone for a walk and would see her at breakfast and then washed and dressed before creeping out of their bedroom.

As Pru descended the main stairs, she heard distant voices emanating from the kitchen and other rooms where servants were preparing the house for the family to start their day. Pru knew that if she left by the front door one of the servants might spot her and also that her footsteps would be heard on the

364

gravel, so she turned right at the bottom of the stairs and carrying her shoes in her hands, ran along the corridor in her stockinged feet. She was reminded of the times she had run down this same corridor on her way to meet Jack all those years before and for a few seconds allowed herself to imagine she was doing the same thing once again.

She reached the side door, unlocked it and, after a little bit of a struggle, unbolted it at the top. Finally she was outside. She slipped her feet into her shoes and ran along the familiar pathway into the woods, feeling free for the first time in months. She stopped when she reached the pine trees and breathed in deeply, relishing the delicious scent she recognised and loved so much. It reminded her of the large pine trees near their home in Jersey.

As she strolled out of the wood, Pru slowed to gaze at the long meadow leading down to the green expanse in front of her where, in the distance on a slight incline, stood the circular folly where she and Jack had first made love. Her heart ached to think how much they had missed in the past twenty-two years. Pru gazed longingly at the low morning mist hanging in the dip between where she stood and the folly, the diffused light making the pretty building remind her of a princess's castle from a fairy tale. Her mind drifted back to the years of the Great War when so much had seemed possible and the urgency of living had forced her to make decisions she would have never imagined before.

She took a deep breath and, not wishing to miss the chance of taking this walk alone, began making her way down the meadow towards the folly. She passed the walled garden to the right where Jack kept his hives. She couldn't decide whether to keep going to the folly or look at the walled garden first. She had imagined coming here so many times over the years, hoping to take a peek in the windows, willing nothing to have changed inside. It was a silly notion, she decided, losing her nerve, and deciding to look around the walled garden instead.

She wasn't ready to have her delicious memories of her and Jack's precious hours together in the circular room taken from her just yet. How different must it be now that Jack had moved in permanently, she wondered? She would wait until later in the day when there was no chance of disturbing him in his private space but in the meantime she stopped and stared at the folly once more, thinking back to the happiest time in her life when her darling Emma had been conceived. She realised she was crying and tried to snap herself out of her sense of sadness. There was no point in raking over old memories, not if she wanted to enjoy being here with her friends and Emma.

Enough. She turned away and made her way through the long grass speckled with daisies, buttercups, poppies and cornflowers, and stopped to pick several of them on her way to the gate into the walled garden.

She stepped through the gate and something caught her eye – Jack. He was in his beekeeper outfit and didn't seem to have noticed her, so intently was he focusing on his work. She watched from the gate, not wishing to disturb him as he replaced what seemed to be the lid on one of the hives. Then, he picked up a can with smoke coming from it and walked over to another hive.

She enjoyed seeing him like this, when he was completely at ease and lost in what he loved doing. Suddenly he froze and Pru tensed as he stood upright and slowly turned to face her.

She wished he didn't have that strange hat with the netting over his face because she couldn't tell if he was annoyed and whether she should leave straightaway. He didn't move but seemed to be looking in her direction.

'Despite that netting across your face, I would have recognised you anywhere,' she said.

They stared at each other in silence and she wasn't sure what to do next. Then, after bending to place the smoking can on the stony pathway, he straightened up and began to remove the strange hat.

Pru barely breathed as the netting gradually inched up to uncover his face. Finally, it was gone and she stared at the face of the man she had dreamt about and longed for.

'You never told me what they did to you when you were captured and taken to that chateau,' she said, looking at the crisscross of scars on one side of his face. Staring at him now that she was not in shock – as she had been, seeing him standing so unexpectedly on her doorstep that day – she was able to take in his beautiful mouth and once perfect lips and how they were now pulled down on one side. She hated to think how much he had suffered. If she hadn't been so stunned and furious with him when he came to fetch her in Jersey and then refused to look at him on the journey to the manor, she might have noticed the deep sadness in his eyes.

He swallowed. 'Not pretty, is it?'

The sound of his deep, melodic voice sent the same shockwaves through her as it had done over twenty years before. 'It's still you though, Jack, and that's all that matters to me. And it's all that will matter to our daughter.'

'We need to talk, don't we?'

'We do.'

'Would you like to stay here or go to the folly? No one will disturb us there.'

Countless times over the years she had imagined something similar happening but each time she had woken and it had all been a dream.

'Yes, that's a good idea.'

They reached the folly steps and as he strode up them she could see he was trying to hide his slight limp. He opened the door and Pru walked in and sat on the sofa. It was a newer sofa but still set facing the small fireplace she recalled from when she had last been in here. He closed the door and removed the rest of his beekeeper outfit.

Eventually, Jack turned to face her and she followed his gaze as he looked from the sofa to a chair by the window, obviously trying to decide which one he should sit on.

Pru patted the cushion next to her. 'Sit here, Jack.'

A pained expression crossed his face and she wasn't sure why he wouldn't just do as she asked. Then it dawned on her that if he sat next to her, his damaged right side would be closest to her and that maybe it bothered him. Without asking, she moved to the other side of the sofa and pulled her feet up under herself. 'Please. Sit down.'

He did as she asked. They studied each other silently.

'I'm not the same man you knew back in 1917,' he said eventually.

He thought she wouldn't love him? Was that what he was

insinuating? She felt indignant that he thought she was so superficial as to let his scars change anything that might be between them.

'And I'm not that naïve young girl. We've both been through a lot, Jack.' She raised her hand to touch his right cheek but he grabbed her wrist before she managed to and lowered her arm.

'Don't do that.'

'Does it hurt?' She didn't imagine that it would, not now that the scars were faded and old.

'No.'

'Then why not?'

He went to stand, but she took hold of his shirt and held on to it. 'Don't go, Jack.' He stilled. 'Talk to me. I need this, even if you don't. I've waited over twenty years to speak to you again and I'm not letting you leave me without giving me some answers. What happened to you?'

'What happened? So much…'

She listened as he told her about being captured and held with Corporal Falkner, who had been killed in front of him, and felt any residual anger at him dissipating completely as he spoke. How could anyone think straight after experiencing such horrors?

When he had finished, she took his hand in hers. 'Jack, I need to bring Emma here to meet you. Properly. Are you happy for me to do that today?'

'I've been waiting twenty-two years to meet my daughter, Pru. You can bring her as soon as you like.'

They stared at each other for a moment and then Jack put his arm around her and drew her to him. Pru rested her head against his chest and breathed in his scent, once so familiar to her. She hoped this wasn't a dream because to wake up from this would be too cruel. 'Jack?' she whispered eventually.

'Yes?'

'I just needed to say your name,' she admitted. 'And to hear your voice again.'

He lowered his head and after a second's hesitation pressed his lips against hers and kissed her. Pru went to kiss him back but thought of Peter and Emma and emotions she hadn't expected rushed through her, overwhelming her.

'I'm sorry, I can't do this.' She stood. 'I … I need to think.' She hated herself for causing him pain but needed to get away.

FORTY

Pru

JUNE 1940

Pru ran down the steps from the folly, kicked off her shoes and picked them up to run back to the house. She reached the woods and, unable to catch her breath, slumped down against the trunk of a pine tree. Bringing her knees up and wrapping her arms around them, she dropped her chin onto them and sobbed for all that she and Jack might have had.

Was this how it was going to be now? Was she going to feel guilty towards Peter? After all, it was his unexpected death that had brought her back here. That and the war, she reminded herself. If he was still alive, she would be with him in Jersey, not here having intimate moments with the man she had once loved most in the world.

She felt movement by her face and gave a start. Opening her eyes, Pru saw a handkerchief in front of her. She looked up and saw Sam, his face distraught.

'Aunt Pru? Are you unwell?'

She shook her head and took the handkerchief from him. 'Th-thank you.' She wiped her eyes and blew her nose. 'I must look wretched,' she said, trying to sound less broken than she felt.

He crouched down next to her. 'You look fine. Has something happened?' He tensed. 'It's not Emma, is it?'

She lifted her hand. 'No, Emma's fine,' she soothed, hating to think she had caused him to panic.

'You've heard about the islands being bombed then.'

Bombed? Pru stared up at him horror-struck. 'What do you mean? When?'

Sam cringed. 'Damn. My father will kill me for frightening you like this.'

'Never mind Monty, Sam. Tell me what's happened.'

'Jersey and Guernsey were bombed yesterday,' he said apologetically. 'I'm not sure about the other islands.'

'Was anyone hurt? Killed?' she asked, terrified to hear the answer and aware that if Jack hadn't almost forced her to leave the island she could be one of the bombing victims. She shuddered.

'Yes. I'm afraid so.'

She covered her face with her hands, trying to take in this shocking news.

'Is it something I can help you with?' Sam asked gently.

She shook her head. 'It isn't but thank you for asking.' He was the sweetest boy. She looked up at him and wondered what would become of him. He was so young, so good and so brave. She prayed that he would be fine and wished he hadn't chosen to become a pilot, like Jack. She couldn't bear it if something happened to Sam too. 'You're a good boy, Sam.'

'Would you like to go back to the house?'

'I would.'

'Have you eaten breakfast yet?'

'Not yet.'

She didn't feel hungry and the last thing she wanted was to sit calmly in the dining room and force herself to eat anything, but she realised he wasn't sure what to do and, not wanting him to worry, she agreed to go inside with him. 'I think I've had enough fresh air for the morning.'

He didn't smile as she had hoped he would and Pru could see he was still anxious for her. 'I'm fine, Sam. I just needed a moment outside, that's all.' He didn't need to know about her encounter with Jack. She wished now that she hadn't been so quick to run off and had given herself time to calm down before doing so. After all, she did have a lot to thank him for, bringing her here as he had.

Sam held out his arm and Pru took it and rose to her feet. She slipped her mucky feet into her shoes and smoothed down her skirt and ran her fingers through her hair, trying her best to look presentable before returning to the house.

'You've been through a lot recently, Aunt Pru,' he said. 'I'm not surprised you're feeling rather emotional. To be honest, I think most people are.'

She was happy to let him think her distress had been caused only by the German army invading the Channel Islands and her hurried evacuation, which, on reflection, she realised could have added to her upset.

They went inside to the dining room but before they got there she stopped at the bottom of the stairs. 'I think I'd better go to my room to freshen up a bit,' she said, needing to find Emma and speak to her about Jack.

She ran upstairs and quietly opened their bedroom door in case her daughter was still asleep.

'Mum?' Emma asked, buttoning up the front of her dress. She covered her mouth when she saw Pru's face. 'Whatever's happened?' She rushed over to Pru and steered her to the bed. 'Here, you'd better sit down.' She bent to take a better look at Pru, who wished she had thought to visit the bathroom first to splash some cold water onto her face.

'I'm fine, love,' Pru said, trying her best to reassure Emma. 'Take a seat, will you? I have something I need to speak to you about.' Emma looked terrified. 'It's fine,' Pru soothed. 'Nothing to worry about.' That wasn't quite true, she realised, but she didn't want to upset Emma as she had already done Jack and then poor Sam.

'Would you like me to fetch you a glass of water, Mum?'

'No, sweetheart. I just want you to listen while I tell you everything I've been withholding from you, then you can ask me anything you like.'

Pru had no idea where to begin, but not wishing to waste any more time or worry Emma, she simply started from the beginning – from the moment she first met Captain Jack Garland. She was grateful to her daughter for sitting patiently and not saying a word as she listened to everything Pru had to share with her.

'So, there you have it,' Pru said finally. 'I'm sorry I let you worry about me and that I never told you everything about Jack before, but as I said, your father made me promise not to say anything while he was alive.'

'I know, Mum,' Emma said, sighing heavily. 'But why not tell me about Jack after Dad died?'

Pru closed her eyes tightly. She had thought she was doing the right thing at the time, but maybe she had been wrong? 'I believed Jack was dead and I worried that telling you about your real father and not being able to give you any resolution about what had happened to him might be too much for you to cope with in your grief.'

'I still can't quite come to terms that my father is the beekeeper. It's incredible.'

'Incredible in a good way?' Pru asked, narrowing her eyes and hoping that her daughter would say yes.

'Yes.' Emma shrugged. 'I liked him. But when I met him, he was wearing that strange hat with the netting so I still don't know what he looks like.'

Pru wanted to prepare her daughter. 'When I knew him, he was very handsome.' She smiled at the memory of the tall, handsome American pilot she had fallen head over heels in love with. 'He's still very handsome to me,' she admitted. Resting a hand lightly on Emma's knee, she added, 'However, he is very scarred now on the right side of his face. He suffered horribly in the war.'

Emma's face fell. 'Poor man.'

'It's fine; you'll forget about his face when you start speaking with him,' she said, certain Emma would never hurt Jack by showing any shock when she did meet him properly.

FORTY-ONE

Jack

JUNE 1940

J ack watched Pru run off and wished he could go after her.

Buddy bounded into the room and nuzzled Jack's leg. 'Where've you been, boy? Out trying to catch poor rabbits again?' He brushed dust from Buddy's black fur. Getting a dog was the one stipulation Monty had insisted upon when agreeing to let Jack live in the folly, and Buddy was that first dog's grandson. Jack and his dogs had been perfectly happy on the estate over the years with few people to bother them, his only visitors Monty and Sam – when he was younger and home from boarding school – coming to the walled garden to watch as he worked on his hives or harvested the honeycombs.

His dogs and his bees. If anyone would have told him when he was younger how much enjoyment he would have from his years as an apiarist, he would have thought them delusional. But he knew that his bees had saved him from himself and from the depression brought on by losing Pru and then the trauma of his final time in captivity.

376

The Beekeeper's War

Seeing Pru that time he had travelled to Jersey, and how she had made a new life for herself, one that didn't include him, he had wanted his world to end. And it had, in a way.

If only he had managed to escape a few months earlier, he thought, still haunted by the timing of his return. He would have been the one to marry her and bring up their child. Jack closed his eyes miserably; their lives would have been so different.

It was all his fault.

Jack sighed. Pru. She was still the most beautiful girl he had ever laid eyes on and he knew that he still loved her with all his heart. He shouldn't have tried to kiss her, and he wished now that he hadn't. He would have to take things one step at a time, but he needed her to know he had been serious about marrying her back in 1917 before everything went pear-shaped.

Jack decided he needed to go to the house to speak to Pru and Emma.

FORTY-TWO

Pru
———

JUNE 1940

'**G**ood morning, ladies,' Monty said as Pru accompanied a silent Emma into the dining room. 'Please sit wherever you wish.'

Pru realised Sam was watching her intently and managed a brief, tight smile in his direction.

'Did you both sleep well?' Sam asked, as if he hadn't witnessed her sobbing earlier. Pru was grateful to him for his discretion and returned his smile. She saw him look at Emma.

'Yes, thank you,' Emma said eventually.

Pru waited as she was served scrambled egg and bacon and then watched as Emma was given the same. Aware that Jean was watching her from one end of the table Pru tried to act as if she was fine. They were served cups of tea and she wondered how she was going to eat and drink anything, feeling as drained as she did.

She felt Emma's cool, trembling hand on her own.

'Are you all right, Pru?' Jean asked, looking a little nervous, Pru thought. She understood why. They had seemed to make

378

up when Jean was showing her around the manor and she suspected her friend was anxious that she had woken up feeling upset with her and Monty still.

'I'm a little at sixes and sevens,' she admitted. 'I will be fine but so much has happened in the past few days that I think it's going to take me longer to come to terms with it all than I imagined.'

Jean's hand clutched at the neck of her blouse. 'I presume you've spoken to Emma about everything?'

'I have.'

Jean gave a tight smile. 'I know this is all very unsettling for you but I promise you Monty persuaded Jack because he didn't want you to feel conflicted, and, if I'm honest, neither did I.' Jean looked past her and Pru assumed one of the footmen had entered the room with more food. 'And Monty thought that if you saw Jack's injuries, being a nurse and someone who was in love with him,' Jean added, her voice tight, 'he suspected you would feel torn and want to nurse him. Jack agreed that it wouldn't be fair to put you in that terrible position. Isn't that right, Jack?'

Pru stiffened. She hadn't expected Jack to come to the house. Not yet, at least.

'It is, Pru,' he said, his voice quiet. Sam rose and pulled back a chair for him. She watched him as he walked around the table and sat next to Sam.

'I hope you don't mind me coming here now?'

Pru realised Jack was asking her and not her hosts. 'It's fine. I've told Emma everything so there's no need to hold back.' We may as well get everything out in the open, she thought, exhausted.

'Thank you.' His eyes moved and settled on Emma for a short while. 'Hello again, Emma.'

'Hello...' She hesitated and Pru suspected Emma wasn't sure how to address him. 'Jack.'

Jack looked Pru in the eyes again. 'Jean's right,' he said. 'I'd seen for myself how happy you were. If you'd heard I was still alive and living here, would you have wanted to see me?'

She could hear the hope in his voice and knew she must be honest. 'I ... Yes,' she admitted. 'But only to know you were safe and well.'

'Then I'm relieved you didn't.' He frowned. 'As much as I would have wanted you to, I was broken both spiritually and physically. These scars on my face aren't the only damage they did to me.' He raised his hands for her to see the damage inflicted on them.

Pru winced and felt Emma stiffen. 'I'm so sorry, Jack.' She couldn't bear to think how Providence had played such a cruel joke on them, for him to find her only when she was already married to Peter. 'It could have all been so different,' she whispered, desperate not to cry but unable to help herself. She felt as if she was mourning the future they had dreamt of – all over again. She felt Emma's hand take hers. 'I'm sorry darling. You know I loved your father, but...'

'It's fine, Mum,' Emma soothed, one hand on Pru's shoulder and the other on her arm.

'Please don't cry,' Jack pleaded. 'I never meant for this to happen.'

'None of us did,' Jean said, and Pru couldn't miss the sadness in her friend's voice.

'Maybe it was meant to be,' Jack said, although she couldn't think why. 'I'm fine now and you were married to a kind, decent man by the sound of things.'

Pru sniffed. 'I was.'

'And we've found each other now, haven't we?'

Pru wasn't sure what that might mean for them both but nodded. 'We have.'

They all sat in silence until Emma spoke. 'Mum, you haven't touched your food.'

Pru wiped her eyes with the back of her hand. 'I need a handkerchief.' She sniffed.

Sam pulled one from his jacket pocket and reaching across the table, handed it to her. 'Here you go, Aunty Pru.'

'Thank you.' She blew her nose and studied the sad expressions of those closest to her. 'I'm sorry. I don't mean to cry. I think I'm probably a little overwhelmed.'

Emma patted her arm. 'Mum, you and Jack have over twenty years to catch up on. Maybe the two of you should go and talk privately without the rest of us present.'

Pru looked at her sensitive, thoughtful daughter and knew that whatever choices they had all made they were at least the best ones where Emma was concerned. The thought calmed her slightly.

Jack stood. 'I think that's a wonderful idea.'

'Mum?'

'You really don't mind?' Pru asked Emma guiltily. 'We were supposed to be spending the weekend together.'

'I'm fine, Mum. We can see each other every weekend from now on if that's what we choose to do. This morning, though, you and Jack need to talk things through.' She looked across the table at her father. 'Isn't that right, Jack?'

Pru watched him and saw the pride in his voice as he stared at the child he had fathered and still had to get to know. 'I would like that very much,' he said.

'Then that's what we'll do,' Pru said, standing, grateful for Emma's understanding.

Jack walked round to her side of the table. Pru looked down at Emma. 'I'll see you later?'

'Yes, Mum. You two go and take your time. You have a lot to discuss.'

Sam downed his cup of coffee. 'I'll take Emma out for a spin in my car, if she wants?'

'Yes, please,' Emma said.

Happy to see her daughter smile again, Pru rested a hand on Emma's shoulder and bent to kiss her cheek. 'I'll see you in a while then.'

FORTY-THREE

Emma

JUNE 1940

E mma watched her parents leave the dining room together. Her parents. It was strange to think of her mother being in love with someone else. Someone so completely different to her dad. She hadn't missed the conflict of emotions in her mum's eyes when she was in the same room as Jack. And the chemistry between them was almost physical.

It was strange to see her mum that way, but also magical. Her mother and Peter had always been kind and considerate towards each other and until Pru had broken the news to Emma about her true parentage it had never occurred to her that there had been anyone else in her mum's life. Seeing her and Jack together now though revealed an entirely new side to her mum, and for the first time she imagined her as the pretty young nurse who had been desperately in love with the American aviator. Was still clearly in love with him, although Emma wasn't sure if Jack realised it yet.

She had imagined the reason her mum hadn't told her anything about him when she had discovered her real parentage was possibly that he had abandoned her and her mother. Discovering that he had been living in plain sight here was all a bit surreal.

She had been shocked to see his scarred face for the first time but also noticed how her mother didn't seem to notice anything when she looked at him, apart from the fact that the man she loved was in front of her.

Emma looked across the table at her aunt, surprised to see she was watching her.

'You don't understand why I did what I did, do you?' Jean asked.

Now wasn't the time when Emma wished to spare her aunt's feelings. 'I understand why you all did what you did, but I don't know if I could ever keep a secret like that from someone who was so close to me.'

'I can see why,' her aunt said. 'And I probably would have thought the same as you, but you have to remember that as much as I love your mother, and I do, Peter was my brother. I had to keep the secret for his sake as well as for your mother's.'

'We are truly sorry,' her uncle said. 'Sometimes you have to make difficult choices and this was one of those times,' he explained, a sad look in his grey eyes.

'Also, Emma, back then Jack wasn't the strong man you saw today.' She turned to Monty for back-up. 'Was he, Monty?'

'He wasn't. Jack's body wasn't the only thing his capturers broke, Emma. They shattered his mind too. And for a very long time he was a shadow of the man we all knew.'

Emma listened intently, aware that her mother needed to hear this to help her forgive Jean. She realised Monty was still speaking. 'The thing is, Emma, Jack saved my life. If it wasn't for him, I wouldn't have made it back to Blighty and met Jean. I owed him everything. Jack had intended asking your mother to marry him as soon as he returned in 1918. He was crushed to discover she had married Peter by then and had given birth to you, but it was too late to do anything about it; not if he still loved her, which he did.'

Emma was only just managing to take everything in. 'He seems like a very brave man.'

'He is. Jack is the bravest man I've ever known. He would give his life for you and he almost did for me.' He gazed at her for a moment. 'This hasn't been easy for any of us,' he added.

She cleared her throat. 'Sorry, this is all a little too much for me, too.'

Sam immediately stood. 'Emma, shall we leave my parents to talk for a bit and go for a drive? Would you like that?'

She smiled at him gratefully. 'That would be lovely. Thank you, Sam.'

'You two go off now and try to enjoy yourselves,' Monty said, reaching out to take her aunt's hand in his.

'We will,' Sam said, accompanying Emma out of the room.

As Sam's MG glided through villages and along green-banked lanes, Emma slowly began to relax. She closed her eyes in the warm summer sunshine and tried to come to terms with all she had learnt that morning.

She felt Sam's hand rest lightly on hers. 'Feeling a little better?'

'Slightly, yes. Today has been rather an emotional one so far.'

'You're not wrong there.' He took his hand from hers and changed gear, replacing it straight afterwards. 'I felt terrible for poor Aunt Pru and you having to listen to everything that had gone on.'

'Did you know about Jack?' Emma asked.

'I know Jack, of course,' Sam said. 'He took me fishing and showed me all about the bees and I used to love helping him with the honey, but I didn't have any idea that he and Aunty Pru meant anything to each other.' He gave her a sympathetic smile. 'Like you, I was brought up believing Uncle Peter was your father.'

'What's he like? Jack, I mean. What's he really like?'

'He's a good man,' Jack said. 'Quiet though, and he's always preferred to keep to himself.' He thought for a moment. 'Dad has said a few times how if it wasn't for Jack he would never have made it back from the war.'

'What a strange time it is for us all,' Emma said, relieved to have a break from all the drama. 'I thought my mother's life was a quiet, simple one before Dad died. Then I discovered all this.' She waved her hands in the air. 'It's all rather incredible.'

'It is.'

'Do you think Mum and Jack will rekindle their relationship?'

'Maybe,' Sam said, slowing the car and turning down another lane. 'Would you mind?'

Emma gave his question some thought and discovered that she didn't mind at all. 'I suppose it would be rather lovely after having been kept apart all this time through circumstance,' she said quietly. 'I just want my mum to be happy. She's been a bit lost since Dad's sudden death and if Jack makes her happy, then that's good enough for me.'

Sam drove on for a bit. 'Is it strange to think of him as your father?'

'A little.' It dawned on her that she had no idea where he was taking her. 'Are we heading anywhere in particular, or is this a mystery drive?'

Sam grinned at her. 'I know where we're going but you'll just have to wait and see. I hope you like it. Just relax and enjoy the drive. We won't be too much longer.'

She was happy to do as he suggested and resting her arm on the lowered window, watched the flower-covered countryside fly past. Eventually she breathed in a familiar scent of sea air. 'We're going to the sea?' she asked, immediately excited.

'Maybe.' He smiled. 'There's something I want to show you'

Sam slowed the car a few minutes later and turned off the road. He parked the car and, after helping her out, went to the boot and took out a rug, flask and some cups.

'That's not much of a picnic,' Emma teased.

'It's not meant to be,' he said, giving her a wink. 'I had expected us all to eat a full breakfast before coming. No more questions now; just follow me. He glanced down at her shoes. 'We have quite a walk yet but you'll soon see why we're here.'

She laughed wondering what he was planning to show her. They walked along a steep downhill path before coming to some steps. 'There must be over a hundred of these,' she grumbled, watching her footing and not looking forward to the trek back up to the car afterwards.

Halfway down she noticed an arched rock standing to their left. 'Oh my word!' she gasped, gazing at the impressive spectacle rising from the sea at the end of the headland. 'It's beautiful, Sam.'

'I'm glad you think so.'

'What's it called?'

'This is Durdle Door.

'I love it.'

They reached the shingle beach and Sam shook the rug and lowered it

'You can sit now,' he said. waiting for her to do so.

Emma made herself comfortable on the woollen plaid picnic blanket and waited for Sam to sit next to her.

'I know it's warm but I thought we might enjoy a little refreshment, so I brought this flask of coffee.'

Emma smiled at him, grateful for his thoughtfulness. 'That would be nice, thank you,' she said, realising how thirsty she was, having not had anything to drink yet that morning. She waited for him to unscrew the lid from the flask. He handed her the two cups and poured their drinks.

'I asked Mrs B to add the milk,' he explained. 'I hope it's the right amount for you.'

'I'm so thirsty, I'm past caring.' She grinned, breathing in the delicious scent.

Finally, having replaced the lid, Sam took his cup and took a sip.

Emma did the same, enjoying the hot drink as she

swallowed the first mouthful. 'This is exactly what I needed today, Sam.'

The final words of her sentence were barely out of her mouth when several planes raced across the sky towards them.

'Oh!' Emma shrieked, almost spilling her drink in surprise. 'What are—' She glanced at Sam to ask what was happening and noticed the look of longing and pride on his face as he stared at the majestic aircraft. She realised he had also brought her here to see his beloved Spitfires in flight. 'Your comrades? The other pilots?'

'Yes,' he shouted over the roar of the engines as they flew overhead.

They twisted around watching the aircraft disappear over the cliffs inland before Sam turned back to her. 'I wanted you to see what I'll be doing when I'm not at the manor.'

'I see,' she said, still unsure exactly what his point might be.

'Emma, now that we know we're not blood cousins and have never actually been related, do you think you might consider being my girl one day?'

For someone as self-assured as Sam, Emma was surprised to see his cheeks redden in shyness. She leaned forward and did what she had been longing to do – kissed him. 'I'd like that very much.'

FORTY-FOUR

Pru

JUNE 1940

As soon as they had left the house, Jack reached out. 'May I hold your hand?'

Pru nodded and slipped her hand into his. The pressure of his hand around hers was instantly soothing. She was slowly regaining control of her emotions and she looked up at him as they walked along the path towards the woods, realising that yet again he had ensured he was on her left side so that the undamaged side of his face was closest to her. She was going to have her work cut out for her if she was ever to convince him that his scars only served to remind her how precious he was to those around him. She knew too that she would always love him. The realisation surprised her.

Eventually, Jack broke the silence. 'Do you think you can ever forgive me?'

She thought about it and decided that there was little point in brooding about decisions made over twenty years before. And anyway, she mused, all of them had done what they'd thought was best for her. 'Yes, I forgive you, Jack.'

'That makes me very happy,' he said, quietly smiling down at her. 'And Monty and Jean? Do you forgive them for lying to you?'

Pru groaned. She couldn't ignore that Jean he been put in a terrible position. 'I'm hurt, but I can see why Monty did what he did and that Jean had little choice but to act as she did. Although...'

'Although?'

'Even if we couldn't have been together, I would have preferred it if she had said something, anything, to let me know you were alive. I would have found it difficult to keep my promise to Peter,' she admitted, 'but I would have done it.'

Would she? She liked to think so.

'It's done now,' he soothed. 'There's nothing we can do to change the choices we all made back then.' He gave her hand a gentle squeeze. 'We need to try and focus on the future now.'

'That's true.' There was so much suffering already going on in this new war. She thought of her beautiful island and her heart ached to think it had been bombed.

She heard him groan. He stopped and she did too. 'What's the matter?' she asked, wondering if he was in pain.

'None of this would have happened at all if I hadn't made love to you back then, Pru. You wouldn't have fallen pregnant with Emma and would have still been here when I was discharged from hospital. We've lost so much time, Pru, and whether you like it or not, I am to blame.'

She turned to him and grabbed hold of his shirt. 'I'll never forget that day,' she said angrily. 'You're right, if we hadn't made love, I wouldn't have Emma in my life – but that would be a tragedy. It's just sad that by having her I couldn't also have you.' She shook her head when he went to speak. 'My memories of being with you in the folly kept me going all these years. And anyway, I haven't forgotten that I was the one who encouraged you to make love to me, not the other way round.' She knew she was blushing but didn't care. 'If anyone's to blame, then it's me.'

He rested his hand on hers. 'I think we should agree it's pointless thinking about that now we've found each other again. I have a daughter to get to know and make up time with, and this time no one else's feelings will get in the way of what we want.'

He was right.

They walked through the woods and Pru allowed herself to imagine she was that young nurse so desperately in love for the very first time.

'I had an engagement ring that I insisted on stopping off to buy before leaving Ashbury for my mission,' he said quietly. 'I was going to propose to you.'

She imagined his hurt to discover she had left and was already married with a small baby by then. 'Oh, Jack.'

'I'm only telling you this because I need you to know that you meant everything to me back then, and you still do.' Pru went to speak. 'No, please let me finish. I might lose my courage and then never tell you and I believe you need to know.'

'Go on,' she said, seeing the pain the memories still caused him and knowing he needed to release it finally.

'It was thinking of you and my love for you that kept me going when I didn't think I could bear anything more from those monsters at the chateau.' His voice had a faraway softness about it. 'Then, when I came back to Ashbury and discovered you were gone, married and raising my baby with another man, I wished I had died instead of Falkner.'

'Oh, Jack. You poor darling.' She raised a hand to his face, needing to comfort him.

He took her hand away. 'I survived.'

'Only just,' she whispered.

'But I did,' he insisted. 'And now we're here, together, and we have a chance neither of us ever imagined being lucky enough to enjoy.'

'What are you saying?' Her heart pounded so loudly she was sure he could hear it.

'Pru, I need you to know how much I loved you then so that you understand how much I still love you.' He slipped his arm around her shoulders.

'Life can be so cruel, can't it, Jack?' Pru said, thinking of all they had missed.

'It can,' he agreed. 'And then something like this happens and you know everything will be fine.'

They stepped back into the bright sunlight and Jack let go of her hand.

Pru said nothing but watched to see where he was going, surprised when he stopped in the middle of a mass of daisies and buttercups and began picking them. He looked so sweet. This man who had meant so much to her for so long, who had suffered so cruelly but who was happy to have her back in his life again. She didn't think she would ever be as happy as she was now.

When he had a small posy in his hand, he walked back to her and handed them to her, smiling.

'I promised you back in 1917 that once the war was over, I would make sure you had fresh flowers every day.'

Pru tried to recall him telling her as much. 'Did you?'

'I did. Now we're together again, I intend to make good on that promise.'

She gazed down at the perfect, pretty posy in her hands, brushing the daisies against her nose and enjoying the gentle tickling. 'I like that idea.'

'I'm glad.' He looked down at his damaged hands. 'I'm aware you were only widowed six months ago and I don't wish to appear insensitive when you're still grieving, but...'

'Are you trying to tell me you would like us to pick up from where we left our relationship all those years ago?' Pru asked, hoping she wasn't imagining where he was going with his thoughts.

'I am, Pru. When you're ready though. I don't wish to rush you.'

'You're not rushing me, Jack,' she said, realising that their walk had brought memories racing back to her and reignited the love she had for him when they were younger.

'The only person other than the two of us whose feelings matter to me right now is Emma, and I know my daughter would want me to be happy.'

'Then Emma and I have a lot in common.'

'We should talk about Emma,' Pru suggested.

He took her hands in his and pulled her closer to him. 'I've longed to see her and now that you've both returned and I have time to get to know her, it's like being given the most precious gift.' He smiled at her, his blue eyes filled with happiness. 'She's a beautiful, sweet, brave girl,' he said smiling. 'Just like her mother.'

Pru could barely contain her joy at hearing him say as much. After all the secrets that had been kept from her, and those she had kept from her daughter, Pru knew now was the time for complete honesty.

'Every single day, whenever I looked at her sweet face, I thought of you and knew that no other man could ever make me feel like you did.'

He swallowed and Pru could tell he was trying to contain his emotions. 'Do you truly mean that?' he whispered, and she knew how much it had taken him to ask her.

'Yes, Jack. I've always loved you. I never stopped.'

He pulled her into his arms and kissed her. She closed her eyes and allowed herself to be transported back to that special place where kissing Jack had always taken her.

Eventually, he moved slightly back from her, still holding her around her waist as he gazed at her. 'Would you consider marrying again?' he asked, his voice hoarse.

Pru's stomach did a little flip. 'You're asking me to marry you?'

He smiled and gave a slight shrug. 'I already have the ring; it would be a shame to keep it in its box for another twenty-two years, don't you think?' He laughed. 'I've no idea if it's still fashionable, but we could always have the setting changed if you don't like it.'

She took his face in her hands, not caring that the delicate petals of the flowers she was holding were creased as they were pressed against his skin, and kissed him.

'I don't know about you but I think that our daughter

might be happy to give her blessing to her parents finally getting married, don't you?'

Pru nodded, happier than she could ever recall being. 'I think you could be right, Jack Garland.'

'Then, my precious Pru, I'd like to ask you formally if you would do me the honour of agreeing to be my wife?'

'I would be happy to, darling Jack.'

He kissed her again. 'I think we should go and break the news to our daughter, don't you?'

Acknowledgments

Firstly I'd like to thank everyone who has read my books and taken the time to let me know how much the characters and their stories meant to them either through a review or via email. Thank you, I appreciate your support more than you know.

Thanks also to my mum, Tess Jackson and godmother, Irene Reynolds for not minding me using them as inspiration for the quirky sisters, Terry and Tiz in this book. They are secondary characters in *The Beekeeper's War* but ones I felt compelled to include.

To my wonderful publisher and editor, Charlotte Ledger. You are always so kind and knowledgeable and I'm truly grateful to you for commissioning me to write *The Poppy Field* and ultimately making my dream come true to become a full-time author.

To my editors for this book, Julia Williams, Tony Russell and Dushi Horti. Thank you for all your hard work and for helping make this book a much better version of itself.

To Lucy Bennett for another gorgeous cover. Thank you, I love it.

To everyone else in the One More Chapter team for all your hard work and all that you do for me.

To my fabulous writer friends especially Blonde Plotters, Kelly Clayton and Gwyn GB and my OMC pals especially Glynis Peters and Christie Barlow for making each day so much fun.

And of course to my amazing husband, Robert Carr and my children, James and Saskia, who are always supportive of everything I do and make me smile and feel very loved every single day.

Dear Reader,

I hope you enjoyed reading Pru and Jack's story. I loved writing *The Beekeeper's War* and at times it seemed like the characters were writing it for me and my fingers simply typed the words that they were dictating.

Follies fascinate me and I have always yearned for one. Realising that I probably would never have the space to build a folly in my garden I decided that maybe I could include one in a book but until now it has never felt quite right to do so. Finally, I felt that *The Beekeeper's War* was the perfect place for the folly of my dreams and so I've included it in this book. I have also dreamt of having a walled garden and although I don't have one of those either I loved spending time in the imaginary one in this book.

Once again I've written about two nurses and this time both of them are from Jersey where I live. I admire the work that medical staff do enormously and in the thankfully few occasions I've needed their care I have been grateful to be in their capable and kindly hands.

As I often do with my heroes I fell in love with Jack Garland my US pilot and I hope that you like him too and enjoy his romance with Pru. Once again I touch on the Jersey Occupation when the island was invaded by German forces in July 1940 when those able to leave or be evacuated had very few days to make the decision, pack their one suitcase and leave the island. It was a traumatic time for those who left and particularly for those who remained and had to face strict regulations for the five dark years that the island was occupied. As I write this we are getting ready to raise our flags and put up the bunting to celebrate Liberation Day. This is an annual holiday when church bells are rung, services and parties are held to mark the day the island was liberated by British forces on May 9th 1945.

As usual I loved the research for this book and spent many a happy hours in thought when I was picturing the house where the hospital would be and how the rooms were set out. With Monty and Jean's story I was inspired by seeing black and white photos of couples and wondering what happened to them and what they might have faced as a couple throughout their lives. I hope you've enjoyed their story too.

Finally, I'd like to thank you for reading *The Beekeeper's War*. I hope you enjoyed it and if you did I would be extremely grateful if you could leave a quick review. It doesn't have to be long, simply a 'loved this book' or really enjoyed it' or anything like that. Reviews help readers discover authors' books and we all love coming across a reader who's enjoyed one of our books. I know I certainly do.

With all my thanks,
Deborah x

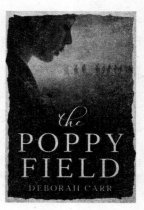

**Don't miss *The Poppy Field*, another epic historical novel by
Deborah Carr...**

Young nurse Gemma is struggling with the traumas she has
witnessed through her job. Needing to escape from it all,
Gemma agrees to help renovate a rundown farmhouse in
Doullens, France, a town near the Somme. There, in a boarded-
up cupboard, wrapped in old newspapers, is a tin that reveals
the secret letters and heartache of Alice Le Breton, a young
volunteer nurse who worked in a casualty clearing station near
the front line.

Set in the present day and during the horrifying years of the
war, both women discover deep down the strength and
courage to carry on in even the most difficult of times.
Through Alice's words and her unfailing love for her
sweetheart at the front, Gemma learns to truly live again.

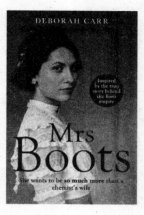

You will also love the *Mrs Boots* series, the epic true story of Florence Boot – the woman behind the Boots empire...

Jersey 1885: On the beautiful island of Jersey, Florence Rowe lives a quiet life working in her father's bookshop. Life for the Rowe family is good, but Florence can't help yearning for more...

When Jesse Boot arrives on the island, Florence is immediately captivated by his tales of life in a busy, bustling city on the mainland. For the first time ever, Florence imagines a life away from the constraints of Jersey society, of being someone more than just a shopgirl. Until her parents reveal the shocking news that they will refuse any marriage proposal.

Can Florence find a way to be with the man she loves and make a new life for herself?

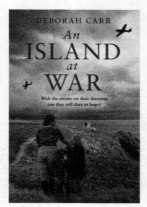

June 1940

While her little sister Rosie is sent to the UK to keep her safe from the invading German army, Estelle Le Maistre is left behind on Jersey to help her grandmother run the family farm. When the Germans occupy the island, everything changes and Estelle and the islanders must face the reality of life under Nazi rule.

Interspersed with diary entries from Rosie back on the mainland, the novel is also inspired by real life stories from the author's own family who were both on the island during the occupation and in London during the Blitz and is a true testament to the courage and bravery of the islanders.

YOUR NUMBER ONE STOP

ONE MORE CHAPTER

FOR PAGETURNING BOOKS

One More Chapter is an
award-winning global
division of HarperCollins.

Sign up to our newsletter to get our
latest eBook deals and stay up to date
with our weekly Book Club!
<u>Subscribe here.</u>

Meet the team at
<u>www.onemorechapter.com</u>

Follow us!
@OneMoreChapter_
@OneMoreChapter
@onemorechapterhc

Do you write unputdownable fiction?
We love to hear from new voices.
Find out how to submit your novel at
<u>www.onemorechapter.com/submissions</u>